One of the world's leading science fiction writers, **Anne McCaffrey** has won the Hugo and Nebula awards for science fiction. Brought up in the US and now living in Ireland, she is the creator and bestselling author of the unique Dragon series.

Also by Anne McCaffrey

Dragonflight
Dragonquest
Dragonsong
Dragonsinger: Harper of Pern
The White Dragon
Dragondrums
Moreta: Dragonlady of Pern
Nerilka's Story
Dragonsdawn
The Renegades of Pern
All the Weyrs of Pern

Restoree
The Ship Who Sang
Decision at Doona
Get Off the Unicorn
The Crystal Singer
Killashandra
The Rowan
Pegasus in Flight
All the Weyrs of Pern

ANNE McCAFFREY

DAMIA

BANTAM PRESS

LONDON • NEW YORK • TORONTO • SYDNEY • AUCKLAND

TRANSWORLD PUBLISHERS LTD
61–63 Uxbridge Road, London W5 5SA

TRANSWORLD PUBLISHERS (AUSTRALIA) PTY LTD
15–23 Helles Avenue, Moorebank, NSW 2170

TRANSWORLD PUBLISHERS (NZ) LTD
3 William Pickering Drive,
Albany, Auckland

Published 1992 by Bantam Press
a division of Transworld Publishers Ltd

All the characters in this book
are fictitious, and any resemblance
to actual persons, living or dead,
is purely coincidental.

A catalogue record for this book is available from the British Library

ISBN 0 593 023757

Printed and bound in Great Britain by
Biddles Ltd, Guildford and King's Lynn

This book is dedicated
to
SARA VIRGINIA JOHNSON BROOKS

'THE FOLDING IS EXTRA'

1

Afra felt his sister's mental touch and told his mother that Goswina had returned to Capella. Cheswina regarded her six-year-old son with her ineffable serenity.

'Thank you, Afra. You always could hear farther, and Goswina better, than the rest of us. But don't intrude,' his mother added, as Afra jiggled about in his eagerness to make contact with his beloved sister. 'Capella Prime will wish to debrief her on her training at Altair Tower. You may continue with your exercises.'

But Goswina's excited about something. Something that has to do with ME! Afra insisted, for he wanted to make sure that his mother *heard* him.

'Now, Afra,' and his mother waggled a stern finger at him, 'you've got a tongue AND a voice. Use them. No-one is to accuse this family of bringing up a discourteous and ill-mannered Talent. You have your lessons and you are *not* to 'path your sister until she comes in that door.'

Afra scowled because, when Goswina came in the door, he wouldn't need to 'path her.

'You won't ever be chosen for Tower duty if you cannot obey,' Cheswina went on. 'Please assume a cheerful face.'

If Afra had heard those admonitions once, he had heard them several thousand times. But he stifled his vexation because what he wanted more than anything else in the world was to be in a Prime Tower, part of the vast FT&T network that handled communications and transportation between the star systems that comprised the Federation. His parents and his older brother and sisters were either part of or working towards being in that great network.

The family were also lucky enough to live in the Tower Complex. As a baby, he had been lulled to sleep by the throb of the enormous generators with which the Prime Talent made the gestalt to perform her miracles of transportation. His first mental effort at fourteen months had been a cheerful greeting to Capella's Prime who had taken the professional name of her posting. Although she had been addressing the Earth Prime with her 'good morning', Afra had heard her voice so clearly in his mind that he had responded. His parents had been shocked by his impudence.

'He was not impudent at all,' Capella had reassured them with one of her rare laughs. 'It was really quite charming to be greeted by a sweet chirping "good morning". Quite sweet. We will encourage such a strong young Talent. Though it would be as well if you can make him understand that he is not to interrupt me.'

Cheswina was a T-8 telepathic sender and her husband, Gos Lyon, a T-7 kinetic. Every one of their children had Talent but Afra's was not only apparent early but was also the strongest, possibly even a double – telepath and teleport. This did not keep his parents from being considerably embarrassed by their youngest son's precocity. So they immediately initiated gentle methods of curbing him without inhibiting his potential Talent.

Either father, mother or Goswina, the eldest sibling, had to be sure to awaken before Afra did and curb a repeat of that performance. For several months, this was a splendid new game for the toddler: to see if he could wake up first so he could chirp 'good morning' to the velvet voice that invaded his mind . . . Capella. Whoever was minding him that morning had to engage his attention in an alternative occupation – like eating. For young Afra loved to eat.

Not that it showed. Like the rest of his family, he was a healthy but lean baby; ectomorphic with the sort of energy levels that burn up calories. Placing a rusk or a piece of fruit in his hand would instantly divert him. As most tots, he had a very short attention span and these ploys worked until he was old enough to understand that his 'good mornings' should be limited to his immediate family.

Goswina, a loving and caring sister, had not an ounce of meanness in her temperament and never found this duty a chore. She adored her clever brother and he reciprocated so warmly that a strong tie was established between them. The mental exercises his Gossie used to divert her lively brother had a salutary effect on her own Talent and she was upgraded to a T-6 by the time she was sixteen. That made her eligible for the special training courses that Earth Prime Reidinger initiated on Altair.

This was a very mixed blessing, for sixteen-year-old Goswina had developed such a deep attachment for a T-5, Vessily Ogdon, that both families had earnestly discussed a possible alliance. However, Goswina was asked to put aside her personal plans for the chance to participate in the Altair course. Only Afra knew how painful that choice was for his sister. Once Gos Lyon invoked family honour, she had complied, demonstrating an obedience that seemed genuine – except to her brother who howled loudly at Goswina's departure.

Afra missed his slender, gentle sister dreadfully. Altair

was so very far away that he could not maintain the light mental touch that reassured him through his daily trials. Afra was not a natural conformist and trouble seemed to seek him out at school, and even at home. He was not as biddable as his brother and sisters had been and his parents found his impetuosity and often 'wild', or 'aggressive' behaviour a trial.

Aware of young Afra's problems, the Capella stationmaster, Hasardar, tactfully had the boy doing small 'jobs' for him, jobs which the worried parents could not take exception to as they were aimed at developing his potential. Afra willingly did the 'errands', delighted to be considered – for once – capable of doing something properly.

One of these errands took him to a large freighter with a packet, requested by the captain. Afra was agog with the prospect of actually meeting spacemen. He'd seen ships come and go from Capella all his short life but had never actually encountered off-worlders.

As he trotted up to the open hatch, he saw big burly space-tanned men, lounging within. He also heard a babble of sound which made no sense at all to his ears. His mind, however, translated the meaning.

'This is no place for leave, boys. Straight as dies, these folk. Methody believers, and you know what that means.'

'Sure, Chief, no hanky-panky, no funsies, no drink, no smokings. Hey, what's coming here? A pint-size greenie! Don't they grow 'em a decent size?'

'Ah, it's a kid.' And one of the men swung down the ramp, grinning. 'Good morning,' he said in good Basic.

Afra stared up at him.

'You got a package for the captain, boy? Stationmaster said he'd have it hand-delivered.'

Afra continued to stare, extending the package with both hands, puzzled by the strange words and especially by the description of himself.

'What does "pint-sized greenie" mean, please, sir?'

Afra flinched at the laughter from the lock and then from the angry glare the chief directed at his crewmen.

'Don't be offended, laddie,' the chief said in a kind tone. 'Some spacers have no manners. You understand more than Basic?'

Afra wasn't sure what response to make. While he knew some people could not 'path, he didn't know that there were many different forms of language in the galaxy. However, as his family would expect him to give a courteous answer to a friendly question, he gave a nod.

'I understand what you say,' Afra replied. 'I don't understand "pint-sized greenie".'

The chief hunkered down, being conscious that it was wise not to offend locals, even a kid. And a kid would be more likely to repeat what had been said to the stationmaster. It was also smart for freighter crews to be on the best possible terms with Tower stationmasters.

'It's like this, lad,' and he rolled back his sleeve, showing a brown-skinned arm, then he pointed to Afra's hand. 'My skin is brown, your skin is green. I'm a brownie,' and he ignored the hoots from his crew, 'and you're a greenie. Just a matter of what colour we got born with. Now, "pint-sized" means small, and I'd be gallon-sized, 'cause I'm much bigger. Get me?'

'More like barrel, Chief!' one of the crew chortled, again using the different sounds though his mind made the comment clear to Afra.

Afra cocked his head at the chief, noticing other differences between himself, a Capellan, and these visitors. The man had brown skin, streaky grey hair and brown eyes. He was the widest man Afra had ever seen, with forearms twice the size of his father's, or even Stationmaster Hasardar.

'Thank you for explaining to me, Chief. It was kind of you,' Afra said, giving a respectful bow.

'No problem, lad. And here's something for your trouble,' the chief said, reaching for Afra's right hand and closing the fingers around a metallic object. 'Put that by for a rainy day. If it rains on Capella.'

Afra looked at the round object, 'pathing from the chief that this was a half credit, a reward for delivering the package. He had never seen credit coins before and he liked the feel of its edges in his palm. He gleaned from the chief that a 'tip' was normal procedure so he bowed again.

'Thank you, Chief. It was kind of you.'

'Tell you one thing, they teach manners on this planet,' the chief said in a loud voice, trying to overwhelm the rude comments his crewmen were making about Afra's courtesies.

Afra didn't catch the meanings behind some of the strange words.

'Off you go, lad, before you become contaminated by this sorry lot of spacers. Ain't any of you guys got some couth? Back inside, the lot of you. You've had your smoking time.'

As Afra trotted across the plascrete back to the station-master, he decided that he wouldn't tell anyone about the coin. It had been given him in return for completing his errand. It was for him, not Stationmaster Hasardar who had said nothing to him about collecting any sort of payment or to expect a tip. If Goswina had been home, he would have confided in her as a matter of course, but his other sisters considered him a nuisance and his brother, Chostel, felt that he was too old to associate with kids. So Afra decided he didn't need to say anything about his coin. He would save it, but not for a rainy day. When it rained on Capella, no-one went anywhere.

This was yet another occasion when Afra found himself deprived by Goswina's absence. And, now that she had returned to Capella, he simply had to renew contact as soon as he could. So, despite his mother's stricture, he reached out his mind to his sister in the main Tower building.

Not now, Afra, Capella said but not unkindly as his mind linked to Goswina's in their conference mode.

Oh, mercy, Afra, not now, was the simultaneous message from a mortified Goswina.

Fearful that his parents might receive official reprimands from the Prime herself, Afra shrank away and coiled so tightly into his own mind that he genuinely didn't 'hear' Goswina until she opened the door of their quarters an hour later.

OH, GOSSIE, Afra cried, tears of joy streaming down his face, as he jumped into her arms.

Theirs was not a physically demonstrative family, as much because they enjoyed a sufficient mental rapport that touch was redundant as because tactile contact between Talents allowed deeper readings, sometimes an inadvertent invasion of the private mind.

Today, Goswina ignored such considerations as she hugged her young brother tightly. Through that close contact, she also managed to convey many things such a reserved girl would find difficult to say out loud. Afra caught rapid shifts through scenes of her landing on Altair, the forested mountains behind the Port City, the raw look of the Altairian Tower, the faces of her fellow students in a hectic montage, with one face dominating the group, rapidly scrolling through the school room sessions, meals, the room Goswina had shared with two girls, then pausing at a musical interlude which was abruptly deleted, overlaid with her excitement at returning to the home she had missed, and her Vessily.

I missed you terribly, Afra.

More than you missed Vessily?

As much, though not quite the same way, Afra, and Goswina's gentle thought teased him. *But it was a splendid trip. I met so many marvellous people. And oh, Afra, how you'll love the Rowan when you meet her. She said that she would consider you when you have finished your training, because you are my brother and because we two knew our temperaments weren't complementary. But I told her that you would be because you're so clever and understanding. I missed you terribly, Afra. Just wait till you see the trees they have on Altair. Whole forests of trees, darling . . . big trees and small ones, different shades of green and blue and many different shapes of trunk, branch and leaf. All of them fragrant. Altair's not as large as Capella but it is a good place. I did so well in my course that Capella said that she will definitely place me in this system,* and, as she held Afra from her to peer into his face, 'to work in a Capellan Tower.'

Did you . . .

'Aloud, please, Afra,' she said, hearing her mother come into the room.

' . . . know that Stationmaster Hasardar gave me some special training, after school hours? He said I had Tower potential, too!' He offered that praise as a homecoming present for her, but he didn't mention the credit coin aloud. Or even in his mind.

'How very good of Hasardar. How clever of you, Afra dear,' she said, releasing him from her embrace and rising to greet her mother more formally. 'Mother, Capella was very pleased both with my course of study on Altair and with the report Siglen of Altair sent her of me.'

Cheswina smoothed her daughter's hair in a brief, loving gesture and smiled.

'You bring honour to our family.'

'Afra will bring more,' Goswina said, looking fondly down at him.

'That remains to be seen,' Cheswina said, her expression bordering on the severe, for she did not believe that it was right to praise a child for what he or she could be expected to do. Reward should never be a consideration of effort. However, Goswina did merit some special indulgence for having brought honour to the family so her favourite dishes were served at dinner that evening and she'd be allowed a visit from Vessily Ogdon.

On returning from his Tower shift that evening, Gos Lyon smiled in benign approval at his daughter. When everyone had eaten a sufficiency of the excellent meal, he handed her an official note. He contained his pride as his overjoyed firstborn communicated to everyone at the table that Capella had appointed her to the staff of the southern Tower, one of the busier local FT&T facilities.

That means you're going away again! Afra cried out in distress.

Silly! I won't be so far that we can't keep in touch all the time. 'Forgive me, Father, Mother,' Goswina added hastily, blushing for such a gross social lapse, 'but Afra was so disturbed . . . '

'Afra must learn to control his feelings,' Gos Lyon said, bending a stern gaze on his youngest. 'Tower staff must always contain their emotions. To splash about personal reactions exhibits a woeful absence of discipline and an abysmal lack of courtesy and consideration. I'll have no child of mine so ill-mannered. One can never learn respect too early in life.'

Later, dear. Goswina shot the very private thought tightly to her brother, so fast her parents would not have caught it, being less telepathically Talented than herself. But she had to do something to relieve the woeful expression on Afra's face and unwind the tension of his small thin body. Shrivelled by the parental disapproval, he had curled in on himself, arms clasped tight across his chest, head down.

Prior to her course at Altair, she would never have dared even think of criticizing her parents. She didn't entirely approve of Altair's social manners but she had also seen a different sort of society that apparently worked quite well. And Afra was so very sensitive to his father's disapproval and, sometimes, very privately, Goswina thought her parents could be a trifle more lenient and understanding. After all, he was the most Talented of them all and needed extra, specially astute handling.

'Now, now,' Gos Lyon said, realizing that perhaps he had been too severe with Afra, 'I know you meant neither disrespect nor disobedience, Afra. Tonight is a time for rejoicing.'

His soft words and gentle tone, as well as the shaft of love and reassurance directed at his son, had the desired effect on Afra and he was soon smiling when Goswina began her almost day-by-day account of her Altairian sojourn.

Afra also 'heard' unfinished sentiments and, once, caught her remembered alarm. He fervently hoped that her 'later' would come soon so he'd find out all those bits and pieces she left out of the public recital.

'Later' was going to really be 'later' for Vessily Ogdon arrived at the door, on time as usual, palpably eager to see his betrothed. Afra didn't like staying in the same room with Vessily and Goswina because he was acutely aware of their attachment. Since Vessily was a T-5 and even older than Goswina, Afra thought that he ought to know how to control himself. He was amazed that his father didn't say anything about leaking emotions to Vessily.

As Afra retired to his room, he heard the depth of Vessily's discontent with Goswina's posting to the Southern Station. But he heard Goswina's telepathic reassurance – and Gos Lyon who was chaperoning the couple, said nothing about *that*! – Afra was also vexed to hear Goswina say exactly the same things to Vessily that she'd said to him – only her tone was much different.

Afra puzzled over that. How could the same words sound so different coming from the same mind? Goswina loved him, but he knew that she also loved Vessily. Afra understood that everyone should have love enough to give special friends, even many special friends. Goswina loved him and she had a special tone for him, but she also loved Vessily – and hadn't wanted to leave Capella for Altair because of Vessily, or so she'd said out loud – and she had *another* special tone for Vessily. That was very strange, and Afra went to sleep pondering that mystery.

Goswina kept her word to him, even if 'later' was the next morning at first light. He woke the moment he felt her mind brush his. Of course, she no longer slept in with him as she had when he was a baby, but her room was adjacent to his. As had long been their custom, he put his hand up on the wall that separated them, knowing that she did the same thing. Not that they needed contact but it was a friendly remnant of childish habit.

What bothered you, Gossie, that you couldn't tell Father and Mother? He shot her a glimpse of the scene of her panicky flight to the parking lot.

Well, it wasn't anything . . .

Huh? That's not what you really think.

Well, one evening, we got permission to go to a concert in Altair Port. She showed him a picture of them all driving off together but she was still concealing something. *You don't need to know every cross on the Ts and the dots on the Is, Afra.*

Sorry!

It's just that Altairian concerts are different from ours. And I don't mean the music they played. I mean, they have a much more . . . flamboyant way of performing.

How? Since his encounter with the freighter chief, Afra had taken every opportunity his duties afforded him to meet other crews, with their variety of skin shades and physical attributes. He also liked hearing the different languages, and the odd things crews said from time to time, most of which he didn't exactly understand. It was often hard to find someone willing to explain variations to his enquiring mind. Some Talents had a way of wriggling past public shields to the real truths but he didn't expect to be able to do that for some years to come. Now that Goswina was back, maybe she'd tell him. But he wouldn't interrupt her with his questions now.

They are . . . far more demonstrative than we would be, and Afra could tell that she was carefully editing the thoughts she let him see. She was falling into his parents' habit of 'protecting' him. He wasn't a sissy. He was over six – nearly seven.

No, you're not a sissy, Afra, and you're a very clever nearly seven or Hasardar wouldn't let you run errands for him. It was an adult concert, Affie, and not something you would understand or enjoy. Afra caught her mental disgust. *It's not as if I'd start acting like a nutty Altairian, Gossie. Please let me see!*

Oh, don't push me around, Afra. I have absolutely no intention of contaminating an impressionable young mind like yours. I said, and Goswina's mental touch unexpectedly firmed against him, *don't probe, or I won't tell you anything else.*

Afra projected compliance because he couldn't bear for Goswina to shut him out and not tell him the exciting thing that was at the edge of her mind.

So Goswina did tell him about her dismay at what she would only term a lewd public display of affection, her mind so tightly shielded that he couldn't catch a *glimpse* of what had made her leave the concert arena so abruptly. Afra hadn't heard 'lewd' before but it couldn't be an acceptable word, considering the way she coloured it in her mind – a slimy muddy yellow brown.

The music had been wonderful. Music always is, Goswina continued, *and then they had to spoil it. The Rowan left with me. I was glad because she was much too young to see that sort of thing, even if it is her native planet and she might be accustomed to such displays. That's when I found out that she was the reason so many Talents were invited to go to Altair. You see, the Rowan is really a Prime so of course she couldn't leave Altair, what with the way space travel sickens Primes, so FT&T set up the course to introduce possible Tower crew to her, when she's old enough to have her own Prime Tower.*

You didn't get space sick, did you? Afra would have been disgusted, even with his beloved Gossie, if she had.

Of course not, but I'm a T-6. The sickness only affects

Primes. All of us on the course thought the Rowan was just a T-4. Goswina's thought brightened with delight at having been the first to learn the truth. *She's not much younger than I am but ever so much stronger. She's being trained in her duties by Siglen, just as our Capella was. I suppose all Primes were young once, like the Rowan,* Goswina added thoughtfully. *She's an orphan. All her family, everyone who knew her, were killed in an avalanche when she was only three years old. They said that the whole planet heard her crying for help.* Goswina did not add the other things she'd heard about how Siglen had behaved at that time because it wasn't proper to criticize a Prime for any reason whatsoever. *But the Rowan is very strong, and so clever, and generous, and brave. I could never have done what she did when those awful boys attacked us.*

ATTACKED YOU? There're indent gangs on Altair? So that was what Goswina hadn't told the parents. Not that Afra blamed her. They'd've been very upset at the insult to their daughter and there could have been embarrassing repercussions. *What sort of a barbaric place is Altair?*

Now, Afra, it isn't barbaric. It's really very – very sophisticated; much more worldly than Capella is with no Method to guide them. And I wasn't hurt. I was scared. Anyway, the Rowan took care of them. Afra could hear something akin to righteous satisfaction tingeing Goswina's thoughts. *She just flicked them out of the way as we'd brush sandflies and without any gestalt to help her. Then, cool as you please, she ordered a cab and we got back safely to the Tower complex. That's when I told her all about you.*

Me?

Yes, dearest brother of them all, you. Because your minds will match. I just know they will. Afra heard her hand slap the wall for emphasis. *And she has promised me that she will see that you take the course at Altair too, when you're old enough.*

She will? But I'd have to be away from you . . .

Afra, dearest, Talents like us aren't more than a thought away.

I couldn't think at you when you were on Altair.

Well, I'm home now . . . and the Southern Station is well within your range, brother dear. Now, it's time for us to be up. And for you to study hard so you'll be ready when the Rowan needs you.

As Afra grew up, that promise began to assume more and more significance – mainly as the passport off Capella and the strict, almost stifling, code of conduct expected of him by his parents. His interactions with freighter and passenger crews, with occasional visitors whom Hasardar had him conduct from their personal capsules to the Tower, had broadened his experience of different cultures and systems.

He encountered the gallon-sized brown chief on a regular basis over the next nine years. Chief Damitcha liked the odd dignity of the 'pint-sized greenie', though that description rarely crossed the chief's mind after he learned Afra's name. It was Damitcha who introduced Afra to the art of paper-folding, origami, which had been part of his ancestors' culture.

Afra had been fascinated to see Damitcha's thick fingers deliberately and delicately creasing, folding and producing the most elegant creatures, objects and flowers from coloured sheets.

'Old fashioned sea sailors used to carve things in their off-duty hours,' Damitcha explained, deftly making a bird he called a heron, with outstretched wings, long legs and neck. 'Scrimshaw, they called it. Have museums of the stuff on old Earth and I seen it once on leave there. But spacemen gotta watch weight and so paper's perfect. Beats the hell outa watching fractiles or such like. Keeps my fingers supple for finicky board repairs, too.'

When Afra begged to be taught how to do origami foldings, Damitcha produced an instruction tape for him and even gave him several sheets of his special coloured papers. Afra told Goswina about this hobby but Goswina was so involved with being a new Tower technician and wife that her response was more automatic than enthusiastic: all part of her detachment from her previous ties. Afra did understand that she had other claims on her time, that she still loved him but that working in the Tower was far more exciting than listening to her little brother. Hasardar was handier and could be relied on for approval and amazement at what Afra could create out of a sheet of paper. He pinned samples of Afra's handiwork on his bulletin board and took the manipulable ones home to amuse his children.

On his next trip into Capell, Damitcha presented Afra with a box of origami papers, all sizes and many beautiful shades and patterns. He brought historical tapes about Oriental arts and even a small paper book on Japanese brush calligraphy.

As Afra grew older, and assumed other duties, Damitcha would join him in Hasardar's office for chats, for meal breaks, for long evening discussions. So Afra learned far more details about other systems than were taught in his classroom.

Damitcha retired from active service with the freighting company and, though he frequently sent messages to his 'pint-sized greenie' to which Afra usually responded, the boy did not find another so congenial. The curiosity that Damitcha had generated in the young Afra would never fail and the boy continued to make far more contact with other cultures than his parents knew, or would consider advisable for their impressionable son.

However, that same curiosity troubled Afra for it made him uncomfortably aware that he found great interest in matters his family considered quite trivial or useless. Afra spent hours in his early teen years examining his inner self, trying to find the flaw in him that wanted more than he could have on Capella; that was fascinated by 'other worldly notions'; that resented the loving supervision of his parents and the path they had chosen for him to follow. The fact that he knew they loved him burdened him in his striving to be different. Their main concern was to keep the family's honour unsullied, which meant adhering to proven ways. With their love, wisdom and (they thought) insight into the characters and abilities of their children, Gos Lyon and Cheswina were convinced that they knew what was best. Especially for Afra.

From Goswina on down, his siblings were quite willing to have their lives ordered by their parents. As minor Talents, they each moved serenely into secure careers in the service of FT&T and that was as far as any of them looked. Goswina's happy marriage and her skills as a technician made her conclude that following parental example would also lead Afra to happiness. So she did not understand his rebellion, nor that he had been exposed to different standards over the years.

Certainly his interest in 'other worldly' things extended to unusual species, like the barque cats on the liner *Bucephalus*. Damitcha had told him about these strange space-faring variants of Terran felines.

'We don't have one, but next time the old *Buc* cradles down here, ask the chief – a woman named Marsha Meilo – if you can see theirs. They gotta new litter but – sorry lad, they're not planet beasts. They stay in space.'

Afra looked up 'barque cat' and the screen showed the current prize-winning sire, Garfield Per Astra, a magnificent beast of tawny brown with his undercoat a tan, with black stripes, and face markings that made him look both benign and exceedingly wise. His eyes were yellow, like Afra's, but that wasn't what endeared him to the boy as much as his air of arrogant independence did.

There were many holos of the unusually marked felines, long histories of their pedigrees, breeding and nurture, their deftness in finding tiny holes in hulls and giving warning to the crew, their almost incredible talent for survival in spacewrecks. FIND THE BC! was the motto of every space salvage group. Any vessel harbouring a barque cat would have BC ABOARD in huge letters in various positions on the hull.

The next time the *Bucephalus* rocked into a Capellan cradle, Afra deserted his immediate task and was in the group hovering by the crew gangway.

'Whatcha got, kid?' a spaceman asked, noticing Afra, who was almost dancing about in his anxiety to get someone's attention.

'Chief Damitcha of the freighter *Zanzibar* gave me a message for your Chief Marsha Meilo.'

The crewman vacillated between annoyance and curiosity.

'Yeah? What's the message?'

'I'm to give it to her,' he said.

'Oh, he did, huh? Didn't know he knew . . . What's the matter, kid?'

For Afra had just seen the barque cat who strolled indolently to the gangway to peer out in as supercilious a manner as the highest Methody preacher.

'Oh, that's Treasure Island Queen,' and the crewman's pride in the beast was obvious.

Afra extended his hand to the cat, for they were on a level, Treasure on the ship and Afra on the ground. The crewman kicked his hand away and Afra jumped back in alarm and hurt.

'Sorry, kid, we don't like our barquie picking up any planetary germs. No touchee. Just lookee. She is a beauty, ain't she?' and the crewman, rather ashamed of his defensiveness, hunkered down to pet the cat.

Afra, hands clasped tightly behind his back, could not tear his eyes off the sleek and elegant creature. Treasure, luxuriating in the crewman's caresses, murmured her appreciation and turned her aristocratic face towards the wide-eyed boy.

'Hmmmmrow!' she said, plainly addressing Afra.

'Hey, kid, you rate. She don't usually speak to landlubbers.'

Afra *listened* with all his heart and *heard* the satisfaction of Treasure's mind for the caresses she was enjoying. Delicately she sniffed, as much in Afra's direction as in general at the atmosphere of Capella, but he took it as a personal accolade and desperately wanted to be able to stroke her, to have such a lovely creature for his own.

You are the most beautiful creature I have ever seen, Afra dared to say.

Mmmmmmmrow! Mmmmmrrr!

There seemed to be no mental equivalent for that except pleasure. Abruptly she leaped away from the door and out of his sight. Just then a group of uniformed men and women emerged and quickly the crewman gestured for Afra to make himself scarce as he stood to attention, saluting those who filed out of the ship.

Afra mulled over that incident for several days before he asked Hasardar about barque cats.

'Them? Well, for one thing, they're not allowed planetside. Those spacers keep them pretty much to themselves. Oh, they trade them between ships, to avoid inbreeding . . . '

'Inbreeding?'

'Too close a blood tie – weakens the strain, they say.'

Afra didn't have a chance to ask more questions. He knew without asking that his parents would not permit him to have any kind of an animal. Not in the Tower enclosure. But that didn't keep him from checking with all the bigger ships to see if they had barque cats. Spacemen were only too happy to brag about their beasts and if Afra couldn't touch, he could admire, and 'path them. Mostly they responded, which tickled him and actually improved his relations with all ships' crews. 'That yellow eyed greenie that the barquies talk to' became his informal designation in Capella Port. His fascination with the animals helped ease his loneliness and he studied pedigrees, and asked questions of any barque cat crew, until he probably knew the lineage and distribution of the animals as well as any spacefarer. His most precious treasure was a packet of holographs of various dignified barquies given him by their proud owners.

But, as Afra grew older and his Talent strengthened, he became less tolerant of the parochial attitudes of his parents despite his love for them. Reared as he had been to restrain his emotions, he mentally chafed against the loving bonds and the parental assumption that he would be delighted to take a place – more exalted than theirs as a T-4 which they did not resent – in Capella Tower.

By his fifteenth year, he had begun to find ways of sliding away from his family's supervision – first mentally when he attended the Capella training sessions and met Talents from nearby systems. Then, physically, when he would clandestinely join his student friends in the few innocent and mild diversions available on his Methodistic planet: diversions his peers regarded as kid stuff. Then, psychologically, when he had the chance to add more adult tapes and disks to those Damitcha had given him. He learned vicariously what 'diversions' could be had on other planets. He began to appreciate just how unsophisticated Capella was, how narrow its moral code, how much more diverse and rich other lifestyles were.

He knew, as all Talents did, that the Rowan had left Altair to become Prime on the new FT&T installation on Callisto, Jupiter's moon. He heard, for he made certain that he did, of all the personnel shifts and changes required to suit the Rowan. Older members of the Capella team criticized her for such vacillation.

'Much too young to be made a Prime. That needs a mature, stable, responsible personality. What is FT&T coming to?' was the consensus. No-one mentioned what was so obvious to Afra: that there were far too few Prime Talents to wait until the Rowan was 'old' enough – whenever that would be – to accede to a Prime's duties.

Afra was also perversely excited by such reports of hiring and firing. That sort of thing never happened on Capella. Once drafted to the Tower, that's where a Talent stayed – until he or she retired after a suitable length of service.

Young Afra, now an apprentice in Capella's Tower, was in a position to learn that the Rowan had a powerful thrust, never dumped capsules into cradles, hadn't damaged cargo or passengers, and expedited both in- and out-system traffic, despite the handicap of great Jupiter occluding Callisto at irregular intervals.

Of all the Talents surrounding the young Afra, only Hasardar seemed to appreciate his restless disquiet. Yet Afra could not bring himself to apply even to him for advice on how to break out of the stultifying future that had been arranged for him.

When he gained manly status at sixteen, he felt it was time to remind Goswina about the Rowan's promise.

'Oh, Afra dear, you are only sixteen,' and though Afra could not doubt that she still loved him, he felt that she regarded him as little more than a child. Certainly he was no longer as important a love for her. But a mother should favour her sons above a brother. Which, sadly, he had to accept, knowing more of human relationships than he had ten years before.

'Callisto's one of the most important stations in the Federation,' Goswina went on, her thought backing up a tone that said she didn't feel he should complain about his obvious future. 'Besides, now that the Rowan has her own Tower, they don't give the courses at Altair anymore.'

'But you've heard how often staff gets changed at Callisto. And you said that I'd complement her. You must remember that, Goswina! Maybe it's me she's looking for.'

Goswina gently smiled at her brother's fervour. 'Now, dear, I hear that Ementish will retire in two years. You'd do very well in that posting. In the meantime, I'll see if you can't work at one of the southern subsidiary links. You'd be young to be on your own in some of those isolated waystations, but you'd be getting such good practice at catching and sending.'

'Sending drones?' Afra was contemptuous. He'd been catching drones at Hasardar's bequest for two years. The novelty had long since worn off. For his dear Goswina to recommend such a posting was a blow to his self-esteem. He was a T-4, 'path and 'port. He could do better than that for himself.

'You did rather let the family down, you know, Affie,' she went on, sweetly chiding. 'Father expected you to get highest honours, not just a mere First . . . '

'Mere First?' Afra was appalled for he had worked very hard to achieve that standard. No student in his year had been given a highest honours degree and he had been one of only three Firsts. But, once again, he sensed that her deeper thoughts were distracted by what scholastic achievements her young sons were likely to make. 'Thanks,' Afra said, trying not to sound bitter and, before she could ask him to mind his nephews, excused himself from her neatly kept house.

So he began to look at the other job opportunities for T-4s. As all his training, all his background had been to prepare him for the Tower, he was woefully short of the requirements for other sorts of assignments and would have to go through an apprentice year to refocus his Talent. Besides which, he wanted to get *off* Capella.

He toyed with the idea of asking Capella's help: she was always pleasant to him when he encountered her in the Complex gardens or in the leisure facilities. But Capella might think him ungrateful, wanting to leave his native planet, and his request would most certainly embarrass his family.

His chance came when he heard that the Rowan had fired yet another T-4 from Callisto Station. It took every bit of credit he had in the meagre personal account he had started with Damitcha's coin to courier his profile to Callisto in the mailbag. He had spent almost a full day to compose the accompanying note, and several hours before he was satisfied with the slanting lines of his calligraphy, much influenced by Damitcha's book. The note was brief enough, mentioning only that his sister Goswina remembered the Rowan most fondly from the course at Altair and would the Rowan consider his application to Callisto Tower.

He endured suspense greater than when he had awaited his test results and he'd thought that period had been nearly insupportable. He figured that he couldn't expect an answer for several days, despite the speed with which FT&T mail packets were flipped about the galaxy.

Therefore, he was totally surprised when Hasardar called him on the vid.

'You've lucked out, lad,' Hasardar said, waving a red transport chit, the kind that meant priority handling. 'Soon's you can throw some things together, you're to find a capsule to fit your long bones.'

'A capsule? Where'm I being sent?'

'Callisto, you lucky dog. The Rowan's looking for a T-4 and you're to get a trial.'

Afra stared at Hasardar, momentarily paralysed by news he had candidly never thought to receive.

'You're to go to Callisto, Afra?' his mother demanded in a feeble tone, as stunned as he was.

Having had no inkling as to the nature of the station-master's call, Afra had not activated a privacy setting so his parents had heard every word.

'Yes, indeed, Cheswina,' Hasardar repeated, rather surprised by the Lyon family's muted reaction to their son's great good fortune, 'Afra's been ordered to Callisto.'

'But how would Callisto have known of Afra?' Gos asked, staring at his son as if the young man had changed shape.

Afra affected a shrug, keeping a very tight control on his thoughts even though he knew his father couldn't, as well as wouldn't, stoop to probing.

'Maybe the Rowan Prime remembered her promise to Goswina,' Afra said, delighted that his voice didn't crack with excitement. 'Which is very good of her, you must admit. A promise made a decade ago. Who'd expect a Prime to remember?' He knew he was babbling as much from jubilation as a sudden fright that, in surprise, his parents might deny him the right to go.

'A Prime is exactly the person who would remember,' his father told him reproachfully. 'Our family is indeed honoured. But didn't I hear that you were to be assigned to a substation? I know you're being considered as a replacement for Ementish in our Tower?' There was a wistful emphasis on the possessive pronoun.

'Father, I can hardly refuse to go to Callisto, can I?' Afra said, pretending a reluctant obedience to a Prime directive but he could scarcely shout out his inner joy when his parents were so distressed at his news. 'I must gather travel necessities.'

'Come when you're ready, Afra. You can be despatched any time in the next hour,' Hasardar said. 'It is only an interview,' he added tactfully and disconnected.

Cheswina was trying hard to control her dismay at the prospect of her youngest child's abrupt departure. She did not feel that Afra was ready to meet the world on his own, though she had started looking for a suitable wife for him. There were plenty of girls who'd look favourably on her tall thin son because he was T-4.

Gos Lyon rose from the breakfast table. 'I am deeply concerned, Afra, about your being sent to such an unstable Tower situation.'

'It is just an interview,' Afra said, reinforcing his aura of dutiful compliance.

'I have heard,' Gos Lyon continued, both expression and mind radiating an anxiety that even a T-10 would have sensed, 'that the Rowan is a very difficult Prime to work with. Her station personnel are constantly being changed. You would be foolish to risk . . . '

'Humiliation?' and Afra hooked the unspoken word out of Gos Lyon's mind. 'Father, there would be no shame, or blame, if the Rowan did not find me acceptable.' Afra felt every fibre of his being denying his words, every ounce of his strength shielding his true thoughts from his distraught parents. 'There would, however, I feel, be an implied insult if I didn't at least appear for this interview. I will pack a few things . . . ' Indeed there was little in his room that he could not leave behind – with the exception of his holos of barque cats, his origami flock, his supply of paper and Damitcha's book. ' . . . and report as requested to the Rowan on Callisto. It is so generous of her to remember her promise to Goswina.'

Before his control on his real feelings weakened, Afra strode from the room. As he tossed a change of clothing, Tower shoes, holos, origamis and the book into a carisak, he probed deftly at his parents. His father was clearly stunned and most perturbed, uncomplimentarily concerned that his youngest could handle the courtesies involved. His mother's mind was running about in circles; would Afra present himself properly, would he be restrained and mannerly, would this Rowan person appreciate that he came from a good family and had been raised to the high standards demanded of Tower personnel, would he . . .

Afra closed the sak and returned to say farewell to his parents. This moment was far harder for him than he realized – especially when he wished so fervently that he would not be back in the few days his parents felt he'd be gone.

'I shall bring honour on the family name,' he said to his father, lightly touching Gos Lyon's chest over his heart. 'Mother, I shall be extremely well-behaved,' and he caressed her cheek softly.

His throat suddenly closed and he felt an unexpected burning behind his eyes. He hadn't anticipated such a reaction when he had wanted so desperately for so long to leave home. Much too abruptly for courtesy, he flung himself out of the house and strode as fast as his long legs would take him to the personnel launch cradles of the station.

He'd seen the procedure often enough to know exactly what to do. The personnel carrier was comfortable enough; certainly, no different from any of the drills or the few short distances he'd been teleported. A T-10 he knew checked him, grinned as he closed and locked the cover, slapped it in casual farewell and only then did Afra remember that he hadn't contacted Goswina.

Gossie . . .

Afra! You have a genius for picking the most awkward moments . . .

Gossie, I'm going to Callisto—

Afra, Capella's firm mental voice interrupted him then, *on the count of three . . . I wish you good luck, Afra.*

The next moment he knew he was being 'ported across the incredible spatial distance to Callisto. That didn't take as long as he had somehow assumed it would. He was aware of the 'portation, the sensation of disorientation that he knew he was expected to feel. Small wonder Primes, being so sensitive, had problems even on passenger liners. He was certainly aware when the changeover was made, when Capella released his capsule into the Rowan's control.

Afra? Did you tell your sister that the Rowan kept her promise?

The Rowan's mental tone, so different to Capella's, to anyone else's he had ever encountered in his lifetime, chimed silverly in his mind. The contact had a brilliance, a vivacity, and a resonance which immediately enthralled him.

I told her I was coming to Callisto.

Well, you're here. Come to the Tower. You are welcome, Afra. A silvery laugh shivered in his mind. *You know, I think Goswina was right. We'll see.*

The cover was unlocked and a rather anxious looking man, wearing stationmaster's tabs on his collar, extended a hand.

'Afra? Brian Ackerman.' The man's anxiety began to fade as they clasped hands. 'Capella grows 'em long, doesn't it?' he said, grinning as Afra got to his feet, standing centimetres taller than the stockier stationmaster. 'The Rowan can play games but don't let 'em get to you, huh?' he added in the tight low tones that suggested to Afra that Brian had his mental shields in place to deliver that brief advice.

Afra nodded soberly and followed the stationmaster to the Tower. It was only then that he noticed, and swallowed against his surprise, that Callisto Tower was a domed facility. In fact, a combination of domes plus the big ship launch area with cradles that ranged from the single he'd been landed in to the immense complex metal affairs that accommodated large passenger liners or naval vessels. Above them, loomed Jupiter. Afra controlled the instinct to hunch away from the giant planet. No doubt he would get accustomed to its dominating presence.

He also found himself breathing shallowly, and controlled that reaction as well: there was plenty of air on this moon.

'You get used to it,' Brian Ackerman said with a grin.

'Is it that obvious?' Afra asked.

Brian grinned. 'Everyone feels the old man and, sometimes, the whole alien feel' – he made a sweep of his arm to include the domes – 'can really get to the planet bred.'

They had reached the facility by then, a Tower more by grace than fact for there was only the one raised section that could be termed a tower. The administrative building was compact, three storeyed, the only windows the clear plexiglas that wrapped around the tower portion, giving the Prime three hundred and sixty degrees of visibility. Lights under the fascia boards of the roof beamed down on the plantings, counterfeiting sunlight enough to encourage growth. Luminous Jupiter's light did not support earth vegetation. To Afra's surprise, he saw a small copse of trees at the back of the terrain-hugging residence off to the right of the Tower complex.

'The Rowan's,' Brian said, noticing his glance, and then palmed the door open. 'She lives here. Primes don't travel much, you know, but she's good about sending us downside on leave.'

Inside the main room, consoles and work tables were placed along the walls, neat enough now as personnel were apparently closing down operations. There was a buzz of friendly chat and considerable interest in Ackerman's companion.

Afra caught mental buzz that identified him as the Capellan T-4. *No longer a pint-sized greenie,* Afra thought very quietly and grinned. If he suited the Rowan, he might even be able to see old Damitcha who had retired downside to Kyoto.

Vague reassurances were aimed in his direction, some of them wistful, some of them pessimistic about his chances but there were smiles enough to make him feel welcome.

'You were the last shipment in today,' Brian said. 'Coffee?'

'Coffee?' Afra was surprised. That was a caffeinated substance which was, of course, unavailable on Capella. Something to do with the expense of it. 'I wouldn't mind a cup.' He fished that phrase out of Brian's mind.

'D'you like it black, white, sweetened?'

'How do you like it?'

'Never had any?'

'No,' and Afra smiled ruefully.

'Well, try it black and see if you like it. Then we can add milk and sweetener to your taste.'

Afra was trying not to probe around for the Prime. There were so many people milling about, some of them flustered with the day's tasks, some hoping to leave for home pretty soon, that he wondered if she were down here. No-one matched the vivid mental picture Goswina had given him so long ago. Then he realized that the Rowan would be ten years older and more mature than that mischievous girl.

Just as Brian handed him a mug with an opaque black liquid, he knew the Rowan was in the room. He turned slightly to his left, towards the beverage dispenser which Brian had just left. Three people, a man and two women, were serving themselves. Afra's attention fell on the slenderer female figure, a mane of unexpectedly silver hair falling to her shoulders although her face was young, and oddly attractive though not in a classic style of beauty. He felt the first spurt – and ruthlessly suppressed that sense – of strong affinity.

Although the girl wasn't very tall and had a pale, rather than slightly greenish skin tone, she had the lean look of a Capellan. But there was no doubt in his mind that she was the Rowan.

Full marks to you, Goswina's brother Afra, she said and, audibly excusing herself from her companions, she jerked her head towards the steps to the Tower level. *If you'll join me?*

Her very casual manner was quite a change from Capella's formality.

I had my craw full of protocol and elaborate convention on Altair, Afra. I run a Tower, not a tea party. I also don't usually 'path conversations. For Goswina's brother I'll make an exception today.

He followed her up the winding metal steps, a bit surprised that she didn't have a ramp as Capella did.

'You'll find I'm not at all like Capella, or Siglen, or any of the other Primes you might have met.'

'Capella's the only one I've ever met.'

They were in the Tower room now, with her conformable couch, the various monitors and consoles that were standard furniture for a Prime's domain. Great Jupiter was visible, and the stark moonscape beyond the FT&T domes. The Rowan gestured for him to take the seat by the auxiliary console. Then she leaned back against the outer wall and cocked her head. He felt no contact from her mind but, unless he was completely mistaken, there was a bond growing between them. He hoped so for he had never met anyone like her before – so radiant, so vital, so vivid. Strength was an almost visible aura about her. And his father had always maintained that Primes contained themselves?

'I'd take you for Goswina's brother. You've the look of her. Sort of.' She smiled, an expression that only increased his attraction for her. 'What did they say when you got my message?'

'They were surprised. Then my father said that a Prime would remember a promise.'

'Ah!' Her grin was mischievous. 'So your family didn't know you had applied to me directly?'

Afra shook his head, unable, however, to break eye contact. So he gave a rueful shrug and attempted a self-deprecating smile.

'Aren't you supposed to take up a position at Capella Tower?'

'When Ementish retires.'

Her grey eyes danced. 'And that fills you with so much elation that you had to give me first refusal?'

'Capella is a good planet . . . '

'Goody good, I'd've said . . . '

Afra cocked an eyebrow at her qualification. 'When we took the Tower course, I met Talents from other systems.' He shrugged again, not willing to belittle his home world.

'And you wanted to see more of the galaxy?'

'One doesn't see much of the galaxy as a T-4 in a Tower

but I thought that it might be . . . challenging to spend some time elsewhere.'

She gave him a curious look. 'What are those odd shapes in your carisak?'

It was the last question he expected of her but he also realized that the Rowan would be unpredictable.

'Origami. The ancient art of paper folding.' Not at all certain he should act brashly, he 'ported his favourite swan – in a silvery white paper – into his hand and offered it to her.

With a wondering smile on her face, she took it from him, turning the bird this way and that, delicately opening its wings.

'How charming! And you just *fold* paper into that shape.'

'What's your favourite colour?' he asked.

'Red. Crimson red!'

He extracted a red sheet from his supply and, when he had it in his hands, he rapidly folded a flower which he offered her with a little bow.

'Well, that's not a mental exercise at all, is it?' she said, examining the flower. 'Flip, flop and you've got a small masterpiece. Is that what people do on Capella for entertainment?'

Afra shook his head. 'A freighter chief named Damitcha taught me – while Goswina was on Altair. I missed her, you see. Origami helped.'

The Rowan's expression altered to one of compassionate apology – and he felt the lightest mental touch, reinforcing it.

'She missed you, too, Afra. I heard all about you.'

'And you remembered your promise.'

'Not quite, Afra,' she said, propelling herself towards her chair and whirling around to seat herself. 'Because there's no course on Altair any more and you're already trained. So let's see if Goswina was right, that our minds will complement each other in the running of this Tower!'

She let him hear what she then said. *Reidinger, I've found me another T-4. Afra of Capella. He folds paper! Which is at least original. And he keeps holos of barque cats.*

So she'd seen those, too, in her mental sorting of his belongings.

ROWAN!

Afra winced as the bellow singed his mind edges. The Rowan grinned mischievously at him and signalled that he wasn't to mind the noisiness.

Well, he can't be any worse than the one who was certain that Jupiter would fall on her. Or that absolute dork from Betelgeuse who couldn't take the least bit of teasing. Much less that martinet you thought was just the sort to steady me while I was learning my job! No, this time, Reidinger, I *get to pick one. And that's that!*

Then she winked at Afra. 'I had an illegal barque cat once. I named him Rascal and he was but the ungrateful feline deserted me on the liner that brought me here.' She gave a little shrug and a wry grin. 'Not that I blamed him the way I carried on.'

'They hear us, you know,' Afra said, thinking that a safe enough remark.

She looked surprised. 'I suspected Rascal did. We enjoyed a friendly empathy but has one spoken to you?'

'Hmmmmm-rowwww!'

The Rowan threw back her head and laughed with delight.

'You're one up on me then, Afra.'

'Not for long, I think,' he replied, pure relief at surviving these initial moments, jolting the uncharacteristic retort from mind to mouth.

She laughed again, idly swinging the chair from side to side. 'Shall we keep score?'

'How much can I lose before you fire me out of here?' He didn't believe it was himself answering a Prime like this.

'Well, I just don't know, Afra. The problem hasn't

come up before,' she said, winking. 'The others have been such blockheads, they couldn't have capped a phrase if I'd handed them the hat! And,' she waggled a finger at him, 'if you hold your own against Reidinger when he vets you, you'll do yourself a favour there, too. Enough of this! I'll show you your quarters.' She slid gracefully to her feet and beckoned him to follow. 'We're off for the next six hours, you know, so there's time for you to settle in before the station's operational again. Then we'll just see how good Goswina's little brother Afra is!'

2

Callisto personnel had better quarters than Afra expected for a moon installation. He was frequently told that Callisto had been state-of-the-art when it was constructed eight years ago. Every new safeguard device since then was immediately incorporated into Callisto's dome. FT&T was not risking its Callisto Prime, and her station crew benefited.

Married personnel had quarters with their own garden and recreational area under their secondary dome. Single staff had two room apartments plus a large dining and recreational lounge. A well-fitted gymnasium centre used by everyone occupied another secondary dome, reached by a short tunnel, though the locks on both ends were standing open. The Tower facility, small capsule cradles plus the generators, underground fuel tanks, main water storage was mainly underground with access in a third small dome: the passenger and naval vessel size cradles under a fourth with airlocks and auxiliary tunnels to the main facilities. The Rowan's private residence with its small copse and garden, off to one side of the main complex, was under a fifth while the main dome offered primary shielding to all. Emergency upright shelters were strategically situated in case of a major strike penetrating the first and second domes and each living unit automatically sealed and had emergency oxygen supplies for twenty-four hours – the maximum time estimated for help to arrive from other stations in the system.

Afra found his apartment more than adequate, even to an imitation fire on a hearth in the lounge room, flanked by two conformable chairs and a rather battered low table. To one side of the mantel was a complicated orological device that displayed Earth time and Callisto's time in terms of revolutions about its primary, and a second orrery depicting Callisto's orbit around immense Jupiter as well as the erratic orbits of the other moons. If he read it correctly, he had another five hours and fifteen minutes before he should report back to the Tower.

Although there were cupboards, shelving for tape, vids, gamescreens, and far more closets than he needed for his one pitiful carisak, there was plenty of space for other furniture, suggesting he could make his own choices of additional pieces.

The ubiquitous communications desk was exceedingly well appointed with a patently brand new console and auxiliaries. When he turned it on, an introductory message filled the screen, inviting him to initiate personal codes and install any programs. He was informed that he had a monthly limit of free calls to his home system, that he could order necessities from Earth on the weekly supply drones at no cost or immediately at a special rate for FT&T employees. Facetiously keying a query on his credit balance, he gasped in surprise at the amount of draw he was permitted for an out-of-system transfer, the allowance provided for redecorating and furnishing his quarters, and how to obtain downside authorization and credit facilities for FT&T personnel.

'Another matter no-one ever explained to me,' he

murmured. 'Or maybe the parents expected to manage my credit for me, too.'

He placed the barque cat holos on one shelf above the console and his flock of origamis on the next, fussing over their placement. He leaned the calligraphy book against the side of the third shelf and snorted. Well, he suspected that he'd find plenty to fill out those shelves.

He investigated the bathroom, noticing the warning of daily personal water allotment, peeked into the tiny refreshment cabinet which included many exotic choices for a Capellan Methody lad, and went on into the sleeping room. The bed was as firm as he liked it and big enough for several bodies the size of his. That opened up another vista for him, heretofore scrupulously unmentioned, even if his parents had been considering the stabilizing influence of a nice girl for him. He grinned. Earth was not that far away and Brian Ackerman had mentioned that downside trips were possible. Tempting!

Then he noticed the second orological display.

'They don't risk your forgetting the time around here, do they?' Even in this privacy, he felt a trifle silly talking to himself. 'I need some music.'

'If you will name your preferences, these can be supplied on a select or random basis,' said a velvet alto which could be either male or female.

Delighted to have a voice address in-room system, Afra rattled off a list of his favourites and the soft string instrumental opus began the moment he paused to decide what else he'd like to have on tap.

'Thank you.'

'Courtesy is not required.'

'It was where I was reared,' Afra replied bluntly.

'Is a response required?'

'It would be appreciated. I promised my parents to remember my manners.' Then he covered his mouth against a laugh. All those drills on courtesy and he had a v.a. system to use them on? Even Goswina wouldn't be amused by the irony.

'Thank you,' the alto voice responded.

'You're welcome,' Afra said.

Then he noticed the time he'd been wasting. He dumped the remainder of the carisak's contents on the bed and, taking his kit, clean clothes and station shoes, went to the bathroom for a quick shower before his first experience of duty on Callisto.

Fortunately for his performance that day, Afra could handle all Tower procedures with routine efficiency, almost without thinking about the intricacies required, but he had never worked at even half the pace required of Callisto personnel.

We are the main forwarding facility, the Rowan sent him halfway through the hectic period. *We handle more traffic than any other Tower. You're doing fine. Don't fret. I don't think we'll wear you down today.*

Huh! Afra restricted comment to that one challenging monosyllable and kept right on working. It was exhilarating, to say the least, for his duties as the Rowan's second were to be sure of the orderly flow of destination placements, weights of cargo whether animate or inanimate, and special instructions from the tertiary rank.

Cargo-handlers (7s and 8s of kinetic Talent) who took travel documents from cargo pods of all sizes, single and double personnel capsules, and the various larger transit vessels, 'lifted' them into the Tower for sorting according to priority. 10s scurried about the landing field making certain all relays arrived in good condition, and always checking animate cargos. Inside the Tower, 6s and 5s assigned priorities and found destination coordinates. Brian Ackerman made sure there were no delays in those duties and established that everything Afra, in turn, passed up to the Rowan was in order, and kept the flow smooth to the Prime.

On a busy day, and Callisto was always busy, Afra as the T-4, was also required to reduce the burden on the Prime by expediting any inanimate cargo to reserve her capability for heavier, delicate and animate transfers. Afra could gestalt with the generations, albeit without the same range and strength as the Rowan. He had always secretly felt that he had more range than he'd ever been permitted to use on Capella – if only because he *felt* he could. Afra was also too well disciplined a Talent to be foolishly overconfident. But, working with the Rowan, he became aware of a sense of extended resources and deeper strengths which he had never experienced working with any other Talent. It was as if the Rowan added a new dimension to his Talent.

And that, my dear Afra, is exactly how it should feel between Prime and her backup, the Rowan said in between shifting two heavy freighters. *If it isn't there to begin with, it won't come, not for all the wishing in the world.*

That was enough to give Afra a second wind for the pace was beginning to get to him. Inhaling deeply, he carried on.

When the last drone had been spun out to its destination and the generator gauges on his board dropped down to zero, Afra was too expended momentarily to move. The muscles along his back ached and he had a mild throbbing at his temples. Then he grinned to himself. He'd survived. He hadn't made a single error – that he could think of. He felt someone standing beside him and craning his head to the right, saw the Rowan grinning at him. Lightly she touched his shoulder, just enough for him to sense a mental flavour of deep green and mintiness from her.

'We did good work today.' Then one of her arched black eyebrows lifted sardonically, 'That is, if you can keep up this sort of pace.'

'Try me,' Afra said, taking up the challenge. 'Just try me.'

'You just bet I will,' but her grin got broader and

her eyes twinkled. 'C'mon, I owe you a cup of coffee. Anyone want to go downside? We're in occlusion.'

A chorus of 'I do' and waving hands answered that offer.

'Grab what you need and find a capsule,' the Rowan said. 'I won't send you down yet, Afra. But plan on next full occlusion. Reidinger wants to interview you. Oh,' when she felt him tense, 'don't worry about him. I,' and she jerked her thumb at her chest, 'say who works in *my* Tower.'

Lightly she climbed back up into the Tower and, although the generator gauges did not so much as flicker, Afra could see the capsules arrowing away from Callisto in Earth's direction.

You've seven to catch down there, Reidinger, she said.

THEY'RE NOT SCHEDULED, was the roar from the Earth Prime.

Let your apprentices catch. My crew need the downside time.

So, how did that Capellan manage? Reidinger added and his words echoed in Afra's mind, confusing the Capellan until he realized that the Rowan was backfiring the conversation. Capella would never have done *that*, Afra thought, astonished, and held his breath for her reply.

He held up well today. I'll give him a three-month trial.

Not before I've seen him, you won't!

Sure thing, and the Rowan's tone was not only saucy but very confident.

Most of the Tower personnel disappeared when the Rowan made her transportation offer. Only Brian Ackerman remained, discussing a few matters quietly with Joe Toglia. Afra continued to sit where he was. He felt drained and even the few steps to the beverage dispenser seemed too far but he could certainly use a caffeine boost.

Then he saw one cup move under the spout, the dark liquid splash in and move aside for a second cup to be filled with sugar and milk added. As the cups made their way to his station, the Rowan came down the stairs again.

'Thanks,' he said with a wry grin of appreciation as she approached. She caught the back of a chair and, hauling it behind her, sat down beside him. He lifted his cup and she touched hers to it in the traditional fashion. 'Thanks a lot, Rowan.'

She gave him a sideways glance. 'Couple of things we got to straighten between us right away, Afra. Just let me know when you need a boost and tell me when you've foozled. I prefer to correct as soon as possible. Understand that and we could make a good team.'

Afra nodded his agreement, mentally too tired to project after all the exercise he'd had the past six hours. She continued to sit and sip at her coffee, the silence between them comfortable. In fact, Afra did not remember being so comfortable with anyone else before – except with Goswina when he was a boy. And before, he added deep in his mind, Goswina went to Altair. By the time they had finished their drinks, he felt somewhat restored. The Rowan recognized it, too, her grey eyes sympathetic.

'Take a long nap, now, Afra. Let your brain idle,' she said, rising and replacing the chair. Then she left the Tower.

Afra took her advice. Nor was that the only time he did so.

He was in the Tower for five weeks before Reidinger contacted him directly, though not in the bull roar he invariably used in his exchanges with the Rowan. At that, the strength of Reidinger's powerful touch direct to his mind was sufficient to dismay Afra. He had never encountered such a dense mind before. Capella had been firm and strong but nothing compared to Peter Reidinger, the third of that name to be Earth Prime. The Rowan was very strong, with hints of a substance equal to Reidinger's but never displayed. But Afra was now familiar enough with the Rowan to be comfortable, if still in awe. Reidinger was different. He was the most powerful man in Federal Teleportation and Telepathic. And on his approval, no matter what the Rowan had said, depended Afra's continued appointment to Callisto Tower. However, Afra managed a creditable, he thought, response, calm, unflustered, and above all, mannerly. His parents would have been proud of him.

Atta boy, Afra, the Rowan said when Reidinger's presence had withdrawn. *He loves to dominate. Has most of FT&T scared witless – saves him a lot of trouble to* have *instantaneous obedience but it* can *be inhibiting. You just carry on as you did and don't let him fluster you. Remember,* and here the Rowan allowed a wicked chuckle to weave into her tone, *he doesn't scare me and if I want you, I'll have you. Tell you what, Afra. Before he can bellow at you – and he will – present him with one of your origamis . . . say a bull in full bellow! A scarlet bull. Take the wind out of his sails. Distract him and you'll have the upper hand.*

Are you sure the upper hand is good for a lowly T-4 from Capella?

The Rowan projected an even more malicious grin. *Sweet-talking words is for a woman: standing your ground is a male prerogative.*

In retrospect, it was not Reidinger who awed Afra in point of fact, but the sheer size of the Blundell building, surrounded by the immense cargo and passenger terminals, cradles and auxiliary structures. Afra stood by the personnel capsule in which the Rowan had sent him from Callisto and gawked. The FT&T complex was larger than the capital of Capella. Beyond it stretched the commercial and residential towers of the largest single metropolis of the Central Worlds, receding into a distance his eyes could not adequately measure.

He was, however, aware of air tinged with an unknown

odour which his mind told him must be 'brine' since the FT&T complex bordered an ocean.

'Afra of Callisto Station?'

He whirled and saw a youth in the uniform of an FT&T apprentice, a stocky lad with oddly flecked green eyes, dark hair and a fresh complexion.

'Yes,' and he echoed the acknowledgement telepathically, testing the messenger.

The boy grinned and held up his hand in the formal greeting between Talents. 'Gollee Gren. I'm supposed to be a T-4.'

'On escort duty?' Afra smiled back, remembering his service in the same capacity on Capella.

'When no-one else is available,' Gollee said, not the least bit disconcerted by such duties. 'This way. You've got to clear security and that takes time.'

Even when it's obvious who I am?

Gollee shrugged, his grin droll. 'Don't be offended. They even go through the rigmarole for visiting Primes.'

'Don't lay it on too thick, Gollee. Primes don't visit.'

'Well, you know what I mean. Even T-2s get the treatment. No-one gets into the Great God Reidinger without clearance.'

Gollee had gestured towards the airy shell of concrete and plasglas that formed the entrance to the huge Blundell FT&T Agency Headquarters.

It did take time to clear security, scanners, retina search, personal interviews – though it was clear they had Afra's dossier on screen as he was interviewed. Afra was tempted to remark that a telepathic check from any T-3 or 2 would allay any suspicions, but the attitudes of the T-8s processing him suggested he'd better not interrupt the process with an impertinence. The security guards did not have his height but outweighed him by many kilos. They were especially concerned about his origami and subjected it to so many tests that Afra was alarmed that they'd ruin the little gift.

'Surely you realize that it's only folded paper? Here!'

He tore a sheet from the pad on the desk and with practised skill, folded a replica. 'See?'

The guards 'saw' but were palpably unimpressed with his dexterity, though Gollee was. Eventually they had to concede that it posed no threat.

Finally the security badge was grudgingly handed over. With a mental sigh of relief, Gollee led him towards the bank of grav lifts.

Gollee punched an intricate code, his fingers flashing so fast Afra's eyes could not follow nor was he able, in that instant, to read Gollee's suddenly shielded mind.

They're even stricter about that, Gollee said in an apologetic tone. *I've only just been assigned to guide duty and they really do mind-burn anyone who disobeys or bends the drill.* They would have to, of course, Prime Reidinger being so important to Central Worlds,' he added aloud and motioned for Afra to step with him into the programmed shaft. 'How long have you been doing that paper-folding? You made it look so easy.'

The upward motion was unusually rapid for a grav shaft.

'Basically origami *is* easy. Once you get the hang of it.'

'Where'd you learn? Is it a Capellan thing?'

'No, it originates from a place called Japan.'

'Oh, in the Pacific Ocean somewhere.'

'So I understand.'

Then, suddenly, a narrow aperture opened into which the current pulled them. The access snapped shut behind them. Gollee grinned at Afra's reaction.

'No way you can get into the Prime's quarters without the right clearance. The entire building is shielded and sealed . . . especially this part.'

'I don't think I'd like to live like that.'

'We never will. We're not Primes.'

A second, more generous opening appeared and remained long enough for Afra and Gollee to step out into the lobby which was elegantly decorated in soft greens and comfortable seating. Fractiles were displayed on a corner screen and soft music fell pleasantly on the ear. Gollee made for the door – the least ornate of several opening on to the lobby – to his left.

'Stand square,' Gollee murmured as they reached the door which then slid into the wall. They walked across a second lobby and to the centre door in its wall. 'You're on your own from here but I'll be waiting to guide you back. Good luck.' His expression suggested that Afra needed all he could command.

Afra squared his shoulders and eyed the solid wood panels and remembered the Rowan's advice. Would security have informed Prime Reidinger about a red paper bull and spoiled his gambit? The door slid open to admit him into the spacious suite occupied by Peter Reidinger.

'Come in, come in,' and the powerful mental voice was just as powerful and intimidating in its audible mode as its owner was physically impressive.

'Thought you might like this, sir,' Afra said, advancing quickly toward the semi-circular desk behind which Reidinger sat. It was a case of moving swiftly or having his knees knock treacherously. He was glad that his hand didn't shake as he leaned across the wide desk and placed the delicate red bull in front of Earth Prime.

Surprised by both approach and gift, Reidinger regarded the little figure. Then he threw his head back and roared with laughter.

'A bull by all that's holy! A bull! Horns, snout and . . . ' With one long and surprisingly well-shaped finger, Reidinger prodded the bull to a side view, 'and balls!' He guffawed again. 'That white-haired bug-eyed Altairian loon suggest it?'

'She's not bug-eyed,' Afra replied, indignant at such a description of the Rowan whom he considered rather beautiful in an unusual way. And when Reidinger regarded him in amused surprise, 'And no loon either.'

The Rowan had said he must stand up to Reidinger. He wouldn't have done so for his own sake but he certainly would for hers.

Reidinger smiled enigmatically, leaned back in his conformable chair, and steepled his fingers. Afra did not like the knowing way Reidinger eyed him and stiffened, tightening his shields – in case it would do him any good in the presence of this man.

'You were raised on Capella, Afra Lyon,' Reidinger said, his face suddenly expressionless, his hooded eyes inscrutable. 'Which is noted for its adherence to the manners other worlds ignore. Manners which are not ignored in my Tower, I might add.'

Afra inclined his head at this tacit reassurance of his mental privacy.

'The Rowan did suggest a red bull,' he said then, with a slight smile, aware now that Reidinger certainly displayed bullish characteristics.

With index finger and thumb, Reidinger picked the bull up by one horn and examined it closely. 'Origami!' he said suddenly. 'I've heard of it but not actually seen examples. Show me how you did this!'

'Paper?'

Reidinger opened drawers, frowning more deeply as he discovered nothing but paper's technological replacements.

'Paper!' Suddenly pads, flowered and pastel stationery, and large sheets of transparent plastic, littered the pristine surface of Reidinger's desk. 'Pick.'

Testing the various weights, Afra found one that would crease well, thin enough to fold easily but not tear. He squared it off and folded one corner away from him to the top, running a finger to form the first crease. Reidinger's eyes never left his hands until he deposited a small pale blue cow beside the horned bull.

'And an udder, by all that's holy!' Reidinger slapped both hands down flat on his desk, the breeze blowing the little cow over and sending the bull backwards. Tenderly, Reidinger righted the blue cow and drew the bull back to its original position. 'Where'd you learn how?'

'The chief on a freighter that regularly cradled at Capella. He's retired now and lives in Kyoto, Japan, in the Pac—'

'I know where it is. Been there yet?' Reidinger cocked his head at Afra.'

'No, sir.'

Reidinger widened his eyes. 'Don't you want to?'

'Yes, sir, when I . . . I . . . ' Now Afra faltered. Not quite brash enough despite the apparent success of this interview to commit himself to future plans.

Reidinger leaned back again, eyeing him speculatively. Then he gave a bark of laughter, shifting his weight so that the chair assumed an upright position.

'If you've managed to endure five weeks with that white-haired,' and Reidinger grinned unrepentantly, 'grey eyed . . . bird-like Altairian, I suspect you'll stay the distance. In fact . . . ' Then Reidinger caught himself up, cancelling that start with a flick of his fingers. He stood, a massive figure, big-boned and muscular, his eyes on a level with Afra's despite the Capellan's unusual height. He extended his hand, palm upwards, across the desk to Afra in a clear command for tactile contact.

It was most unusual but Afra responded without hesitation though he could not stifle his gasp at the shock of rippling power and how much Reidinger learned of him in that split second's contact.

My little loon's lonely in her Tower, Afra Lyon of Capella . . . And Reidinger's tone was as gentle as the hint in the words.

Afra was overcome with confusion. None of the exhaustive homilies on etiquette from his family covered this contingency.

'Be her friend, too, Afra,' Reidinger added in a brisk,

business-like tone as if he were recommending a particular brand of technology so that Afra almost wondered if he'd mistaken that quick mental message. 'Now, get out of here and let me get back to work.' He settled back into his chair and swung it to the consoles that were ranked behind his desk. 'Gren's to take you into the city,' he added without looking around. 'You won't survive comfortably on Callisto with a bed, two sagging chairs and a battered table. Spend some of the money FT&T's paying you on yourself for a change.'

Respectfully, Afra bowed and, turning around, left the room. In the lobby, Gren sprang to his feet, his whole body expressing concern and interest. His face broke into a smile.

'You survived?'

'The bull did it!'

Gren's smile broadened. 'Clever that. Ooops.'

In alarm, Afra watched as Gren's eyes suddenly crossed and, as suddenly, refocused. Gren shook his head and swallowed. 'I wish he wouldn't do that to me,' but then he looked at Afra and his grin returned. 'I'm *under orders,* no less, to take you anywhere in the city you want to go.' He winked and Afra caught a tinge of sheer sensuality from Gren which made him blink. Gren was his age but had obviously not had the strictures of Method to inhibit physical experiences. 'You've got a two-day leave of absence. So,' and he gave an impudent bow, 'what's your pleasure, T-4 Afra?'

'Mercantile, I think,' Afra said, gratefully seizing that opportunity. 'And something to eat.'

'Stomach's settled, huh?' Gollee's knowing look was sympathetic.

They retraced their way, Gollee informing Afra that his security clearance was valid for his lifetime. Gollee took him to the T-10 clerk who stored such badges and then down to the ground floor where he ordered transport for them.

Afra's first contact with the metropolis remained a series of brilliant impressions: the staggering choice available in the furniture showrooms (he surprised himself by choosing simple things, reminiscent of homely Capellan counterparts), linens in plain shades, rugs in geometric designs, rather plebeian lamps (from the look on Gollee's face) and two lovely Asian vases filled with flowers held in stasis forever at their peak, book tapes by the gross (titles he'd only heard of) and two paintings, both antique but pleasing to him. (Gollee tried to steer him towards modern artists but Afra found them too frantic in design, material and colour.)

In clothing, he allowed Gollee to guide him, for the youth's own dress was quietly elegant and well made. For someone who had never had more than three tower-jumpsuits and one good outfit, Afra enjoyed buying apparel that subtly diminished his alien complexion and accentuated his broad shoulders and erect carriage while imparting a stylish bulk to his lean frame. He liked the look of some of the trendy boots and had a pair fashioned, while he and Gollee watched, in the size, colour and style of his choice.

When Gollee realized that this was a major shopping effort, he called the FT&T cargomaster and arranged for a pod and cradle number to which all Afra's purchases could be sent, and transported back to Callisto on the next shipment, or whenever Afra came to the end of his credit.

Then, clad in a new outfit of dark green, soft leatherene boots and a fashionable tunic and trouser combination, Afra invited Gollee to take him to a mid-range eating place where they would replenish lost energy.

'I know just the place,' Gollee announced, with another of his reckless winks. Shortly they were seated at a table in an eating house with a pleasant ambience. There was soft music, subdued lighting, excellent appointments and a discreet menu which appeared in the top of their table as soon as they were seated.

The selection was literally other-worldly for it listed dishes from every one of the Central Worlds. Gollee appeared to be far more sophisticated than his years for he rattled off a description of items which Afra had never heard of. Afra tried not to let his ignorance or confusion show. Then Gren held up a hand to beckon an attendant. As the man came in answer to the summons, Gren looked earnestly at Afra.

'I know some of the specialties of this restaurant that I think you might like.'

'We-ell.' Gren's self-assurance and the good natured way in which he had steered Afra throughout the day easily convinced Afra to accede. He gave a rueful smile. 'I haven't had much experience with off-world dining.'

The waiter regarded Afra in surprise while Gollee's encouraging smile became very worldly indeed.

'One man's homeworld is another's tourist spot. My friend is in from Capella. How about serving us a platter of dainties that'd tempt him to appreciate Terran cuisine?' The attendant seemed reluctant. 'Is Luciano on today?'

'Luciano?' That did impress the man.

'The very same.' Gollee nodded pleasantly, as if discussing menus with Luciano was a habit. 'Would you tell him that the G-man is showing a friend of his boss about this aul' sod and we need to consult.'

The waiter raised his eyebrows. 'G-man? I've heard about you.' He gave a hitch to the white apron tied about his loins. 'I'll tell him you're in again.'

Luciano himself appeared between the platter of dainties and the soup. He gave Afra a friendly nod as Gollee introduced him.

At that moment, Afra had a mouthful of an unexpectedly peppery savoury and just caught himself resorting to telepathy to answer. He flapped his hands, first indicating his busy mouth and then giving the concerned chef the 'OK' sign.

'Spicy? Not spicy enough? Too spicy?' Luciano asked with professional concern.

'Too spicy, I'd say,' Gollee suggested with a laugh. 'I'm accustomed to your brand of seasoning but Afra must think he's being poisoned. Look at his face and how his eyes are watering.'

The arch look on Luciano's face startled Afra so much that he ventured to splutter around his mouthful: 'No! No! 'Sgreat. I like . . . spices.'

Luciano was instantly mollified. 'Ah, a man with educated tastes.'

'Not only that, Luciano,' Gren said, grinning with sheer malice, 'he got the ol' man by the balls and had him laughing.' Gren shot the astounded Afra a conspiratorial wink, 'And that's no bull, my friend.'

'You did that?' Clearly Afra had ascended ranks in Luciano's estimation. 'To the great man?' And the fiery Italian gestured in the direction of the distant Blundell complex.

Afra washed the rest of his mouthful down with water so that he could remedy this slightly skewed version of the morning's business.

'It was just a short interview . . . ' he began.

'With Prime Reidinger, which he survived unscathed,' Gren said, nodding his head up and down, his eyes wide with admiration. 'Afra made him a gift and got him to laugh.'

'The great man laughed?' Luciano awarded Afra a respectful glance.

'And,' Gollee paused significantly, 'Reidinger immediately gave him a two-day leave. I'm to see this tourist doesn't get into trouble his first time on Earth.'

'Ah, how wise of you to bring him here to eat, Gollee,' Luciano said, beaming with approval. 'And you have a formidable guide, Afra,' he said, meaning to reassure, 'for this one knows the very best places to go for whatever pleasures you might desire.' Luciano winked, setting one thick index finger to the side of his nose. 'You're in the best hands with this one. Have no fear. No worries. Gollee will see you truly enjoy your first visit to this ol' Earth.'

Afra was startled, not only by the Italian's remark but also by the underlying nuances which were exceedingly sensual.

'You bet,' Gollee responded, grinning with an anticipation which Afra sensed was as sensual as Luciano's. 'Best way ever devised by the kindly gods to relieve the pressures to which man' – and it didn't take much Talent for Afra to guess that Gollee made regular use of that relief – 'is exposed. What with one thing and another, Afra's had a tense and pressured day. Don't you worry, Afra. I know just the place.'

'And you will need to eat properly to enjoy yourself to the fullest,' Luciano said, rubbing his hands together briskly. He extended one towards Afra politely in reassurance. 'I will make sure that your energy level is sufficient to sustain you.'

In order to mask his agitation, Afra hastily bent over the appetizer platter, pretending to concentrate on his next selection. He certainly couldn't let Gollee see how much the innuendoes had disturbed him. He knew that Terran customs concerning sexual relations were considerably more relaxed than Capella's but to discuss such a topic over a meal, a meal which was going to be designed to stimulate and support the activity, was a shock. Yet both Gollee and Luciano seemed to consider it the normal conclusion to a stressful day.

'And I have a very special wine . . . '

'We're underage,' Afra protested feebly.

'Of course, I know,' and Luciano spread his arms in a gesture of complete understanding. 'We have a very good stock of grape juice.' And he cocked a wink at Gollee who grinned broadly back at him.

When the 'grape juice' was presented – in ordinary

water glasses – Afra realized that it was unlike any fruit juice he had ever tasted, filling his mouth with a rich tartness and expanding in the most pleasant way to the back of his throat and into his stomach. But, as he had also never tasted wine, he was unaware of what had actually been served.

Gradually, as the meal progressed and he and Gollee ate through the various delicious portions presented to them, he noticed that he was visibly relaxing. And, where at first the thought of losing his virginity had troubled his conscience, he began to see that if both Gollee, who was his age, and Luciano who was quite mature, considered a visit to a pleasure house an appropriate part of the day's conviviality, he ought not – out of courtesy – object to his host's plans for him. Then, too, Reidinger had assigned Gollee as his guide and Gollee had mentioned that he often did escort visitors. Surely it would be churlish of Afra to affect prudery. Afra flushed suddenly at the memory of Reidinger's 'pathed comment. Surely . . . He put that thought sternly from him. Perhaps it would be the better part of discretion to relieve his tensions here on Earth so that he could return to Callisto with no lingering stress.

So, when the meal was finished and the last glass of grape juice drained, Afra had no compunctions about falling in with the next item on Gollee's hospitable and helpful agenda. When Afra's guide led him to a large, well-maintained building in a discreetly parklike suburb, he was no longer the least bit apprehensive. The ambience of the interior was welcoming and Gollee was greeted warmly, Afra as well. He didn't even cavil when asked to undergo the obligatory physical scan and permitted a blood sample to be taken from his earlobe. He didn't even blush when required to place his ID disk in the processing slot so that his last anti-fertility jab could be noted. But then, Gollee was chatting away with the proprietor during these preliminaries so Afra could hardly protest a routine which was not at all intrusive, but mutually protective.

The choosing of a partner was also mutual, not that Afra noticed, but he was rather surprised when five attractive women approached him, smiling agreeably, and conversation was initiated. When the Coonie wandered into the lounge and right up to Afra, he was charmed.

'This can't be a barque cat!' he exclaimed.

'No, indeed, it can't,' laughed the tallest of the five girls who wore dark curly hair in a close crop to her well-shaped skull. She had unusually pale blue eyes which fascinated Afra for he'd never seen the like. 'This is a Coonie cat: the nearest we surface dwellers have to barquies. They're not quite as intelligent,' at which point the Coonie growled a protest, delighting Afra, 'but they've qualities of their own. Amos, this is Afra. Afra, meet Amos.'

To the Capellan's surprise, the Coonie immediately jumped in his lap and, standing up on his hind legs, put his paws on Afra's jaw and sniffed his mouth.

'You've made a friend!' the girl said, genuinely impressed. 'Amos has standards.'

Afra wasn't certain how to react until he saw the approval in Gollee's expression. And when Amos jumped down again and wandered out of the room, Kama of the pale blue eyes, moved just close enough to Afra so that their legs touched.

Somehow there was a transition from the pleasant lounge and verbal sparring with Kama seated so enticingly close to a private room. When it became apparent to her that Afra wasn't at all sure how to proceed once they were alone, she became quite supportive.

'I'm your first? Well, the important thing is to do what comes naturally,' she said, gently massaging the tense muscles along his shoulders. 'My first time was special for me. I could do no less for you, especially,' she added with a throaty chuckle, 'when Amos approved of you.'

Afra's nerves made the first attempt more of a disaster than a release. Kama gave him the most tender of smiles and suggested that they just relax side by side and become more accustomed to each other. She also kept running her hands about his body with feathery delicate touches so that very shortly he was ready to make a second attempt. Not only was that eminently successful for both of them but Afra was totally aware that her ecstasy was as genuine as his. That spurred him on to further efforts with Kama impressed by his stamina as well as his ingenuity.

When they woke a languorous time later with the room still dark, Afra shyly asked if her cooperation was limited by time or deed.

'Not with you, my dear,' Kama replied and energetically pulled him to her, 'not ever with you!'

When he returned to Callisto, he was both refreshed and exhausted, and stumbled into his quarters, falling over the packages that littered the lounge, and even the bedroom. The orrery warned him he had only five hours before he was on duty again. He told himself to wake up in four so he could wash and find something more appropriate than the glad rags he shucked any which way as he made for his bed. He had also shucked a great many inhibitions though it actually took some time for him to determine which ones.

During that work period, he discovered just what a temper the Rowan had. He was so aghast at a *PRIME* in a tantrum that he was beyond surprise. Familiarity with Callisto Tower allowed him to react automatically to the minor crisis, soothing the Rowan and flicking the required placement into her lap in the Tower. Then he initiated the defence he had effectively used to blot boredom and proceeded with the transfers in his usual calm and imperturbable fashion.

Only when the Tower closed down hours later, did he realize that everyone else's nerves were frazzled.

'How do you do that, Afra?' Brian asked him when the Rowan had stormed off to her own quarters, raw emotions swirling after her.

'Do what?' Afra asked, looking up from the bird he was folding. His hands and fingers were as deft as usual.

'Ignore her when she's broadcasting like that?'

Afra looked up with a grin. 'It certainly puts us on our toes.' There was no way he would admit that he had been stunned by her temperamental display. He had also been more fascinated than disturbed by it.

Brian gulped. 'Is that why she does it?'

Afra shrugged, opening the little blue bird's wings. 'She's the Prime. She can do what she pleases.'

Brian frowned. 'She always does,' he said sourly, and went back to sort out the mess of flimsies, pencil files and wayflippies that littered his desk. 'At least it was all cargo.'

Busy with unpacking his new possessions, Afra missed the first tentative knock on the door to his quarters. But a mental presence then impinged on his awareness so he heard the second rap.

'Come,' he called out, 'lifting' two cartons away from the door so that it could swing open.

It did, slowly, and he was astonished to see the Rowan peeking around the door, as if unsure of her welcome.

'Come in, come in,' he said, 'whisking' wrappings and styro packing pellets into an empty box and closing its flaps.

The Rowan slid in and closed the door behind her, regarding him with grey eyes wide and worried.

'What's wrong?' Her colour was wrong and her manner a dramatic contrast from the virago who had stormed out of the Tower a scant hour past.

'I want to apologize to you, Afra,' she said in a muted voice.

'*She's a lonely lonely girl.*' Afra quickly hid this recall of Reidinger's unvoiced assessment.

'Because I can take downside leave and you can't?' He couldn't feel her reading him nor would he breach Talent ethics by attempting to read her – in a remorseful mood or not.

'I think that was at the bottom of it,' she said and sighed deeply as she sank into one of the huge lounge pillows that he had just unpacked. Then she shook her head savagely: 'No, it wasn't. I must be honest with you if we're to continue as a viable team.' She locked her grey eyes on his yellow gaze. 'You've lost a certain tension. I can't.' She held up her hand when he opened his mouth. 'Reidinger's approved of you, you know.'

'I didn't.'

She gave a little shrug that was more a twist of her shoulders than a lift. 'You wouldn't have been returned here if he hadn't.'

'I thought Primes made their own choices . . . ' and Afra grinned at her.

She managed a weak smile but her body lost much of its tension. 'I didn't even have to argue with him.'

'He liked the bull!'

There was a genuine smile on the Rowan's narrow face now. She craned her neck up to look at him and he courteously dropped to a sitting position on the new table he had assembled.

'He liked the touch of square balls and *that,*' she pointed her finger at him, 'was your idea!'

'But it was *your* idea to distract him with an origami.'

Her grin broadened. 'But you still had to take the initiative and you did.'

Afra cocked his head at her. 'Were you listening?'

Eyes wide with denial, she shook her head vigorously, her loose and slightly damp hair clinging to her cheek until she pulled it away and tossed the strands back. 'Not me. I suppose if I really *needed* to, I could get into

Reidinger's lair. But I would certainly have to have a very good excuse. I see you put your downtime to good use,' she added, changing the subject as she looked about her with interest in his purchases.

Afra managed to control a rush of blood to his face, thinking of how he had spent some of that time. 'Yes, well,' and he 'lifted' over an as yet unopened parcel, 'I didn't bring much with me, you know . . . '

'I do . . . '

'And I seem to have all kinds of allowances for the transfer so . . . ' He used his strong hands to fracture the seal and brought out the lamp, crafted like one of his origami herons in a delicate ceramic. 'I couldn't resist this . . . ' He held it up and she responded with generous compliments.

'What else did you get? Besides' – and her smile was mischievous – 'reams of origami papers?'

She helped him unpack the rest of his purchases and approved of the disposition of furniture and furnishings.

'Would you care for something to drink or eat?' he asked her, finally recognizing the onset of hunger and thirst in himself now that the day's demands had eased.

'No, not tonight, I think, Afra. If you would be kind enough to join me tomorrow evening, I would be glad of your company.' She threw back her head, making eye contact. 'I'm a good cook.'

The Rowan was subdued the next morning but her work was steady and her manner much improved over the day before. Still, by the end of the shift, Afra steeled himself against the Rowan reneging on dinner.

He was positively startled when she asked: 'Is six too early?'

Afra shook his head. 'No, not at all.' His eyes lit appreciatively. 'Can I bring anything?'

The Rowan gave him a deep smile. 'Some origami paper, as I know I won't be robbing you.'

With a wad of various colours and sizes of paper, Afra paused nervously outside her quarters. He took a deep breath and pressed his hand against the door plate.

Come, the Rowan said and the door slid open.

Afra took one step inside and went no further as he took in the Rowan's spacious quarters. He had been more than pleased with his rooms but this – this was palatial! Of course, she was a Prime and less than this sort of luxury would have been insulting. Nevertheless, his eye was drawn here and there by the clever disposition of sculpture, paintings and the style of the furnishings. She had simple but extremely elegant taste.

And, judging by the subtle aroma that drifted across the lounge area, that extended to her cooking. He took a deep breath.

'Smells great!'

'Tantalizing, huh?' The Rowan called, ducking to peer at him from the kitchen hatch. 'It ought to taste even better than it smells,' she added and beckoned him to join her.

She had three pots simmering on the hob. She pulled a spoonful from one and turned towards Afra.

'Taste?'

Afra self-consciously bent down to sip from the proffered spoon. Mischievously the Rowan drew the spoon back, slowly enough that Afra at first didn't catch on to her ploy. He made to grab her wrist but pulled back, shocking that he would ever accidentally touch a Talent, especially a Prime, without invitation.

The Rowan caught both look and feeling. 'So serious!' She noted sadly. 'Do young Capellans ever have fun?'

Afra felt his cheeks redden as memory sprung unbidden. The Rowan's smile fell and she forced the spoon into his hand.

'I've never done it before, Rowan,' Afra blurted out in apology, both for his dalliance and the broadcast of it in her company. 'I . . . it . . . ' he struggled for composure,

'I mean, I had dinner with Gollee Gren, he's a T-4, my age. They seemed, I mean – they acted as if that's what everyone does on Earth. Gollee – Luciano – and I really did feel stressful. I do feel much less taut today. I – I hope I worked well—'

A suddenly magical smile pulled at the Rowan's lips. 'I shall also hope you performed well last night.' Her smile deepened as he gasped in shock at her reply. 'Well, I hope so for your sake, Afra. And hers.' She turned back to the stove and stirred one pot vigorously. 'First times are special.' She cocked her head at him. 'I was eighteen and he was special, too.' With an abrupt flick of her hand, she turned off the heat and began ladling the food into serving bowls. She gestured to Afra to take two and led the way to the dining room with the other two.

Seated, she explained the dishes. 'Sort of a smorgasbord of Chinese food – ginger beef, chicken cashew, kung pao chicken and—' she crinkled her nose at the last dish, finishing conspiratorily, '—something frozen from the BX.'

'And you did this since the generators shut down,' Afra protested, amazed that a Prime would go to such effort for a T-4.

The Rowan dismissed that consideration with a wave. 'Minutes! Lusena . . . ' Her voice trailed off.

'A friend?' Afra asked to end the uneasy silence that filled the room.

'The only mother I remember,' the Rowan replied. She tipped her head in a shrug. 'And more than a mother. Have you ever lost someone close to you?'

Afra shook his head, wishing for something to divert her sad shift of mood. 'No. But I cried for nights when my sister—' He broke off too late and regarded the Rowan sheepishly. 'I was only six and she and I always enjoyed a special rapport. I forgave you taking her from me when she said that you'd save a place for me.'

The Rowan grinned. 'Goswina called up the image of such a charming little boy. And she was so anxious not to sully family honour because we both knew we could not work together. I did sense that your family would have been so pleased had we come to terms.' Her grin turned mischievous again. 'I'd always wanted a little brother. You seemed perfect for the role.'

'Green skin notwithstanding?'

Rowan laughed. 'Skin's only the outer layer, Afra.' She reached up to ruffle his hair. Caught off guard by such an intimate gesture, Afra nearly ducked away but then submitted meekly to the fondling: quite different to Kama's. 'Sorry to maul you about, Afra. I realize that Capellans are too Methody to indulge but I don't think you're as Methody as you were.' She cocked a knowing eyebrow at him and he managed to suppress a blush, if only to thwart her intention. 'Rebellious yet collected, controlled, studious, clever-fingered, quick-minded, slyly humorous, openly amusing. The many faceted Afra.'

Abruptly she altered mood again. 'I'm glad that Goswina mentioned you. We work well together.' Then she compressed her lips, scowling until he looked at her, wondering what he had done wrong. Her grey eyes pierced him. 'Afra, mostly I need a friend.' She preempted his hasty assurances. 'I can't leave Callisto. I can never conduct my own search for a mate. I have to wait to see what Reidinger finds to send me.' She grimaced, quite distorting her beauty. Then, as she flicked her long silver hair to her back, she added, 'That I have to accept as part and parcel of being a Prime but I *have* to have one friend.' She regarded him steadily.

Afra had never experienced such an onslaught of emotions before. His face went numb and his mind raced in the tightest possible confused circles, hoping she wouldn't probe at such a delicate moment. The Rowan was offering a deeper relationship than any he had ever had with another human being, even with Goswina. Less than Reidinger had hinted at but, for many reasons, more than Afra had any right to expect. A Prime was begging him to drop the careful choreography of acquaintance in the hopes of the most miraculous of friendships.

Slowly, dropping his mental shields, Afra extended his hand to her, palm up. The Rowan looked at it, catching her breath and appearing for a long moment as if she would retreat further into herself. Impulsively Afra grabbed her hand. She jerked at the touch, then made her fingers unclench.

What would you have me do, my friend? Afra asked across this tactile bonding, tighter than mere telepathy. Slowly the Rowan relaxed and slowly her marvellous smile lit her face to beauty.

Afra made his bow deep and respectful. He doubted she ever made amends to any of the other Tower personnel. A Prime and the second in command of a Tower needed to cultivate their rapport – a rapport which must develop and intensify. To what degree? Afra wondered, once again recalling Reidinger's remark. Was that behind the Rowan's apologetic behaviour? In the seconds it took to complete the bow, Afra decided it would be very unwise to anticipate. The Rowan was a lonely person but not necessarily lonely for *him*, in spite of what Reidinger tacitly suggested.

3

Over the next few years, by a serendipity Afra never quite understood, the relationship between the Rowan and himself deepened but never in quite the direction Reidinger would have preferred. Their professional rapport was shortly so fine-tuned that even the other Tower staff knew that Afra was the aide she had been searching for.

On the emotional level, Afra became increasingly able to gauge the Rowan's moods and, if necessary, would warn the Tower personnel to slap up their shields and endure. He could sometimes turn her state with an adroit pressure of positive reassurance. Sometimes he couldn't and the tension in the Tower would become thick enough to cut. Once or twice, when he felt she had gone beyond the bounds of permissible emotional display, he'd reprimand her, in kindly tone, heavy with surprise at her lack of control: though he hated to borrow any of his parents' attitudes. On those few occasions when he did reprimand her, her turbulence would generally abate to a tolerable fury.

As stationmaster, Brian Ackerman suffered more than anyone else. When he threatened to quit, Afra would appeal to Reidinger. Of course, Afra never 'heard' what Earth Prime said to the Rowan but she would be reasonably docile for the next week or so.

Callisto was, in many ways, far more difficult a Tower than any other, including Earth's. So there was greater pressure on its Prime and Tower staff. Some lower T ratings weren't sufficiently flexible and were replaced but gradually, over the next few years, a balance was achieved and maintained. Afra also suggested a roster of temporary replacements when some key personnel reached an overload point. As a T-4 in gestalt with the station's generators he was able to, and did, send people downside for a few days' relief though, generally, the Rowan would oblige even if she was in a bad mood.

Since Afra could 'port himself with an assist from the station's generators, he availed himself of those periodic longer occlusions when great Jupiter, or several of the smaller moons, made traffic in or out of Callisto impossible. That was when he learned more of the planet of his ancestors.

The first visit he made, however, was to Damitcha in his forest retreat. Though the old chief was genuinely delighted to see his young friend, his mind wandered and, even during the brief stay, Damitcha became confused, thinking he was in Capella Port, or Betelgeuse, and wondering how Afra came to be so far from his home system.

More frequently, Afra accepted Gollee Gren's company on tours of the pleasure houses that abounded in the immense and sprawling capital of Central Worlds. These excursions were both relief and tantalizing for Afra. He met many lovely women, skilled and innocent, but none of them could hold his interest very long. He returned most often to the calm and understanding Kama – even if she teased him that he came more to dally with Amos, the Coonie, than with her. But she knew that he found solace in her company and she would arrange her time so that they could spend days together if he asked.

Back at the station he and the Rowan would engage in elaborate games, sometimes play-fighting with all the ferocity of mates. Sometimes, when the mood threatened to turn intimate, the Rowan would break away, hiding her head from the hurt she had imposed upon him. Afra's stern Methody upbringing helped him to school his expressions and turn his words to safer stances.

Their relationship evolved into something approaching elder sister–little brother but with an intimacy such blood affiliations could not attain. Afra, for his part, found it easier to accept *that* role than the young lover of an older woman. The Rowan used her greater age on him unmercifully until the two finally grew tired of it, dropping the petty bickering for the silence of dear companions.

Perhaps following the dictum that familiarity breeds contempt, the Rowan took increasingly to spending most of the station down-time in his company. Afra, for his part began to accept the gender differences between them in an attempt to aid him in his dealings with his less cerebral relationships. If Kama guessed, she never mentioned it. Nor did the Rowan ever seek to find out more about Afra's 'downside' friend.

That consideration only underscored Afra's comprehension of the Rowan's loneliness which tore at him viciously, sometimes at the expense of his seeking out Kama. His deep compassion for the Rowan constantly teetered on the verge of offering to provide her physical as well as mental comfort. He fought within himself over the fear that by not providing her with a physical bond that he was denying her the lover she so desperately wanted. But he feared more the consequences of his being wrong: of robbing the Rowan of the only person to whom she could spill her soul in an attempt to provide her with someone with whom she could share her life. And, deep within himself, Afra feared that perhaps she would accept; for he did not want to be the youngster in his love, he desired to be the consoler, the anchor for a young spirit blown by the winds of life.

But, as her loneliness manifested itself more frequently, Afra began to hope that she might turn to him. Certainly he was the most likely candidate in the galaxy, even if he knew that she could not requite his abiding love for her.

Unconsciously, he sought alternative solutions to the Rowan's agoraphobia, a problem that seemed to affect all Prime Talents, of being unable to teleport without violent reactions. After her first space voyage, the Rowan had arrived at Callisto Station in a near catatonic state. While Afra knew that Callisto, also, had had the same violent reaction to space travel, he wondered if there might not be a cure, especially for one as young as the Rowan was. If, he reasoned, the Rowan could escape Callisto Station and 'bring Mohammed to the Mountain' she would at least have the opportunity to dabble without it being immediately known to all her fellow workers. So he suggested that she try to overcome her space *cafard* by making small ventures off the surface of Callisto in a special capsule, cushioned against any movement and opaqued from any source of exterior light or view. With his mind to minimize the act of 'portation, the Rowan tried to neutralize her agoraphobia. Gradually, she was able to endure being 'ported beyond Callisto for short periods. Afra did not dare force the exercises.

Then the eighth planet of hot Deneb, bombarded by an alien task force, made contact with Callisto for desperately needed medical personnel to cope with the plagues spurted from space at the colonial planet. And the mind that made contact was male, young, powerful and unattached.

When the Rowan proposed a mind-merge to defeat the invaders in Deneb's skies, Afra was both elated and wary. But the mind-merge with Jeff Raven, successful as it was in destroying the intruders, was not sufficient to induce the Rowan to leave Callisto and join this potent young male on his home planet. Her despair hit a paralysing nadir so deep that Afra, and Brian, feared for her sanity.

Afra's rage on learning that Reidinger wanted to use the affair as a way of breaking the Rowan's phobia surprised everyone in its intensity. Reidinger in particular had come to consider the young Capellan of a placid temperament. While he put his anger on hold with the appearance of the very distraught Rowan, he intended to do battle again with Reidinger as soon as possible, after all, he had been *handling* the situation quite adequately, damn it!

The day was draining, more from the tragic air of the Rowan than the efforts of moving cargo. At the end of it, as Afra considered how best to help his Prime, a young man in plain travel gear arrived in the control room.

'You come up in that last shuttle?' Ackerman asked the stranger politely. Afra lost the answer as he scrutinized the man. He was tired but carried himself with a composed air marred only by a slight wistfulness and a greater nervousness.

'Hey, Afra, want you to meet Jeff Raven.' Ackerman's voice called him back to awareness. Raven, Afra noted to himself. Deneb, another part responded coolly. Deneb here? Afra had trouble believing it: Primes did not travel. Jeff Raven's eyes met his.

'Hello,' Afra murmured, rueful that his introspection had betrayed him.

'Hello,' Raven returned, his grin altering imperceptibly. Afra kept his expression fixed but he *knew*. He flicked his gaze away, unsure of his continued control.

What the hell is happening down there? asked the Rowan with a tinge of her familiar irritation. *Why . . . ?*

And then, in violation of all her own rules, she was there, standing in the middle of the room. She flicked a quick glance to Afra who jerked his head in the direction of Jeff Raven.

Deneb stepped to her side and gently touched her hand. 'Reidinger said you needed me.'

Reidinger said you needed me, the words rang through Afra's mind like bells. He watched closely as the Rowan reacted. Well inside his shields, half-ecstatic, half-destroyed, Afra thought: *Give her the care she needs! Give her what she will not take from me!*

And then the two Talents left, making their way up the stairs to the Rowan's once lonely Tower. Afra broke the awed silence of the other station crew by grabbing a cake from the box in Ackerman's motionless hand.

Eyes watering with the conflicting emotions that tore at him, Afra called out: 'Not that that pair needs much of our help, people, but we can add a certain flourish and speed things up!'

Over the next few days Afra spent his free time adjusting to the fact that he no longer needed to worry or hope that the Rowan might one day come to him for more than verbal comfort. Then he recognized, with growing anxiety, that despite all his hopes and fears the Rowan was stuck in a terrible limbo: loving but unable to be in the arms of her lover. Jeff Raven had shown that Prime Talents could cross the void of space without the terrible disorientation that Siglen's travel trauma had imposed on all her charges but the Rowan still had to conquer that imposition in herself.

Afra was delighted, if exhausted, when the Rowan awoke him early one morning to demand his aid in overcoming the neurosis. As much as he wanted to help her immediately, he recommended that she rest first and start the new attempt the next morning.

With two hours before Callisto cleared Jupiter's shadow and the station could begin its workday, Afra gently nudged the Rowan's capsule out, using his gestalt with the station generators to push it slowly into a Mars orbit.

Afra was delighted when he heard the Rowan's sour comment.

I can't just sit here in the cradle . . .

You're not, you know, he told her. *You're hovering near Deimos.*

She panicked and Reidinger screamed at him but it was worth it. Afra was sure that in time he could help her break her fear for he perversely determined that, now she had found her mind-mate, she was going to be free to be with him on Deneb.

When Afra brought her capsule back to the station and palmed open its door, he took her hand and pumped her energy levels back up. He was careful to get his shields back up before she could read him: not just because he did not want her to know his plans but also because he still was not completely sure of his emotions.

You don't need to treat this as so commonplace an occurrence, you know, she said with some asperity.

Why not? It should be! He returned with a smug grin. She pinched him. *Yow!* He sidled away from her.

His pleasure was short-lived, however. The next morning, when the Rowan thought of going to Earth, he balked.

'We've got some pretty heavy stuff to shift,' he warned her. But she glared at him and Afra found himself wondering if he could endure her during the necessary adjustment period. The Rowan told the staff they could prepare for the day's work without him or her, then glared at him.

'I want to go back to Deimos again. Now!'

'As you wish.' Afra gave in gracefully. Gently he pushed her back out close to Mars' largest moon.

Is Earth visible from this position? she asked him.

He rotated the capsule and told her how to use the controls to get a magnified view of Earth and its Moon. But the blackness was too much for her and, the moment he caught the explosion of fear, he yanked her back.

Easy, Rowan! he said, soothingly. But her reactions were so strong that they disturbed Jeff Raven way out on Deneb.

Scared me half to death, you did! Raven told her.

Jeff, Afra replied with some fear of reproach, *she's all right.* Afra added to the strength of his response by initiating a metamorphic massage to the Rowan to reduce her tension. Inwardly he was angered: *what* was blocking her so much? Was *he* trying to inhibit her? Was he rushing her in order to threaten her resolve? Afra detested even the thought that such petty jealousies could lurk in his heart. *I want her to be happy,* he told himself sternly. *I will be happier if the Rowan is happy.*

The day passed uneasily, with Afra walking a tightrope for fear of setting the Rowan off. But she worked more like an automaton, neither jocular nor snappish. They were just closing down the board for the day when an emergency cargo signal came through.

Some Fleet nerd to judge by the ID . . . Brian Ackerman started sourly. Silence spread among the rest of the crew until Afra turned to the personal capsule. Jeff Raven stepped out, tossed everyone a jolly salute and charged up the Rowan's Tower two steps at a time.

'There's nothing on this list we can't handle ourselves!' Afra exclaimed, thrusting the cargo manifest back into Ackerman's outstretched hand. 'Get those generators back on line!'

'But, Afra—' Ackerman began pleadingly.

'No buts!' Afra's yellow eyes burned hot. 'We will not disturb them.' He gestured peremptorily around the control room. 'Have Mauli and Mick report here, they've worked with me before.'

'Yes, but only when the Rowan was in gestalt, too.' Ackerman complained.

Don't task me, Brian, Afra snapped back, his normal aplomb shaken enough that he 'pathed. He jerked his head in silent apology, adding aloud: 'We *owe* them this much.'

Ackerman sighed deeply, nodded in agreement. He turned to the others standing around the control room. 'You heard the man, people! We've got work to do!' He grinned conspiratorially at the tall Capellan.

'Just don't try to resign because *I'm* bullying you!' Afra teased, waggling a finger.

'Wouldn't dream of it!' Brian responded heartily. 'Now, here's the first load . . . '

'That's the last load.' Brian said, handing the datasheets to the Capellan. 'Afra? The last load.'

'Oh? Yeah,' Afra looked up wanly, limply taking the sheets. Beyond him, Mauli and Mick reeled slightly in their seats. He walked over to them slowly. 'Mauli? Mick?' He looked down at them. 'Last one.'

The twins slowly rose to their feet, swaying. Afra grabbed their hands, apologizing. 'Tactile contact will make it easier.'

Fortunately it was a small cargo lighter. Afra suspected that Brian had saved it especially. With a great effort the three heaved the empty ship back to Earth orbit.

Hey! Watch it! Reidinger swore, steadying the tumbling ship as it popped into orbit just above the Earth's atmosphere. *Any closer and you would have drenched Sri Lanka!*

Afra ignored the comment, as they had done throughout the day in their contacts with Earth Prime. The excuse given out was that the Rowan was furious with Reidinger and not talking to him. The Rowan had *never* done that before but Afra was sure she would be amused by the ruse when he had a chance to explain it later.

'Afra—'

'—we can't do this again,' Mauli and Mick told them in their twin-speak.

Afra gave them a long searching look before he nodded rueful acceptance.

'We've got a passenger liner due through tomorrow, anyway,' Ackerman confided, the next day's cargo manifest on his screen. 'You're beat, I'll tell the Rowan in the morning.'

Afra shook his head. 'No, I will.' He looked around the control room at the exhausted crew. 'Thank you.' Then he went around the room, shaking the hands or patting the shoulder of each and every person. 'And please thank those outside who helped us today. I'm sure the Rowan will thank you, too.'

'They didn't do it for *her*,' Brian muttered under his breath. Afra did not hear him.

Afra knocked louder on the Rowan's door in his fourth attempt to rouse the pair the next morning. He had slept soundly but had woken quite early, nervously considering how to admit his weakness to the Rowan when Callisto Station had to go to work. There was that large passenger liner which, no way, could he and the twins 'port. He tried through the comsystem to rouse them again. No luck.

For a long time Afra stood at the door, fists clenched, breathing deeply as he considered the impropriety of the next logical act. Finally, as softly as he could, he 'pathed to the two forms inside.

I do beg your pardons!

A series of emotions and feelings washed over him: restfulness, satiation—

Rowan! You're broadcasting . . .

He caught snippets of her rousing Jeff, his tired response as he told her it was his day off and her gentle admonition that *yesterday* had been his day off.

She's right! Afra called desperately, adding by way of caution, *Reidinger doesn't know you're here . . .*

Why not? was Jeff's half-amused response.

He's not . . . Afra faltered, better tell them later. *He's in a very touchy mood.* As Afra expected, the Rowan, always very diligent, was ready to get to work but, to his surprise, Jeff held her back, all ready to rebel for another day off.

With all respect, Rowan, Raven, he remarked, falling back on the courtesy his parents had drilled into him, *we managed well enough yesterday but there's a passenger carrier coming in that requires the Rowan's gentle touch.*

Even that polite statement was received rebelliously by Jeff Raven who insisted on a half-hour hold while he and the Rowan broke their fast. When they'd eaten, they didn't exactly race to the Tower where, reluctantly, he returned to his responsibilities on Deneb. Afra's mood was mixed as he tried to be understanding of their need for each other and control his resentment of being unthinkingly abused.

But his silent dedication and that of the rest of the staff were well repaid in the Rowan's gentle smile, easy manner and efficient work throughout the week. Afra was disconcerted that he had to pace himself and the others gingerly to allow them to rebuild the stamina they had squandered in their support of the Rowan's day of rest. So it came as somewhat of a surprise when the Rowan, on the fifth day after Raven's joyful appearance, psychically screamed. *JEFF RAVEN!*

What's the matter, Rowan?

He's gone. His touch is gone! Instantly Afra rushed up the stairs to her Tower. Her panic had reached down through Afra to Brian Ackerman and Bill Power who followed the Capellan into the Tower.

We'll link! Afra told the frightened Rowan.

She opened to them, Afra marshalling the others in a mental pyramid with her as the apex and calling up the full power of the station's six generators. After a horrifically long moment, a panicked Rowan, terror-stricken, turned to him. 'He isn't there! Surely he's heard us!'

Afra had never expected that he would have to be the comforter of a bereaved Rowan. He had survived the stress of her meeting Jeff Raven, falling instantly in love with the man's charismatic personality: he had accepted that he would remain on the outside of that relationship in the role of supportive friend, steadfast companion. But how could he possibly cope with a bereft and doubly desperate woman who had lost her soul's mate? The Rowan needed his aid, *now*. He extinguished his fear, took the initiative and reached for her hands.

'Breathe more slowly, Rowan,' he ordered her in tones he forced to be calm. 'There can be many reasons . . . '

Rowan?

Afra squeezed her hands reassuringly at the faint call: 'You see, I told you . . . '

The Rowan jerked her hands out of his. 'That's not Jeff!' *Yes?*

Come at once! Jeff needs you!

Afra saw her determined expression and caught her arm as she started out of her chair. He could not imagine her trying the jump to Deneb after her black terror in viewing the Earth. 'Now, wait a moment, Rowan.'

'You heard!' She returned in resolute tones. 'He needs me! I'm going!' *I want a wide open mind from everyone on Station!* She added mentally, circumventing Afra. Then she was not there, in the Tower, but settling in the launch. *Where's my linkage, Afra?*

Afra's hands were tightly, painfully clenched to his sides. *Must I lose you, too?* The painful whimper came from the depths of his soul. He realized that if he did not refuse her, if he provided her the jump power to Deneb and she died, he would have as good as killed her with his bare hands.

Afra, do it now! the Rowan shouted. *If Jeff needs me, I must go! Do it before I realize* what *I'm doing!*

Rowan, you can't attempt . . . The thought jerked out of him.

Don't argue, Afra. Help *me! If I've been called, I must go!*

Afra turned slowly in the high lonely Tower to gaze

down at the sealed capsule and his beloved friend inside.

I'll be waiting for her at the usual point . . . came that faint firm mind-tone. Afra recognized its essential femininity, its assurance of the transfer and its over-riding anxiety for Jeff Raven. That confident assurance decided him, though logic informed him that Jeff's was the only powerful mind Deneb had so far produced. As he released his fists and assembled the psychic power of the station, the Rowan gripped his psyche strongly, bringing him tightly into the merge. It was as if she was convinced that if she held him so tightly he could not resist or alter it. She was wrong. Afra allowed himself a moment's amazement to realize that he *could* resist her, could stop this transfer. Then the coordinates were in her mind and she pressed against the generators and, with his sudden willing cooperation, was gone.

Long after the generators wound down to silence, Afra Lyon stood in the lonely high Tower of the Rowan, tears streaking his face as he worried and wondered and prayed as he had never done before that the Rowan was safe, that she could help her beloved and that he had not made the wrong decision in sending her to Deneb VIII.

His tears had dried, his fears had seeped away, and he had somehow fallen into the Rowan's chair when he heard a soft step behind him.

'Afra?' It was Brian Ackerman. He came around to stand in front of him and then gripped his shoulder to make him attentive. 'Can you hear her?'

Afra drew a deep breath, gently flicked off the station-master's grip and stood up. He shook his head. 'No, I can't.'

Ackerman winced and closed his eyes for a moment against what must now be done. 'You'll have to tell Reidinger.' He spoke carefully, weighing the impact on the tall Capellan.

I know. The voice of Earth Prime startled them both. To Afra only, he said, *I owe you a great debt, bold Lyon.*

And a myriad of images followed that thought: Reidinger knew that Afra had run the station the day Jeff Raven came through; he knew of Afra's valiant efforts to cure the Rowan of her claustrophobia; he guessed Afra's role in maintaining the balance of her sanity; guessed his role and power in the Rowan's trip to Deneb. Sadly the Earth Prime added. *I may have to draw deeper into your debt.* And Reidinger shared the fear that Jeff Raven would not live, offering Afra the position of the Rowan's comforter and Jeff Raven's surrogate. *You have always loved her, I know.* Reidinger added with flashes of sexual intensity.

Angrily, Afra shook his head. *You cannot even* begin *to understand!*

And Afra found himself locked tight against a powerful mind, a mind which could have picked clean his darkest secrets. *No, my friend, I do. In my fashion,* and Afra perceived a sincere fatherly interest, more tender than ever imagined, locked deep within Reidinger's gruff exterior, *I love her too!*

Afra sensed a change in Reidinger's thinking. *But you, my impetuous friend, I fear for you. It was one thing to be little brother to the virgin queen and attentive courtier to the royal couple. But some alternative might be needed to anchor her sanity. You are there and already have her trust and appreciation . . .*

Although Afra had always known how ruthless Reidinger could be in the care and maintenance of FT&T and his precious Primes, this half-formed suggestion made him more amused than indignant. Especially as they didn't even know for certain that contingency plans were needed. There could be any number of reasons why Jeff Raven had been unavailable to the Rowan: though it *was* rather difficult to find a logical one.

With all respect, sir, we don't need to go into that just yet, I think.

You know something I don't? Reidinger seemed to leap on him.

No, but I refuse to be negative. Especially where the Rowan's concerned.

Do you know how valuable *that girl is?*

To FT&T?

Don't roar at me, Capellan Lyon!

Then abruptly his mind-tone altered to one of immense and incredulous belief. *She did it. She pulled him back, though I can sense only the most delicate of flickers. She knows she's saved his life.*

A wave of relief that was close to orgiastic surged through Afra at that report. He had to grip the arms of the chair to keep his balance, so intense was his sense of reprieve from disaster. He knew that Reidinger shared his reaction.

Thank God, if you believe in one, for that mercy.

I do, I will. My gratitude for sharing the news. You will keep us informed of the conditions on Deneb?

Of course! Reidinger said reassuringly. By way of parting, he shot, *And Afra, I'll want you to retest when all this is over. You can't be merely T-4 with all the shenanigans you've enacted lately. T-3 at the least so I'm upgrading you. And paying you accordingly, starting today.* He chuckled. *We'll argue over backpay later.*

Afra started to protest the unexpected, and possibly undeserved promotion. But to argue with Earth Prime? Reidinger's laugh cut through that thought.

Please! Argue! You need the practice! Then, including Ackerman back in his conversation, Reidinger added, *I think it best that we all pretend I don't know where the Rowan is.* Afra was perplexed by that. *Let's just say that I've got games of my own to play, young Lyon. Until I tell you, the Rowan is not to know we talked. If she contacts you, behave accordingly.* And then he was gone.

Brian and Afra exchanged surprised looks. 'Well, you know he likes to play his games, Afra,' Brian said first.

Afra nodded, brows furrowed. 'We will tell the others

that he doesn't know and we'll continue as we did when they had their day off.'

Two days later the Rowan contacted him late at night. Afra was surprised that he could receive her, even with the gestalt of her generators over that distance. Maybe he was legitimately a T-3. He didn't mention that as he carefully made a note of the supplies she requested.

I may have to break them into smaller parcels than usual, Rowan, he said when he examined the complete list.

That's all right. The generator here can't handle too much, the Rowan replied forgivingly, then added, *How are you holding up? I don't know how long I'll have to stay here on Deneb to be sure Jeff's going to recover completely from his shrapnel wounds.*

Bet he'll watch where he steps from now on.

Does Reidinger know where I am?

Afra chuckled. *We're doing well enough. Generator three has magically developed a glitch which has reduced 'your' ability to handle heavy traffic.*

Oh, Afra! Thank you! Across the light-years, Afra felt the gentle caress of a grateful friend. He thanked Reidinger's God for deliverance from a less appealing role.

In another few days, Afra heard from Reidinger; the contact announced by a deep chuckle echoing in his mind. *I singed her ears off, Afra! But she gave as good as she got and begged me to send you a couple of T-2s.* Reidinger's 'voice' took on a different tone. *Who do you want?*

Afra shrugged. *If it's all the same with you, we're doing well enough just now. Just keep our loads like this and we'll manage.*

Reidinger snorted. *I just finished telling her I wouldn't have her burnt out catching cargo unaided, do you think I'm fool enough to burn out her best man?*

Afra was not aware that Reidinger was broadcasting until Brian Ackerman turned to him with a grin of agreement.

Sadly, Reidinger added, *I myself am too busy to handle the increased load of Callisto so I'm sending you a pair of T-2s. I'm sure you'll treat them well.*

How's the Rowan, Reidinger? Brian asked, boosting himself off Afra.

Don't you ever *tell her,* Reidinger returned with that incredible tenderness that so surprised the two stationers, *but I think she's doing just fine!* He paused. *Oh, and by the way, do you want to switch brands of whisky this year?*

Brian Ackerman's eyes widened in amazement; it was well-known that when he used to threaten to resign from Callisto Station on a yearly basis, he was bribed to remain with a case of his favourite tipple but it never once occurred to him that Earth Prime knew that!

Uh, no, I've gotten rather used to the Paddy's now, Brian managed to respond. Beside him, Afra doubled over in a laughing fit.

Torshan and Saggoner duly arrived and the Tower staff, worked just slightly ragged in keeping with a cunning plan laid down by Brian and carried through by Afra, were more than pleased to have their aid. Although there were several teething troubles, the calm togetherness of the loving pair of T-2s and Afra's demanding performance standards soon had the station operating at nearly peak efficiency within the week.

The routine was set in the next week and by the third week the station personnel had nearly forgotten life under the Rowan. It was shattered when a personal capsule arrived unheralded in a cradle.

Belay that! Afra called to a cargo handler who nearly crushed it with the capsule scheduled for that cradle. Afra was hot with anger at the near catastrophe. *Who the hell put that capsule*— he began and then touched the mind inside it. *ROWAN!*

Pandemonium broke out as the rest of the station heard his mental shout. Suddenly everyone 'ported in around her, patting her, talking to her, hugging her. The Rowan turned bright red in the face of such open affection. Afra sent a personal message on a tight beam to Torshan and Saggoner to explain the sudden disruption of his usually orderly station. They accepted his explanation calmly, saying that they would work around the celebration.

The next day's work, due to the Rowan's return, progressed with an incredible ease. Afra had forgotten how effortlessly she handled even the heaviest loads. Once the work was finished, Afra was contacted by the Rowan.

I need to talk to Reidinger, she told him, almost daring him to challenge her.

Is that wise? Afra replied, fretting that, somehow, she had discovered Reidinger's duplicity.

He can't be that bad! she responded, adding that Reidinger had no call to be angry over her absence. Afra responded diplomatically but somewhat defensively on behalf of Reidinger.

He gained a lot more than I risked, she told him.

Afra examined her carefully, noting the faint augmentation to her aura. His eyes narrowed. Was she putting on weight? No, at least not without good cause. *I know,* he responded warmly. Did the Rowan know her condition? Probably not since she'd had other concerns to divert her from noticing a physiological change.

I'd like to surprise the old geezer, she continued.

Geezer? Afra spluttered, thinking that she was due for a few surprises herself, especially as she'd never been able to meet Reidinger face to face.

You've contacts at Earth Prime Headquarters. Can one of them sneak me in without having to announce my arrival?

The question startled him so he continued to banter with her while thinking furiously under tight shields.

First he'd have to warn Reidinger, and then Gollee, but he did assure the Rowan that he knew someone who might do him a favour. He begged a few minutes to arrange matters.

Reidinger? Afra called in the tightest telepathic shaft he could manage.

Wha'? was the gruff response. *This better be good.*

Hurriedly, Afra explained.

And it was good enough for he could 'hear' Reidinger's grin quite plainly. *Excellent! I have to talk to her anyway and it'll be better if she thinks she's got me at a disadvantage. Here's what we do . . .*

Afra absorbed the instructions with a growing sense of betrayal. Reidinger perceived that and broke off. *Afra, you* know *that I want the best for her. She* needs *a father figure, someone to rebel against. And I need her spirited, rebellious. We all do.*

Privately, Afra remained unconvinced but he couldn't quarrel with Reidinger. And it might just have a beneficial effect on the Rowan's growing recklessness. Now that she could travel without ill effect, who knew to what lengths she might take her new freedom?

Thank you, Reidinger said, *I'll tell Gren.*

Afra turned his attention back to the Rowan. *Well, Gollee's agreed on my especial request to escort my* anonymous *young friend as far as he's able but security has to be placated. He'll meet you at the landing field entrance.*

Reidinger must have been listening discreetly to Afra's answer, for Afra caught him swearing. *Keerist! Security! I'll have to warn them or my security beams'll fry her when she jumps in!*

Afra turned hastily to call out to the Rowan but she was already gone. Angrily, he growled, *Reidinger!*

Like gold dust, lad. Earth's Prime Talent called back gently. *I'll treat her like she was my own blood. Uh-oh! She's here!* Reidinger faded out, and came back with: *I meant to tell you – will tell you later . . .*

Afra did not hear from Reidinger until the next morning as he was finishing his usual skimpy breakfast. 'Altair?' Afra shouted aloud when Reidinger told him of his assignment for the Rowan. *HOW COULD YOU?*

I had *to!* Reidinger retorted sharply. Afra, who had spent years learning to read emotion, caught an undertone of pain in Earth Prime's voice. It was the pain of command, the malaise that comes from having made too many disagreeable decisions; also, very deep, was the pain of a person who was just plain *old.* Afra hastily accessed his data console's readout on Reidinger – he was approaching his one hundred and tenth birthday.

Afra considered telling Reidinger of the real reason for his anger at the Rowan's reassignment but decided against it: the Rowan and Jeff Raven had the right of making *that* disclosure. Besides, Afra chided himself, he was not *sure* that the Rowan was pregnant. Nor that the child would be a boy and very talented.

Besides, Reidinger added in a very small tone, *I had to free you and Ackerman to perform a very special mission.*

Don't you think Callisto's been disrupted enough without removing us? Afra returned tartly. He frowned at himself, both annoyed and amazed that he could react to the man who *was*, for all intents and purposes, Federal Telepath and Teleport.

I wouldn't dream *of moving either of you!* Reidinger responded. *However, I have to think of the future beyond me and, frankly, while Jeff Raven's a good man, he does not have the skills required to run a Prime station. I want you—*

Afra was ahead of him. *Me? To teach the Rowan's husband? Has it occurred to you that the man might not even want me around his wife? Let alone himself and his children?*

It has, Reidinger responded sadly. *And I think it would be the greatest of catastrophes.*

Afra spluttered, spreading his hands in dismay. While he would be deeply saddened, he could not see how his personal feelings would amount to a catastrophe.

Reidinger made it clear to him. *What good are they to me if they can only work together? Do you* honestly *think that the Rowan would choose a man so petty? Come, you know she almost chose—*

Stop! Afra called, eyes closed painfully. *The Rowan is my friend and more. I love her like a sister. If her happiness requires that I step out of her life, then not you, nor the FT&T nor* anyone *will stop me!*

So you'll run away at the slightest possible excuse, will you? Reidinger hurled in response. *Green by colour, green by nature, is that it, Capellan? Are you afraid to look upon their love? Do you love her so little that you cannot welcome her husband with open arms?*

I never said that! Afra returned heatedly, yellow eyes flaring. *I will gladly work with Jeff Raven. He's a remarkable man and he well suits the Rowan. But you must understand, there are secrets, things the Rowan and I have shared that – that may make it very difficult for him to work with me.*

Give it a try, then, Reidinger said. *If it doesn't work out, we'll try something else. But don't prejudge the man—*

I already have, Afra returned with a grin. *She's chosen him which makes him special. Besides which, the man has such a way with him, he can charm anyone.*

Reidinger's response was laughter. *As he charmed even Earth Prime?* Afra was astonished that Reidinger grasped that hidden qualification. *I have always thought that you were a wise perceptive lion. Just think of this assignment as another way in which you help the Rowan – as well as FT&T.* The interview was over, Reidinger's mind faded out but not without a final warmth and an ill-concealed ache.

The interview left Afra mentally drained and emotionally confused. He had liked what he saw of Jeff Raven and could not but rejoice that the Rowan had finally met her mate. It gave him hopes that perhaps someday he too could be so happy. But he had not lied to Reidinger when he fretted that his brotherly intimacy with the

Rowan could prove a source of friction between himself and Jeff Raven.

Brian Ackerman buzzed his commlink. 'Afra, where's the Rowan?'

In response, Afra downed his breakfast, tossed the container towards the dishwasher and jumped to the Control Room. Brian started irritably with Afra's arrival. 'Her replacement's due in soon, Brian. Better let everyone know.'

'Replacement?' Ackerman echoed in his confusion.

A newly painted personal capsule appeared in the nearest cradle. *Afra?*

Here, Afra responded, sending a mental image. And Jeff Raven appeared in the room.

'I'm sorry we didn't have time to talk the last time I was here,' Jeff Raven said to him, extending a hand, his wide smile as charismatic as ever, His face still bore the marks of his recent near-fatal accident, but the vigour of the man was restored. 'But I guess we'll have plenty of time *now* to correct that.'

Bracing himself, Afra took the hand and returned the firm grip with one of his own. Feeling the generous surge of gratitude and respect before the clasp was broken, Afra could reply with complete honesty. 'I look forward to it.'

Jeff turned around the room nodding at those he knew and smiling at those he did not.

'If you haven't guessed yet,' Afra said to the Tower at large, 'this is Jeff Raven who's here to replace the Rowan. She's been upgraded to a whole planet, her native Altair.' He did not have to tell them that Siglen was no more.

'Afra,' Jeff called politely, 'a word with you.' Afra approached and Jeff looked around the room critically. 'Let's talk in the Tower.'

When they entered, Jeff looked around it. 'At least there are two couches,' he remarked cryptically. Then he looked at the Capellan. 'If we're going to work together, there's something we must clear up—'

Afra raised a hand, forestalling him, having already prepared for the worst. 'I can leave. Reidinger'll get you a replacement easily. There's a very good T-4 at Blundell, Gollee Gren: you may even have met him. You two'd probably work quite well together—'

Hold on! Jeff Raven broke through his apologetic dissembling. He regarded Afra searchingly for several moments. Then he grabbed him, hugged him tightly, thumping him on the back with sturdy fists. *Thank you!* Afra was confused. *Thank you for her sanity, for her happiness, for everything! I couldn't exactly convey all of that downstairs when we shook hands . . . not with everyone wide open for input . . .*

'Wh-what?'

'I think she would have gone insane if not for you, Afra Lyon,' Jeff said aloud. 'You weathered her rantings and ravings, her tantrums, her fears and always you were there to give her the support she needed.' He paused, drew another breath, 'While I was convalescing on Deneb, she was forever talking of family – even if mine is a bit overwhelming in the close quarters we had to share – but, whenever she thinks of family, your face comes to her mind.' Jeff grabbed Afra's forearm, reinforcing what he was saying. Then he shook his head, giving one of his lopsided grins. 'Look, Afra, you *are* her family, but when we make our union formal, would you do me the honour of standing to my right as my best man?'

Afra took an involuntary step backwards as the words sank in. He slipped out of Raven's grasp. He swallowed, found words.

'I guess I've been over-reacting but I've been afraid that you might resent my relationship with the Rowan.' He bowed deeply. 'I see that I was unutterably at fault.' He straightened, nodding to Jeff Raven's tight smile. 'You must understand that . . . over the years here . . .

well, we've become attached . . . not really involved, but emotionally attached in a special way. I know she regarded me as the brother she never had.' Hesitantly he licked his lips. 'To be perfectly honest, Raven, had you not appeared, I was perfectly willing—'

Jeff held up a hand. 'I know,' he said softly, 'and I thank you.' Seeing Afra's puzzled look, his expression turned rueful. 'Your hesitation only confirms what we both know now – she was never the right person for you. I don't know how I got so lucky. I devoutly hope that one day you will know the intensity of the bond we share.' His smile altered to one of sadness. 'Unfortunately, not many of my relations survived and all my remaining sisters and older cousins are already committed so you can't marry into my family.' Jeff shifted his position and drew a breath. 'Sometimes I babble too much, or so my mother tells me. I'll give you a chance to answer me: are you willing, as brother by bond, to stand with me when I exchange vows with the Rowan?'

A slight grin played across Afra's face but he bowed again, deeply. 'The greatest honour that you – both – could bestow on me.'

'Then why the grin?'

'Well, you *are* planning on uniting soon, aren't you?'

Jeff's question was preempted by Ackerman's call. *Afra! We've got cargo to move or we'll be backlogged for a week!*

'That was *really* why I asked you up here,' Jeff said. Afra was confused until Jeff added, 'I've never run a station before. I want you to know that whatever you say, I'll do. I consider myself your pupil.' With a wink, he added, 'I'm under orders from herself to trust you completely. I believe her exact words were: "Do what Afra says and don't mess up!" '

When Afra looked sceptical, Jeff gave him a pleading look. 'Very well, Jeff, as we're under *her* orders.' Afra made for the door.

'Where are you going?'

'To the Control Room,' Afra explained. 'Only the Rowan works up here.'

'I'll get lonely,' Jeff responded in mock serious tones. He waved a hand at the second chair that had been installed for the duration of Torshan and Saggoner's Primacy. 'Why not stay here with me? There're two feeds and it'll be easier.'

'My consoles at the Control Room are programmed for my particular duties.' Afra explained.

'I'll learn the running of a station quicker the sooner I understand your duties as well as my own,' Jeff responded. He waved Afra to come back to the centre of the room. 'Do what you can now and we'll have the technicians rig up more consoles here.' Afra was reluctant. 'Wouldn't it be more efficient to have the Prime and all the station crew in one room?'

Afra's eyes bugged out, Raven was practically *quoting* him! 'The Rowan never thought so.' Afra temporized.

'Hmm,' Jeff mused, 'Probably safer for the rest of you, given her volatile nature.' He cast a telling glance at Afra. 'And *you* would never think to argue with her. But my dear love is not here now and she *said* to listen to you in all things. So tell me, Afra of Capella, what do you think of consolidating the station's operations?'

A slow smile spread across Afra's face. *Ackerman, initiate the Epsilon Plan!*

Are you serious? Ackerman's response was incredulous with excitement.

Please, was Jeff Raven's response. *If it is a plan to consolidate operations, I can think of nothing more dear to my heart.*

Immediately! And Ackerman was gone, bustling off to set up a plan he and Afra had lusted over for many years.

Epsilon is the Greek symbol used to calculate efficiency, Afra said in reply to Jeff's unspoken question. He tapped a console. *You have just ingratiated yourself for ever to Brian by making his dearest wish come true.*

'The first cargo is a freighter, Prime,' Afra said aloud. 'The data is on your number two console.'

Within a week an ecstatic Ackerman reported a 20 per cent increase in the station's throughput. Afra noticed that the Callisto crew were eager to aid Jeff Raven in any way at all. His easy manner, willingness to cut administrivia to its least parts, and his relationship with the Rowan all served to cement their devotion to him.

Jeff took a break at the sixth day to visit the Rowan at her Altairian Tower.

'Will you be arranging for the ceremony?' Afra asked with studied nonchalance as Jeff prepared to leave.

'There's no rush,' Jeff replied absently. Afra grew silent. *Ready!* Jeff called.

Then he was gone and the generators wound down while the offshift crew raced to perform the little maintenance that was necessary.

Afra was rather pleased, two days later, when Raven returned with an incredulous look on his face.

'You knew!' He accused Afra. 'You knew and you didn't even tell me!' His eyes narrowed. 'How did you know?'

'I've been her friend for eight years, Jeff,' Afra responded evenly, not showing a trace of the smugness he felt. 'There's a slight variation in her that I was able to perceive.'

'Who else knows?'

Afra shook his head. 'No-one.' He looked apologetic. 'I would have told you but, after all, it isn't precisely the sort of information one lobs off the way one launches cargo.'

'But she didn't even know, until last week, or so she told me. And she told me as soon as she suspected.' Jeff gave him a scrutinizing look, leaving unvoiced his amazement that Afra should know such an intimate fact.

Afra was by that time well enough attuned to Jeff Raven

that he held up his hands in protest. 'An intimate fact, yes, but I've had to become very much aware of the Rowan on both the mental and physical levels for the last eight years. I'm delighted that the perception is verified.' He said that last with some stiffness of manner.

Jeff sighed and nodded. 'Sorry. I think *I* know my mate intimately but I also know, and accept, that there are many levels of intimacy, my good friend!' His grin dissolved Afra's coolness.

'Are you glad it's a boy?'

Jeff stared at him, astounded. 'I didn't know . . . ' and he shook his head in bemusement, 'and I don't think the Rowan does either that our child is male. I never realized that you're a precog, too.'

Afra shrugged. 'I'm not, but the child is a boy. Or did you want a daughter? I could be wrong.'

Jeff gave Afra a slow grin. 'I haven't yet learned to cope with my lovely Rowan. I'll hope you're right. I'll need more time before I have to deal with a miniature Rowan. Though it could be fun. How about you? Game for a repeat?'

Afra grinned back. 'I don't see as I have the option. I'm in too deep to change.'

At that Jeff chuckled, throwing an arm around the tall Capellan's bony shoulders. 'So what happened here while I was away, eh, Afra?'

Afra! Raven called at the beginning of his third week as Callisto Prime, *there's a T-4 here!*

Afra popped up to the rearranged Tower. He still had misgivings over the appearance of the revamped Tower. Wires ran all over the place and were a potential danger to the unwary but Ackerman cheerfully assured him that was to allow the Tower to be rearranged to the Rowan's old style if suddenly required.

'We'll have the new ducts laid in the next downshift,' the stationmaster added.

'Ah,' Afra was unruffled, 'Jeff Raven, meet Gollee Gren, T-4.'

Jeff nodded politely to Gollee who seemed to have lost his usually glib tongue in the presence of a man who was becoming a living legend.

'Glad to meet you,' he said absently, turning back to the Capellan. He very pointedly raised an eyebrow at Afra.

'You're not going to be here for the rest of your life, Jeff,' Afra began diplomatically. 'At which point you will probably want to know that you can work with another T-4. Besides, Gollee needs the training.' Afra grinned maliciously when Gollee opened his mouth to protest, a response not lost on Jeff Raven.

'I see,' Jeff said noncommittally but it was obvious to Afra how little he liked the notion.

Afra sighed. 'The best way to prove you've learned something is to teach.'

Jeff eyed him thoughtfully. 'The Rowan never mentioned this aspect of your personality.'

'The Rowan never asked me to train her, either,' Afra replied with a saccharine smirk. He wasn't sure which reaction pleased him more: Jeff's or Gollee's. He stepped away from the second couch. 'I'll be within call here if either of you need me,' he added with an overly courteous bow to both as he waved a reluctant Gren to take the seat and tapped a display. 'First launch is Earthward, Reidinger to catch . . . '

As he had hoped, Gren's mischievous stance matched Jeff Raven's 'homeboy' nature perfectly. By the end of the day the two were working the station's cargo effortlessly.

During the next several months, life at Callisto Station devolved into steady easy routine with Gren and other Talents arriving at scheduled times to work with the Denebian to broaden his ability to handle gestalt with different personalities. Afra and Ackerman noted that Jeff worked best with Gren, a report which Reidinger received with a grunt.

I've been hoping *to find a use for that one!* Reidinger exclaimed.

What, met someone you *can't handle?* Afra asked, amused.

I seem to have a problem with T-4s and -3s, Reidinger replied imperturbably. *It'd worry me except there're so many of them I can fire 'em when I please.*

Afra refused to rise to the bait.

The Rowan's return to Callisto Station five months later as a visit turned into a permanent reassignment the instant Reidinger learned that she was pregnant. Reidinger singed Afra's mental 'ears' when he admitted that he had known of the pregnancy. *Well, if I can't trust you, I'll have to set up my* own *spy.*

Afra was genuinely pleased to have the Rowan back at Callisto. While he had enjoyed working with Jeff Raven, he had to admit to himself that perversely he found greater comfort in his link with the unpredictable Rowan.

'Oh, by the way, Afra, the Rowan's been pestering me to ask you something,' Jeff said abruptly one evening as the station closed down.

'Oh, what?'

'If you'll stand as l.p. to our son?'

'Ell Pee?'

'Yes, *loco parentis.* Admittedly it's a Denebian custom but, considering the hazards on my planet,' and Jeff's grin was rueful, 'it ensures that someone whom the parents of a child trust will oversee its upbringing. The Rowan liked the idea as being much more personal than being made Ward of the Planet. We'd both be glad if you would be willing to stand in an l.p. capacity for our child.'

Afra was deeply touched and it was several seconds before he could speak. 'Nothing is going to happen to you!'

Jeff silenced him with a gesture. '*We* certainly don't plan on it but—'

'And you've a planetful of relatives . . . ' Afra hedged.

'They're there, of course, but it's the Talent aspect of

our child that we both want to sustain, Afra, and no-one on Deneb's got much Talent training. I know you are critical of the way you were reared on Capella, but I can say with objectivity that you've a large advantage in such training over me. And, besides, the Rowan and I agreed on you, Afra.' Jeff's blue eyes were frank. He quirked his head, his characteristic smile beginning to tug at his mouth. 'What do I tell her?'

Afra smiled a soft sad smile. 'Tell her that I would be a bad choice: if something happened to either of you I would surely be dead beforehand.'

Jeff laughed. 'Don't be morbid. You're not precogging again, are you?' When Afra vigorously denied that, he was audibly relieved. 'Besides, I've firsthand experience of how good an instructor you are, you know.'

Afra bowed deeply, once more falling back on ingrained courtesies to respond. 'Jeff Raven, please tell your lovely wife that I am deeply honoured and will be glad to serve *in loco parentis* to any children of yours and to the best of my ability.'

Jeff gave him a curt satisfied nod and a hearty clout on the shoulder. The Denebian never learned the non-tactile etiquette of Talents but somehow, such familiarity from Jeff never offended. 'Good! It's settled, then. Now, tell me, what do you know of babies?'

It turned out that Afra knew quite a lot about babies, having dealt with his sister's children on several occasions and having even minded the Ackerman kids when Brian and his wife needed a night off.

At the end of their chat, Jeff sighed deeply. 'You will let me know if the Rowan's keeping something from me, won't you?'

'Are you going somewhere?' Afra asked, startled.

'Yes, hadn't you heard?' Jeff's attitude was ingenuous surprise. 'Apparently Reidinger's decided to get his own back by making me a sort of roving Prime.' He drew up to his full height and made a mock bow.

Afra laughed. 'Remember when the Rowan told you Reidinger'd take it out of your hide?'

Jeff shrugged, his expression comical. 'For a worthy cause.' Then he winked, his expression turning slightly malicious. 'He might as well make use of my ability to travel. I'm the only Prime who can zip about as it pleases me.'

'Why don't you challenge Reidinger to travel now we all know that Siglen imposed the neurosis?'

Jeff gave Afra a long hard look, his eyes sparkling with mischief. 'I really should, shouldn't I? The old sly geezer. He'd probably growl something about teaching old dogs new tricks.'

'I think,' Afra said in a slow thoughtful tone, 'that I'm just as glad Reidinger can't. His mental bark is bad enough! I'd hate to know he could 'port wherever he wished and chew me out face to face.'

Jeff cocked one eyebrow and grinned with deliberate malice. 'Oh, well, you could always bull your way through.'

Afra blinked, gawped and then burst out laughing at Jeff's sly reminder.

'And he still has both bull and cow on his desk,' Jeff added. 'I think if you had to, you'd give as good as you got. Another reason why we want you as l.p. for our son. Say, you can't, by any chance, hear the baby, can you?'

'No.' Afra's response was definite and a little bit sad.

The birth of Jeran Raven was a cause for joyous celebration throughout Callisto Station and beyond. Everyone under the domes heard the healthy mental cry of the baby as it was born and the communal welcome added to the gentle ambience from the three adults present at the delivery. Attentive Primes also heard it; Afra had to carefully supervise the removal of kilos and kilos of rare flowers, sent by an ecstatic Peter Reidinger, from the Gwyn-Raven quarters. The arrival of floral offerings almost undid the careful schedule Afra and Brian had worked out to keep Callisto operating with a reduced workload while their Prime had limited capability.

Afra was working late, catching up on the rescheduling when the door buzzer to his quarters rang. 'Come!'

He rose and strode to greet his guest at the door. It was Jeff's mother, Isthia Raven. Afra had seen her about the station during the last days of the Rowan's confinement but had purposely not intruded upon her.

'You have not come to see the child, Afra Lyon,' Isthia began immediately.

'I've been busy and had no wish to disturb him or his parents . . . ' Afra hesitated slightly, not certain how to address this blue-eyed lady with a cap of crisp black curls.

'You may certainly call me Isthia.' Afra inclined his head. 'Rowan told me about you, how closely you work together.' She looked at him keenly. 'Are you afraid of newborns, then?'

Afra laughed. 'Hardly. When would it be convenient for me to come? Rowan seems to need a lot of rest these days.'

'She does, but *you* are always welcome. Come this afternoon and get it over with.'

'I scarcely consider it an obligation to be "got over",' Afra said.

Isthia gave him another of her searching looks. 'No, I don't think you would. But you are down as *loco parentis* and you haven't so much as cast an eyeball over my grandson. Yet you and the Rowan have been very close.'

'Not,' and Afra felt it advisable to reassure her on that score, 'as close as she and Jeff, if that is what you're worried about.'

Isthia regarded him with wide-eyed surprise. 'I'm not the least worried about it now that we've met for it is quite plain to me that you are an honourable person.'

Afra gave a slightly impudent bow which she dismissed with an irritated wave. 'Are all Capellans so inhibited?'

'All Capellans are raised to be courteous under any conditions.'

Isthia gave a bark of laughter. 'Good shot. We Denebians tend to speak our minds.'

'I'd noticed. It makes a nice change.'

'Well, I can see why the Rowan and Jeff rely so much on you. I just wanted to be certain myself that you'd be suitable as a default parent.'

'Is that what all this is about?'

'Of course,' Isthia replied stoutly. 'I like a man who doesn't balk at taking difficult paths or walking tight-ropes. But you could be easier on yourself now and then.'

Mildly surprised at the line this conversation was taking, Afra looked at her quizzically.

'Don't try that on me, young man,' Isthia commanded, eyes twinkling to remove the sting. 'You must come to Deneb some time. Let your mind rest from your very strenuous labours.'

'It would be my pleasure. Yours must be a fascinating world to develop such amazing Talents.'

'Develop Talent? Oh, I suppose so.'

Afra was nonplussed by her casual dismissal. He sensed that she had considerable Talent herself though Jeff had never mentioned that she'd been tested. If her attitude was indicative of the general population, it was no wonder Jeff and Rowan worried about Jeran's potential Talent.

'Come to think on it,' and Isthia's expression altered suddenly to that curious blankness that Afra had been taught heralded a precognitive episode, 'you will come to Deneb . . . ' She hesitated as her eyes, suddenly clouded, rested unseeing on his face. A chill raised gooseflesh on his arms. ' . . . to rest your mind and renew life.' Abruptly she shook her head, eyes clearly blue again. 'Did I go off just then?'

'I didn't notice anything,' Afra said smoothly, as much because of her earlier dismissal of Talent, as because her clairvoyancy genuinely had startled him. He felt uncomfortable with such cryptic talk. 'May I offer you refreshment?'

'That would be very pleasant. You don't happen to have tea, do you?' she asked wistfully.

'China or Indian?'

'Indian,' she said, a hopeful smile on her face.

'Earl Grey or Darjeeling?'

'Darjeeling,' she replied with happy relief. 'Marvellous institution, tea. A man who serves tea is certain to be an asset to the Raven Clan.'

'I beg pardon?'

'Well, you did agree to stand *in loco parentis* for Jeran, so you are, in effect, bound to the Raven clan.'

Afra was puzzled but caused the kettle to boil before he looked back at Jeff Raven's indomitable mother. 'If this is some form of ritual bonding . . . ' Some pioneer planets had revived rather barbaric customs.

'No, no ritual. Just acknowledgement of fact,' Isthia responded. The kettle whistled.

Tea-making, on the other hand, did require certain minor rituals which Afra dutifully observed, patently to Isthia Raven's delight. And for the rest of the visit they exchanged pleasantries.

Afra found himself waxing effusive in the presence of this remarkable woman and was genuinely unhappy when she took her leave.

'Oh, we'll talk again, Afra.' She warned him. *Be certain of it!* 'And when are you coming to visit your new responsibility? Not to mention his mother. She's fretting that her maternity is repulsive to you.'

Never! The response flew out of Afra before he could control the impulse.

Isthia merely smiled. 'She'll be glad to hear that.'

★

Jeff Raven insisted on helping Afra and the Callisto Station whenever he was available while the Rowan was on maternity leave. However, she became quite agitated when he protested her return to the Tower a scant ten days after her labour.

Arrgh! It was my body that strained, not my mind! she said in a fine fume over his protests. *Men!*

However, with Jeran not yet established on a regular sleeping cycle, the Rowan was apt to tire easily or be forgetful. It was a 'memorable' period, as Isthia later commented. Afra and Isthia spent much time together, volunteering for baby detail, merely chatting or playing bridge with the Ackermans, a game which both Afra and Isthia had missed sorely in the past.

Jeff was surprised when Reidinger summoned him to Earth for a conference.

'Why can't he just 'path me?' Raven complained to Afra when the formal message was received.

'I suspect he has his reasons,' Afra responded soothingly, expression carefully neutral. 'Do be sure to say hello to Gollee when you're down there.'

'And Luciano! Ye gods! What food!' Jeff licked his lips in anticipation. 'Be certain, I will!'

Hours later he returned. *You knew!* Jeff swore at him.

Reidinger is one hundred and ten, you've been trained on Tower procedures, you work like a maniac, you know every Prime there is, I thought it rather obvious. It was just a question of timing, was Afra's phlegmatic reply.

You didn't tell her, did you? Jeff asked with some alarm.

Of course not! There are certain surprises that must be personally delivered, Afra replied in a pointed reminder to the knowledge of the Rowan's pregnancy.

'Good! I can't wait to see her face!' And Jeff jumped to the Rowan's quarters to spread the glad word.

Brian Ackerman had watched the whole exchange

from a considerate distance but his curiosity overwhelmed him when Raven departed.

'What was that all about?' he asked. Afra shrugged noncommittally. 'Good news?'

Earth Prime! The mental seepage from the Rowan's mental exultation vibrated through every mind on the station.

'You could say that,' Afra said with a slight smirk. Then he added thoughtfully, 'You know, the Rowan usually shields and we've not had much "noise" from young Master Jeran but he sleeps most of the time. But hadn't we better get the bright boys working on a way to shield infantile babble emanating from the Rowan's place?'

Ackerman took on an abstracted look which turned puzzled. 'He's not loud enough to worry about. Oh, yes, she's not likely to stop with just one, is she? I remember her telling me she wanted a large family. Of course, she may change her mind. My wife did but, yeah, maybe we ought to look into the problem before it becomes one.' Ackerman jotted a quick note down on his ever-present pad.

Six months and two days later, late one night as Afra was just about to give up on an intricate origami dinosaur he had been trying to create for young Jeran, his buzzer beeped.

'Come!' he called, half-irritated, half-relieved at the distraction.

It was Brian Ackerman. Afra greeted him with a ready smile. 'You're here to tell me they've got the mental shielding prepared?' Afra asked suavely as he passed a cup of soothing tea to the greying Ackerman.

Ackerman looked startled. 'No, I was saving that for tomorrow,' he allowed with a groan. 'Jeff Raven asked me to drop by.'

'Whatever for?'

'Well, he should be—' The door chime interrupted him.

Jeff Raven apologized profusely to the two men for such a late night meeting. 'It's the only time I can be sure she isn't listening in.'

'Why?' Afra asked carefully.

Jeff raised an eyebrow. 'Well, I've something to ask you and it's difficult to leave her what with the way she's been acting lately. She's asleep right now with Jeran on her lap.'

'So?' Afra refused to be drawn. 'The way she's been acting and her sleepiness are perfectly normal, you know.'

Jeff gave Afra a second keen glance. 'I wasn't talking about . . . Oh, no! It's much too soon.'

'That isn't why you're here?' Afra asked, annoyed with himself for assuming the reason for Jeff's visit.

'Not exactly but I'll take the bad with good. Well, is she or isn't she? And cut that guff about there being some things that are announced privately!'

'Well . . . ' But Afra felt Jeff reach for the truth.

'One day I'm going to throttle my mother.'

'Isthia?' Brian asked, apprehensively for he respected the woman and knew that Jeff did.

'My mother's been filling my wife with some nonsense about sibling bonding. It was why Mother insisted on freshening every year.' Jeff did not approve of either theory or practice. 'Is it a boy or girl, Afra?'

'A girl.'

'So she figured out how to achieve that, too?' Conflicting emotions of exasperation and respect crossed Jeff's mobile face. Then his expression altered to worry. 'What I came to discuss with you is a very private 'path I had from my mother. She wants me to come to Deneb to check out an unusual happening. She thought she felt something, a presence.'

'Wasn't the Rowan fretting about some malign presence just before she gave birth to Jeran?' Afra enquired.

Jeff nodded. 'She, my mother and Elizara. Mother thinks she's experienced the same phenomenon again.' Jeff shook his head. 'I got no glimmer.'

'How can we help?' Brian asked.

'I don't know,' Jeff replied worriedly. 'But I felt I'd better put you on the alert. My mother's not one to cry "wolf" even if she hasn't fine-tuned her Talent yet. Only women on Deneb have caught the trace of whatever it is. Considering the Rowan's sensitivity, she might just get another jolt from it. That's why Isthia warned me. To let me know. We all know that that woman of mine can go off half-cocked from time to time and pregnant women are notorious for it.'

The other two men exchanged looks so pained that Jeff Raven laughed. 'Just restrain her from doing something impetuous right now – especially now – but I've got to get back to work.'

'You'll be on Earth, won't you?' Ackerman wondered.

'Maybe. It's hard to tell. I've been doing a lot of hopping about in my role as heir apparent.' He looked gratefully at the Capellan. 'It was most shrewd of you to have me work with Gollee Gren before this was announced, we make a great team.'

Ackerman nodded knowledgeably. 'He doesn't talk much but he hears a lot, this Capellan Lyon of ours.'

Jeff slapped his knees and rose from the couch. 'So, do I have your word?'

'Certainly,' Ackerman said affably, rising also.

Afra was more hesitant. 'There are some secrets best left with their owners.'

Jeff inclined his head in respect of the sentiment. 'I'll trust your judgement, Afra.'

Jeff's presentiment was accurate. Barely a week had passed before the Rowan presented herself to her second-in-command and the stationmaster, requiring teleportage to Deneb.

Ackerman took the lead. 'Now, look, Rowan, Mauli will do anything you ask but I'm damned if Afra and I will take the responsibility for you two, and Jeran, haring off to Deneb without at least checking with Jeff.'

Despite the Rowan's threats, the two were adamant that she check with her husband first. In a huff the Rowan did so. Brian Ackerman wondered if he'd been set up for a quick game of 'good cop, bad cop' when Raven, dutifully informed, acceded to her request. He caught a hint of amusement beneath the Capellan's cool exterior.

'Why'd she take Mauli and not Mick as well?' Brian grumbled as the generators wound down from the kick they had imparted to push the Rowan and crew out to Deneb.

'Mauli's female,' Afra said, adding when Brian almost snarled at him, 'remember that Jeff said the trace Isthia heard was only audible to women. And it may well be that Mauli's unique echo ability will give the Rowan greater range in hearing whatever it is that's traceable.'

'A sex-linked calling?' Ackerman was dubious.

'It *is* possible,' Afra replied, adding subliminal images of maternal instincts.

'Like Jeff said, Isthia doesn't call "wolf".' Brian wasn't too happy.

Afra shook his head. 'No. I'd be happier if it was a wolf.' He turned away, heading off toward his quarters.

'Where are you going?' Ackerman wanted to know.

'To rest,' Afra called over his shoulder. 'I rather think we'll need it.'

He was right. The next day the Rowan was back but Jeff Raven was off cajoling and collecting Fleet scouts to assess the threat that the Rowan, Mauli and the other sensitive women on the planet had 'heard' approaching Deneb. Jeff, risking his life in a little scout vessel, made a visual contact with the alien spaceship. That was sufficient for the Rowan to put Callisto Station on Yellow Alert. With his urging and the support of Mick and Brian

Ackerman, Afra unconditionally informed the Rowan that he would be watching and listening if she would take a much needed rest.

Several hours later, Jeff Raven's explosive mental *WOW!* went through the station like a bolt of lightning. Afra and Ackerman discreetly listened in on the ensuing conversation with the Rowan who had been roused by the cry. Jeff could now report that what the Rowan had named 'Leviathan' – the huge and very alien ship carved out an immense asteroid – was on direct course to Deneb and that the intent of its 'Many' mind was nothing less than the conquest of Deneb VIII and perhaps as much as the destruction of the human species altogether.

Afra interjected a comment once in the telepathic conversation, not only to make a well-intentioned point but also to assure himself that he could 'reach' Jeff at that distance.

The Rowan quite rightly insisted on going out to the threatened planet where she could focus and merge all local Talents should such a measure be needed. Afra left unspoken his concerns for Jeran; such a psychic storm would have untold ill-effects on the young mind. The Rowan apparently had no fear for herself at all. Afra need not have worried: Reidinger absolutely prohibited it, reminding the Rowan of the dangers, pointing out that her quarters were the only ones currently shielded against psionic backlash (Brian had managed that without even telling Afra). So Afra exercised his right to be *in loco parentis* for Jeran much sooner than he ever expected to.

Young though Jeran was, his mind responded to Afra's and he was quite content to sit in the Capellan's lap watching origami birds and fish and animals appear. When Jeran advanced from clapping and laughing with delight to reaching out with unskilful grasp to gain possession of the fragile creations, Afra patiently taught him how to use just his forefinger and thumb to hold the origami. And when Jeran fell asleep in his arms, Afra found that trustfulness particularly appealing. He regretted having to transfer the soft warm body to its crib.

The stress which the rest of the Tower personnel had so skilfully controlled with the Rowan present rose significantly as they allowed their concern over the severity of the onslaught to leak into the open.

A tray containing cups of steaming liquid appeared in the Control Room. Afra sniffed enquiringly and smelled only the best of coffees and teas, superior in quality and freshness to any available on the station.

Compliments of Luciano! Gollee Gren said, a chuckle of delight at his surprise in his 'pathing. *As long as I can and you need, there'll be non-stop refreshments at Callisto Station!*

The broad band statement was answered from everyone on the station with a welling of profound gratitude.

The refreshments were devoured and Gren had to make replenishments twelve times during the course of the vigil as this time Callisto, Earth, Betelgeuse, Altair, Procyon and Capella all stood ready to support beleaguered Deneb.

Reidinger's orders came up electronically at light speed rather than instantaneously via telepathy. Afra discerned why as soon as he read them. He approved of Reidinger's plan but it was dangerous to split the Talented forces in the path of the enemy. It was a gamble.

Afra worked diligently to ensure that the staff of Callisto Station was properly briefed and rested. Even so, the tension built acutely as the events around Deneb were relayed throughout the Nine Star League.

'Hey, that thing has slowed.' Jeff's voice, relayed telepathically, was linked over the station's commsystem. 'It's going to go into orbit around Deneb!'

'Why?' That was the voice of Isthia Raven, being echoed again by the comm telepath. 'I will not believe its intentions are pacific!'

Afra heartily agreed. The Leviathan had passed through ten Welcome & Identify beacons, breached the mine field laid out beyond Deneb's heliopause and sent out destroyers to engage the Fleet.

'No, certainly not in that orbit,' was Jeff Raven's droll response. 'Just far enough away for its missiles to be effective and too far for any retaliation from the ground – if we had any missiles of any kind. Ruddy bitches are going to pound the hell out of us again!'

No, they're not! Everyone in the Control Room started when Reidinger's emphatic tones burst forth. *Angharad Gwyn-Raven, the A focus is yours. Gather it! Jeff Raven, collect the B focus. Prepare!*

Afra! The mental 'voice' of Jeff Raven contacted him with a firm grip as he contacted the male minds that were his strike force. The Rowan would be gathering every female Talent in her focus.

Here, Afra responded calmly, letting 'go' of his mind at Jeff's touch.

Good! Raven returned with a sense of relief. *I cannot get Gren to respond at this distance.* Jeff's voice held a note of tension in it.

Don't worry, Afra hastily assured him and simultaneously sent out mental alerts to Gren and Ackerman who were standing by. *We've built a pyramid, with you at the apex.*

Slowly at first, then with increasing speed, Afra felt the lesser Talents of the solar system aligning themselves behind himself, Gollee and Ackerman. He was aware of a mental engorgement, passing through him to Jeff, as if he himself had swelled to the size of a small moon. *Callisto and Earth are with you,* Afra sent, passing forward a mental baton which was the combined will of all the male Talents that Earth, Callisto and all the planets of the solar system could muster.

Betelgeuse joins the Prime.

Procyon is on line.

Capellan men send greetings and are ready for the merge.

Altair here.

And far out at Deneb, Jeff Raven found himself the centre of a maelstrom of power. The timing was perfect, for as the Rowan-focus had finished pulverizing the minds of the 'Many', it was time for the Raven-focus to shove Leviathan to its doom.

NOW! Jeff Raven called and every kinetic male Talent was united in full gestalt with all available generators in the Nine Star League to divert Leviathan to a new trajectory – straight to the huge star that was hot Deneb.

That's what we should have done with the first attackers, the Raven-merge said.

We did warn them! The Rowan-merge replied.

And then, job completed, energies spent, the two foci of massed minds fell apart to their constituent pieces. Collectively the personnel at Callisto Station gave an exhausted groan, many falling over at their posts, sapped of all energy. The generators, suddenly freed of their load, whirled up to overspeed and circuit breakers tripped them out.

Jeff? Afra managed to find enough energy to call. He was not sure he heard a reply, like a man shouting across a windy field. *Reidinger, the generators have all dropped out. We're all shagged here, but nothing that a day's rest won't cure.*

I'll tell him, Gollee Gren sent back with overtones of a yawn.

'Keerist! I don't want to do that again!' Brian Ackerman swore.

Afra toggled the all-call on the station commsystem. 'Get to bed, people, rest. We're shutting down for the next twenty-four hours. Maintenance crew, work it out so that the generators are ready to go on-line by then.'

Brian looked over at him and grinned. 'Afra Lyon! I think that's the first time you've ever made a command decision!'

Afra was too tired to respond.

★

The Defence of the Denebian Penetration, as that act of alien aggression came to be called in the popular press, was the last act of FT&T under the auspices of Peter Reidinger. The stress had been almost too much for him and Jeff Raven's stellar performance had opened any door that had previously remained closed to the Denebian's good nature and steady charm.

'Not,' Reidinger growled, 'that I won't keep an eye on you!'

That problem, however, was not the least one to be considered with the successful defence. The one that concerned Afra the most was one that caused him considerable anxiety because he didn't know if he was misinterpreting some very odd remarks Jeran was making. And it was some weeks before he finally figured out where the toddler's observations came from and arranged to meet with Raven to discuss it.

'You're tense and your shields are wobbly,' Jeff said as soon as he met Afra in his office – once Reidinger's lair – on Earth. 'What is wrong?'

'It's your daughter.' Jeff's eyes widened. Afra went on quickly, 'With all the energies flowing through the Rowan during the Defence, I think your daughter has been affected.'

'How bad?' Jeff asked, face gone pale.

'Oh, not bad!' Afra replied, sounding very positive. 'It's just – just that I've heard Jeran talking to her.'

'Already?' Jeff was astonished. He sent a quick tight band to his mother.

Yes, was Isthia's considered opinion, *I'd say Afra is right. I wasn't too sure of it when Angharad was still on Deneb but if Afra's noticed the phenomenon, I accept his opinion. How is it manifested?*

On rather an infantile level, Afra said wryly, *but there is a mental contact between the two children. Jeran doesn't quite understand what's fretting her but he knows she's not happy 'in there'. He doesn't know how to answer. How could he?* Afra added.

Jeff was thoughtful. *The baby's reacting to the stress the Rowan felt? So we have to tell him what to tell her, carefully censured for a foetal mind?* Afra nodded.

I can see why you didn't want to upset Angharad. She exhausted most of her reserves in the Merge. I wouldn't want her stressed right now.

Jeff's grin was rueful. 'Yes, it could be disconcerting to have your toddler suddenly tell you that your daughter's unhappy where she is.'

'I have a suggestion,' Afra went on, 'which I've already discussed with Elizara as the Rowan's obstetrical adviser. Jeran's merely repeating the baby's anxiety. Let's have him make a physical contact. At a moment when the Rowan is distracted and won't either inadvertently curb the link or physically prevent it.'

It should work, Isthia remarked when he had finished. *Though I've never heard of a sibling talking to a foetus. Could we please have Elizara in on this conference?*

When the practitioner joined them, she suggested that while foetuses were not normally aware at this stage of gestation, she'd rule nothing out in the case of Angharad Gwyn-Raven.

There was a tremendous amount of raw power coursing through the Rowan's mind, strong as that is, Elizara said thoughtfully. *After all, I was part of it. I didn't think of such a side-effect but there certainly could be a leakage into the physical. An unborn child would assuredly be vulnerable in this trimester and could become charged.*

Isthia's tone reflected her concern. *I feel that Afra's suggestion should be implemented as soon as possible and, preferably, without Angharad's knowledge.*

Indeed, especially without her awareness, Elizara agreed.

'It might not be a bad time for an official acknowledgement of your union,' Afra suggested subtly.

'Official?' Jeff made a face.

Yes, Jeff Raven! Marry the girl! Isthia shot back across the stars.

It hardly seems necessary to go through an official acknowledgement at this late date, Mother!

To you but not to her. The force of Isthia's reply rocked Jeff back in his seat. He turned to Afra, a slow grin forming. 'Still willing to be best man?'

Jeff wanted Deneb, Reidinger wanted Earth and the Rowan got Callisto as the site of the wedding. Jeff had to give in to the political overtones of this, the first union of two Primes. 'Much though I hate it, it's a great chance to cement certain alliances firmly with the Gwyn-Raven dynasty.'

Reidinger had fought bitterly to have the brief ceremony held on Earth. And, indeed, the Rowan was sorely tempted. But that would have allowed FT&T too free a hand with invitations, whereas limiting guests to space available in the Tower Compound restricted the numbers to a manageable quantity. She also didn't want just anyone 'porting in on them on what ought to be a private and personal occasion. Fortunately, Rowan had more cooperation than she expected. It took the best efforts of Jeff, Isthia, Afra, and Elizara to soothe Reidinger's vociferous protests. Elizara might have had a private word with her great-grandfather because, suddenly he subsided in his efforts to get the Rowan to Earth. Afra told the Rowan that it was only because he had promised Reidinger that every angle of the ceremony would be taped.

'I know it doesn't matter on Earth,' Isthia had said as a final argument, 'but some purists might fault a bride who is not only pregnant but has a child old enough to be ring-bearer.'

Afra instantly assumed the task of instructing the 'ring-bearer'. With a gentle but firm pressure, he also told Jeran that he could reassure his sister and how to send such a mental message.

'You tell her that she's quite safe now, and that you'll protect her, too.'

With brows knitted in concentration, Jeran repeated that message, taking some comfort in it himself.

Like I take care of the origami? he asked. Afra had hunkered down to his level so child and man were nearly on the same level.

'As gently as you take care of the origami,' Afra said, and reinforced that message mentally. Jeran's brow cleared and he beamed at Afra, his mind as tranquil as it was determined to perform his two tasks perfectly.

The ceremony was simple but poignant. Because the 'old man' – Reidinger – could not be present to give her away, Gollee Gren, as his representative, lent his physical presence while Reidinger did the talking.

'As usual,' Gollee had said with a malicious smile. Reidinger might not have been there in person but his inescapable mental presence was felt by all who were.

Mauli, Elizara, Rakella, Besseva, Torshan and Captain Lodjyn of the scout that had carried Jeff on his close reconnoitre of the Leviathan, all were happy to be the Rowan's attendant-witnesses. Afra felt quite nervous in his place of honour as groom's man and he had a right to be. He had assiduously studied and performed all the traditional duties of best man, relieving the bride and groom of most worries in preparing for the event. Ackerman headed the groom's men who included Bill Powers, Chief Medic Asaph and Admiral Tomiakin.

Jeff paused dramatically when it came time to say 'I do', a twinkle in his eyes until he had the Rowan glaring fiercely at him in alarm.

Reidinger broke the tableau, swearing *sotto voce* 'It's a bit late now for cold feet! If you don't marry her, I will!'

Jeff paused long enough to give the old Earth Prime a hefty mental buffet, then turned back to the Rowan. The adjudicator coughed delicately, repeating 'Do you wish to form a permanent union with this woman?'

'I most certainly do!' Jeff said in a clear firm voice that carried throughout the dome.

'And you, Angharad Gwyn, do you wish to form a permanent union with this man?'

The Rowan cocked a head at Jeff but could not bring herself to drag the scene out. 'With all my heart, I do.'

Just at that moment, as Jeff and Angharad bent to seal the ceremony with a kiss, Jeran slipped from Isthia's loose hand and rushed to cling to his mother, hand upraised.

Good boy! Isthia sent to the youngster in a tight shield. *Talk to her, say hello to your sister!*

Elizara gave an approving wink, then cocked her head as if listening. Eyes widening in astonishment, she nodded. She caught Afra's rapt expression, traced it to the eldest Rowan child and raised her eyebrow provocatively at him. Afra acknowledged it with the merest flick of an eyebrow.

Jeff and Angharad, locked in a kiss made more special by the moment, knew nothing of the tight psychic interchange.

The navy had a special surprise as they made their way to the reception, a double line of uniformed men forming a bridge of steel with their archaic, polished swords.

Elizara caught up with Afra at the reception. 'It worked, you know.'

'Yes, I thought I felt her accept Jeran.'

'Nevertheless an *in utero* link is most remarkable. It's been just a concept.'

'Till now.' Afra grinned. 'My sister tried some sort of pre-natal reassurance but she would never admit to me just how successful she was. Do you think it will comfort the child now?'

'I felt her relax,' Elizara said, smiling tenderly, then added more briskly. 'Let's hope the Rowan never realizes how dangerous that merge might have been for her daughter. She'd never forgive herself. At least,' and Elizara's smile turned mischievous. 'At least today she had her mind on other matters and may never realize what was achieved.' She gave a girlish giggle which surprised Afra who had always found the practitioner the model of decorum. Then a thought distracted her. 'Now all we have to worry about is the effect on the two children!'

'They'll surely be closer than usual,' Afra replied.

'Which will please the Rowan, I know, but what about future siblings? We can't be sure we can mind-bond every child the Rowan has.'

'Why would we need to? The circumstances are unlikely to be repeated,' Afra said blithely and gave a diffident shrug.

One final surprise crowned the event, at least from the Rowan's viewpoint. The liner which had brought so many notables to Callisto for the ceremony had been the same one which had transported her from Altair to Jupiter's moon. It wasn't until Jeff had carried his officially acknowledged mate back to their quarters, that the significance became apparent.

'WHAT is that?' Jeff demanded, pointing to a large spotted furry lump in the middle of their bed.

The lump stirred, extended limbs, yawned widely, showing long white fangs, and then deigned to regard the intruders with vivid eyes.

'Rascal? Rascal!' the Rowan cried, her voice incredulous, her expression joyful.

'It's some rascal all right,' Jeff replied tartly, 'and it'll get out of my bed immediately. I have other plans . . . '

'You don't understand, Jeff, it's Rascal, my barque cat!' And the Rowan plunked herself down, reaching out to tickle the chin of the beautiful beast. 'Oh, Rascal, you've come back to me.'

'Mmmmrrrow!' said Rascal conversationally. He then graciously accepted her homage.

'Come, Jeff, pet him. Make him feel welcome.'

'Frankly, I don't wish to make—'

'Jeff Raven!' And the Rowan gave him a thoroughly indignant glance. 'Barque cats are special. We're honoured by his presence.'

'We are?'

To keep peace on such an important night, Jeff did as the Rowan asked. Then she did as he asked and Rascal learned to find somewhere else, safer, to spend his nights.

4

Her face displaying a look of surprise and disappointment, Damia's baby legs gave out from underneath her and she *plopped* on to her dry-padded bottom. For a moment she considered crying but the disdainful look from Rascal assured her that he would provide no sympathy. Now why had she been standing, anyway? she mused. Year-old Damia's thoughts were not coherent for any great length of time and she often found herself wondering what she had been thinking of moments before. Missing. Something was missing. A faint shadow of the frown she had seen her mother use so effectively – her mother! That was it! No mother nearby!

Damia pushed off the ground and stood, wobbling to survey her realm. She tottered slightly as she turned her head. Aside from the towering form of Rascal, Damia sighted no other living form. No ankles or warm kneecaps entered her view. Determinedly she raised a foot to step forward only to lose her balance with an inelegant wobble and return unceremoniously to the floor.

Well! She had the Rowan's indignant tone down pat

but still hadn't managed to convince her mouth to form more than 'gah'. On all fours she crawled towards the doorway.

Rascal deftly interposed his elegantly marked body, whiskered nose stopping just short of her own. Had she been older she would have recognized the barque cat's expression as identical to the old British Bobby's: ''ello, 'ello, 'ello! Where do we think we're going then?' However, it was obvious that the cat stood between her and her objective. She backpedalled and worked her way around the cat only to have it deftly interpose itself between her and the door *again*. Damia gave a squeal of indignation, dropped her head, and butted against the barque cat. The cat out-massed her; she wound up slipping on the carpet. Damia continued pushing for several seconds before she realized that she was making no progress.

She backed up and took stock of the situation. She determined to stand up in the hopes of outrunning Rascal, especially as the barque cat stood conveniently close to provide a prop to raise herself up. Pleased with her solution, she reached forward for the cat but Rascal refused to cooperate, sagging out from under her hand.

It was too much, Damia adjusted her squeal of rage upward into an interminable bawl. Her aggravation was such that she failed to notice the approach of ankles.

'Damia?' A tenor voice murmured. 'Shh! Your mother's having a nap!' A mental image brushed her mind of her mother curled up on the bed, covered by a blanket much like the one that usually covered her.

Nap? Mothers no nap! Damia does! she thought.

Astonishment rippled at her, followed closely by sardonic humour. *Tired mothers nap.*

Damia not nap now. Damia play now. The other mind registered reluctance. Damia persisted. *Please?*

Not so loud, child, the other mind chided gently. *You'll wake your mother up.* There was a gentle concern in the other's voice.

Who you?

Afra.

A face descended into view. Damia squiggled backwards on her bottom and regarded it. Blond hair, blond eyebrows, green skin, yellow eyes blinked at her, lips upturned in a smile. Afra, she thought to herself, fixing the face and the name together in her mind, adding them to the others she knew: mother, father, jer, cer, tanya, grandmother.

Afra sensed curiosity from the baby. At her age, coherent thought was intermittent and, as she had yet to talk, not vocalized but he 'touched' more in her mind than he expected.

'It's been a rough day at work for your mother and me,' Afra told her soothingly. 'We ran extra shifts to get the local defence net into place. Your father's stuck down on Earth tonight.' He laughed. 'So I came over to see if I could lend a helping hand.'

A light tan Coonie with dark brown face markings crossed in between them, casting a critical eye towards Damia. Haughtily it decided that Damia was neither threat nor food and turned to Afra with a chatter of sound. Afra reached down and gave it a friendly pet. Damia absorbed this and reached a hand out. Unlike the rascally Rascal, this large furry thing bent into her feeble efforts. Encouraged, Damia continued as the Coonie swaggered back and forth, demandingly. The first raccoon-type beast had been a gift from Kama to Afra, to give him something to care for on Callisto. Others had admired the creature and, obtaining permission from the Rowan to import 'a few' more, several families in the compound now enjoyed their endearing antics. Rascal condescendingly tolerated their presence in his established haunts, like the Gwyn-Raven house.

'Ringle likes you,' Afra told her, then sighed. 'Now what should I do with you, minxlette? Your mother really needs the rest.' He turned his head towards the doorway.

He looked back to her again with a smile. 'How about you and I play together for a bit?'

Damia greeted the suggestion with a delighted burble and held up her chubby arms to this new playmate.

'She's much more articulate than either Jeran or Cera at the same age,' Afra told the Rowan one night two months later as he passed an evening in the Gwyn-Raven quarters. The two older children were happily doodling crayon scrawls on a large piece of paper spread across the floor. Damia was asleep, cradled in his lap.

'Articulate? She won't talk for another six months!'

'But I can isolate definite concepts in her mind and hear sounds that are *almost* words,' Afra replied equably. 'You know, like the shorthand speech Jeran and Cera have developed, not quite standard Basic but certainly real communication.'

The Rowan placed a hand lightly on his shoulder and chuckled. 'This child of mine has bewitched you, Afra.' She shook her head. 'When she starts to talk, even baby talk, I'll know.' The Rowan frowned, wrinkled her nose with a dismayed sniff. 'Sorry, I didn't catch her in time and you've just been anointed.'

Afra looked down at the sleeping form, whose face took on the drowsy smile of a baby who has relieved an uncomfortable hydrostatic pressure.

'Won't be the first time.'

The Rowan laughed, shaking her head. 'You should be having children of your own, Afra.'

He cocked his head at her. 'In my own time.'

'But you'd make such a marvellous father. You shouldn't be limited to l.p.-ing. Just look at how Damia succumbs to your charm,' and the Rowan indicated her sleeping daughter. 'I can't get her to do that. You didn't "encourage" this nap, did you?' she said in a half-accusatory voice.

'Heavens, no,' Afra replied, raising his hands to protest

his innocence. Everyone in the Tower had been made aware of how the Rowan felt about any subtle mental control of her children. They were to grow up as normally as possible, with no mental tamperings, until Talent manifested itself in the due course of their development. That all three children were potentially high Talents had been established at their births but the Rowan didn't want their abilities forced, as hers had been.

The Rowan gave him a suspicious glare.

'Honest, Rowan!' Candidly Afra thought that a little adroit mental control might minimize the problems she'd been having with Damia but she was the parent. And Damia was definitely cut from a different mould than her older brother and sister. 'You saw yourself how Rascal and the Coonies wore her out playing.'

The Rowan had to admit that. 'Will they survive her, I wonder?'

'They survived Jeran and Cera. Actually, I think they have more fun with Damia. She's more inventive.'

She had laughed as much at Damia chasing barque cat and Coonies as Afra had. Damia had been so intent on catching one or the other and all had eluded her until she'd collapsed in fatigue. Now the Rowan snorted in amusement at the recollection.

'Shhhh! You'll wake her.' He peered down at the beautiful face of the sleeping child.

Jeff Raven 'ported himself into the room. Afra looked up in greeting while the Rowan gave him a frosty glare. The Rowan had definite views about Talent protocol.

'Use the door!' the Rowan said, reproving him.

'That would've roused the baby,' Jeff replied, unrebuked. 'She *is* asleep, isn't she?' When Afra nodded, he let out a sigh of relief. 'This one's worse than the other two, Aff: she has the uncanniest knack for waking up only on those nights we're shagged.' Jeff looked at his lifemate. 'Let's take a breather after this one? OK, love? We need sleep.'

The Rowan shook her head vigorously. 'I want a big family, Jeff. I know what it's like to be lonely.'

Jeff scowled in pretend horror. 'What? Greedy? Three bonuses aren't enough?' FT&T substantially rewarded Talents who produced offspring, in hopes of increasing the numbers of the Talented throughout the League.

Afra absorbed their repartee like a moth circling a candle: eager for the warmth but fearful of the flame. Within this circle, he enjoyed family life – however vicariously – and coveted these evenings, secure in the affection of both the Rowan and Jeff: the sort of family life that he had never had, never imagined was possible.

Jeran and Cera paused long enough in their mildly competitive application of colour to blank paper to smile at their father. He patted them affectionately, for Jeff had no trouble being demonstrative with his children. Then he became the host, offering to top up glasses before he poured one for himself and settled next to the Rowan on the circular couch.

'Has David calmed his Administration down?' Rowan asked.

Jeff gave a shrug. 'I sincerely hope so. Van Hygan and that ordnance fellow proved – to me, at least – that the factories are working overtime to turn out the components, that the Fleet is scheduled to move as soon as they have sufficient units, so it's only a matter of time before Betelgeuse, too, is securely ringed with early warning devices.'

'Which leaves Altair, Capella, and all the systems in between still struggling?'

'That's it,' Jeff said with a sigh, and he sipped his wine. 'Not that there's been a peep on any DEW unit.' His knee started jiggling, an indication of inner anxiety. The Rowan laid a hand on it and Jeff gave her a sheepish grin, instantly covering her hand with his.

Afra looked away, suffering a pang of jealousy for the bonding between his two best friends. Yet, if after long lonely years and vicissitudes, these two had found each other, perhaps he shouldn't give up hope. Kama had certainly indicated often enough her willingness to be more than bedmate and sometime confidante. He liked her, but his affection for her was a dull gleam beside the radiance that suffused Jeff and the Rowan. He stared down at Damia's small face, trying to imagine the features older, the mind mature. Detachedly he wondered what her life would be like, who she would marry, which Tower she would run (for he was certain she had Prime potential), whether he would have the joy of bouncing her babies on his knee. Would she be a handful like her mother or would she take after her father and be a biddable child like Cera and Jeran? Afra was willing to bet the former – with suitable individualized embellishments – but he was now deftly accustomed to handling the Rowan's outbursts with a carefully controlled silence. But here now was this wondrous baby, just beginning her life and she was sleeping on *his* lap! Afra marvelled that any soul could be so trusting of him. As he had told both Jeran and Cera, when they had been babies sleeping on his lap, *I love you, little darling!*

'Afra!' The Rowan's voice broke his reverie. For a moment he feared that she had 'heard' him but he gathered by her tone that, instead, she had been trying to gain his attention. She was standing, hands reaching down towards baby Damia. 'I'll take her. It's time she was properly put to bed.'

Afra was reluctant to yield her. 'If you pick her up, she'll wake,' he said. 'Then goodness knows how long it'll be before you get her to sleep again with her batteries partly charged.' The Rowan wearily conceded his point. 'Just this once, 'port her to bed.'

The Rowan's expression altered and anger clouded her eyes.

'Afra, you know . . . '

'I think Afra's right. Or have you forgotten how long it took you last night . . . '

'She had a touch of colic,' the Rowan said by way of excuse.

'She doesn't tonight, and she's asleep,' Afra said. 'We've a heavy schedule tomorrow. She's so soundly asleep she won't even know she's been shifted.'

The Rowan hesitated, torn between stated ethic and opportunity.

'Just this once?' And Jeff added his encouragement: the warm look in his eyes and the slightly sensual curve to his smile suggested to Afra, as well as to the Rowan, what plans her husband had in mind for her. 'And, appreciating your scruples in the matter, my love, I'll 'port her.'

She wavered just long enough and suddenly the warm weight of the sleeping child was lifted from Afra's lap as Jeff took advantage of her hesitation.

'I'd better make sure . . . ' the Rowan said and hurried from the room but, as Jeff and Afra grinned at each other, neither heard any loud protest from the 'ported sleeper.

Jeff clapped his hands together, attracting the attention of the older two. 'C'mon, put your crayons away. Bedtime.'

Without protest, Jeran and Cera broke off their activity and began to stuff their colours back into the box. They were already dressed in their nightclothes and each with solemn expression held out a hand to their father to be led away to their cots.

'Say good night to Afra.'

''Night, Afra,' the two chorused dutifully.

'Sleep well, Jeran, Cera,' he replied politely.

'Thanks, Unk,' Jeff said with a grin as he led his children off.

Afra finished his wine, somewhat regretting the absence of Damia on his lap. She was a great leg warmer. Sighing, he rose and made his way back to his own quarters. He treasured these evenings for they anchored his soul and countered the depression he often felt for not being able to establish a similarly satisfying 'marriage of true minds' for himself.

Over the years he had consoled himself with being the brother the Rowan had lost in that avalanche, keeping *philia* and *eros* separate. He had also come to recognize the unexpected reward of his upbringing on a Methody world, despite its legacy of emotional control and detachment. Although he had learned to break out of the rigid undemonstrative demeanour that his parents had instilled in him and could, on occasion, express his emotions, that early training kept his unrequited love for the lonely Rowan separate from his affection for Angharad Gwyn-Raven. The tense atmosphere of the busiest Tower in the League was no place for a person to act like a pressure vessel. So, with Kama for his sexual needs, the Rowan for his intellectual comfort and Gollee Gren for his still irrepressibly rebellious nature, Afra managed to keep himself balanced.

Afra could tell by the way the Rowan walked into the Tower that she'd had another bad night with Damia who was teething. With Jeff on his annual Tower Inspections throughout the Nine Star League, the Rowan was having a spate of unrelieved childcare. Some of her personnel, Afra included, devoutly hoped that this would certainly delay, if not deter her, from considering a fourth pregnancy, which was on her agenda, if not on Jeff's. The Rowan's first priority ought to be a smooth-functioning Callisto Tower.

'Bad night?' Afra asked sympathetically.

The Rowan rolled her eyes. 'The other two weren't like her at all,' she said, a hint of despair in her voice.

'My firstborn was like her,' Brian Ackerman added, handing the Rowan the sheaf of flimsies for the morning's outgoing traffic. 'One night I caught myself holding Borrie at arm's length and screaming at him to shut up.'

Brian scratched behind his left ear, embarrassed to relate that reaction. 'She'll grow out of it, Rowan. You'll see.'

'But when?' The Rowan's tone was both wistful and rueful. 'Will I last long enough?'

'Ah, it seems a long time when you have to go through it,' Brian said with the encouraging, slightly patronizing smile that the survivor will give the victim. 'But it won't be long now.'

'Why don't you have Tanya cope with her tonight?' Afra asked. The very competent T-8 who managed the pre-school crèche had established a good rapport with Damia who napped quite easily when required to do so under her care. One of the other mothers had suggested, within Afra's hearing, that perhaps the Rowan, being so highstrung, was unconsciously stimulating her daughter into these wakeful nights.

The Rowan rolled her eyes expressively. 'I couldn't do that, Afra. Tanya has to cope with her all day long. I can't ask her to take night-duty as well.'

'Ask,' suggested Afra. 'She can only say "no".'

'I don't wish to make her feel she *has* to because I can't cope.' There was a slightly hysterical edge to the Rowan's voice.

'What about a pukha?' Afra suggested.

The Rowan stared as if she couldn't believe her ears. 'My daughter is *perfectly* normal. She is not the least bit traumatized.'

'I didn't mean to imply she was,' Afra said at his calmest because he could see the dangerous glint in her eyes. 'But pukhas do soothe the restless child.'

'She's teething, I said.'

'Gotta better idea,' Brian said, hoping to divert the brewing of a Rowan-storm. 'We don't have any live traffic this morning. Nothing Afra and me can't handle.' Somewhat gingerly, he took the Rowan by the arm and turned her back towards the Tower door. 'Also, right now Damia's Tanya's responsibility, all legit, no favours required. So, you go get yourself six good hours of sacktime until the outer system stuff comes through. Right?'

Almost magically, the fury went out of the Rowan and she put her hand on Brian's shoulder, expressing her heartfelt relief at his entirely sensible suggestion.

'Oh, could I?'

Quick to take advantage of her compliance, Afra made a shooing gesture, and 'pathed her a firm nudge, planting the image of her stretched out on her bed, her hands folded virginally across her chest.

'Don't lay me out quite yet, please,' she replied with some asperity but then she managed to grin. *Before I change my mind,* she added to Afra and half-ran out of the Tower and down the link to her quarters.

Afra followed her mental touch until the door to her shielded house closed behind her, but he had no doubts that she made her way straight to her bed. He'd been maladroit to bring up the subject of a pukha for Damia but he hated to see the Rowan so dragged out. She'd handled alien monsters with less strain. He set the remote alarm to ring in her room in six hours and then went up to the Tower room to start the day's business.

There was indeed nothing that he and Brian couldn't handle with full gestalt and a little assistance from the higher T-ratings in the Tower. Sometimes he wondered why so many single cargo pods were routed. It'd take less time and effort to link same-destination packages together and flick 'em out in one lot. Afra made a note to suggest the idea to Jeff on his return to Earth.

Some four hours into Rowan's respite, Tanya contacted him.

Afra, the Rowan didn't by any chance remove Damia from daycare, did she?

No, Tanya. Why? Afra felt the first spurt of panic.

Damia isn't anywhere in the crèche. She was asleep in her cot when I last looked.

Did you ask Jeran and Cera?

Oh, them! Tanya's tone was disgusted. *They told me she went out waving her wand.*

Hold it a moment, folks, and Afra spoke to everyone in the Tower, *missing person problem.*

Damia? Brian asked and groaned. Why did kindly notions dissolve into disasters? *Can't you spot her, Afra?*

If you'll give me the quiet to do so. Afra had already begun to cast his mind about. He could usually 'hear' her infantile stream of consciousness anywhere. Whether or not he could trace her wherever she had got to in the Compound was another matter. He'd better or the Rowan would skin him for garters. Afra started at the daycare rooms, casting about the main compound.

Then Brian and Joe Toglia came stamping up the stairs to the Tower and began flicking on the screens to interior monitors, examining one area after another of the four domes that comprised the station. The screens showed no small figure trundling about.

'How long's she been walking?' Brian asked Afra.

'Long enough to be pretty good at it.'

Cursing under his breath, Brian programmed a decko of the tunnel links. There were so many places that could shelter a small body from the optical sensors.

'She's not tall enough to reach the doorplates, is she?' asked Joe, thumbing through views of the basement levels of the supply section.

'Wait a minute!' And, with sudden inspiration, Afra leaned across the console and accessed the remote in his own quarters. And there Damia was, toddling about his living-room after Ringle and two other Coonies, trying to bean them with the dowel-wand in her hand. 'And that's how she activated the doors . . . waving her wand!'

Afra 'ported into the room, sweeping the stray child into his arms.

'Af'a! Af'a!' she squealed with delight, patting his face

with her free hand and waving her 'wand' furiously with the other. He carefully unwrapped her fingers from the dowel before she stuck it in his eye.

'Damia shouldn't leave Tanya!' he said, knowing how futile scolding this imp could be. Merrily she grinned up at him, her huge blue eyes rounder than ever with her excitement.

'Af'a! Af'a?' She began to squirm free, 'Ingul, Ingul,' and she twisted her head to find Ringle, arching her back to get free.

'No Ringle now, Damia. I'm taking you back to Tanya.'

'Tan'a? Tan'a.' That name emerged as a sort of guttural grunt and the twisting became more violent. 'No, Tan'a. Ingul. Wan Ingul.'

'Not now, baby!' Bearing in mind the Rowan's dislike of exposing her children to Talented actions, he secured her writhing form in his arms and walked her back to the crèche where an anxious Tanya waited at the door.

'Ingul, Ingul,' Damia was saying over his shoulder, suddenly ceasing to fidget. 'Ingul. Goo Ingul.'

Turning his head, Afra saw Ringle dutifully following him.

'How could she have got out, Afra?' Tanya said in a near wail as she reached out to relieve Afra of his burden.

'She had a wand, a dowel stick with a star on the end of it,' Afra told her.

'And used that to activate the doorplates?' Tanya was amazed. 'The little minx. Well, I'll get Forrie to touch code them tomorrow. She won't try that one on me again. Where's the Rowan?' Tanya anxiously looked across the compound. Afra could well imagine how she had dreaded confronting an irate mother, especially a Prime, whose child she had just misplaced. Damia tried to launch herself head down out of Tanya's arms, both arms reaching for Ringle who had entered the crèche.

Deftly, Tanya righted the child, placed her on her feet so that she could reach Ringle who scampered off, Damia following as fast as she could churn her short legs.

'The Rowan arrived this morning looking like hell warmed over,' Afra began.

'She did look exhausted when she dropped the children off,' Tanya remarked, and made a rueful noise with her lips.

'So we sent her back home for some rest.' Afra did not mention his abortive mention of acquiring a pukha for Damia, though these 'comfort toys' could be programmed for any number of responses to soothe a fretful child. 'Tanya, how do *you* get Damia to take her naps?'

The girl regarded him with surprise. Not for the first time Afra thought that she was little more than a child herself, for all he knew she was twenty-nine. She was a daintily made girl, all brown: brown eyes, brown hair, light brown skin, with small hands and feet. If Gollee Gren hadn't expressed an interest in her, Afra would have been tempted to try his luck.

'Well,' and Tanya pointed to the rocking chair just visible in the nap alcove, 'if she won't settle, I rock her and sing a lullaby. She goes right to sleep for me.' She caught her lip with her teeth, looking sheepish, and fluttering one hand in dismay. Afra could 'hear' her distress at seeming to criticize her Prime.

'Just a lullaby?'

'Just a lullaby,' she replied firmly. 'You know how the Rowan feels about mental coercion. Actually, any song will do the trick. I use different ones so I don't get bored.'

'I know how the Rowan feels but what she doesn't know, won't hurt,' Afra said, having come to a decision. The Tower demanded some adjustment to her directive. He called Ringle to him. 'And it will sure help all of us.'

Brown eyes widening, Tanya's jaw dropped in consternation. 'Afra, I don't think we should.'

'We both know that a mild therapeutic post-hypnotic suggestion doesn't in the least inhibit the developing mind of the Talented child,' Afra said as he reached down to stroke the obedient Ringle.

Trotting up behind him came a giggling Damia, dark curls bouncing on her shoulders. So Afra captured his victim and asked Tanya to teach him the tune and the words. By the time he had learned them and implanted the command in Damia's mind, she had yawned herself to sleep in his arms.

'I'll send Forrie to change the doorplates,' Afra said and went whistling back to the Tower, crisis over. At least, he amended privately, this one.

When the Rowan, much refreshed, returned to the Tower, everyone was very careful not to think of the morning's brief crisis. And Afra waited for an opportune moment to suggest a sure-fire remedy for Damia's nocturnal restlessness.

Brian listened, his mouth slightly ajar, as Afra recounted a totally fictional account of how his sister, Goswina, had dealt with his sleepless nephew.

'A rocking chair?' the Rowan asked in surprise.

'Rocking chair,' Afra said and implanted the appropriate image in his mind for her to see. Then set it moving, and placed a Rowan and a Damia in it. 'Between the motion of the chair, the repetitive rhythm in his mother's reassuring voice, my nephew was soon fast asleep.'

'I'm willing to try anything. But I don't know any lullabies. Jeran and Cera never needed any.'

'I know a good one,' Brian said. 'My mother used to say how often she had to rock me when I was teething.' In a rather strong baritone voice, he launched into a rendition of an ancient folk tune about what a daddy would buy his li'l baby if it would hush.

Afra countered with Tanya's 'Rock-a-bye baby'. 'That one was a sure-fire sleep-inspirer.'

What's going on in the Tower? asked Jeff Raven. *It is working hours.*

Sorry, boss, Afra said with absolutely no remorse.

Ready, my lovely? Jeff asked the Rowan, *we have some paying customers.*

And, instantly and of one mind, Callisto Tower turned into a smooth functioning facility.

'Wanna play,' Damia told her two siblings. They were all in their home play-room while their mother was in the kitchen, preparing lunch. Jeran and Cera were building a complex structure of blocks. Damia had been in a corner crooning to herself as she trotted her herd of ponies about an obstacle course and in and out of their stable. The intense silence of her siblings' concentration attracted her.

'G'way,' Jeran told her.

'Y'g'way,' Cera added, waving her sister off.

'Wanna play,' Damia repeated. Then changed her tactics. 'Can't I play with you?'

Jeran blinked at her, recognizing grown-up syntax for their parents never used baby-talk. 'No, Damia,' for he could speak just as good grown-up as she could, 'Cera and I are playing together.' He waved towards her corner. 'You play with your horses.'

'Ponies,' Damia corrected him absently in a vague hope of provoking further attention from her brother. But Cera nudged him, indicating a block in her hand and, in their private garble, requesting his opinion on its placement.

Recognizing the futility of enticing them from their game, Damia turned away. She looked at the corner where her toys were strewn. She thought of calling Rascal who always came to her, or the Coonies but she'd already spent half her morning with them.

'Bored! I'm so bored!' She looked about her. The baby gate blocked her exit from the play-room. But that was the way out, to more exciting play. She walked over to it, examining it carefully. She had watched her mother putting it up many times now and observation had shown her how it worked. The gate was braced in place by a simple lever that locked down. A simple jerk up would release the brace and the door could be pulled aside or knocked over. Normally Damia could do nothing with the information she had acquired because the lever was on the outside which she could not reach. Today, however, her mother had inadvertently reversed the gate and the lever was inside.

Tentatively, more from curiosity than plan, Damia tapped the lever. It jerked up and the baby gate fell softly on to the carpet in the hallway.

Jeran heard the noise and looked around at her. 'Damia ba'guh.' Cera added, scowling. 'Dam ba!'

Against this censure, Damia could not bring herself to explain that she'd only touched it: getting it to drop out of the door was an accident. However, the gate was down, Jeran and Cera wouldn't play with her, but Afra would. He always did. She would find Afra.

Safety was a paramount consideration on Callisto Station and reigned over security. Consequently all doors were the automatic sliding type, with ultrasound sensors. Early in Jeran's babyhood, the Rowan had ordered the sensors raised so that the boy could not leave the house. Jeran never wanted to, nor did Cera. As the Rowan hadn't heard about Damia's adventure with her 'wand', it hadn't occurred to her to alter the sensors to touch-control plates. All Damia had to do was find something long enough for her to break the circuit.

A long stemmed flower from the dry arrangement on the hall table, acquired by climbing up on a chair and removing a suitable one from the vase, made a good substitute for her wand. The door slid politely out of her way.

Every dome had a hallway where the personnel tubes

connected and where elevators, freight and human, expelled their cargo. Below ground were the powerplants, hydroponics garden, life support, recycling machinery, gravity generators – all the equipment required to keep Callisto Station operating. Also in the basement were the long-term survival units awaiting a catastrophic disaster. The personnel tubes were plasglas covered, allowing personnel access between the four lesser domes. Along the tubes were personal safety capsules to guard against the unlikely event of a pressure breach.

Damia had travelled all the tubes but always in the company of adults. Now she spent many moments carefully considering each tube. With a determined look plastered over her misgivings, she started off down her chosen tube.

She stopped several times to look back yearningly towards her home but always she trudged onward. She had chosen correctly: the tube opened up on to the large park that was the 'doorstep' for Callisto Quarters. To her right was the large gymnasium with its indoor pool, to her left the two-storeyed Married Quarters and straight on, through the park with its dwarf trees, was the three-levelled Bachelor Quarters. As most of the residents were indoors, eating or involved in other chores while Jupiter occluded Callisto, no-one happened to notice her progress.

'Afra!' she cried in cheerful anticipation, toddling as fast as her slender legs could carry her.

However, she had left her long stemmed flower behind her and had nothing close to hand to trip the sensor. She grew quite frustrated, poking at the undemonstrative door, jumping up and down, hand above her head, trying to reach the plate.

Afra! Afra? she said, unaware that, in her anxiousness to contact him, she used an ability that she ought not to have discovered so prematurely. She had also launched her mental call into his quarters, not realizing that Afra was lunching with Brian, nor that she'd have needed more 'volume' to reach him. However, she did startle Ringle awake.

With an understanding chitter of acknowledgement, the Coonie started towards the door. As the Coonies all needed access to the park for their toilet, maintenance had equipped them with ultrasound collars. Ringle walked up to the door, paced by it and it opened.

'Afra!' Damia entered jubilant and halted her headlong progress into the room when only Ringle greeted her. 'Afra? Afra, play with me!' She toddled off to find her playmate, not noticing that the door silently closed behind her, having been open long enough for any animal to exit. 'Where is Afra?' she asked Ringle who had followed her in her perambulation.

Ringle chittered, turning away from her and pacing towards the kitchen. He was always hungry and Damia had given him sufficient tidbits on previous visits here to allow him to hope for more.

Emergency! the Rowan 'pathed on the widest band possible. She stood on her front steps, the baby gate dangling from one hand. *Damia's got out. I don't know where she's got to. I've checked every remote screen and there's no sign of her.*

How long's she been gone? Afra was the first to ask.

How do I know? the Rowan exclaimed, half despairing, half angry. *I was getting lunch. She'd been safely in the play-room with Jeran and Cera who, in their fashion,* and that was added in a terse tone, *have no idea where their sister went. Jeran said she knocked the gate down.*

Remembering all too well Damia's tendency to seek him out, Afra replied. *If you haven't seen her on the remotes, then I've a good idea where she might be.*

Relieve my mind? the Rowan asked cryptically.

Afra had no trouble seeing her tapping her foot with impatience.

My place.

How in the world would she get there?

Walked, was Afra's laconic answer.

I'll meet you there. And the Rowan's tone was severe.

Afra 'ported himself from Brian's dining area to his living-room and sure enough, Damia was busy feeding Ringle leftovers from his refrigerator. She was convulsed with the giggles because Ringle was 'washing' each handful before he popped it into his mouth.

The Rowan arrived only a moment later, anger and relief warring for dominance. But Damia's laughter was infectious and, as Afra saw the Rowan's expression soften, he allowed himself to grin.

Suddenly aware of observation, Damia swivelled about. 'Afra!' Abandoning Ringle, she raced to him, only then aware of her mother. She teetered to a stop, her expression one of total innocence. 'The gate fell over, Mommy. Honest it did. They never play with me and I was bored! Afra always plays with me.' Grabbing his hand, Damia tilted her head up. 'Don't you, Afra?'

He squatted down to her level. 'I do when it is the time to play, Damia. But you must wait for me to come. Do you understand? You mustn't come looking.'

She nodded solemnly, one hand bringing her comfort finger to her mouth.

The Rowan hunkered down, too, her eyes on a level with her fractious daughter. 'You know you're not supposed to wander around the station, Damia. Don't you?'

Damia shook her head. 'I wanted to play. Jeran and Cera won't play with me. Ever.' She tried to squeeze a tear out of her eyes.

'How'd you get in?' Afra asked, knowing that Damia was trying the wrong tactics on her mother.

'Ringle let me in!' Damia pointed to the Coonie who was now finishing his impromptu meal.

Afra and Rowan exchanged surprised looks.

'Ringle heard me,' Damia went on, 'he let me in.'

'How could he do that?' Rowan asked Afra, then looked accusingly at her daughter. 'You must tell the truth, Damia.'

'I tell the truth,' and Damia's face began to contort as a prelude to tears over such adult intransigence.

'If Ringle heard her, he'd come to the door,' Afra said quickly, to forestall Damia's tearful reaction. 'His collar would open the door. It'll close automatically.'

The Rowan let out a long, exasperated sigh and gathered her daughter in her arms. 'All right, Damia. Now don't cry. But you mustn't run about the compound on your own. Promise, you won't leave the house without someone with you?'

Clinging to her mother in an excess of contrition, Damia vigorously nodded her head.

'Now, your lunch is ready, young lady,' the Rowan said, hoping that she had made her point without frightening her wayward child.

'Ringle's had his, and I'll go back to mine,' Afra said, ushering the two out of his apartment. 'And I'll get a cat-flap put in my door. Damia's too big to crawl through one of those.'

There was relative peace for a few weeks. Afra was not the only one nervously anticipating the next Damianism. As it happened, there was a great deal of traffic in that morning, heavy stuff that needed careful handling. Tanya's frantic cry for help was therefore not welcome to anyone in the Tower.

I can't stop Damia, Afra, the girl cried. *And I know the Rowan's terribly busy but I'm afraid Damia will hurt someone.*

Afra signalled for Joe Toglia to take over as he spun his chair over to the nearest free monitor and called up the remote in the daycare centre. He could see Tanya, cowering by the communit, as the other children cringed under the small-scale furniture. Jeran and Cera serenely played some intricate game while a stream of toy bits and parts, and occasionally something heavier, was rained at them by an enraged Damia who was blubbering in fury.

'Play with me! Look at me! Talk to me!' she was screaming. As soon as she exhausted the objects on the shelf beside her, she moved to the box of connectable shapes. Fortunately her aim was skewed or – and Afra couldn't quite believe this – Jeran and Cera were deflecting the projectiles, for most items dropped well short of targets who blithely ignored her.

Instantly Afra 'ported the box out of reach and, when she squealed in outrage, cleared the next likely ammunition out of range.

No, Damia, he said in as disapproving a tone as he had ever used with her. *That is not allowed.*

'They won't talk to me!' Damia cried, sobbing with frustration. 'S'not fair! They never talk to me! They never play with me.' Then she ran to the pile of things that had fallen short of their mark and would have pelted Jeran and Cera with them if Afra had not made a clean sweep. 'And that's not fair, Afra. That's not fair at all!'

Tanya! Afra called. *Grab that little minx and make her take a nap! Damia, you will go with Tanya this instant and stop making such a display of bad manners. Such a temper for someone who will run a Tower!* He was slightly appalled to hear one of his mother's favourite admonitions emerge from his lips.

To his amazement, Damia gulped back the next of her indignant sobs and submitted to Tanya's ministrations. She was asleep before Tanya got through the first verse. Jeran and Cera continued their game as if nothing had happened.

'I think, Rowan, that you had better speak to Jeran and Cera,' Afra told her when Jupiter occluded Callisto and everyone could take a break.

'Why? What have they done?'

So Afra explained the scene in the daycare room. 'It's

my opinion that they do that deliberately, knowing it will upset her. She does indeed feel left out.'

The Rowan considered this, slightly defensively. 'They have this bonding. And Damia is much younger . . . '

'That doesn't give them the right to exclude her, especially when they do it deliberately.'

'She shouldn't lose her temper that way.' The Rowan set her mouth firmly. 'She's constantly demanding attention.'

'Perhaps, but Jeran and Cera could include her in their games once in a while. You know they never do. And don't tell me they're more advanced. Damia's advanced, too.'

The Rowan had to admit that, for Damia's vocabulary was at least as extensive as her siblings', and certainly her small muscle control was excellent. So she did have a talk with her elder children, quietly and positively, and, after they had listened attentively to her, they had one of their short-speak conversations that so excluded her she experienced reluctant sympathy for her youngest.

'We will teach Damia to play one of our simpler games, Mother,' Jeran said in his prosaic way. 'That should satisfy her.'

The Rowan told Afra later that it had been all she could do to keep from giggling at his pomposity.

'You see, then, Damia had a valid complaint,' Afra said.

'Yes, she did,' and then the Rowan sighed deeply. 'I want all my children to love and understand each other.'

Afra gave a derisive snort. 'Wait till they're old enough, my dear. Right now, they're cruel, heartless, mean little monsters.' Rowan gave him a startled stare. 'Well, they are, but I'm sure they'll grow out of it.'

Tanya contacted the Tower ten days later – tactfully waiting until the break.

'Jeran and Cera played a new game with Damia, and

with half the other children,' she told the Rowan, trying very hard not to laugh.

'Then why—'

'Because the game was colour-oriented,' and now Tanya did burble with laughter. 'Your three are green and the others are a sort of pied-piper of whatever other colours were left in the water-paints. I can't get nine children clean by myself so could parents be excused for fifteen minutes? Fortunately it is a water soluble emulsion. And they did take their clothes off first.'

That mischief had not originated with Damia but she did her own variation several days later when she tried to paint Rascal and every Coonie in the compound. This time with an oil-based paint she had evidently found where the maintenance man had left it while he ate lunch.

Everyone was annoyed with her for that one and the Rowan insisted that she help the owners clean their pets' fur. She also insisted that everyone let Damia know how much they disapproved.

'Maybe she'll come to realize that she could hurt the animals with a trick like this. They've feelings, too.'

Damia was indeed much chastened by human censure but neither Rascal nor any of the Coonies seemed to avoid her. In fact, there were half a dozen who would happily throng to her at her peculiar warbling whistle. During the outdoor activities that Tanya conducted every afternoon, Damia was usually surrounded by the pets while she waited for her turn. As her brother and sister could ignore extraneous matters, Damia could inhabit a world that consisted of herself and the animals.

One afternoon, while others were gathered around Tanya, Damia was cajoling her four-footed cohorts to try and catch the ball on a string that she was dragging behind her as she ran pell-mell around the park. She ran out of breath by the pool door which someone had left slightly ajar.

She peered inside. This pool was much much larger than the one in her house where she often swam with her parents. While she knew that the pool was here, she'd never had occasion to visit it. And, at this time of the day, it was empty. Suddenly Ringle batted her string ball through the door, on to the tiled surface around the pool. The string whipped out of her hand and Ringle triumphantly carried it off down the pool side.

'Ringle, that's not playing the game,' she said, running after him. But the soles of her sandals were slick and she skidded, her feet going out from under her. She fell heavily on her shoulder and tipped over into the pool with a huge splash.

She was competent enough in water not to panic, and surfaced. The Coonies shrieked at the top of their lungs and Rascal, who'd been the last one in the pool, responded by throwing himself into the water, raising a wave that hit her right in the face, swamping mouth and nose. She started to choke, couldn't get her breath and became frightened.

Afra! Help me! she cried, flailing her arms about in panic, trying to reach the pool ledge. The Coonies, in trying to reach her, got in her way and she went under the water.

The next thing she knew, hands were dragging her to the surface, hauling her from the pool, pounding her back to open her airways.

It's all right, baby, it's all right. Afra's here, and she was held against a wet but reassuring human body.

DAMIA! cried her mother and suddenly the Rowan was there, reaching to take her from Afra, holding her so close that Damia was amazed to discover that her mother could tremble. She could 'feel' her mother's fear and that so shattered her confidence that she burst into tears.

It took time to calm her down, calm the Rowan down,

dry soaking Coonies and Rascal, and then more time for Damia to insist that it had not been *their* fault. The door had been open and she had slipped on the wet edge.

'But you *know* you're not supposed to go into a pool room without someone with you, Damia,' her mother said, with an edge to her voice that Damia now recognized as disapproval. 'And Coonies do not constitute someone else!'

'I wasn't *going* swimming, Mommy, I was playing with my friends.'

Over her head, the Rowan looked hopelessly up at Afra who was wringing out his shirt. 'She's never in the wrong, is she?'

'Actually,' and Afra paused to towel his sopping hair, 'she often isn't. She's simply inquisitive, inventive, isolated.'

'Well, I'm doing something about that!' the Rowan said, 'with or without Jeff Raven's complete cooperation. Damia *needs* a companion.'

Afra managed to hide his grimace in the towel and then stopped rubbing his hair as he reviewed her phrasing. 'With or without Jeff's complete cooperation'? He dropped the towel and stared at her.

'Angharad Gwyn-Raven, do you mean what I think you mean?'

She gave him a wide-eyed stare of innocence, still rocking her daughter. 'I want my children to have a happy childhood, and not feel excluded or forced to play with animals.'

'Damia loves the Coonies.'

'Exactly! I want her to have a brother to love.'

When told of the afternoon's escapade, Jeff sighed deeply. 'She's like me at the same age. Mother couldn't keep me in the yard with a logging chain.'

'So how did she keep track of you?'

Jeff grinned in reminiscence. 'Dad was good at training animals . . . ' He laughed when he saw the exasperated expression on the Rowan's face. ' . . . He sicced a wolf bitch on me as guardian. She followed me everywhere and if she thought I was likely to get in trouble, she'd trip me up, knock me down, sit on my back and howl. Sometimes she was howling a long time but I didn't come another cropper even if my knees and ribs were always bruised from being knocked flat by 30 kilos of white wolf.'

'Barque cats and Coonies are sufficient livestock in a dome.'

'Oh, I know that. Merely apprising you that Damia's escapades follow a well-established genetic pattern.'

'We can't have more animals but we can provide her with another sort of suitable companion,' the Rowan went on, bringing the conversation neatly to where she wanted it.

'I gather that you are in the process of providing that companion,' Jeff remarked with a bite in his tone.

The Rowan took a backwards step, nervously biting her lip. 'How did you know?'

'It's been what? Two months? It shows.' Jeff returned. He stepped forward, laid a hand on her belly. 'How did you do it?'

The Rowan dipped her head. 'A lady must keep some secrets. It's a boy, you know.'

'To give Damia someone to care for.'

'Beside Afra,' the Rowan added.

'Her affection for him is natural. He's family.'

'But she called *him*, not me.'

Jeff perceived her conflict. 'And how many times have you impressed upon the children that they are *not* to call you when you're in the Tower?'

The Rowan slumped disconsolately. 'But I *have* to make them understand that.'

'I agree. So Afra becomes the next best person to turn to. Let us be thankful that he is also willing and extremely able. We might even get him to like the feel of trusting young arms about his neck enough to do something about starting his own family.'

'Your last effort at matchmaking did not work?' The Rowan was secretly pleased. 'You should leave match-making to the women of your family, love.'

'I don't recall any efforts on your part.'

'I've yet to meet a woman good enough,' the Rowan said brusquely. When Jeff raised an eyebrow in turn, she added, 'Afra should have someone really special. I owe so much of my happiness to him.'

Her pregnancy was not going well. She had managed to endure three months of morning sickness, clinging to the consolation that those symptoms would gradually ease. But they persisted; her waspishness grew to uncontrollable proportions, her ankles hurt abominably and she was absolutely convinced that the gravity in Callisto Station was set too high. She blamed everyone in sight for her condition, including Brian Ackerman who defused it with his best 'would that it were true' look but especially Damia for her requirement of a little brother and Jeff for not stopping her in her wilful theft of his sperm.

Her condition established a vicious cycle where her temper would set off the children and depress the station staff such that her temper would get worse and so the effect would escalate. By the sixth month of her pregnancy, the staff was completely gaunt-faced and jittery.

What she absolutely hated, and could not admit to herself, was the fact that Afra would *not* get irritated with her no matter how irascible she became. She longed for the chance to rant at him so desperately that she knew it was completely irrational. He was nearly obsequious in his genuine concern for her and always caringly thoughtful of her needs and condition.

In her pregnancy with Damia and Cera before her, Afra had always been willing to take the children off her hands so that she might rest as best she could in her condition. This time, however, she was unwilling to let Damia out of her sight, letting, instead, the elder two stay with 'Uncle Afra'.

Afra took the whole situation phlegmatically which irritated the Rowan because it did *not* irritate him. He even went to the extreme of getting Damia's solemn promise to be extra careful of her mother in her gravid state, a promise which the child carried out faithfully until the Rowan shrieked at her one day as she attempted to serve breakfast in bed. After that Damia became a sullen, dispirited child prone to unprovoked fits of crying.

But a prolonged sulk was not in Damia's nature. Heartened by the solicitous nature of the Coonies and by Rascal's steadfast loyalty, she took to exploring the nooks and crannies of Callisto Station escorted only by the felines. She was not 'heard' by anyone as she traipsed about on her great adventures because she had learned of necessity to shield herself from the Rowan, projecting a totally false image of her surroundings: generally her own room.

So while her ailing mother thought her safely playing at home, she conducted her personal rebellion. She loved the personal safety pods the most. These lined the corridors and subterranean ways of Callisto Station, provided against catastrophic pressure loss. Gaining entrance was easy: she merely walked up to one and the translucent panel slid open. Inside there were marvellous accoutrements: a plush seat with all sorts of computer controls adorning a keypad, a computer ready to aid her in any emergency and room enough for her coven of Coonies. Best of all, the computer would carefully and patiently explain every aspect of the capsule until she had it memorized. She would play in these for hours; Damia Queen of Space, Damia Space Police, Damia Rescue Run.

At the end of every game, where Coonies played

medics, pirates, injured and police at her whim, Damia would carefully peer outside her capsule and, the coast clear, quietly exit it, carefully closing the door and observing the green 'A-OK' light. Then, depending on the hour and her hunger, she would either return to the Rowan's quarters or traipse on to the next capsule and the next game.

Her discovery of the cargo cradles at the base of the Tower was an eye-popping revelation. She scrunched herself tight up against the corridor wall, watching in awe as the cradles magically filled and emptied again as cargo was shunted back and forth to the large composite ships waiting patiently in orbit above for their cargo to be marshalled and the Rowan to push the result off to its destination planet.

Cargo capsules were long and box-like, exactly the same as those used on ships and trains for surface transport on worlds. Passenger capsules were different and came in many shapes and sizes. All had airlocks at various strategic locations and most had view panels. But most intriguing to Damia were the personal safety pods which blistered the sides of the larger passenger transporters.

She was sufficiently sensitive psychically to know that the capsules were being manipulated by various Talents in the Tower. Once, with a thrill of recognition, she felt Afra's sure mental touch as a string of passenger capsules were separated and landed in individual cradles. Small domes enclosed them and soon maintenance personnel were busy, working around them.

'That Altairian freighter's late!' the Rowan snapped at Afra up in her Tower. The expedient of reducing the gravity on Callisto had eased the weight on her swollen feet but did nothing to alleviate her temper. Afra turned carefully to face her, eyes showing the strain of his mental manipulations.

'There's a problem in the life support system of the passenger and crew quarters,' he explained. He closed his eyes in concentration, something he normally did not require and looked back up at her. 'Powers is handling it.'

'We're going to blow the whole day's schedule!' the Rowan replied in what was nearly a wail. She directed her frustration solidly at Afra.

'No, we're not.' Brian Ackerman returned steadily, relieving Afra of the brunt of the Rowan's ill-will. 'I've already worked around the problem. I've got a fifteen minute window before things start piling up.'

Afra considered that and nodded. 'Should be about right.' He sent a thought to Powers. 'Bill says it'll be tight but he'll push for it.'

'In the meantime, Rowan, while it's not normally your task, if you could pull apart that Procyon composite that'll keep Afra free to stitch together the Altairian.'

The Rowan started to protest but Ackerman gave her such a pleading look that she relented. 'Where're the sheets?'

'On two.'

The Rowan turned to her second console and, referring to it, commenced to pull the capsules off the Procyon ship *Lysis*.

The passenger capsules called to Damia. They screamed of adventure, of far off places, of Damia Star Guard. She glanced backwards at the cats for support, ignored Rascal's counsel of caution, and proceeded boldly forward towards the tunnel leading to the first passenger capsule.

Bill, Bill, she'll blow a fuse if it's not ready! Ackerman sent privately to the Assistant Supercargo.

Powers' response was laced with strain. *We're pushing it now, Brian.*

In the Tower, unseen, Ackerman nodded approvingly. *Just keep it up.*

Damia marched unconcerned by techs and maintenance personnel on her way to the passenger capsule. The cats followed her at a discreet distance, blended into the landscape in the way of all cats.

One of the shipboard personnel looked at her and mistook her for a passenger.

'You'd best get back aboard, little lady,' he told her politely.

'I don't know how,' Damia replied.

The technician took pity on her, no matter that the station personnel were throwing a fit, and led her aboard the passenger capsule.

'You know your way from here?' he asked, worried that he would lose too much time if he had to search out her parents.

'Oh, yes!' Damia responded, eyeing one of the safety capsules eagerly. Damia Space Guard on a real spaceship!

'Have a good journey!' the tech called as he left.

'Thank you, I will!' Damia said as she had heard Tower personnel do so many times. The tech left, shaking his head at the excellent manners of the child.

Quickly, Damia scampered into a personnel capsule, holding the door open long enough for all her feline entourage to enter. When the door closed, the capsule activated.

'Wollen Sie des Hilfe?' the computer asked politely.

'What?' Damia had never encountered any language other than Basic.

'How may I help you?' the computer replied, shifting languages.

'Oh, I know what to do.'

The response fell into one of many distressed voice ranges the computer was programmed to detect. It set its System Alert flag. Had the passenger capsule been attached to the composite ship, a ship-wide alarm would have been sounded. As it was, the circuit was broken and would remain so until the capsule was connected with the ship.

Hurry, Bill, hurry! Ackerman called urgently. Afra must

have picked up a bit of spill from his message for the Capellan raised an eyebrow. *She's got that ship all put back together again and she's looking for something else to throw!*

Done! Powers said proudly. Beside Afra the display board chirped, red lights turned green.

'The Altairian's ready, Rowan,' Afra informed her, mentally casting a call to the generator technicians to prepare for the load. He glanced at a clock; Powers had left five seconds to spare.

'About bloody time!' the Rowan snarled. 'Wait a minute, the ship's not together yet!'

I'm taking care of that now, Afra responded calmly. Privately, however, he was irritated that the Rowan would choose to misinterpret his statement. She knew that he still had to stitch the ship together. He lifted the first capsule from its cradle but paused, there was something *familiar* about it.

I'll do it! the Rowan snapped waspishly, snatching the capsule brutally from his mental 'hands'.

'Bumpy ride, Captain,' Ackerman warned on his comm link.

All three capsules were slapped on the stern of the Altairian freighter at once by the Rowan in her temper.

'Ready for boost,' the Rowan announced.

'Red light! Red light!' the captain shouted over his comm link. But it was too late, the generators rose to a shriek and suddenly—

Afra! A terrified voice cried from the void.

Damia! Afra's response was immediate, with a speed he had never needed before, he lurched for the fleeting child, twisting the Rowan's thrust and snatching Damia from the pod.

'Emergency!' Ackerman snapped. 'Kill the generators!'

Get that ship back! the Rowan cried, flailing to maintain her grasp on the massive freighter.

Afra! Damia wailed.

I'm here! Afra called. *Come here, baby.* And there she

was, falling into his arms. He grabbed her, clutched her fiercely.

'Afra!' Ackerman shouted, pointing to the Rowan. The Rowan was slumped, knuckles white as she strained by sheer power of will to hold the hurtling ship. With a cry of fear, Afra launched every ounce of his mental powers to one mind: *Jeff, help!*

And then he was there, a reassuring presence surrounding them all, body almost visible in the room.

Damia's safe! Help the Rowan! Afra cried, sagging to the floor, his arms lapping Damia's fright-stiffened body.

I'm here, luv. Let me in to help! Jeff called from across the void to Earth.

Ackerman watched amazed as near visible forces flickered through the Rowan and once again she and Jeff Raven joined souls.

'Gods above!' a voice crackled hoarsely through the comm link. 'In-again-out-again-gone-again Finnegan! What did you do with us?'

Ackerman looked out above the Tower and saw the Altairian hovering in view. He let out a deep ragged sigh.

5

'All I can say is that I'm glad it worked out all right,' Captain Leonhard of the Altairian freighter said as the situation was explained to him. 'As far as my passengers know, we had a shipboard malfunction.'

'You're very kind, Captain,' Jeff Raven replied with sincere gratitude. They were in a shielded conference room in the bowels of Callisto Tower. Ackerman and Afra were also seated around the table. The Rowan and Damia were at home, both recovering from the traumatic incident.

'However, it worries me some – what would have happened if your wife had not kept "touch" with my ship?'

Jeff? The touch of his mother's mind distracted him as he prepared an answer.

'Excuse me,' Jeff told the captain, closing his eyes to indicate that he was 'pathing to someone. *I gather you heard it, too?*

The whole galaxy heard that shriek. What happened? Isthia asked as calm as ever. Jeff sketched her the complete details quickly. *Afra* pulled *her off the ship?* Isthia exclaimed as Jeff finished.

What surprised me most was that he could! I don't know whether or not it's good that she obeyed our injunction that she doesn't bother her mother in the Tower. This was the moment she should *have.*

A two-year-old child, even your Damia, would not understand such distinctions, Isthia replied in a sad tone, then she continued more briskly. *What is surprising is how Afra got all that power to make the save? You say he nearly knocked the ship out of Rowan's hands?*

Jeff Raven frowned. *I hadn't thought of that.* He brushed it aside. *I've got to run, I'm busily unruffling the captain's feathers. He wants to know what would have happened if the Rowan had lost her grasp on his ship.*

What will you tell him?

The truth, of course, Jeff responded promptly.

That his ship would have been lost in limbo for all time? I don't think that's something you want known.

No, it's not, Jeff said grimly. *I'll tell him that we would have gone looking for him instantly.*

That's clever and very true! His mother's tone became thoughtful. *Should I come? Angharad seems unusually distraught, not that I don't think I'd be in a similar situation. I'm forever thankful I had a planet on which to raise you lot.*

This pregnancy has *got her down,* Jeff said, allowing his mother to see the anxiety he took great pains to hide from everyone else. *But not quite as much as Damia appealing to Afra* in extremis . . .

That's not quite it, I think, Isthia remarked in an enigmatic fashion that Jeff did not have time to query for, beside him, the space captain coughed politely. *We'll take this up later. The feathers are hackling.*

Well, don't you *get upset, dear,* Isthia said in farewell.

'Staff interruption,' Jeff remarked by way of apology to the waiting captain. 'As to your question: why we'd initiate a search immediately.'

The captain heaved a sigh of relief. 'That's good to know.'

'And remember that we've *never* lost a ship,' Ackerman added jovially. 'You can't say that about the old reaction drive days when I dunno how many ships went missing. Never heard from again.'

'No,' the captain responded, shaking his head, and glad he lived when ships could expect safe transfer, 'I suppose you can't.' He rose. 'I've taken up too much of your valuable time.' He nodded at Raven and the others. 'I don't like interrupting a Tower's busy schedule longer than necessary but I had to clarify the problem in my own mind. The passengers, you know, will need reassurance.'

'Of course they will,' said Jeff, rising to grip the captain's hand firmly, 'and please convey the Tower's apologies for that minor glitch.'

'Minor?' Ackerman muttered under his breath as the door closed behind the captain. 'Minor? With one generator seized up and cargo to be cleared up all over the place?'

'Be grateful the damage *can* be cleared up, Brian,' was Jeff's last comment on the incident.

Pleading extreme exhaustion, Afra took the rest of the day off. The curious chittering of Coonies greeted him as he entered his quarters. He smiled wanly at the anxious expressions on their masked faces as they pressed in on him. Had Damia sent them to him? No matter, he appreciated their company which, since Damia had monopolized them as playmates, he had little of.

But he didn't have the energy to respond to their overtures and dropped down on to the wide couch to stare unseeing at the fireplace. He *was* exhausted, but that was not why he needed time off. *You could have* killed *her!* He shouted at himself in white hot rage. *Do you realize the awful risk you took, grabbing at her? And grabbing at a child instead of the ship which was equally at risk?*

The door chimed. 'Come in, Jeff,' Afra called, knowing beyond prescience whose hand was on the buzzer.

Jeff Raven, slightly haggard underneath his outward diffidence, entered Afra's apartment warily, noted the collection of Coonies and, receiving a gesture from the Capellan, took a seat in a chair opposite him.

'I know why you're here,' Afra said quietly. Without any regard for etiquette he summoned the nearest piece of paper to him – oddly it was a sheet of fine origami paper – and a pen. He scrawled a date, a short sentence and signed it without any change in outward temperament. 'Here.'

Jeff raised an eyebrow, examined the message, balled the paper up and threw it across the room. The Coonies took it as a toy and commenced to dribble it about the apartment.

'I've had enough guff from a distraught wife and hysterical daughter. I'm not about to tolerate nonsense from you, too, Afra.'

'But I broke the most important law of Tower protocol – I interrupted a thrust and nearly caused the loss of a passenger ship.'

Jeff stopped him with a look. 'Saving my daughter in the process.'

'But what if you *hadn't* been able to retrieve the Altairian . . . ' Afra persisted.

'We did but if you hadn't hauled Damia, she would have been very dead.' Jeff shuddered uncontrollably at that thought and saw that Afra had blanched to a grey.

'If I hadn't encouraged her to use the Coonies and Rascal as playmates, she wouldn't have taken to wandering about . . . '

'So it's the Coonies' fault, too?' Jeff asked amused.

'No, *I'm* at fault,' Afra said, unwilling to unload responsibility.

'Oh? And you led her to believe that the passenger

capsule was a good place to play with the Coonies? C'mon, Afra, let's permit a little common sense to infiltrate the breast beating.'

'No matter,' and Afra dismissed his arguments with a chop of one hand, 'the fact is that I broke the gestalt with the Rowan – I could have killed her and still not saved Damia!' Afra's control broke with those last words, his voice rising in self-contempt and loathing.

Jeff waited for the yellow-eyed Capellan to collect himself. 'Have you thought to wonder where you got the strength to do what you did?'

'Where? What—?' Afra broke off, his eyes widening in surprise. He looked to Jeff who nodded in slow affirmation.

'Consider what would have happened if Damia had tried the jump *blind* without your aid.'

Afra did and his skin blanched pure white.

'I came here to thank you for saving my daughter's life,' Jeff said slowly, 'even if you had to get a two year old to help you save herself. And those bloody Coonies.' He paused, watching those same animals playing soccer with crumpled paper. He let out the rest of his held-in anger. 'I most certainly did not come here to listen to silly twaddle about who's guilty for what and who's responsible for everything else in this system!' He launched himself out of his chair suddenly, clasping Afra tightly by the shoulder, shaking him firmly in emphasis. 'You're family, man, right or wrong, up or down, in or out. Get it? Now, what have you got to drink? I'm parched,' Jeff grinned at him. 'All that fast talking with Captain Leonhard.'

Afra instantly rose. 'I could make some tea or coffee?'

Jeff cleared his throat noisily. 'Surely you've something stronger, Afra? Or maybe I should start sending you a case or two the way Reidinger did for Brian. Though I've known a time or two when there's been some pretty good rotgut available on this station.'

From the kitchen, Afra produced a clear bottle containing a clear liquid.

'I use it for colds. It's effective.'

'Well, I felt damned near frozen today for a few seconds there,' Jeff remarked. He downed half a glass and his eyes bulged. 'First class,' he managed to say on a forcefully expelled breath. He waggled the bottle at Afra. 'You need some, too.'

'No,' and Afra shook his head, making a cup of a soporific tea that had often soothed jangled nerves. The rotgut was too much of a stimulant in his present condition.

They arranged themselves in the high chairs surrounding the bar-height kitchen table.

'Have you eaten?' Afra asked as his manners continued to surface out of the reaction to the day's trials.

'No, have you?'

Afra had to think for some moments before shaking his head.

'Let me,' Jeff offered, noting the other's exhaustion and added with a grin, 'I'm not a bad cook!'

'Chinese doesn't take much time,' Afra suggested.

'Rowan got you on that cuisine, too, huh?' Jeff said. Then he shook his head. 'Actually, I think I'll have dinner sent up, if you don't mind.' Afra looked puzzled. 'Luciano has obliged me on several occasions.'

'He has?' Afra was surprised. 'Though I wonder about rich food on my stomach . . . it hasn't settled yet . . . '

'I'll advise Luciano to prepare something restorative for nerve and mind.' Jeff sent a quick mental cast to Gollee Gren back on Earth, who had the good sense to swallow his curiosity and promised to expedite the request.

'While we're waiting,' Jeff continued, 'we can talk about our problem child.'

'She didn't mean to—'

Jeff raised a hand. 'I know that.' He sighed, an admiring look on his face. 'She's very much like her mother, you know.'

'But different.'

'The Rowan can't handle her,' Jeff remarked almost rhetorically. 'Nor can Tanya.'

'Are you suggesting some hypnotics?' Afra wondered. They had used only the most subtle hypnotic suggestions to keep Damia from becoming completely unmanageable. Afra had instigated the first. This successful implant had been followed, always with Jeff Raven's full knowledge and approval, by others, but only after certain restrictions became necessary. As today had proved, Damia appeared to be one jump ahead of everyone's estimate of her capabilities. She was also growing increasingly resistant to the more 'delicate' suggestions and, with the Rowan *firmly* opposed to 'tinkering' with her children, stronger impositions would be noticeable.

Jeff sensed Afra's uneasiness and shook his head firmly. 'No, I don't think hypnotics are the solution.'

Jeff? Isthia Raven's 'voice' distracted him.

'Mother, I'm here with Afra,' Jeff responded, speaking aloud for Afra's benefit and echoing telepathically.

Hello, Afra. Isthia responded, widening her telepathic 'voice' to include him. *Are you recovering from that remarkable rescue?*

Somewhat, Afra replied. He had long since given up at pretence when dealing with the Raven matriarch.

Except that he's torturing himself with guilt in the process, Jeff added.

Tut! Isthia chided. *Guilt's for small souls, Afra. Your immediate response was nothing short of heroic and I won't allow you to escape that designation. I'm sure Jeff agrees.*

Oh, I do, but he won't. He's threatened to resign.

Nonsense!

You are not Tower, Isthia Raven, Afra replied, rousing from his lethargy. *You cannot be expected to know that I broke one of the strongest rules of Tower procedure . . .*

Saving a child? Priorities always supersede mere procedure. There was such a trenchant criticism in her retort for bureaucracy that Afra had to grin. *At least you heard the child.*

Damia did not call the Rowan, Afra replied glumly.

And how is Angharad? As if in answer to Isthia's question, the station's generators screamed to full power, crescendoed, then rose again to another crescendo and another as cargoes were hurled rapid-fire to their destinations.

I'd say she's decided to work off fright and anger constructively, Jeff responded mildly. He winced at the shriek of the generators as they hit launch peak. *Fortunately Ackerman's giving her cargo. At that, some of the fragile goods are going to be worthless.*

Oh dear! Isthia's response included a soft caress of understanding. *What do you plan to do?*

Afra and I were just discussing that, Jeff replied. *We've ruled out more hypnotics.*

Good. I doubt they'll work, the child's too quick. Across the light-years, Isthia frowned. *What alternatives have you considered?*

None, yet, Jeff replied. *We were going to try the full-stomach method of meditation. Then I'll have to see what the Rowan wants.*

She may not want me, after this, Afra said dispiritedly.

Stop it, Afra Lyon! Isthia shot back hotly. *Mind you, not even Angharad will tolerate your wallowing in such a slough of self-recrimination.* Isthia paused briefly. *Well, now, maybe a good yell will shock you back into appropriate manners, you Methody Capellans being so fierce about proper conduct. But then, Angharad's not likely to consider protocol more important than her daughter's life.*

Afra was dumbfounded. *But I nearly lost that Altairian freighter. If Jeff hadn't . . .*

Lord above! He's really into this guilt trip, isn't he? Jeff Raven demanded rhetorically. *If it would make you feel any better, I'm perfectly willing, as head of FT&T to dock your annual salary for whatever amount you feel will compensate us for your interference with the conduct of traffic on this route. But, as Earth Prime, I'm obliged to point out to you, Afra Lyon, that it's highly unlikely that Angharad Gwyn-Raven will accept your resignation.* Jeff paused to regard Afra's unyielding expression and sighed in exasperation.

Isthia sighed, like an echo of her son. *I'd thought that years of exposure to Reidinger and Angharad would have eroded your Methody upbringing. What is it offenders have to wear on Capella? Sackcloth and ashes.*

Afra shook his head, then propping it into his hands, made a deliberate effort to break out of the fugue which tormented him.

Of course, actually, as Earth Prime, I'm not supposed to interfere with local Tower discipline so I won't.

That is, said Isthia, *no further than you've already done.*

Listen to the generators, Afra, and Jeff grinned. *She's working it all out of her system. Maybe you should, too. No? I guess that's only sensible. You're shagged.*

Afra, dear, Isthia put in, *I love you incredibly but you really* must *pull out of this negativity. It simply doesn't suit you.* Then she grew thoughtful and added, *No, you're fighting something . . . resisting with every ounce of your mind. That's why you're displaying so much negative emotion, isn't it?*

Afra blinked. He had not actually been indulging in self-pity, or – the notion amused him – wearing mental sackcloth and ashes. In fact, he wondered that Jeff had not perceived what did, terribly, worry him. Now that he had shown Damia how to use her innate telekinesis, he had opened an avenue of escape for her that would lead to far worse expeditions than today's. He'd already done the Gwyn-Ravens irreparable harm with that *in utero* link between Jeran and Cera: the link which caused that pair to so isolate themselves from Damia that she was excluded from any natural relationships with them, an outcast within the family unit that should have sustained her. She was also the youngest of the pre-school children but so much more advanced than the nearest child in age that she had no suitable playmates. If there had been even one station child who'd been compatible, he knew that Damia would have been content and certainly less trouble-prone. Afra groaned, shaking his head in his hands.

What is it? Jeff asked.

The Rowan will not like it, Afra responded obliquely. His shielding was sufficient to keep long-eared Isthia from penetrating his tired mind. Or perhaps she had arrived at a similar conclusion.

Aha! she cried triumphantly.

I know that sort of an 'aha' from you, Mother and it means trouble for someone, Jeff said with a groan not unlike Afra's.

Wearily Afra explained. *I was thinking that most of Damia's problems would be solved if she had other Talented children nearer her age and accomplishment. She is the youngest in daycare by over a year. If she had a human playmate her own age . . .*

I don't want her down on Earth, Jeff began, *and the only place where there're more is—.* He stopped short and regarded Afra solemnly. *You're right, the Rowan won't like it. Not at all.*

But she must see the sense of it, Jeff, Isthia said. *This isn't the first time Damia has instinctively appealed to Afra as a source of reassurance and assistance. He* can't *be bailing her out of every little scrape. Or if he does—* Isthia kindly left the thought unspoken but Afra could still see the Rowan's desperate lunge to grip the Altairian freighter and could imagine what would have happened had not Jeff Raven been there to help her prevent the freighter from plunging into the void unguided.

'How do *you* feel about this, Afra?' Jeff asked the tall Capellan softly.

Afra's response was a long time coming. 'It is not what *I* feel that matters, Jeff. It is what is best for Damia.'

'It'll be hard on all of us,' Jeff said in response to Afra's unspoken plaint. *Mother, not a word of this to anyone!*

Particularly not within Angharad's hearing. Thank goodness she's involved in slinging cargo about the galaxy, Isthia replied. *There are quite a few Talented children nearby. And a shower of second and third cousins who could be . . . if anyone bothered to show them a thing or two. I'll see what can be contrived here on Deneb. Especially if Damia's just become kinetically active.* More to Afra than to Jeff, she added, *I promise that I will help this difficult grandchild of mine whom you find so adorable.*

With strong and sensitive fingers, Jeff massaged deep into the Rowan's neck, kneading out the worst of the knots in her tense muscles late that night.

'If it hadn't been for Afra!' she exclaimed. 'Oh! That's it, right there!' She swivelled her neck to aid his efforts. 'Ah.' She pulled away from his grasp, taking his hands in hers and gently squeezing them. 'Oh, thank you! That's much better.'

'Anything to oblige,' Jeff replied with a slight bow as he sat on the edge of the bed. The Rowan was below him on the floor, tucked between his legs. She jumped up, brushed his forehead with a kiss, then dragged him up as well. Jeff responded with a firm hug and a tender expression. The Rowan stopped him with a stern expression and a finger on his lips.

To his puzzled expression she said: 'Let's talk in the kitchen.' She turned and, fingers twined with his, dragged him after her by the hand.

The kitchen presented two good places to sit: the barstools and counter near the stove and the larger circular table where they usually ate (or tried to) breakfast with the kids. Jeff raised an eyebrow enquiringly at his love but she resisted his gentle probe until she dropped into one of the seats surrounding the kitchen table.

'Jeff, I'm scared,' the Rowan began. 'If it hadn't been for Afra, we might have lost Damia completely.'

'The ship was going to Altair, luv, not the Horsehead

Nebula,' Jeff chided her gently. 'They would have brought her back.'

'What if she had panicked?' The Rowan wrung her hands together. 'What if Afra hadn't been there? Hadn't handled her kinetic thrust? She could have been lost for ever.' She flung out her hands despairingly.

Jeff captured one in both of his, stroking her palm gently with his fingers. He smiled up at her. 'But she wasn't, luv. Afra caught her.'

Her answer came in a sob. 'He did, didn't he? Why didn't she call me?' Her eyes watered. 'Oh, Jeff, am I such a terrible mother?'

'No!' Jeff's answer was emphatic, firm.

'Then why didn't she call to me?' the Rowan cried. She pulled her hand out of his.

'You were too intent, Rowan. You had a freighter to 'port—'

'So did Afra!' she broke in. 'He had that load too! But she called to him, not me!' Again she pulled her hand free to wave it over her head in more wild gesturing.

'Rowan, love, who knows what goes on in the mind of a two-year-old child – especially Damia's.'

'She's almost three!' the Rowan corrected him almost absently.

Jeff shook his head. 'No matter, she reacted out of panic, called to the first person to come to her mind. At least, she's learned not to bother you when you're working.'

'You see, I *am* a terrible mother!' she wailed.

Jeff let out a hot hiss of breath and turned away, angry with the Rowan for her futile outburst of self-contempt.

'Well, it's certain that you're not doing your new son much good, getting yourself all roiled up like this,' he remarked when he had schooled his emotions. 'Damia's a spirited child which makes her a handful.' He grinned, flicking a finger accusingly in her direction. 'If I recall correctly, you were just about the same age when you startled a whole *planet* which is much more than your daughter's done.'

The Rowan blinked and managed a small chagrined smile. 'Our situations were somewhat different but I take the point.' Then she sighed in despair. 'Only I have no trouble coping with Jeran and Cera . . . '

'Who are even-tempered to the point of being phlegmatic and totally engrossed in their small selves to the exclusion, I might add, of their younger sister. Damia, on the other hand, requires the same delicate understanding you received from Lusena. But we don't have a Lusena here, who can devote every waking hour to the care and companionship of our Damia. Who is, it has been pointed out to me, very much like her mother? Opposites attract, luv, and alikes set sparks. And, in turning to Afra in time of crisis, Damia's only following her mother's good example, isn't she?' He waggled his finger at her. 'Imitation is the sincerest form of flattery.'

Rowan drew breath to contradict, then let it out in a long defeated sigh. Their eyes locked and a long silence ensued. 'If it happened—' she began.

'It'll happen again,' Jeff finished, nodding. 'We may not be so lucky the next time.'

'What can we do?'

Jeff was a long time forming an answer and, when he did, his voice was rueful. 'For all my fingers in Talent pies, I haven't been able to find a T-6 nanny. And I've offered all kinds of enticements.'

'You didn't tell me . . . '

Jeff rolled his eyes at her vehemence. 'We'd need *someone* anyway with the new one on the way. And come on, luv, after today, you wouldn't have complained if I had found someone suitable.' He exhaled and made a less palatable suggestion. 'We could try hypnotic—'

'No!' the Rowan's response was emphatic. 'I will *not* have my children tampered with!'

Jeff continued down the list of possibilities. 'What about a pukha?'

'Damia has not been orphaned . . . '

'She had been through a rather traumatic experience . . . '

'She doesn't *need* a pukha. She's got a mother and a father . . . '

'Remotes, then? There're some excellent robotic—'

'A robot minding Damia?' Rowan was horrified. 'A thing with no sensitivity . . . Why even a pukha would be preferable!'

''Bots can't be distracted from the job they're programmed for.' Then Jeff shrugged that notion aside before the Rowan gathered her contradiction. 'I admit the notion doesn't appeal to me but—'

'Hideous notion!'

'There is one possible alternative,' Jeff began, careful to sound tentative.

'What?'

'It worked with me,' Jeff began, judiciously choosing his words, 'though even a whole planet might not be large enough. We could ask Mother to take all three of them . . . At least until you've delivered this child.'

'What? Admit to all Deneb and the Nine Star League that I can't look after my own children?'

'No, admit to the Nine Star League that you are having a bad pregnancy, yet you honour your commitment as Prime. But, because your children are special, you are willing to sacrifice your daily contact with them to ensure that they grow up as happily as possible,' Jeff corrected her. 'Besides,' he continued on a fresh breath, 'what do you care for the opinion of others as long as the children are happy?'

'But your mother can't possibly—'

'It's not just mother who'd be involved but my brothers, sisters, cousins and nieces,' Jeff corrected. 'They'd all be ecstatic. It'd be a good thing for Deneb. You know how many undeveloped Talents you found in the city. Even young as our kids are, they've had more training than anyone there. Deneb's been reorganizing – give the planet examples of Talented children to stimulate interest in that natural resource. And,' Jeff added, reaching over to pat her belly lovingly, 'you'll be able to concentrate on him whole-heartedly.'

'Maybe if I hadn't—'

'You got pregnant for Damia, if you recall,' Jeff gently reminded her. 'Mother would be over the moon. And Ian's a good lad: he'd certainly be happy to have nephews and nieces to play with!'

The Rowan had to smile at the incongruity of a seven-year-old uncle. Ian was the last born of Isthia Raven and the first baby the Rowan had had a chance to handle. She could in fact visualize him as a good companion for six-year-old Jeran who was much too preoccupied with a sister fifteen months his junior.

'Jeran could do with an older brother and I'm sure Ian would be glad to oblige,' Jeff remarked, neatly accessing the Rowan's thoughts.

'Jeff—' the Rowan began in preparation for a protest. He raised a hand to forestall her then placed it over hers. 'Sleep on it, love.' Gently he led her from the kitchen to their bedroom.

In bed, the Rowan rolled over. 'Jeff?'

'Mmm?'

'Don't mention this to Afra, just yet.'

'Of course not, not until you've made up your mind,' Jeff responded ingenuously.

As the week progressed and the ripples from Damia's 'accident' spread throughout the Nine Star League, with shipments late or lost, the Rowan found it increasingly harder to resist the suggestion.

'It's just that it's so unnatural!' the Rowan railed late one night to her husband. Eyes tear-rimmed, she turned to him. 'Why *can't* I look after my own daughter?'

Jeff patted her soothingly. 'Hush, luv, you could, if you'd nothing else to do with your time. But look at the demands on you? Three highly Talented children, another on the way, long hours in a FT&T Tower.'

'But I don't want to be like Siglen . . . '

Jeff regarded her with astonishment, then laughed, rocking her in his arms. 'Luv, you're no more like Siglen than . . . than Brian Ackerman's a Reidinger clone. Sometimes, when I think how that woman repressed you, babied you, gifted you with a load of rubbishy phobias, I wonder you've turned out as well as you have,' Jeff exclaimed. He cradled her possessively. 'You've chosen not to repress or overprotect your children and they're really rather marvellous. It's just that,' he added ruefully, 'a young Gwyn-Raven marvel is a handful for anyone!'

The Rowan sighed in agreement.

'And you've three handfuls with a fourth on the way.' Jeff moved a hand to rub her belly soothingly. 'And then there's this disturbing report from Elizara.'

'Hmm?' The Rowan stirred uneasily at the change of topic. 'Oh? That, well, yes, she mentioned something about anomalies in my latest lab results.'

'Oh?'

The Rowan dismissed them. 'Elizara said she'd come back to me. It does happen.'

'I'd really rather know a.s.a.p.,' Jeff said with gentle insistence. 'I can't think why,' and he grinned, 'but you're very important to me.' He draped an arm about her shoulders and peered down at her half-hidden face.

She gave him a long, enigmatic look out of the corner of her eye. 'I could . . . ' she hesitated, 'take a leave of absence from the station!' Before he recovered from his surprise, she added, 'Afra could take over . . . with you to give him a hand with the live and heavy stuff.'

The suggestion bowled Jeff over. Sympathetically he drew her against him as he mulled it over, digesting the notion – and also the Rowan's reason for making such a drastic proposal. He knew how important the Callisto post was to her. And, in the normal way of things, she ran it faultlessly. He'd seen Reidinger's private notes about her management. The Altairian freighter episode was unique in every way. He could feel through her that he had delayed an answer long enough to cause her to fret.

'You could. You're entitled to leave,' and he stroked her hair, grinning. 'None of us Primes take even a quarter of the leave we're allowed. I could transfer Saggoner and Torshan here . . . ' And, with the index finger of his free hand, he prodded the bedspread, miming the moves he would have to make. Then he frowned. 'Of course, they've become indispensable to Altair and that system hasn't got DEW yet . . . Gollee could be spared to assist Afra here . . . ' His voice dropped out while he considered the ramifications. Then he made eye-contact with the Rowan and tightened his arm about her. 'There's another possible solution. Mother!'

The Rowan poked at him in disgust, physically and mentally because he was concealing something. 'Your mother can't run a Tower.'

'No,' and Jeff's grin was wide if the sense of him was tentative, almost wary, 'but she sure raises kids well.'

'After all she's *had* to raise? You'd saddle her with Damia?'

'And Jeran and Cera,' and Jeff was dead serious now. 'If Damia has learned to 'port, that pair are too competitive not to mimic the kid sister's trick.'

The Rowan's expression mirrored the fearful tension Jeff could feel in mind and body. 'We're so far from Deneb . . . ' the Rowan began defensively. Abruptly she gave him a sharp poke in the diaphragm that made him grunt: her look altered as she jabbed him again, harder. 'You devious unrepentant dork! That was all pretence about shifting T-ratings. You had this in mind all along! You're no better than Reidinger now you're Earth Prime. The Callisto Station runs best through me . . . even when I'm spewing my guts with morning sickness.'

Jeff coughed delicately. 'Actually, the highest efficiencies and throughput were achieved when *I* was Prime.' The Rowan glared at him, words unneeded. Jeff shrugged. 'Well, you could run Earth!'

'Jeff!' she growled, launching herself on top of him. The Rowan broke off the ensuing play fight with a groan. She pushed herself away from him.

'Are you OK?' Jeff asked solicitously for her complexion had turned an odd grey.

The Rowan nodded raggedly. 'Uh, our little one decided to join in the fun.'

'I'm calling Elizara,' Jeff said in tones that brooked no argument. 'And the children are going to Deneb.' When the Rowan started to protest, he held up a hand. 'This pregnancy is not proceeding normally and I won't risk losing you.'

Elizara arrived so promptly that, despite the Rowan's protestations that Jeff was being overprotective, she was alarmed. Elizara immediately reassured both parents that the child was not under any stress.

'You are,' she said, pointing an accusing finger at the Rowan. 'I've checked, and double checked, the lab reports of your latest tests. You have developed what's known as gestational diabetes, Rowan.'

'Diabetes?' Jeff sat down heavily on the bed beside his wife, drawing her into his arms as if his protection would mitigate the illness.

'It's not uncommon in pregnancies, though it usually manifests itself in the first or second. The condition passes when the baby is born.' She was readying a hypospray as she spoke. 'This injection should balance your glucose levels.'

'But I've always been so healthy. I've had three easy pregnancies . . . ' The Rowan was stunned.

Elizara nodded. 'So you have. This time you're not.

You will have to watch your diet and your workload. Stress must be reduced or you can do yourself, and the child, serious harm.' She turned to Jeff. 'I know that Callisto Station is a vital link in the FT&T network, but I have to insist that the Rowan's schedule is lightened.'

'As of right now,' Jeff said and he 'pathed through the restriction to Afra and Brian Ackerman.

Elizara caught and held the Rowan's gaze. 'Right now, Rowan?'

She nodded, no longer able to deny the consuming weariness she had struggled to ignore. She lay back on the pillows and wanted to weep. 'Oh, Jeff. I'm so sorry.'

'Sorry? What for?' Jeff enfolded her in his arms, alarmed to see tears streaming down her face. 'Not your fault, luv, that your body's done gone and let you down. Mind you, there're not many pregnant women who could hold a megatonne freighter in sheer determination not to let it drop forever out of sight. Not to mention all the other minor little crises you seem to deal with every day. Then, too,' and his grin turned to sheer mischief as he realized that sympathy was not helping, 'if you'd allowed me to produce this embryo in the time-honoured fashion . . . ' He cocked his head, hoping that he'd taken just the right teasing note with her.

She stopped crying and glared at him. 'You can't blame the whole thing on *me*! Sperm's sperm no matter how I acquired it.' Then she caught his expression and began to giggle. 'Oh, all right. I did do this on my own and I'm paying for it! And it is my fault. But you wouldn't help me. Damia is such a caring child. Look how she treats Rascal and the Coonies . . . '

'Paints them pretty colours . . . '

'But she cleaned them up. She just wants what Jeran and Cera already have: a sibling to care for and play with.'

'And you're having your own way, and now we'll take over,' he said, squeezing her affectionately and rubbing his cheek against hers. 'But we'll get you sorted out. We'll make sure that you get lots of rest, all the best exercise,' he sniggered suggestively, 'and no hassles.'

'The children?' she asked almost fearfully, though she 'felt' that he had also taken that decision from her.

'Are going to Deneb. I've already talked with Mother and she's got some ideas that ought to solve her problems and our problems. And,' he paused significantly, pulling back enough to catch her eyes with his, 'you'll agree to give yourself a long break before you ask me – politely and in the normal fashion – for another baby.' He eyed her sternly.

'Oh, I will!' the Rowan replied, earnestly wide-eyed. 'I will!'

Afra caught up with Jeff Raven. Brian Ackerman was right behind him. 'She *will* be all right, won't she?'

'Elizara told you everything?' Jeff asked, allowing Afra to 'see' the concern he had kept from the Rowan. 'She must keep her metabolism balanced. Elizara had a private word with me before she went back to her clinic. Rowan did not wait long enough between pregnancies to get her metabolism back to normal. If we keep her occupied with a decent work load, less than she does normally but enough to keep her pride intact, and if we keep her emotions in check – you know better than I, perhaps, how unstable her emotions have been in this pregnancy . . . ' He grinned as Afra rolled his eyes expressively and Brian exhaled a long and hard-used sigh. ' . . . then she should be fine.'

'What'll happen next time?' Ackerman asked sceptically.

Jeff nodded. 'Elizara has hopes. Nothing can be done now but afterwards there are treatments which can prevent a recurrence.'

Ackerman looked dubious. 'I thought that another pregnancy would *always* cause permanent diabetes.'

'Used to,' Jeff said. 'But Elizara assures me that this is no longer so.' He regarded them thoughtfully. 'The children are going to Deneb. We'll have to do that quickly.' He looked directly at Afra.

'If it's to be done, 'twere better swiftly done,' Afra said, agreeing and forcing a grin from Jeff at the misquotation. 'Today. Brian and I can organize transport.'

'Sure, sure thing,' Brian answered, wondering why he was being seconded to an unenviable chore, but Afra would have his own reasons.

'I'm not sure what tack to take in breaking the news to Damia,' Jeff said, twisting his mouth in dismay. 'The poor little thing's been so subdued lately.'

'I'd be surprised if she wasn't,' Afra said. 'How did you get the Rowan to capitulate the children away?'

'That freighter débâcle helped almost as much as realizing she's risking the baby if she doesn't take care,' Jeff said. 'I just don't want Damia connecting her disobedience with her summary exile.'

'Why will she? If Jeran and Cera are to go with her,' Afra asked. 'Emphasize that the Rowan's sick – which Damia certainly senses already. Jeran and Cera probably do, too. They may be self-involved but they're not insensitive to their surroundings.'

'No, they're not.' In fact, Tanya had told Jeff how agitated the pair had been following the freighter episode. And they had known that Damia had been in trouble. They'd even spontaneously involved her in more than one game in daycare. 'When?' Jeff asked, his decision made.

'Today,' Afra responded immediately.

'Isn't that precipitous?' Jeff worried about the Rowan's reaction to what seemed, even to him, like an almost indecent haste.

'Your mother is ready and waiting,' Afra added, giving Raven the distinct impression that Afra had been in private collusion with her.

Jeff Raven sighed, nodding and thinking of all the matters awaiting his attention back on Earth. 'Very well. Let's do it today then.'

★

Damia had practised very hard at being good for two whole days. Tanya collected her in the morning because Damia already knew that Mother was very tired and was resting all day in bed. Damia wondered if something was wrong with the Tower. Mother never stayed away from there for very long. So, because Daddy had said that Damia must be quiet, she expanded that request to include her hours at the daycare. Occasionally she would glance around to be sure that Tanya noticed how well she was behaving.

She had not *meant* to cause trouble; she had just got frightened when the ship lurched so suddenly. *Her* voyages had always gone smoothly. Then she had 'felt' her mother involved in the lurching and she became afraid that Mommy was mad at her. So, she'd had to call Afra for help. She was sure that he would explain to Mommy and then everything would be all right. But everything was still not right; Damia suppressed a momentary surge of anger at Afra for not making everything better.

Damia? Someone 'called' to her. Afra! It was Afra! She turned around. 'Afra!' she called aloud, rising to run over to him. She knew she was supposed not to 'call' rather than speak but she could not help a little hopeful echo. *Afra?*

Afra squatted down and hugged the small child.

'You've come to play with me because I've been very good and quiet,' she cried in happy expectation. She gave him a coy, beguiling look, blue eyes peering up through jet black hair, trying to think which game she could involve Afra in.

'Tanya said you have indeed been quiet and well-mannered,' Afra replied. 'So if we can play something while I talk with you . . . '

Happily Damia led him over to her corner, a small hand wrapped around his big finger. 'We can play station,' she decided, having discarded several other possibilities as they walked. 'I'll be the Prime and you be my twic.'

'Twic?'

'Two-I-C?' Damia tried again.

Afra chuckled. 'Second-in-command! Certainly,' he gave her a mock bow from his cross-legged seat on the floor, 'your wish is my command.'

Damia placed her hands on her hips and cocked her head at him irritably. 'Afra!'

'What?'

Damia waggled a finger at him. 'You know. Now play right.'

Afra obliged, working up a manifest of cows, cats and clam chowder for their first load. They did three loads before Afra decided that she was sufficiently relaxed.

'Where's the next load?' Damia asked, a pout at the ready.

'How would you like to be a load? A proper one, just like those you've seen leave the station.'

Damia hesitated, not sure she really wanted to play in the pods right now. 'You'll have a proper carisak to take on board for your trip.'

'Trip?' Damia was not enthusiastic but she knew she could trust Afra. If he felt she should be a proper load . . .

'Jeran and Cera will be going too.'

Damia was not happy about that. She'd rather do something that *they* didn't. They were so mean about sharing with her – though they'd been much nicer the past two days.

'Are you?' she asked, looking up hopefully but Afra shook his head. 'Then I don't want to.'

'Ah, but you see, your grandmother has especially invited you to come. You'll like her.'

Suddenly sensing that Afra was *not* playing the sort of game she liked, Damia threw herself at him, clutching his neck fiercely with her arms. 'I want you!'

Afra gently disengaged her, his hands wrapped around

her tiny waist, holding her from him so that he could keep eye-contact as well as reinforce his words through touch. 'Damia, you *need* to go on this trip,' he said in his gentlest, most persuasive tone. 'Your grandmother has made such special arrangements for you.' He ignored her pout. 'You'll have cousins your own age . . . cousins who'll include you in all their games. Indeed, knowing you, you'll probably be leader.'

'I would?' Damia was captivated by that prospect. Being youngest, she wasn't allowed to lead anything here.

'You'll have a whole planet to play on, not a bunch of domes that restrict you to one measly play area and dank tunnels.'

'But I like the tunnels . . . '

'That's only because you haven't seen the wonders of a planet that your Uncle Ian—'

'Uncle?' She wrinkled her nose in perplexity.

'Your Uncle Ian. He's seven.'

'He's not my age then. He's older than Jeran.' She frowned suspiciously at him. 'Who's my age?'

Afra laughed because he hadn't enquired about such details. 'Well, there're so many I quite forget who's who and how old but your grandmother will introduce you. She's waiting for you, you know, on Deneb. Where your father lived as a child.'

'I'm staying here,' Damia declared stoutly, crossing her arms over her chest in bold emphasis.

'Which toys do you want to bring?' Afra asked, looking around at the pile.

'Why can't I stay here?'

Afra considered his next argument. 'Well, you know that your mother's not well?' When Damia nodded, her little face assuming a solemn expression, he went on, 'It's because of your brother to be.'

'I'm going to have a brother?' Damia brightened considerably.

Afra nodded wisely. 'Don't tell your mother I said so, but yes.'
'Will he play with me?'
'I imagine so,' Afra returned. 'Are you going to be nice to him?'
Damia did not commit herself immediately. 'Will he play with me like Jeran plays with Cera?'
'That depends on you,' Afra replied, giving her a quizzical look. 'If you love him like Jeran loves Cera then he'll play with you the same way.'
'I'll love him!' Damia declared excitedly. 'When am I going to see him?'
'Well, he hasn't been born yet—'
'You mean he's in Mommy's belly?' Afra nodded. 'And she's got to get him out?' Afra nodded again. 'Is that why we're going to Gran?' Again Afra nodded. 'Then why didn't you say so?' Afra, who had already had experience with her precocity, wondered why he *had* tried the oblique approach with her.
'We started to play a game of stations, remember?' he said, teasingly. 'Let's gather your toys.'
'Don't my cousins have toys?'
'Yes, but surely you'll want to share yours with them?'
'I guess so, if they're going to play with me,' Damia replied cheerfully.

Damia's mood changed perceptibly when it was time to strap down in the personal capsule. 'I don't want to go by myself,' she cried to Afra. Jeff Raven, lips drawn thin in tight control, stood close by. 'Daddy, make Afra come with me?'
'No, honey,' Afra told her. 'I've got to stay here with your mother.' He picked her up and set her beside her brother and sister, strapping her in against her squirming.
'I don't want to go!' she declared.

What about your brother? Afra asked her privately.

Don't want a brother! I want you! She shot back so strongly that Afra was startled by her vehemence.

The 'noise' attracted the Rowan who 'ported in the direction of her daughter's 'voice'.

'Damia? What's wrong? What's going on here?' she demanded. Her eyes widened as she took in the tableau. 'Jeff! Not yet! It's too soon!'

'Luv, you should be resting.'

'You weren't going to let me say goodbye?' the Rowan cried.

Jeff took her hands in his, shaking his head. 'You're not saying goodbye. You're saying *bon voyage*. The children will only be in Deneb. You can hear them no problem.'

'Jeff!' she started, accusingly. She saw Afra. 'You! You're in it too!'

'Rowan—' Afra started, stepping towards her, arm outstretched beseechingly.

'No!'

'Mommee!' Damia cried, struggling against her straps.

'Oh Jeff, how could you?' the Rowan gasped.

And then Damia disappeared out of her straps and into Afra's arms. The Rowan's eyes widened in shock as she saw her youngest disappear, then her jaw dropped as she saw where she reappeared. She turned to Jeff, hurt amazement on her face.

'She's got the hang of it, hasn't she?' Jeff told her quietly. 'What if she were to jump into the vacuum?'

The Rowan blinked, wetted her lips and looked back to her daughter, speechless.

Say goodbye to your mother, Damia, Afra said on the tightest mental band he could exercise, and with such authority that he felt her objections melting in the absence of any option. He took her to her parents.

And my brother? Damia begged in what Afra knew was a last ditch delaying tactic.

Very quietly, he said, without letting up on his authority.

Damia stretched from his arms to wrap her own around her mother's neck. 'I'll be good, Mommy,' she promised, planting a pair of wet lips firmly on her mother's cheek. 'For my brother.'

The Rowan hugged her back, suppressing the agony of separation. Any weakness on her part would undo all the preparation Afra had managed. 'I'm only just a thought away, Damia dear.'

'Even in the Tower?' Damia asked anxiously.

The Rowan closed her eyes briefly against that soft query.

'I promise, darling, that while you're away – and, if you're a good girl – you can even speak to me in the Tower.'

'Oh!' Damia's voice was charged with relief and she smiled broadly. 'Daddy, too?'

'If you remember that we might be too busy to talk long,' Jeff said, holding up a warning finger.

'Afra?'

'Well, minxlette, I'm not as good at long distance as your parents are, but I'll listen real hard.'

'I'll call real big.'

Then she squirmed to be released from Afra's restraint. He sensed what she wanted to do and let her down. She put her hands on her mother's abdomen and said with an amazingly narrow shaft of thought, *I'll be the* best *sister anyone's ever had.* Her face radiated a contentment that he had never seen on her face since her baby days.

To his intense surprise, Afra became aware that neither the Rowan nor Jeff had heard Damia's promise. He was more relieved than ever that she'd be away from the hazards of a domed station.

'Now,' he said, taking charge of matters again, 'let's just get you settled,' and he picked her up and started to settle her back into the capsule.

'When can we *go*?' Jeran demanded with a flavour of impatience for all this delay. Cera glared briefly at Damia.

'As soon as I'm feeling better, your father and I will come visit . . . ' the Rowan began, speaking to forestall tears, so she was grateful for the suggestion Afra 'pathed to her, ' . . . and see you being the leader of all your new friends . . . ' But she fully intended to tell him just what she thought of his part in this hasty exile of her children.

Will you visit me too, Afra?' Damia demanded.

'Of course,' he replied, 'we're to play stations, aren't we?'

As the capsule closed, her submission vanished. 'No! NO!' she shrieked, voice muffled inside the capsule.

Damia! Jeff had been ready for such a reverse and he clamped such a hold on her mind that she was rendered powerless.

Afra! Afra! I want to stay! Please? I'll be good.

Ready the generators, Jeff ordered the Tower personnel.

Afra?

The generators rose in pitch.

Be good now, sweetheart! Afra felt her fear, like an icicle against his heart but he firmed his mind against her plea, trying to deny how treacherous she must perceive him.

Aaaffffrrra! The squeal of the generators rose to a crescendo. The capsule disappeared. The generators wound back down.

They're here! the distant voice of Isthia informed them calmly. *My, can she scream!*

Afra let out a long-held breath in a ragged sigh.

The Rowan threw herself into Jeff's arms, weeping bitterly. 'I feel the most complete traitor,' she cried.

'You're not the only one,' Jeff replied, noticing the haggard look on Afra's face. 'But we had to. You know that.'

'I do, but oh, Jeff!' Suddenly the Rowan looked up, her expression radiant, despite the tear stains. 'I can hear her! I can still hear her!'

Afra turned away. 'I can't!' And he 'ported himself

back to his resoundingly lonely quarters, hearing Damia's prattle echoing from every corner.

It had taken Deneb seven years to recover from the Beetle attack. City was a thriving centre for the whole planet which now had two other metropolises: Riverside and Whitecliff. Both were seaports located close to extensive mining operations on the other continents. Roads were still mostly the illusion of roads elsewhere in the Nine Star League, but sea-going vessels plied a great trade on the high seas and railroads connected smaller villages along the coastline to the larger cities.

Deneb's Tower was located at the same site the Rowan had renovated so many years ago and it was near here that Isthia and the Raven clan had their town dwelling. This was built around the original smaller house that had partially survived the Beetle bombardment. Wings had been added on as the Raven clan grew and expanded. These now enclosed a large central garden, perfect for a play area. The dwelling was on a large parcel of land, with hills rising through forest to one side, farm land and barns on another two and the City skyline visible in the distance.

Many lessons had been learned since the Expansion from Earth. Denebians, indeed all colonists, had a greater feel of husbandry for the land than had early Earth dwellers. Forests had been marked off as reserves for oxygen generation, mines were always tunnelled when bacteria leeching techniques were not viable, and, most importantly, the clean quiet flitter for medium and long distances had replaced noxious internal combustion-powered, wheeled vehicles. Shorter trips made use of small, sturdy and tractable ponies who thrived on the rough grazing and wandered unchecked in small herds.

Deneb, and all colony worlds, started life indebted for the large cost of the initial colonization of the planet. As such, all colony worlds sought rapidly to provide export goods while at the same time limiting imports to the bare essentials. The best export items were those that commanded the greatest prices for the least effort to ship. Rare or high quality finished goods, *objets d'art*, music, literature all fitted the category perfectly. Knowledge and useful new engineering techniques, patentable to the planet of origin, were even more exportable but much rarer – the great engineering solution of one planet was often inapplicable on another. Raw materials, valuable but bulky, were a poor last choice of a cash-starved colony.

Talent, particularly those rare people who could hurl objects through the depths of space instantaneously, was the greatest boon to a colony's cash flow. Talent was in short supply everywhere and in every kind, from the metal finder who could locate high grade ore precisely and perform remote assays which would cost a regular crew millions of credits and years of time in scant seconds, to the electronic specialist who could detect faults in circuitry by its 'feel'.

The Raven clan had produced a number of such Talents but, until the Penetration had tapped these hidden resources, such natural abilities had gone relatively untrained. The Rowan had identified some useful faculties besides the medical Talents of Asaph and Isthia's sister, Rakella, when she'd had to rebuild the Tower in the days after Jeff's accident. Sarjie had a metal affinity which she now used in the rich Benevolent Mines that supplied much of Deneb's cash balance. Morfanu had been struggling to manage kinetic Talent and had been tested as a T-3. He now handled most of the FT&T transfers to the planet, though he needed assistance. Besseva was telepathic but her range was limited.

Of the untrained Talent of Deneb, Isthia Raven was the strongest but she knew herself that she dabbled in too many things to perfect one. So, to bring her grandchildren here in the safest possible fashion, she had assembled everyone on Deneb known to be Talented. She'd hovered so closely in Morfanu's mind when he 'caught' the capsule from Callisto, that he'd had to kick her shins to divert her.

It took no Talent at all to hear Damia bawling or the fierce remonstrations of her brother and sister.

'Why are you crying? You're perfectly safe! And it's your fault Mother and Father sent us away!'

IT'S NOT! IT'S NOT! Damia was as loud mentally as physically.

No, it's not, Grandson Jeran. I, your grandmother, specifically invited Damia, and you and your sister, to come live with me on Deneb. To Isthia's relief, Damia's howling abated. *I had to argue long and hard with your parents to allow this visit. Now, are we going to start off on the right foot by being pleasant, or do I send away the ponies I brought for you to ride home on?*

Ponies? Damia asked, now merely sniffling.

Ponies? And Cera showed a glimmer of interest. *What kind of ponies? The kind Damia's always playing with?* Her tone was scornful as well as sceptical and her sudden very private aside to her brother on this matter caused Isthia some concern. That bond she and Afra had initiated was far stronger than she'd been given to understand.

Why don't you all put on your best faces and party manners, and we'll see, shall we? Damia? I've told everyone about you and how wonderfully well-mannered you all are. Don't disappoint me. Isthia employed the same positive tone she had always found useful in dealing with her dozen children. These three, after all, were also Ravens. *Are you ready?*

She motioned for her son, Ian, to stand beside her. He'd been jiggling with impatience to see his nieces and nephew. Being the youngest in his family, he envisioned the fun he'd have bossing someone around the way his older siblings had bossed him.

The capsule split, the top rising upwards to reveal the inside. Isthia was relieved to see that, while not beaming, Damia was attempting to smile around her wide-eyed curiosity.

'Welcome to Deneb,' Ian piped up on cue, he looked to each one in turn, 'Jeran, Cera, Damia. I'm Ian, your uncle.' He did not giggle but his eyes were bright with suppressed laughter. He swept an arm back to his mother in continuation of his carefully rehearsed greeting. 'And that's Morfanu who 'ported you here, and your Great Aunt Rakella, and—'

'Ponies?' Cera said, looking accusingly at Isthia, 'you promised ponies . . . '

'We did, didn't we?' Isthia said mildly when Ian looked at her for guidance. He hadn't introduced half those he was supposed to. 'As promised, ponies,' and she nodded to Ian.

Grinning from ear to ear because he could get to show off so soon, Ian 'called' the ponies from where they browsed on the grass growing among the cradles. Obedient to the summons, they trotted to him while the children, still in the capsule, stared with wide open mouths and eyes at the little troop.

Damia was out of the capsule like a shot, Jeran and Cera not a split second behind her. But Damia stopped just short of the first pony, taking in his flaxen mane and tail which Ian had plaited that morning, the darker 'beer' of his hide, his dainty hooves, his bright black eyes, alert with interest.

'Just hold out your hand – flat so Jupiter can't catch your fingers – and let him sniff you,' Ian instructed.

'What's this one's name?' Cera asked, already holding her hand out to the lighter-coloured mare nearest her.

'And this one?' Jeran asked, wanting his answer from Ian before Cera had hers.

'The mare is Birdie, Cera, and, Jeran, your gelding is Cricket,' Ian said, genuinely enjoying his role.

If Afra had been told about the ponies, Jeff, Isthia remarked to her son later that night when her grandchildren had finally been put to bed, *there'd've been no fuss on leaving.*

I forgot you still had to use those wretched beasts, Jeff said ruefully for he had stopped riding the moment he had learned how to teleport accurately. *Afra will be immensely relieved. He was talking about sending out a Coonie or two to keep her from being too lonely.*

Thank you, no. There's enough livestock to be cared for about the place. As it is, it took a lot of persuasion to get Damia to sleep in her bed instead of out in the paddock with Jupiter.

Jeff chuckled. *Jupiter?*

Yes, Damia was so pleased by that. She has a remarkable appreciation of her environment, doesn't she? Anyway, reassure Angharad that all's well.

I will, but I may not mention that she's been displaced by runty-legged manure-makers.

The Rowan knew that the children had arrived safely and were settling in but she'd given himself and Afra such a bollocking for the way they had practically abducted her children that he decided not to risk another storm. She was resting now, more deeply than she had in many months. That was something he wouldn't mention though he was intensely glad to see how effective the lifting of her maternal burden had been.

Those runty-legged manure-makers are the best possible antidote for unsettled kids. Damia had firm control over Jupe in about five minutes. Cera wasn't all that pleased with the effect of a long ride on her tender behind but Besseva slathered her with an appropriate salve. Jeran's being pompous. He's so much like your father at moments!

Jeff chuckled because he knew exactly what his mother meant. *Then I shall expect to see him much improved when we get a chance to visit.*

Ah, about that! Leave it a while. Angharad really oughtn't to travel – too much stress. And let the children settle in completely. Rhodri and Ian took half a dozen tapes which I'll get Morfanu to zip off to you. That should reassure you both.

I am, I am, Mother, and can't thank you enough for pitching in like this.

Oh, I had my reasons.

But when Jeff probed to find out what they were, Isthia refused to admit him.

Besseva, noting Isthia's smug grin, raised her eyebrows enquiringly.

'I've reassured the doting papa that his little ones are safely asleep in their cots,' Isthia said and resumed her smile slightly.

'We're going to have to watch that youngest one,' Besseva said. 'Oooh, but she's powerful.'

'Hmmm, yes.'

'But really, Isthia, aren't they a bit young?'

'Not at all,' Isthia replied stoutly. 'They'll have fewer inhibitions.'

'And get into more trouble, too.'

'Besseva, we've got to develop our own Talents, and that *requires* Talent. One blind man can't lead another effectively.'

'But they're children!' Besseva's voice rose slightly in protest and Isthia, mentally and physically, shushed her. Ian was working in the corner, giving his niece's saddle a good soaping to soften the leather.

'And a little child shall lead them,' Isthia said, her eyes sparkling.

'You are the absolute end, Isthia Raven.'

'On the contrary, I'm the beginning,' Isthia replied. 'And, if I'm going on as I mean for them to begin, I'm going to need a good night's sleep.' She gave a gusty sigh. 'Why do children have the reserves of energy people my age so desperately need?'

'Huh!' Besseva said in contradiction to that complaint.

Lying in a new bed into which she had been tucked by her fascinating grandmother, Damia was still reviewing all the wonderful things that had happened since the capsule had opened. Being *on* Deneb was much better than hearing Daddy talk about it. And why hadn't he ever mentioned that Deneb had *ponies*? She sighed and, to make sure *he* was all right, she 'reached' to touch Jupiter. He'd stopped eating and was idly flicking his tail, as much to discourage the minute nightfliers from settling on Birdie's head as to keep them off himself. His mind was drowsy with sleep.

Just like Rascal's when he was curled up on her bed. Was Rascal missing her? Damia wondered. He'd have no-one to sleep with. A sad feeling made her throat constrict. Poor Rascal! Maybe, just tonight, Daddy would let him sleep on the foot of their bed. She loved having a pony but a pony couldn't sleep at the foot of her bed and she missed the comforting presence.

'Mrrow?' Came a plaintive call from outside her door. Damia had been given a proper bed without railings. She crawled out from under the covers and opened her door. 'Mrrr?'

'Who are you?' Damia called sleepily. A large orange and white cat marched into the room, rubbing himself against her leg. 'Oh, you're beautiful.' Though the animal was as tall as her waist, Damia hoisted him into her arms, once again exerting kinetic energy without realizing what she'd done in her wish to do what she needed. 'There,' she said, plonking the cat down at the foot of her bed. 'Now, you stay there and keep me company, hear? Maybe Rascal'll have sense enough to go to Afra if Daddy won't let him sleep in their room.'

Yes, she thought firmly as she scrambled back under her covers, Rascal'll go to Afra so he won't be so lonely with me gone.

Seeing her settled, the cat circled into the spot of his choice at the other end. His purring put her to sleep as Rascal's so often had.

Afra sat back in the couch, exhausted by the day's

emotional upheavals. He fed the Coonies and they went out for a night of hunting vermin in the tunnels. He could have used their company, especially tonight. He cleared his mind and tried repeatedly to stretch himself across the eighteen light-years to Deneb but he had failed every time to pick up even the merest glimmer of young Damia.

'She'd be sleeping,' he told himself, 'I hope.' I ought to do the same, he continued silently. All of a sudden, a body burst through the catflap.

In the next instant, that body executed a flying leap, landing on his chest so hard that Afra grunted.

'Rascal? What are you doing here?'

Never had Rascal purred quite so loudly in Afra's presence, nor was the animal so determined to settle himself on Afra's person. It was as if . . .

'Did Damia tell you to come to me?' Afra asked, wonderingly. 'Or is it just that you miss her, too, and you came looking for her here?'

The way the barque cat had leapt on to him did not suggest he'd been looking for anyone else but Afra. Planting his hindfeet firmly on Afra's thighs and his front paws on Afra's chest, Rascal then butted his head imperiously into Afra's face. Then, looking squarely, yellow eyes into yellow eyes, Rascal said definitely, 'Meh!'

That apparently settled that and Rascal jumped down, looked expectantly at Afra, before sauntering in the direction of the bedroom. Afra saw him settling himself on the bed with an air of 'here I am, here I stay.'

'You're quite right, Rascal. I'll turn in now, too.' *Good night,* he called blindly across the void to Deneb.

He didn't expect to sleep, certainly not with a heavy lump weighing down the duvet over his feet, but curiously comforted by that companionship, he did.

There were lots of girls and boys Damia's age at the school in which Isthia enrolled them, for Deneb did not run to special daycare centres for pre-schoolers. Damia couldn't appreciate that Deneb was undergoing a much needed population explosion, but she did realize what Afra had promised her was true. Within a few minutes, Damia was seated at a small table with a green-eyed blond girl named Alla, a solemn-faced boy called Jorg, and a freckle-faced red-headed girl named Jenfer who didn't stop grinning all that first morning. There were lots of other children her age, too, just as Afra had promised her, at more small tables in the sunny room with shelves and shelves of toys and books and curious boxes that Damia was dying to open. But because Alla, Jorg and Jenfer sat very correctly at the table, Damia did so too, however much she wanted to play with the fascinating stuff in the boxes. She tested and found one was crammed full of coloured crayons all different sizes.

Both her grandmother and her Uncle Ian had impressed on all three Gwyn-Ravens that they were to be on their best behaviour at school. Or, and the threat was awe-inspiringly frightful, they wouldn't be permitted to ride their ponies. Jeran had had a private word with his sister and had glared ferociously at Damia so that she knew she'd suffer his retribution, too, if she tried any of her tricks.

Damia was far too entranced with her new friends to think of any 'tricks'. She listened, very carefully, to the instructions Linna Maybrick gave the class – hearing it on two levels – and sometimes puzzling at the contradictions. But when she saw the others obeying what was said aloud, she followed their example.

At the morning break, she let Jorg lead the way to the playground where the four tablemates played together, climbing all over the 'mountain' and down into the 'tunnels' and swinging over the 'rivers' and revelling in noise and happy dirtinesses, for the play area was dirty and full of shavings.

Linna Maybrick, their teacher, watched carefully from the doorway. Alla climbed to the top of the 'mountain' and hesitated for a moment at the top of the slide down for it was, for a child, a huge drop. One of the more aggressive older boys was behind her and he lost patience, giving her a push on her way. His thrust was off-centred and caught Alla just as she was bent to sit on the slide. Thrown off-balance, she teetered to one side, a two-metre free-fall to the playground below. Alla screamed. Damia, who had been waiting at the bottom, gave a horrified shout, then 'concentrated'. Linna, who had started running the moment she saw the boy shove Alla, came to an abrupt halt as the little girl *bounced* gently on to the hard ground. Damia rushed over to her friend and helped her up.

'Are you OK?'

Alla nodded shakenly. 'I got pushed.' Then she cocked her head. 'Did you do that?'

Damia turned suddenly shy. If she admitted to doing any 'tricks' she wouldn't be able to ride Jupe. 'Do what?' she asked ingenuously.

Alla narrowed her eyes at Damia. 'Well, someone did something.'

Jorg, who had watched the whole incident wide-eyed, looked at Damia critically. 'You're not from here.'

'I am, too. I live with my grandmother and my uncle.'

She pointed towards Ian who was playing with older boys on an adjacent field. Jorg peered in the direction but his eyes were suspicious when he turned back to her.

'I know about the Ravens. My dad says they're all FT&T freaks.'

Damia didn't know the word 'freak' but she did know FT&T. Everyone she knew worked for FT&T and were proud of it.

'Why, thank you very much,' Damia said while Alla gawked at her in stunned surprise.

So did Jorg, having anticipated a far different response to the insult.

'But you're a freak!' he shouted and she picked up on the pejorative this time.

'There's no need to shout,' Damia said, dismally aware that the three of them were suddenly the centre of attention.

Abruptly Jeran and Cera made their way through the tight knot of children.

'Who called my sister a freak?' Jeran demanded, fists clenched at the ready. Beside him, Cera assumed a similar stance. Jorg nervously retreated.

'Actually, he said I was an FT&T freak, Jeran,' Damia replied, worried lest her brother realize she'd done something that could be accounted a 'trick' even if it had saved Alla from injury.

Jeran frowned intently at his sister for a moment and then, bracing himself again, unerringly settled on Jorg as the culprit. But the recess bell sounded and Jorg was the first one into the school.

Back in class, Jorg quickly spread the rumour that Damia was a freak. She felt miserable, especially as Alla wouldn't even look across the table at her. On the other side, Jenfer's grin turned slightly malicious and she kept staring at Damia.

When Isthia collected her after school, she naturally asked how Damia had liked her first day at school, and was taken aback by the fierce answer.

'I hate it. I'm not going back.'

On the flitter ride to the Raven compound, Isthia deftly drew out the reason for Damia's discontent. She was both saddened and angered that her grandchild had had such an unfortunate encounter on her very first day.

'Jorg is wrong. You are not a freak,' Isthia assured her, 'even an FT&T freak. And you were very quick about saving your friend from injury.'

'She's scared of me now and Jenfer just stares at me, grinning!'

'Stare back at her and I'd suggest you give Alla a

little time to get over being rescued. She must have been surprised to bounce on the ground when she expected to crash.'

Damia considered that. 'Yes, I guess she was more surprised than anything else. Least she wasn't hurt.'

Isthia ruffled her hair affectionately. 'That's right.'

Damia regarded her grandmother solemnly. 'Then rescuing Alla isn't a real trick and I can still ride Jupiter?'

The incident, as embellished by Jorg, set Damia apart from the others and while in time even Jorg was glad of her unprejudiced use of Talent to protect her playmates from the worst ravages of the playground, Alla was willing only to be her acquaintance. The lack of a close friend disturbed Damia and worried Isthia. To compensate, the youngster would often accept greater challenges in school and, at home, would often take off on Jupiter for lengthy adventures.

I fear she is a solitary soul, Isthia remarked in a conversation with her parents.

That's not a Raven trait! Jeff, who had always had a pack of boys to lead on excursions, replied.

No, it's more apt to be a Gwyn trait, I'm afraid, the Rowan said bitterly. *I thought that it was just being Ward of the Planet and having much older foster siblings, but perhaps it is a personality thing.*

You bestow your affections frugally, Angharad dear, Isthia said gently, *but where you do you are selfless.*

But I was so *lonely!* the Rowan cried. *I didn't want Damia to be lonely, too.*

It may be in Damia's nature to be solitary, Isthia replied. *But she's not lonely. There's Jupiter to ride about on, most of the workdogs when they're free, and Marmalade on her bed at night. She's not lonely. She does have companions at school even if she hasn't established a true-blue friendship. That'll probably take a little more time.*

Well, maybe she'll be happier for a brother.

How are you feeling? Isthia asked hopefully.

The Rowan responded with a mental sigh. Jeff added, *She hates to admit it but she's been doing much better since the children left.* Isthia could feel the mental nuzzle Jeff sent to his love. *She can concentrate on growing this new one, can't you, luv?*

I should be able to manage as much as you did, Isthia! the Rowan complained guiltily.

Ah, yes, but I was not running a power Tower nor was my husband absent all day long on another world. Then again, as soon as my eldest was able, I had him minding babies. Your Jeran's a solidly responsible boy, Angharad, and I love him dearly but he's not quite ready to baby-sit Damia.

The Rowan chuckled at the thought of the self-contained Jeran trying to handle his wild-mooded sister. *Well, maybe he'll be able to sit for this one.*

Damia awoke with a gasp. Someone was crying. Someone felt bad. Instinctively, with a sense of compassion which was fundamental to her nature, Damia reached out to calm the person. Her mental 'hand' stretched far, farther than she actively remembered. Whoever was crying was upset because it was cold and wet and had been warm just a few moments ago. Something rough was rubbing against it.

It's a towel! Damia exclaimed as she identified it. *It's all right, you'll be warm and dry in a moment!*

The someone was awestruck.

It's all right, Damia repeated soothingly. *You'll be all right now.*

The someone was calmed, felt sleepy. Warm and sleepy.

Damia continued to send soothing thoughts, herself growing drowsy in her efforts to send the other to sleep. She yawned, turned over and drifted off.

'I've never seen anything like it!' Elizara exclaimed to

Jeff Raven as they took a late celebratory libation. 'That child was all set to cry his lungs out and then—' Her eyes narrowed suspiciously. 'Did *you* do anything?'

'Me? No,' Jeff replied, confused. 'I had thought it was you. It certainly wasn't the Rowan.'

'No!' Elizara agreed. 'Not under anaesthetic.'

'Will it take her long to recover from the Caesarean?' Jeff asked, the thoughts turning from his newest son to his greatest love.

Elizara shook her head, grinning. 'This isn't Deneb where some of your obstetrics are still pretty archaic. Microlaser surgery heals seamless. She'll be fine in three to four days.' She raised a cautioning hand. 'But it will be months before the abdominal muscles recover from the intrusion.'

'So if it wasn't you, it wasn't me and not the Rowan, who?' Jeff, reassured, returned to the original topic. 'Afra?'

Elizara shook her head. 'It was a female touch.'

'Then it was Damia!' Jeff announced firmly. 'That little minx!'

'Really, doting Daddy,' Elizara said in one of her rare moments of mischief, 'isn't that a long way for such a young child?'

Jeff shook his head slowly, his smile rueful. 'I don't think any place is a long way where Damia's emotions are concerned.'

For the first few months of young Larak's life, both his mother and father 'felt' his sister touch his mind, causing him to smile.

'Has to be wind,' Brian replied sceptically when the Rowan remarked on her daughter's range.

Afra would smile. 'She promised she'd be the best sister ever.'

'It's not as if he has much conversation, Afra,' Brian protested.

'Ah, the heart needs no words,' Afra replied and, with a totally uncharacteristically dramatic gesture, placed his hand on his heart. Then he picked up the colourful origami birds he was arranging as a mobile for Larak and, with delicate movements, tied them to the string harness.

Brian shot the Rowan a puzzled look before he left the Tower.

However, at some point in Larak's first year, Damia found out that Alla loved ponies as much as she did, and the two became inseparable. The incidents of contact diminished slightly but occasionally, and for no apparent reason, Larak would giggle. His laughter was so infectious that he could set off anyone else in the house. But every time his parents, or Tanya or Afra, tried to explain these bursts of hilarity, they found nothing, not even Rascal, to account for them.

'Damia checking in,' became the standard explanation.

'A merry child,' his mother said, 'is a double delight.'

Afra forebore to mention that Damia had been a merry child, too. But he did not object to merry Larak and he had become adjusted to the lack of Damia in his life.

'He's here!' Damia cried excitedly, turning to her teacher. 'My brother's here!'

'Shush, Damia,' the teacher scolded, for the girl was old enough to respect classroom manners. 'Continue with your studies. You can see him after school.'

Damia fidgeted her way through school and burst out to the waiting area. Rakella was there.

'Isthia sent me,' she said, grinning at Damia's radiating excitement. All the girl knew was that she would be seeing her beloved brother. Today, even Jupiter was cast in shadow. Damia hopped into the flitter, practically 'pushing' Rakella to exceed the speed limits in the built-up area. She bubbled all the way back to the

Raven compound and burst out of the flitter almost before Rakella had set it safely on the ground.

'Where is he?' she called excitedly, but unerringly she headed toward the kitchen, slamming open the door. She stood there a moment. 'Larak!'

What young Larak saw was a slender figure a head taller than himself with sparkly blue eyes and long black hair. What Damia saw was a splendid dark-haired brother. She held out a hand entreatingly, sensing his sudden shyness. Cautiously, the toddler took it.

'Now that you're here, c'mon!' Damia cried. 'I've so much to show you and tell you . . . ' She started for the back door, all but dragging him after her.

'He's only a baby,' Isthia began, laughing at Damia's single-mindedness but the girl's enthusiasm was contagious and Larak didn't so much as hesitate a step. He happily followed his magical sister. 'Oh, let them go!' Isthia said when someone moved as if to stop her. 'She'll take good care of him. It's what she's waited for for so long, isn't it?'

'All I can say is, thank goodness Jupiter's too placid to buck any more.'

Damia had planned for Larak to meet Jupiter first but they were halfway to the paddock when she began to feel a reluctance, a hanging back on her little brother's part. Looking anxiously over her shoulder, she saw him staring wide-eyed at the wide-spreading branches of the nearest tree. He certainly hadn't seen the ponies sheltering under it. Damia was utterly charmed by his reaction. What fun it was going to be to show her little brother everything she knew and loved about Deneb. She looked down at him.

'That's a good tree, isn't it, Larak? Bigger'n anything in the park at Callisto.'

''Listo?' Larak asked, his expression dissolving into worry.

'Who needs 'Listo when they're on Deneb,' Damia said, quite forgetting her own recalcitrance, but she had imbued her reply with such enthusiasm that her brother's face altered to a happier mode, though he kept staring up at the tree. Abruptly, her original plan to introduce him immediately to Jupiter underwent a selfless change.

'D'you wanna know something, Larak,' she whispered conspiratorially to him, 'I've got a special spot right at the top. Wanna see?'

Big-eyed, Larak could not find a voice to speak and mutely nodded.

'Come on!' Damia replied, waving an arm. She was up three branches before she looked back and saw Larak standing still on the ground, looking up at her with a puzzled expression.

'Ooops, sorry!' Damia clambered back down, lifted him up to the first branch, pushing on his bum until he was firmly perched on it and then scrambled up beside him. 'You've never done this before, have you?'

Larak shook his head. 'Uhuh, 'Mia.'

Damia giggled. 'Damia, not 'Mia. Try it.'

Larak worked his tongue but only got out: ''Mia' again. Damia shrugged it off. 'You can try again later. Let's climb!'

It was quickly apparent to her that his legs did not have the length of hers and, while the branches of the tree shot out of the trunk at steppable intervals, her small brother would have trouble continuing. So, since they were high enough up in the tree not to be visible to anyone, she 'lifted' them both to the top to her special spot, just where the branches narrowed to diameters that would not support even her slight weight. Then she parted the branches to give her brother the full view of the realm they surveyed. Pointing out features – where Alla lived, where she had found a brookside cave she'd show him in the morning, the Tower which was conspicuous on the horizon, the smudge of the City – she finally ran out of breath and looked at him hopefully.

'Isn't Deneb great?'

Larak gave her an adoring look. 'Grea. . .t!' He managed the 't' as a separate syllable and grinned at his success.

I love you, Damia sent shyly in the quiet 'voice' she had addressed him in for the past year.

Larak's eyes widened, first in fright then in recognition. His face burst into a beaming smile. *Love you, Damia!*

'They're inseparable!' Linna complained. 'She cries and he just sits there, weeping silently. Which frankly I find harder to endure than her howling. Put them together and they're sweetness and light.'

'Didn't we go through the same thing with Cera and Jeran?' Isthia asked the concerned teacher.

Linna nodded. 'Yes, we did but the solution was to hold Jeran up a bit for Cera to catch up. But that won't work with Damia and Larak. She's too smart to be held back – she really should be encouraged to go forward at her own speed.'

'Is Larak bright enough to catch up?'

'He's bright but, really Isthia, it would be most unwise to force his pace to accommodate her. That sort of individualized instruction simply isn't possible in a classroom environment!'

'Not in a classroom environment, eh?' Isthia repeated thoughtfully.

'Isthia Raven, what *are* you thinking of?' Linna demanded in her best teacher's voice.

Isthia was impervious since she'd taught Linna the trick. 'And you do agree that there are now twelve other youngsters in this school district that have Talented leanings?'

Linna didn't quite grimace, and her sniff wasn't exactly disapproving, but her eyes were sad. 'The freaks.'

'FT&T freaks,' Isthia corrected her.

'Where do children learn such words?'

'I'm sure I don't really need to tell you that, Linna, but

I am thinking that it's about time we let our freaks get what they deserve here on Deneb.'

'Not that special school you've been trying to wrest out of the Education Committee?'

'Don't you agree it's needed?' Isthia retorted. 'The Education Committee's not the only one to complain about lack of funds but they sure tie the purse strings when I advance the notion that a little expenditure now on proper training and we'd have marketable assets to improve our economy?'

'Our economy?' Linna echoed weakly. 'What about our sanity?'

'Linna Maybrick, are you trying to tell me that Talented children are more difficult to teach than regular children?'

'Oh cripes, no! Children are impossible without exception,' Linna responded emphatically. 'But how will you get permission? And the specialized teachers?'

Isthia cleared her throat. 'Each one, teach one,' she said cryptically, and bent a fond eye on Damia who was patiently showing her small brother how to hold a crayon.

Linna never did hear how Isthia got round the objections of the Education Committee but somehow the Council found enough money to pay the salary of a T-4 teacher whom Earth Prime had located for them, and Isthia Raven agreed to underwrite his living accommodation. 'So we saved a little on salary,' Isthia told her sons and daughters. She also reorganized living space in the Raven Compound to house the Denebian Special School for the Talented until the construction of the permanent facility in five years' time, at which point the Education Committee should have the funds to build it.

'I had to compromise,' Isthia Raven said when Jeff and the Rowan came to visit their children, 'but it could be worse.'

Jeff rather thought she got what she deserved. 'You said "If you want it done right, do it yourself!" once too often, Mother!'

The school was understaffed, the new teacher overworked but Isthia worked as hard as he did. 'And learned more,' she said. 'I just wish I had had the opportunity I'm providing my grandchildren.'

Damia loved it because it meant that she and Larak could share classes. In fact, she *had* to teach him several subjects, including mathematics. She got to be quite good at mathematics herself from such exercise.

Larak was not her only pupil, nor were only Talented children entered in the school but Isthia chose a careful mix from families whose views did not run to 'freaks' or fear of Talent. Children from Larak's age to sixteen, who would be physically and mentally challenged by the opportunity of 'unstructured' classes were asked to enrol. So Damia found herself learning to control her temper at the difficulty some older students had in learning what she had to teach and her jealousy at younger students who stamped *their* feet at her 'slow' pace.

It was the sort of school only a gifted computer could plan for: with students and classes to mix and match in such complex calculations that it yielded a doctorate for the T-4 in record time. Physical therapy and physical exercise, mental therapy and mental calisthenics all vied with the more regular curricula of other schools.

Damia learned quickly the fallacy of judging a person on the colour of skin, the condition of body or the attractiveness of face.

She also learned, just as quickly, the art of moving cargo containers, juggling bricks and reading waybills, much to the amazement of her teachers.

Cooperation was a primary requirement for all Talented people: civil discord was something intolerable in one with Talent.

Damia's favourite sport was team dodgeball. It was

played both strictly with Talented children and with mixed groups of Talented and non-Talented children. The rules were simple: if you were tagged by the ball, you were out. The object of team dodgeball was to have at least one team member not tagged out at the end of the game. The Talented members of the team were permitted to 1) gain control of the ball by superior strength of mind; 2) pull themselves or pull their teammates out of the way of the ball. There were, however, limits to a 'port: a Talent was not allowed to lift a non-Talented teammate higher than three feet off the ground, or more than two feet laterally, or outside the playing field. Games with only Talented players were brilliant displays of unexpected lifts or the wild orbitings of the foam ball as players jockeyed for its possession. Games with mixed teams were perhaps less showy but more fun for the non-Talented and exceedingly good exercise for the gifted. However, particularly in mixed dodgeball, score was kept with one point for each team member still left when the other teams were eliminated. The size of the teams was arbitrary: some very small teams won more regularly, even on points, than larger ones. There were two unbreakable rules in team dodgeball: no player should be injured, and teams had to be evenly mixed boy–girl, Talented–non-Talented.

Damia grew closer and closer to her little brother, always wanting, but never quite achieving, the amazing rapport which Jeran and Cera shared. She would brag immensely about their combined capabilities and Jeran, who had grown rather less tolerant of his youngest sister as he grew older, would always take special pains to prove to her just how wrong she was. By the time Damia was nine and Larak nearly seven, the rivalry had grown to full scale war.

'My little brother's better than *your* little sister!' Damia would taunt Jeran, who, being older, would invariably agree: 'Yeah, Larak's better than Damia any day!' To which Damia could only shriek with anger.

Jeran had just reached puberty and had started to notice girls in a different light so having one so truculent was particularly annoying to him.

'Larak and I can beat any four of your friends!' Damia declared one day.

'Cannot!' Cera rejoined, coming to the defence of her adored older brother.

'Can too!'

'Prove it!' Cousin Channa challenged.

Damia paused, not expecting this tack. 'All right, dodgeball. Who's your fourth?'

Jeran's mouth fell. He floundered for a suitable way out of the challenge but Channa was Marci's best friend and Jeran just *had* to make Marci notice him. The trouble was that Channa was not all that good in dodgeball, being only moderately Talented and massively clumsy. Worse, the obvious choice of partner for Channa was Teval, her current male interest, and Teval was not only not Talented but an incredibly gawky adolescent.

'Fourth?' Jeran taunted. 'You said you could beat us all!'

'We can!' Damia returned, chin jutting defiantly. 'All the cousins!'

'How many teams?' Jeran demanded.

'*One* team!' Larak put in. And so the lines were drawn. The time was after school and the place was in the field beyond the river boundary of the Raven Compound.

'It'll be a slaughter!' Teval declared from the sidelines. Not being a member of the Raven clan, he was excluded from the tournament but invited by Channa who hoped to impress him with her abilities.

'I hope no-one gets hurt,' Marci Kelani, standing beside him, said nervously.

'No way. Just little Damia's pride!' Teval chuckled. 'The others are OK but she's a little busy britches.' She had tutored him in language class the year before and he had failed to respond to all her best efforts, refusing to learn from a 'little girl'. From the corner of her eyes, Marci gave him an appraising look and, with a flick of her eyes heavenward, decided she did not like what she saw in the boy.

Out in the centre of the field, Jeran looked around at his team of twenty-one cousins with concern. Some of them were a bit too happy to team up against Damia and Larak. He swallowed nervously. 'Are you sure you still want to do this?'

Damia rose above the doubts she felt because, absolutely, there was no way that she could salvage any pride if she backed down in front of everyone. Steadfastly she nodded her head. 'We're sure. Why? Are you scared?'

Jeran licked his lips but shook his head. 'You can call quits any time.' He pulled out the little foam ball. As usual it had a dye bag inside it so that anyone hit would be marked with a fluorescent orange dye that washed off. 'Shall we flip for possession?'

'Smallest team *always* gets possession!' Damia declared hotly and somewhat scornfully that her brother's understanding of the rules was faulty. Jeran let the ball go, Damia 'caught' it and let it hover between them. With a contemptuous mental 'nudge' Damia burst the dye bag. A splurt of dye filled the air.

'GET READY!' she yelled. 'On three! One! Two! Three!' *Ready, Larak?* she shot at him.

If the answering thought wobbled a bit, the boy's face was as determined as hers. *Ready, Damia.*

The ball became a vibrating blur which flew in an intricate pattern at the waiting throng of cousins. Damia knocked out three with the first pitch, then lost control for a moment as the remainder reacted and wrested it from her grasp. The bag came back firmly at her but she 'ported out of its way and shifted her power to Larak who, to the chagrin of the older players, looped it back around in a tight arc. Two more defenders were knocked out.

'She's good,' Marci noted from the sidelines. Alla, Damia's friend, rode up on her brown pony. The moment she pulled him up, he dropped his head to graze. 'Is she all right?' she asked Marci.

Teval snorted. 'Little brat! They'll show her, that's for sure!'

But the cousins were faring badly: in two separate passes Damia and Larak had managed to knock out two more, leaving only fourteen on the opposite side. The cousins were forced to switch completely to the defensive, hoping to tire the two youngest. They didn't attempt to 'take' the ball, only to dodge it without being blopped. The tactic began to take its toll for both Damia and Larak were soon panting and sweating profusely in their efforts to keep the ball both in the air and vibrating with the special effort that kept it out of the 'reach' of the other cousins.

Three more cousins were knocked out in the five minutes it finally took for Larak and Damia to lose 'control' of the ball. Heedless of the danger, Larak dropped to the ground, panting.

'Larak?' Damia called, turning to him. She started towards him.

'They're finished!' Teval cheered triumphantly from the sidelines.

The ball, now in the hands of the remaining cousins, hurled unerringly towards the prone form of the panting boy. But the light ball was thrust upwards and just over Larak.

'Oh, good, Damia! Good!' Alla cried from the sidelines.

Damia took another step towards her little brother. 'Come on, Larak,' she called encouragingly. The others scooped the ball back up from the dip it had taken after Damia had diverted it and brought it back around in a circle.

'I'm tired!' Larak gasped to his sister as she approached him.

'Perfect, two targets together!' Teval chortled.

Damia helped Larak up to his feet. 'Should we quit?' she asked him. Larak shook his head feebly, drawing away from her to stand on his own feet. Damia looked about her, saw the incoming ball and batted it aside with a mental 'flick'.

'Give up?' one of cousins called out hoarsely.

'No way!' Damia returned. She zoomed the ball at the speaker. Either he didn't see it or he, too, was tired but the ball caught him squarely in the chest.

'This is going to go on for ever,' Marci moaned. 'Why don't they quit?' She waved a hand at the remaining cousins.

'Quit? Against a little girl?' Teval sneered. 'They just need a hand.' He picked up a small rock.

'Teval, no!' Marci cried but the rock was launched right at Larak's unprotected head.

'Damia!' Alla screamed, throwing herself at Teval.

Turning at Alla's shout, Damia saw the rock and flung herself at Larak, arms outstretched. She pushed him out of the way but the rock caught her squarely at the base of the skull. She fell silently to the ground. Spun about by the force of his sister's arms, Larak whipped around and screamed when he saw her lying there, her head bleeding profusely. *Damia!*

Jeran was running as fast as he could towards her when the dye ball hit him. It flicked past him and hit all the remaining cousins with such blinding speed that no-one was spared. Then it made a spiralling loop before it slammed into the vengeful smile on Teval's face.

It was dark. The air was bad. Her head felt awful and *They* were trying to get her. Damia moaned silently as she struggled away from the dark and back towards the light. But *They* would not let her. *They* tried to keep her down. *They* chittered at her, not like Coonies, but like evil scraping claws on harsh metal. *They* were after her. *They* wanted revenge. *They* tried to suck her out of her body, tried to eat her soul. Damia whimpered in fear, searching blindly for something, someone. There! Far away, far, far away, like a beacon! A blip of light. She lost sight of it, searched for it, drew it to her, crawled towards it. There! *They* were afraid of the light, it scared them. If she could just get to the light! The light! The soul-eaters would never get her if she could just get to the light. She cried to the lighthouse, cried to the keeper. The beacon flared, light streamed steadily towards her. She was getting nearer – or had the lighthouse moved to her? Damia did not know, did not care. The light bathed her, burnt the soul-eaters and the lightkeeper soothed her with warm words and his warm light.

'Depressed skull fracture,' a voice mumbled in the distance. Damia ignored it, wanting to bat it away with her hands but she was so weak, so weak from crawling.

'Will she be all right?' a tenor voice asked worriedly. The lightkeeper! She heard his voice! She willed her lips to form a smile. See! I've found the light, see?

'Look!' It was another voice, one she felt she should know, a kind voice. 'She's smiling!' The voice approached, beams of kindliness washed over her. 'Oh, Damia, you're going to be all right! Sweetheart, you'll be all right!'

The mumbler coughed. 'We'd better let her rest. I'll have the nurse look in on her later.'

'I'm staying here,' the lightkeeper responded sharply in tones that brooked no argument. A hand touched hers and she felt the warm yellow glow light its way up her arm, fill her body and knew that the lightkeeper had found her, had driven away the soul-eaters. And she remembered that the lightkeeper had a name. *Afra?*

I'm here, the lightkeeper whispered. *Rest, Damia.*

The hand let go and the darkness crept into the shadows of her sight. *Afra!*

The hand grabbed her again, light flared and banished the darkness. *I'm here, love! Rest. I'm here, there's nothing to worry about.*

A smile formed on her lips and she rolled over, small soft tanned paw still in Afra's warm rough green hand.

'Afra!' It was dark, Damia awoke with a start.

'Here.' Her hand was squeezed gently by his bigger one. 'Rest. It's night.'

Damia went to sleep, secure in the soft mental touch of the yellow-eyed Talent.

The bright sun of morning woke her. Damia turned in her bed, scanned the room and was startled to find no-one there. She double-checked frantically. When the door opened she nearly jumped with fright.

It was Isthia. 'Ah, you're awake!'

'Where's Afra?'

'He went back.' Isthia caught her expression. 'He was burnt out, sweetie, and desperate to give your Mom the good news.'

Damia started at Isthia's choice of words: burnt out.

'We've all been worried,' Isthia went on, not noticing her granddaughter's reaction. She shook her head. 'Your father and mother were frantic. They've been here but Afra stayed. You seemed calmer when he was in the room.'

'He had the light,' Damia murmured, incredibly drowsy but she forced herself to get the words out. 'Can he come back? Would he come if you said I needed him? He hasn't visited Deneb but half a dozen times in all the years we've been here.'

Isthia clucked at her. 'Afra's been very good to come as often as he has, Damia. He has other friends to visit than young girls who make impossible challenges.'

'Was not impossible! Neither Larak nor I had been hit when Teval threw that stone!'

'He's not likely to throw another,' Isthia said, her expression grim.

'Why, what did you do to him?' Damia asked with a certain understandable vindictiveness in her voice.

Isthia shrugged. 'I did nothing. Didn't have to,' and she let a smile twitch at her lips. 'I wouldn't have thought a foam ball could be flung that hard.'

'Who?'

'Larak, of course.'

'You see, it wasn't an impossible challenge. It's so good to make Jeran eat crow . . . '

'You eat your meal, young woman, or you'll find me an unpleasant challenge!' Isthia said and set down the tray she was carrying.

When Damia had finished the light meal, she lay back, wondering if she *dared* ask for Afra again.

Oh, she's all right, Damia heard her grandmother saying, projecting tremendous relief. *And, fortunately, all she understands about that wretched game was that she and Larak won. She hasn't an inkling of what that exhibition demonstrated of her potential.*

How could she? and Damia recognized the weaker voice of her aunt Rakella. *Not even Jeff could explain it and Angharad still doubts it.*

Afra had a theory, and Damia heard her grandmother mulling it over in her mind before she projected her answer. *He thinks that Damia is a catalyst: she steps up anyone else's ability. Afra says that's what she did when he rescued her from the capsule that time. THAT was why the power surged in the Tower: Damia tapped it. He didn't and neither did Angharad.*

A Talent with an extra go-gear? Rakella asked.

Something like that.

Then both voices drifted out of her 'hearing' and she drifted off to sleep again.

★

A week after Damia was allowed back to school, she had an unexpected visitor. She was in her room wondering if she dared sneak out and visit Jupe when she heard Isthia's voice giving directions: 'Her room is the one at the end, on the left. I'll bring down some drinks later.'

Whoever it was paused for a long while at her door.

'Well?' Damia called, her curiosity overwhelming her. Teval's head slowly peered around the door. If the light wasn't deceiving her, his nose was thicker and there were discoloured patches and barely healed cuts on his face.

'Damia?'

'What do *you* want?' she demanded, suddenly deciding boredom was better than this guest.

Teval shook his head, entering the room. A heavy schoolbag swung from one hand, nearly dragging the carpet.

'I've been assigned to teach you self-defence,' he said, looking miserable.

'I can learn that watching a tape!'

'You've also got to pass a practical so I got assigned as your mat partner. 'Nother thing; you're supposed to be my teacher.'

'Your teacher?'

'Remedial language,' he mumbled, blushing in his misery. 'I failed my exams.' He held out the text-tape.

That didn't surprise her but she decided it wasn't fair to kick someone when he was down. Damia upended the bag. 'Am I supposed to teach you all these, too?'

'Not exactly. I've got to bring you your homework assignments and help you catch up on what you've missed.' He looked sheepish. 'You're taking almost all the same stuff I am, except maths and language and you're way ahead of me there.'

'What if I don't want you?'

'You've no choice, Damia Gwyn-Raven!' Isthia called from beyond the door, entering the room with a tray of beverages and a light snack in her hands. She put the tray down and looked at her granddaughter critically. 'Actually, you do,' she corrected herself. 'If you don't take Teval Rieseman here as your tutor and you don't tutor him on those subjects assigned, we will have no choice but to release him from the Special School.'

Damia looked horrified. 'Expel him?'

Isthia nodded. 'Fighting is against school rules,' she said sternly. 'He threw that rock without any provocation whatsoever. By rights he should already be expelled. But someone intervened on his behalf.'

Both Teval and Damia were surprised. 'Who?' they asked, almost in unison.

'Afra Lyon.'

'Afra?' Damia was confused, almost angry. How could Afra do that? Didn't he know that this was the boy who had tried to hurt her Larak? That he'd cracked her skull? Then she knew that, of course, Afra had known the whole thing. So why?

'Why?' Teval beat her in asking the question. 'I thought he was her uncle.'

'He used to be my special friend!' Damia exclaimed heatedly, glaring fiercely at her grandmother to answer the question. Isthia handed her a note. Damia opened it, turned it around, frowned, turned it over and finally looked up at Isthia.

'I can't read it.' She handed it back to Isthia. Isthia glanced at it. 'I can't read it either.'

Perplexed, Teval leaned over and looked at the writing. 'That looks like the printing in some old books my grandfather used to have. He was Russian, I think.'

'What's it say?'

Teval lifted his shoulders with an indifference that didn't match the emotions which Damia suddenly felt roiling in his mind. 'I don't know! My family was killed by the Beetles. I only recognized the script, not the words.'

Damia could feel the pain emanating from him and, while she had always thought Teval was a dork, in that unguarded instant she learned that she had misjudged him badly. He'd had a little sister, just about the same age as Larak, when the Beetles came: he'd had a mother and father, and the Russian grandfather. Now he lived with an uncle who worked too hard to have much time for his nephew. It was like Afra to know more about Teval Rieseman than she, Damia Gwyn-Raven, had bothered to find out in the years they'd spent as classmates.

'Why don't we study Russian as your language?' she suggested gently. 'Then we'll find out what this message says.'

It took them many months and they were good friends, but still not without their quarrels, when they finally translated the one-line message. It read: 'Friends don't fight with rocks.'

'Let's go hunt Beetle junk!' Damia suggested one day to Larak as Deneb VIII sweltered in an unusual heat wave.

'Uncle Rhodri said he'd found all the near stuff.' Larak, at eight, sometimes questioned his sister. But it was so hot, he didn't like the idea of hunting Beetle metal. It stank and, if you touched it, it went 'sting-pzzzt'. He hated the feel.

'I need new stirrup leathers and that takes cash. Uncle Rhodri pays good for Beetle metal. And I don't have enough money. Grandmother's stingy.'

'I'll lend you my cash,' Larak said, more so that he wouldn't have to go hunting than because he was generous.

'No, Larak, that's very nice of you but I'd rather spend money I've earned. And, besides, if we keep sitting here, Gran'll discover another nice cool job for us.' She could see that that appealed to her brother. They'd already been nabbed for some dirty, dusty garden chores.

'But we're not supposed to hunt Beetle metal unless we tell Uncle Rhodri.'

'We'll tell him *when* we find it so he can send the 'copter to collect it,' she replied.

'Do I get to ride in the 'copter again?' Larak began to be enthusiastic now. He'd been allowed to ride back in the big navy vehicle the last time they'd found some Beetle metal. He was going to learn how to fly a 'copter when he grew older.

'If we find metal, you might,' Damia replied, not specifically promising the treat but she saw the anticipatory shine of her brother's eyes. 'OK, here's what we do . . . '

It was, after all, easy to slip out of the Compound, even with backsacks carrying 'provisions'. She'd got handlights as well as food and made Larak roll up a blanket though he'd protested that it was too hot to need a blanket.

'Well, we might just need to stay the night,' Damia said in explanation. 'I've food enough. And the forest's always cooler.'

Larak agreed, though he demurred when she wanted him to bring a shirt, too.

'Against branch lash,' she said curtly. 'Now, go get ready. And be quiet. You know what long ears Gran has and we don't want her stopping us with more jobs to do. Meet me at the paddock.'

So Larak went 'quietly' to gather the things his sister wanted him to get. Larak liked being with Damia. Which was more than he could say about the company of his older brother and sister. For all his efforts, Larak had never been able to establish a good rapport with his older brother. He had astutely identified Cera as the source of his older brother's apathy. Since Damia was a lot of fun to be with, he'd given up on the other two. Anyway, Jeran was now on a probationary assignment to Deneb Tower, taking on-the-job training and Cera, moping about the place without him, was no fun to be around at all.

They met at the paddock where the ponies drowsed in the heat of the afternoon.

'Now, we know there's nothing to the east, south or west of us because Uncle Rhodri says those directions are all clear of sting-pzzzt,' Damia said, 'so we'll go north, through the woods, which will be cooler. No-one's really done much that way. Not even Jeran when he organized his search party.' She was slightly contemptuous because Jeran had been so *sure* that he'd find tonnes of the stuff. 'So, let's be off!'

Taking Larak's hand, she struck off across the paddock, and into the first of the trees.

They were panting from the heat but the moment they got in the shade, they could feel an appreciable difference in the torrid heat of the day.

'Hey, it's cooler,' he exclaimed, delighted.

'Told you it would be. Come on!'

Damia led on, weaving her way due north, with little variation despite the press of trees. She signalled their first break when they crossed one of the logging roads. Revived by the rest and drinks from their travel bottles, they continued.

Larak would have liked to stop longer and enjoy the coolness but Damia insisted that they wouldn't find any Beetle metal this close to the Compound. And no Beetle metal meant no 'copter ride. Larak got to his feet and trudged along behind her.

When they came to a brook, gushing down a rocky bed, Larak did insist that he had to cool himself down. So they shucked out of their clothes and splashed about in the pool. Damia shared out one of their sandwiches and ordered him to fill his canteen again.

Shortly after they resumed their march, they broke through the forest into a lovely mountain pasture. They quartered this because Damia thought it the very spot where Beetle metal might have dropped. Then she had to explain to Larak, once more, how their mother and father had destroyed the Beetle ships, breaking them open and scattering the pieces far and wide, thus saving the whole world, and beyond.

By then they had reached forest again and, of course, had to sit to enjoy the coolness, have a cool drink, eat a few biscuits. The sun was lowering but Damia knew they had a good few hours of daylight.

'We'll find a cave, with a stream,' Damia told her brother as he gamely plodded on behind her. 'We'll have a great night out.'

'When'll we find Beetle metal?' Larak asked plaintively.

'Why, we could trip over it any time now."

'I don't want to *trip* over it.'

'Well, then, let's just concentrate on locating some good sting-pzzzts, huh?'

Obediently Larak cast his mind about and that kept him occupied until the blister on his left heel began to do the stinging.

'I gotta stop, 'Mia. I gotta blister.'

'We'll stop when I've found us a cave and a stream so you can stoop that blister cool,' Damia said, with a patient sigh over Larak's blister.

She hoped he could hang on a while longer. She had no idea how far they had tramped but it wasn't far enough for they hadn't found Beetle metal yet. She was determined to find some. Meanwhile, raising her forearm, she rubbed her forehead dry of sweat and, shifting her backpack, went on.

Larak was a real trooper, she thought, when she saw him limping though he didn't complain. He was the best brother. She was getting a bit anxious about a suitable camping site. Uncle Rhodri had taught all his young relatives basic woodsmanship when he'd organized his Beetle metal hunts.

They found the stream first so Damia suggested that Larak take off his boots – the cold water would ease his blister – and they'd walk upstream until they found a campsite. Maybe not a cave, but a nice clearing.

By the time Larak had slipped and fallen into the stream four times, and bruised his toes, he was ready to quit just when they rounded a bend and found that an old rockslide had indeed formed a sort of cave.

'What if there're animals?' Larak protested nervously, peering into the shadowed opening.

Damia had not considered that aspect and was miffed. Uncle Rhodri had shown them tapes of all the animals on Deneb, mainly small, but some had poisonous bites. Some nocturnal species could be most unpleasant, trying to creep into a camper's sleepsac. But they only had blankets with them. Nevertheless, caution was advisable. She pulled the handlight from her belt and shone it into the cave. Carefully, she looked in every corner. 'See? Nothing there! Now, let's get this camp organized. I'll get us firewood, you can set out our supper.'

The first attempt at fire starting did not go well. They had built it in the cave, which immediately filled with smoke. So, against Damia's better judgement, they built another fire, in front of the cave. Soon they had a good roaring blaze going. And none too soon for night had fallen and the woods closed in about them, with only the gap above the stream to let in starlight.

So they happily munched on the rest of their sandwiches before Damia grandiosely extracted a half sack of marshmallows from her sack, scrupulously divvying them up. Larak limped over to a sapling to pull long enough branches to roast the marshmallows on.

'Now,' Damia said, dropping her voice into the creepiest tone she could affect, 'all we need is a good ghoulie story!' Just then her marshmallow fell off her stick. 'Rats!'

'Rats aren't very ghoulie!' Larak complained.

'Of course they're not. I said "rats" because I lost my marshmallow.'

'I'll tell you a story,' Larak declared and launched into the telling of the Headless Horseman which had scared him the first time he'd seen the tape. Larak was a good story-teller so Damia didn't mind hearing it again. Towards the end of his recitation, her attention wandered and her eyes darted to the edge of the dark. A light night breeze had come up and there was an odd scraping sound: a dim memory tugged at her.

'Now, you tell me one!' Larak demanded when he had finished.

'Soul-eaters,' Damia muttered to herself, for the scraping noise reminded her of her nightmare terror.

'Soul-eaters? What are they?' Larak's eyes grew round.

'Nothing.' Damia gave a convulsive shudder. She really didn't want to remember that awful dream.

'No, tell me!'

'That's too scary and it's not a story. I'll think of another one, a better one.'

'No, I want to know about soul-eaters,' Larak insisted. 'Where did you hear about them?'

Damia shook her head. 'I didn't hear. They came after me.'

'Sure!' Larak snorted derisively.

'When I was hit on the head,' Damia continued, more to herself. She sat on her haunches, not really wanting to, but nevertheless reconstructing her recollection. 'It was dark. They were darker. They chittered like beetles on the outskirts and they tried to drag me away.' Her voice went shrill and she gripped her arms about her knees. 'They were going to get me, to eat my soul! Chittering, chittering!' She had dropped her voice, not as part of a story-teller's effect, but because she was succeeding in scaring herself with the memory.

'Damia! Stop it! You're scaring me!' Larak threw his arms around her, his mouth trembling, his eyes watering with nervous tears. 'Damia? Tell me this is a story. Tell me there aren't any soul-eaters out here!'

But Damia had triggered the recollection and was trapped in it, talking her own way out as she had struggled in the dream. 'They got me by the foot, then slithered up my leg, and always making this awful chittering. I could just make out a light. I knew that if I could only reach the light, I'd be safe. But they kept holding me back; they got my other foot and then I saw the light—'

'Light?'

She didn't register the pure panic in Larak's voice, didn't see what he was doing. 'Then, I reached the light and Afra had it! He turned them away! Turned them back! He scared them with his light and then he touched me with it and—' Her eyes refocused and she shook her head, shielded her eyes. There was much too much light, illuminating the cave behind her, the clearing around her. 'Larak?'

Larak was at the edge of the clearing, a burning faggot in one hand, spreading the flame to every dry branch and root he could find. To make enough light to keep the soul-eaters at bay.

Larak!

More scared than singed, Angharad, Isthia assured her daughter-in-law when the situation was finally under control. Overhead a water-carrying 'copter made another pass at the remains of the forest fire. *We pulled them out as soon as Damia's scream woke us. She was too disoriented to 'port.*

What caused the fire? Jeff wanted to know.

Larak. He used a firebrand to light the forest. Said something about soul-eaters and light. He was scared witless. Isthia replied. *He's sleeping now.*

And Damia? another voice, which Isthia placed as Afra's, asked with some strain.

She's all right, Isthia quickly reassured him. *What time is it on Callisto?*

Early, Jeff said with some acerbity.

I was awake. Couldn't sleep, Afra replied and a mental yawn followed. *I'll turn in now. Rowan, Jeff, Isthia.* Isthia felt Afra's touch fade out.

Well! the Rowan declared tetchily. *When is that child going to stop playing her 'tricks'? I really don't want Ezro learning from that sort of example.*

I think she's been well and truly frightened, luv, was Jeff's verdict.

I would remind you, Angharad, Isthia said, her tone stern, *that Damia didn't start the fire: Larak did. She has always looked out for her younger brother and protected him. Or have you forgotten the incident with the stone?*

Anyway, Jeff interposed quickly, *she's due to start Tower training so she'll be too tired for night-time treks. How far did you say she hiked?* Isthia detected a note of admiration in her son's tone.

Once she learns how to 'port over distance, the Rowan said thoughtfully, *she could actually commute from here to Earth everyday. Just as you do, Jeff.*

I'm not sure the galaxy is safe once Damia learns how to 'port distances.

The Rowan mulled that over. *Well, I do feel that now is the time for Damia to return to Callisto and start using some of the skills she's learned. Isthia, we've impinged on your good nature far too long . . .*

Nonsense, Angharad. It's been – educational, Isthia responded with a chuckle. *Because of Damia, and Jeran and Cera and Larak, I got the Special School I wanted and Deneb is now actively looking for Talents to train.*

Was that your reason for offering to take my children? the Rowan asked. She'd always known that Isthia had had some devious reason.

Not the main one, Angharad. There was Ian to be considered, too, you know.

Jeff guffawed. *And he's tested out a T-4. You did well by the brother!*

What do you test out these days, Isthia? the Rowan asked.

I've never really wanted to know, Isthia replied smoothly.

Best leave with honours even, luv, Jeff said.

But I think it is time for us to give Damia the benefit of working in a busy Tower environment. Know that I – we – are deeply grateful to you, Isthia. And the Rowan was entirely sincere in that.

Isthia gracefully accepted the thanks for she was as fond of the mother as she was of the daughter.

She's starting to sprout since you were last here, Isthia told them.

So soon? Jeff mentally counted on his fingers.

Let's say that she's germinated, then, and should shortly sprout, Isthia amended her original statement.

Are there any suitable candidates there? Jeff wondered.

T-1s? The Rowan's tone was frankly contemptuous.

Love, when a woman's fancy turns to men she does not always stop to check their pedigree, Jeff remarked carefully. Isthia could feel the Rowan's cheeks redden across the light-years.

There are no candidates here, Jeff, Isthia said in response to the original question. *In fact, with Larak here it's as well you consider bringing Damia home.*

Both parents were shocked.

Goodness! Isthia chuckled. *You two think the* worst *things! I meant that Damia would be ambivalent about dating a boy if it might compromise the special relationship she and Larak have for each other. Tsk! Tsk!*

I take your point, Jeff said, somewhat abashed. *It would be easier for her first romance if she did not have to worry about the jealousy of her little brother.*

Exactly, Isthia replied.

Jeff made his mind up. *Very well, send her back when term is over. I'll arrange for her continued education here. Not that it will be as good as what she could get on Deneb, of course,* he added with a wink in his 'voice'.

Of course!

It was only after contact was broken that Isthia recalled what she had wanted to ask Jeff. Or rather Afra. To intercede on her behalf with Capella to find a high T-rating who would teach on Deneb. There was something positive to be said for a Methody upbringing. She hoped that a little more Methody might rub off Afra on to Damia when she returned to Callisto. Isthia was rather sure that he'd have a hand in her education. From comments that Jeff had dropped and her own observations of Angharad, Afra was likely to have taught her the self-control she'd needed to run Callisto Tower as efficiently as she did. Jeff had provided the emotional security Angharad required.

Isthia sighed, remembering his father and wishing, as she often did, that Jerry was still alive. But he wasn't and she was. And this wasn't furthering the aims she had set herself for next year: delving more deeply into metamorphic manipulation. Unfortunately, Capellans didn't believe in that.

6

The hands which were thrust into Afra's view were no longer those of a small child but were still slender, graceful just like their owner.

'What do you think?' Damia asked, turning her hands palms up and palms down for his inspection. Afra looked up from where he had been kneeling, into the intense blue eyes in an oval face framed by long raven-black hair. Damia had let her hair go long in the four years since she had returned from Deneb.

'Think of what, witch?' he asked, flicking to her back the one strand of white that emphasized the blackness and lustre of her hair.

'This!' Damia stretched to her full height, running hands alongside her body. It was only then, with the girl standing boldly upright, one leg slightly before the other, that Afra realized she was not wearing her swimsuit. She quirked an eyebrow at him provocatively, daring him to look away. Afra responded by scrutinizing her body carefully from graceful neck, to firm breasts, to graceful hips, sculpted legs and finally to delicately boned long toes.

'You're maturing nicely, Damia,' Afra told her when his inspection brought him back up to her eyes. He patted the water beside him. 'Water's warm.'

Clothing in the gymnasium at Callisto Station was strictly optional and decorative rather then veiling.

Damia stamped a foot and squealed, 'No! The tan! Afra, the tan!'

Afra looked back at her body. He cocked his head: it was *slightly* darkened. He put a green arm up next to hers and shook his head. 'Not my shade, I think.'

Damia let out a screech of indignation. 'Afffrrrra!' She stamped her foot so hard that her breasts shook.

Afra gave her a teasing smile. 'Yes?'

She pulled a bottle off the nearby deck chair and handed it to him. 'Will you put this on me?' she asked, her tone turning sweet. 'I don't want to lose what little tan I've got.'

Afra took the bottle of before-swim tan lotion and eyed the adolescent carefully. He sniffed the bottle, put a little on one finger and rubbed with his thumb. 'How much and where?'

'Just enough to get me oily and everywhere, of course.' Her tone was just short of patronizing.

Afra obliged, starting with her backside. 'Your hair will get oily.'

'I don't care! I'll wash it later.' She lifted it out of his way with a hand. She twisted her head back slightly to watch his expression. It annoyed her that he merely laved her down gently, working from shoulder to buttocks to ankles with no change of expression. Her eyes twinkled in anticipation when it was time to do her front but Afra was just as careful and just as nonchalant when he lathered her breasts as when he lathered her nose.

Still, he did avoid one area. Damia coughed discreetly. 'You missed a spot.'

Without batting an eye, Afra oiled up his hands and

dutifully went over the indicated zone. 'I guess you'll wash that, too.'

To her intense pique, Damia blushed.

Afra avoided her face until she had recovered, spending the time ostensibly fumbling with the bottle's top. He hefted the closed bottle and, with a gesture, asked, 'Put it back over there?'

'Oh, sure,' she replied absently. She patted her firm belly for attention. 'Do you think Amr will like it?'

'Your belly? I can't see particularly why,' Afra said, peering wistfully to the empty pool beside him.

'Afra! Not my belly! The muscles! Look!' And she tensed, revealing an exceedingly well muscled body, with abdominal muscles showing clearly under soft tanned skin.

'Nice,' Afra replied absently. 'Let's swim!'

'Oooh! I should know better than to try to compete against a pool with you!' And with that she dived in.

Hours later, she appeared in his apartment. 'What do you think?' she asked, twirling around to let the skirts of a diaphanous purple evening dress swirl about her. She had done her hair up in a bun, with her witch's streak spiralling around the outside. Long dark lashes accentuated piercing blue eyes. Dimples formed around her mouth as it curved gently in a smile.

'I think,' Afra said as he strode into the living room with his dinner, 'that you were taught to knock.'

Damia pouted but her eyes twinkled mischievously.

Afra knew that look. 'You know how your parents feel about you 'porting around the station.'

'Are you going to tell?'

Afra shook his head immediately. 'I told you when you returned that you were welcome any time, anyhow. The door is even keyed to your retinal pattern.' He gave her a measuring glance. 'But it is good manners to knock.' He put his plate down on the coffee table and gestured at her dress. 'I *do* like it, you know.'

'It's for our date tonight.'

'Date?'

'Me and Amr.'

'Sweet sixteen is a good age to start dating. Where are you going?'

Damia's face fell. 'Weeelll,' she hedged, finishing in a rush, 'Amr's picking me up at Earth Station.'

'So this is not merely a fashion parade. Do your parents know?'

'They won't have to.'

'What are you hiding from them now?' Afra asked with some exasperation. Damia pursed her lips, bowed her head. Afra took in the look and let out a sigh. 'A special boy?'

'He's not a boy! He's eighteen – almost!' she responded hotly. 'I've been seeing him for months now. Tonight's special.'

'So I had gathered,' Afra replied softly.

Damia stared at him. 'You're not angry?'

'That you're ready to become a woman? Why should I be?'

His detached response perturbed her. Afra was aware of that but ignored it. Damia's affection for him had blossomed quickly into an infatuation as puberty changed her from girl to young woman. Afra respected that and handled the change in the intensity of her emotions as best he could but refused to release the storm that would surely strike if he made any overt acknowledgement of it. It took a supreme effort on his part as he recognized how much joy he took in her presence but he refused to abuse and relinquish his position as her best friend and confidant.

'Will you 'port me to Earth then?' she asked him flatly, eyes flaring.

'You'll be careful—'

'I know what to do!' she shouted back. Before she could draw breath to berate him further, she was on the steps at the entrance of Earth Station. 'Hmmph! That showed him.'

Call me when you want to come home, Afra sent along with a special stamp that Damia had come to accept as a quick peck on her forehead. Despite herself, she smiled fondly.

Damia had met Amr at Luciano's when Uncle Gollee had had to cancel a lunch date. Amr Tusel, with swarthy good looks and a ready smile, had proudly informed her that he was a T-9 and training to be a stationmaster. Damia, too worried that she would frighten him away, had not revealed her own Talent but professed astonishment at his prowess. At eighteen it would be a while before a T-9 would assume stationmaster duties. They had spent that whole first night dancing, and Amr had walked her back to Central Station which despatched people to any part of the world. His consideration and his kindness had impressed her but their first kiss had her toes curling and her body flooded with emotions she had not felt so intensely ever before.

Since then, Damia had established that they would meet at Earth Station because (truthfully) it was closer to home for her. They had seen each other for over six months, catching films, tri-vids, cavorting at amusement parks and dancing the night away. As time passed, they spent more time engaged in passionate embrace than in conversation. Several times in the past weeks Amr had had to break out of their passion for fear that they would violate the few remaining blue laws.

He had not figured out who she was, having never seen the lofty Jeff Raven nor any of the Gwyn-Raven clan, but Amr had figured out that she was young and a virgin. With a sense of honour and a Talented compassion, he had surmised that he was being considered for that most delicate of consummations. The prospect had frightened him and for a while they did not see each other. When he relented, Damia had grown reticent in her own right and it was only with a loud and lengthy argument that she finally set the date.

Being dormed at Trainee Quarters, Amr had no room of his own for such an assignation and Damia had dodged the possibility of using her house by saying that her parents were always around and that would inhibit her.

The hotel was just across the street. Damia had left an overnight bag at Earth Station several weeks before when she had first made up her mind and had retrieved it before she met Amr.

He approached her with a smile on his lips and gave her a quick kiss. He stood back, taking in her appearance and shaking his head in admiration. 'You are beautiful, Damia.' He took her bag from her, waving her onwards with a hand. 'Lead on, fairest of Venus' daughters!'

Amr conducted the course of the evening. They checked in, left their bags with the bellhop, asking them to be taken to their room. Dinner, a full course menu, was first followed by a leisurely stroll and then the dance floor. They danced until the DiscoTech was reluctantly closed. The last dances were slow ones and Damia's passions had been aroused. The urgency abated slightly on the trip up to their room but Amr teased her back into passion.

Passion was not new to Damia: she and Amr had spent many evenings locked in tight embraces but always before she had broken free when her passion threatened to overwhelm her. It had been incredibly frustrating. Tonight Damia felt free to unleash her full emotions.

Gently Amr drew her into his arms, sliding them down her stately shoulders to her delicate waist. He pulled her body close to his as they kissed with rising passion. As passion rose, their clothing fell.

Soon they were on the bed, Amr running crafty hands all over her body and Damia lost in a shower of feeling that threatened to drown her. As her passion peaked for the third time, Amr gently entered her. At first Damia was too distracted by all the other sensations of her body to notice. She froze for a moment when she did, looking up at him with a frightened expression but Amr smiled tenderly through his passion and gently flexed his flanks. Damia moaned, grabbed him tightly, wanting him *in* her. In her ecstasy she opened herself up, pulled him along and they rose and rose, crashed, rose again and again.

You're Talented! Amr cried through his passion. Damia heard the accusation in his tone, unwillingly offered to stop but Amr thrust himself deeper in her, thrust his tongue into her mouth, crying: *No! Oh gods, no! I've never felt this before!*

They continued, Damia reviving Amr's flagging passions until they were both afloat on a wave of emotion, drained, recharged, sizzling electric ecstasy pounded over them, through them, around them wave after wave. The exertions and emotions finally were too much for Damia and she drifted languorously from orgasm to sleep.

Damia awoke with Amr's eyes glittering on her, following the line of her body like daggers. She was sore, sore in places she had never known she had. Muscles she had only just discovered registered their abuse with loud flares of pain as she moved one leg in front of the other.

'Do it again, please?' Amr's voice was hoarse, small.

'Oh, it was great!' Damia answered. Amr moved an arm to encircle her but Damia moved – painfully – away. 'I'm too sore, Amr. Too tired. None of the tapes mentioned that.'

'Nor what you've done to me,' he replied, eyes dull. Anger crept into them. 'Have you no notion of what you've done to me?' His fingers clenched into fists. Tears welled in his eyes, tears of anger, of honour lost, of despair. 'Do you?' His voice grew louder until he was shouting: 'Do you? Do you? Whore, slut! Bitch!' With a look of pure terror he caught his hand mid-stroke as it moved unwilled to strike at her.

Afra! Damia cried in despair.

She disappeared as Amr fought to produce an apology. Gone, he closed his eyes and cried softly in deep sobs, curled into a foetal ball.

Nothing was mentioned about hating after loving! Damia sobbed to Afra as he finished towelling her off and pulled her into his arms to wrap the towel around her. She rested her head on his chest and bawled. *It was so . . . so . . . and then he* screamed *at me!*

You were careful, weren't you? Afra asked her, keeping his tone calm and soothing.

Of course I was careful! I've had the implant for months now! Damia retorted angrily. Afra pushed himself away from her, tilted her head up so her eyes met his.

'Damia, you kept your shields up, didn't you?' Afra asked.

'Shields? Afra, we made love!'

Afra's expression altered, pain flickered across his face. 'You were in a hotel?' Damia nodded dully. 'The one across the street from Central?' She nodded again.

What room number?

Afra! she protested.

We have to know how Amr's handling this, he said, then strengthened his 'pathing. *Gollee, we've got an emergency.* A muffled response came back to him. Afra made a face. *I need you to look after a T-9, Amr Tusel. He's over at the Excelsior.* Afra paused, his face expressionless as he looked down at Damia. *I think he's been burnt out.*

Gollee Gren became instantly alert. *I'll handle it, Afra.*

'Burnt out?' Damia echoed aloud. 'Afra, he was fine!'

'Was he fine when you left him, Damia?' Afra asked her softly. 'Did you guard your Talent when you made love?'

Damia was devastated. 'Nobody told me!'

'I did,' Afra said quietly, lips thin. 'I said, be careful.'

'I thought you meant—' Damia broke off, finally absorbing the enormity of her recklessness. 'Will he be all right? Will he recover?'

'Possibly,' Afra hedged. But she cocked her head at him challengingly. 'Probably not,' he admitted, recognizing the morality involved.

'Oh, Afra!' Damia wailed, throwing herself in his arms. *I'll never love again!*

'I wouldn't say "never", Damia,' Afra said at his driest. He picked her up and carried her over to the couch. 'Just never be so careless ever again.' He placed her beside him on the couch, cradling her torso with his arms. 'Love, Damia, but be caring and careful with it.'

No, I'll never love again, Damia mumbled earnestly as her 'voice' faded with fatigue. Afra made no reply, holding the youngster until she drifted into sleep. Then, very carefully, he insinuated a tendril of thought to ease her pain.

Afra was aware of Damia's gaze before he opened his eyes. He looked down at her, still resting on his chest and met her piercing blue eyes. He gave her a slight smile. 'Bet your muscles are sore.'

Damia snorted. 'From sleeping this way or from before?'

'Both.'

Damia regarded him for a long moment, then admitted: 'It could have been you—'

Afra silenced her with a finger to her lips. 'Don't.'

She examined the finger critically, then ducked away from it to kiss it, smiling up at him. The smile faded. 'Have you heard about Amr?'

Afra nodded solemnly. 'He's resting now, in hospital.' He looked down at her. 'I will teach you control.'

Damia bit her lip. 'Would I have done that to you, if we had—'

Afra shook his head. 'We didn't, Damia.'

'It could have been you!' The admission was torn from her lips. She buried herself against his chest. 'Oh, Afra, don't you love me?'

Afra cradled her head tenderly to his chest.

'I wanted to, you know,' Damia went on, implacably young and naïve. 'I tried—'

'I know,' Afra soothed.

She pulled her head back against his hand to look him in the eyes. 'You knew? And you didn't . . . And I . . . And Amr?' she spluttered, growing furious.

Again Afra put a finger to her lips but Damia wrapped her teeth about it, biting hard. Her eyes locked on his as she bit harder and harder but Afra's expression didn't change. When she tasted salty blood in her mouth, Damia spat the finger out.

Tears dripped out of Afra's eyes as he coldly examined the bleeding teeth marks.

'I'm *glad* it hurt!' Damia said, hot with fury, with embarrassment, with guilt.

Afra flicked his eyes to her. 'That isn't what hurts, Damia.'

She broke free of his grasp angrily, strode to the bathroom, pulled on one of his long shirts, grabbed a first aid box and threw at him on the way out. 'Here! That's for your hand. I can't do anything for your heart.'

The door, being automatic, would not slam but Damia kicked it with a resounding thud to achieve the same effect.

'A word with you, young miss!' The tight voice of Gollee Gren shocked Damia so much she jumped.

'Gollee! What are you doing here?' she asked, looking around the lounge at Callisto Station. 'It's not Dad—' Then she remembered. 'Amr?'

'He's all right.' Gren dismissed the issue. He grabbed her, dragged her over to a booth, sat down beside her. 'Just what do you think you are doing, anyway?'

'What do you mean?'

Gren swore. 'After all he's done for you. He's covered

up for your "tricks", he's watched over you, lied and you – you're not even worth your name!'

'Who?' Damia cried in confusion.

'Who?' Gren snorted. 'Trust you to not know! Don't you think? Don't you see?' He shook his head in a vain attempt to throw off his anger. It did not work. He let out a deep breath. 'I got the pictures back from medics.' He nodded to emphasize his point. 'He said that one of the Coonies had bit him but I know those marks. Even when you try to bite his hand off he protects you!'

'Afra?' Damia exclaimed. 'He doesn't even know I exist! That cold-blooded green-skinned yellow-eyed—' She searched for further epithets, found none, 'Capellan!'

'You don't think about anyone but yourself, do you?' Gren snapped back. 'Damia, Damia, poor Damia!' He narrowed his eyes critically at her. 'Well, what about Afra? How do you think he felt when his best friend's daughter comes on to him? Don't you know what you did?'

'He turned me down!' Damia exclaimed, wondering how Gren could have known that and amazed at herself for blurting out such an unsavoury episode.

'You were as obvious as the sun! He had no choice, even if he had wanted to!' Gren said hotly. 'But that's nothing. To punish him for it you go off and maim some poor—'

'THAT'S NOT TRUE!' Damia shouted at the top of her lungs, tears of rage rolling down her cheeks.

'Isn't it?' Gren asked quietly. 'Think carefully before you answer, Damia Gwyn-Raven. And when you are done, you go to him and you ask him very politely to teach you control.'

'I won't! Never!' She was so furious she whispered, visibly trembling to suppress the things she wanted to do, could do to her accuser.

'Your parents don't know about that night, or Amr,' he said, speaking as low and as intensely. 'Yet.' He rose, turning back to her in parting. 'Now, you apologize to him and you learn from him how to control yourself.'

'Or you'll do what?' Damia sneered tauntingly.

Gren looked her over critically. 'I *won't* tell your father.' And he stomped off leaving Damia to wonder why that promise struck her as so sinister.

'Larak!' Damia cried joyfully, running to embrace her brother. 'Whatever are you doing here?'

'Afra sent for me,' Larak told her, hugging her happily. He shook his head. 'I hadn't realized that Mom and Dad took his advice so seriously.'

'Your voice!' Damia declared, recognizing differences over the past year. 'You've grown.'

'I'm not a little boy any more, Damia,' Larak replied, his voice now deepened with adolescence. 'I've put on three inches in seven months! I'll catch up with you soon!'

Damia laughed. 'And pass me out, I'm sure!' She pursed her lips. 'Why did Afra send for you?'

'Didn't he tell you?'

'We're not exchanging confidences these days.' Damia's response was curt, blocking any further conversation.

Larak ignored the implied injunction. He blew out his breath. 'That's new. I thought Afra was your extra special friend.'

'I've grown out of such a childish dependence.'

Larak gave her an appraising look which turned into a different sort of look. He nodded appreciatively. 'If you weren't my sister, I'd ask you for a date! I'm not the only one who's grown up!'

Damia shook her head. 'Thank you. I'm not much into dates now, though.'

'Poor men!' Larak exclaimed. He hefted his carisak. 'Well, lead on! I'm starving!'

Damia grinned. '*That's* normal!'

★

Brian Ackerman caught them up in the canteen. Larak waved a fork at him agreeably, his mouth working through an overlarge hunk of food.

Ackerman shook his head at the change in the young man. 'I nearly didn't recognize you!'

'Even with the typical Raven features? I'm hurt!' Larak had the same easy camaraderie his father possessed. Brian recalled with surprise that he had known Jeff Raven for over twenty years now and the Rowan for slightly longer. At seventy-five, Ackerman was beginning to feel his morning exercises but beyond that, and going totally grey, he felt himself to be much the same man as the one who had met Jeff Raven those many years ago. And the one who had, in desperation, sent his resignation to Peter Reidinger because he could not cope with the young Rowan. The thought of the Rowan made him flick his eyes at Damia. Her features were a delicate blur of the best of the Rowan and the best of Raven but she favoured more her mother in moods, temperament and emotion. Yes, a lot like her mother, Ackerman decided, only more powerful. He wondered if the Rowan was really aware of her daughter's psychic potential. He had his suspicions but Jeff had tactfully kept his counsel on that score.

'What brings you here?' Damia asked with an unspoken accusation in her tone.

'I've got new station assignments,' Ackerman replied.

'Station assignments?' Larak was startled. 'Aren't we a bit too young?'

'That's never stopped you before!' Ackerman exclaimed, a smile forming on his lips. He nodded at the youngster. 'I've read your transcripts, Larak. You're going to be a great twic some day!'

'Twic?' Larak was puzzled, Damia startled.

Ackerman nodded at her. 'It was a name your sister coined, stands for: second-in-command. Only she saw 2IC and pronounced it twic.' He paused. 'Afra must've liked it because he's used it ever since and it's stuck.'

Larak turned a fond look at his sister but Damia looked as though the words offended her. 'So, what's up?' Larak asked, ignoring his sister's expression.

'Altair's up,' Ackerman replied, turning to Damia and winking at her. 'You're assigned there for six months, to work with Torshan and Saggoner. I think Earth Prime's doing what Reidinger did to him – starting you on a round of Towers to give you experience.'

'Gren put you up to this, didn't he?' Damia asked, her eyes snapping with blue sparks.

Ackerman recoiled from the verbal onslaught, confused. 'Huh?'

'Where did these "assignments" originate?' she demanded.

'Headquarters, on Earth, where else?' Ackerman returned, remembering belatedly how poor the Rowan's manners had been when she was angered by something. What's up? he asked himself. 'You've done very well here, Damia. But it's time for you to get about more.' He recoiled a bit at the anger she didn't quite suppress.

'When?' Her question was delivered in a flat tone but both men could sense the tension within her.

Ackerman blinked. 'I guess you can go as soon as you like, Damia, but there's no exact date given.'

'Well, I suppose I should be grateful for time to pack,' she said in a bitter tone.

'Ah, you just got in, didn't you, Larak,' Brian began, trying to rescue himself. It was rather like those times when the Rowan had been in a right snit and no-one knew why.

'Yes, I did,' and Larak fell quickly in with Brian's obvious ploy. 'Haven't even seen my mother yet. Found Damia and she suggested I might be hungry.' Larak's ingenuous grin flashed at Brian. 'Have I got an assignment in that pack?'

Brian ruffled the flimsies. 'Yes, you do, actually,' and

he extracted the right one. 'You're here for six months, working with Afra—'

'So he had to get rid of me first?' Damia asked in a sullen tone.

'Afra has nothing to do with assignments,' Brian said, puzzled by her attitude. Why, when she was a baby, she'd followed Afra around like one of his Coonies. Ackerman shook his head. 'He doesn't know they've come in, much less who's been assigned where. I don't think he'll like it much, though.' Ackerman looked at his watch and rose. 'I'd better log these in officially, kids. I'll see you two later?'

'Certainly!' Larak called back.

Afra had heard the news that evening and was not pleased. When he met Gollee Gren at Luce's restaurant, he started right in. 'What's the idea behind sending Damia to Altair?'

'She needs the experience,' Gollee said simply, flagging down a waiter. 'Please tell Luce that Afra's here.'

The waiter looked dubious. 'Afra?' He looked at the Capellan who nodded politely.

'Afra of Callisto Tower,' Gren amended. 'Luce'll know what to do.'

'Chef Luciano is a busy man—'

'Who'll be very upset if I have to tell him myself.' Gollee whipped his napkin from his lap and made to rise.

'I will tell him.' The waiter rushed off.

'New man.' Gren frowned. 'He'll learn.'

Afra shook his head. 'I haven't been here that often recently.'

'Tell me about it!' Gollee snorted.

'Tell me about Altair.'

'She's got to have a lot more experience before she's ready to run her own Tower,' Gren said, then paused as Afra realized what he meant.

'A *new* Tower? Where?' With more and more systems joining the Nine Star League – which had far more than Nine Stars in it now – there was incredible pressure on F T & T to expand their facilities.

'Aurigae,' and Gollee made a face. 'They've got ores every system will buy. They already have credit by the pod load. They want a T-1 yesterday. But Jeff won't overload her until he's sure she's ready for that kind of responsibility.'

'She's got the capability.'

'She doesn't have the self-control,' Gren said and his eyes were hooded with disapproval. Afra arched an eyebrow and he shrugged, then admitted with a sigh, 'It's also because of the incident—'

'Jeff hasn't heard, has he?'

'Not from my lips,' Gren assured him. 'And no, I don't think he has. Amr's getting therapy and the prognosis is good, but he won't ever make stationmaster. He also has no idea who she really is. So when Jeff was wondering where to send her, I admit I suggested that she fill the Altairian spot, with an eye toward Aurigae. It's preferable to her being at Blundell.'

'Hmm, yes, she was dating the boy for six months. They did a lot of dancing. Someone's sure to remember her face if she starts going out and about on Earth again.'

'I also think working with Torshan and Saggoner will be good for her. Jeff's objective, but the Rowan's not.'

Afra pursed his lips, nodded. 'Yes, that's a factor, too. Damia's always been Rowan's sore spot. It's been pretty intense at times in the Tower during Damia's apprenticeship. I don't know how much of that is their personalities clashing. Even so, she'll learn more control.'

'Oh, indeed she will. She's scheduled to go to Capella after Altair,' and Gollee's smile was malicious. 'She'll learn control.'

'Don't be so hard on the child, Gollee. She's only

sixteen and in an act of passion it's hard enough for anyone to control themselves.'

'*We* manage!' Gren protested.

Afra agreed with a nod, adding, 'But we're not sixteen.' Then he deliberately changed the subject. 'How's Tanya? And the kids?'

'The kids are great!' Gollee returned promptly.

'And Tanya?'

Gren smiled, having lined Afra up for that. 'She's even better.'

'Your daughter, she's what – twelve?'

Gren groaned. 'Thirteen and boy trouble already.' He sighed, reflectively. 'In fact, I had a long talk with her after . . . '

'Good idea,' Afra agreed quickly.

'I can't figure out why the Rowan neglected—' Gren began in protest.

'I don't think she did. I think Damia simply didn't hear,' Afra cut in. 'Cera had no problem.'

'Cera's overcontrolled,' Gren remarked. 'Would she?'

'The Rowan mentioned Cera had reached an understanding. A nice lad, she says, a T-3.'

'Jeff Raven's own population explosion. You watch over all of them, don't you?' Gollee said, amused. 'But Damia more than the rest.'

Afra shrugged. 'She's so much like the Rowan, it comes naturally.' Afra furrowed his brows. 'But Aurigae? That's going to be a tough Tower to run.'

'Who knows? Your Damia may well have found herself a soul mate before she gets to Aurigae,' Gollee said cheerfully.

The food arrived, along with an ecstatic Luciano, and the subject of Damia and Aurigae was not renewed.

7

Iota Aurigae was a blaze at zenith, to Damia's left, glinting off her personal capsule. Capella's light, from the right nadir, was a pulsing blue-white. Starlight from the Milky Way bathed her, too, but the only sound was her even breathing as she allowed her mind to open fully to the mindless, echo-freedom of deep space.

It was as if she could feel the separate cerebral muscles relaxing, expanding, as her tall slender body went gradually limp. She enjoyed these moments of total mental relief from the stresses of Aurigae Tower. But her purpose in these jaunts had a more important application than a mental vacation for herself: she must also be certain that no unwelcome visitors approached the Nine Star League from deep space beyond Iota Aurigae, the furthest human colony from Earth.

Eventually the League would have sufficient sentries to ring the heliopause of every one of its member star systems. But the effective warning system evolved by the combined effort of Fleet and Commercial Engineers was expensive, and time-consuming to manufacture, and almost as tedious to install when completed since each network had to be designed for the star system it would protect. Since the Beetles had twice tried to penetrate Denebian space, that star system had been first to receive heliopausal sentinels. Despite the fact that the home system was already festooned with sophisticated sensors and listening devices in swarms about each of the inner planets and a gigantic listening mechanism on Neptune, Terra received the second system.

Over the next fifteen years, devious politicking, strikes, ultimatums and power plays by nervous administrators on the other Systems – Altair, Capella, Betelgeuse and Procyon – were frequent: each Star determined to have equal safeguards against alien incursions. As the newest, and least populated, of the colonies, Iota Aurigae relied on Damia's weekly reconnaissance.

Which suited both the Aurigaens and Damia perfectly. Perhaps that was why she so enjoyed the independent, reckless spirit of Aurigaens. They didn't give a damn about their 'perilously' unprotected status. They were arrogantly confident of their own resources and besides, wasn't Deneb on the far side of the galaxy from Aurigae? Most of the energetic, hard-working colonists did not really have time to worry about something that 'might' happen.

Then, too, after nearly twenty years, the memory of the Deneb Penetration had faded from active memory into a tale to frighten children with. Damia often wondered how many people – with the exclusion of all Denebians – remembered just how nearly the Nine Star League had come to being overrun by the hive species. Certainly, during her childhood on Deneb, that lesson was reinforced time and time again. And, regularly, the matter of adequate warning systems still exercised the Fleet, Nine Star League Senior Senators – of all species – and all members of the Federated Telepath and Teleportation System.

Much as Damia liked Aurigae's raw and ruthless ways, she did find the utter peace of deep space an anodyne to the constant demands of her position as FT&T Prime. While gradually Aurigae was beginning to supply all agricultural needs and even manufacture needed parts for its technologies, she still had to haul in significant quantities of food stuffs and a multitude of the bits and pieces that Aurigae did not have the time or facilities to manufacture for itself. More to the point, she had to send off immense loads of the raw ores, minerals and rare earths which made the Aurigae colony valuable, and affluent: commodities that in the main went into the manufacture of the low-pulse radar warning systems for other star systems.

Initially there'd been trouble with the Colonial Council in accepting Damia who'd been eighteen when her parents had judged her ready to assume FT&T responsibilities. She'd been furious with the implied criticism that she, a Gwyn-Raven, of a family that already boasted four Primes, was too immature to handle a Tower. Worse, she had caught just a trace of anxiety in her father's mind that she was too flighty to settle down to the hard and tedious work of a Prime.

So she'd shown them all her mettle in her first three months' trial in Aurigae Tower. She'd mentally cajoled or bullied the Tower staff into line in the first week and had never lost so much as a single shipment nor bounced a cargo, no matter how heavy or awkward. Settling her staff so quickly had been a minor personal triumph for Damia, since her own mother had juggled Tower personnel for nearly five years before she'd been satisfied.

Occasionally, even Damia's resilient mind felt the strain and required respite from the insistent murmur of broadcasting thought that beat, beat, beat like a tinnitus in her brain. Ironically, because she had done so well, Aurigaens now tended to take her for granted, to assume the fast and faultless service she rendered in her gestalt with the mighty dynamos of the Tower.

With a flick of a finger, Damia screened out the over-brilliant starlight and opened her eyes. The softened stargleams, points of gem fire in the black of space, winked and pulsed at her. Idly, she identified the familiar patterns they made, these silent friends. Somehow the petty grievances that built up inside her were gently dispersed as the overwhelming impersonality of cold nothingness brought them into proper perspective.

She could even forget her present preoccupation for a moment: forget how lonely she was; how she envied Larak, his loving, lovely wife and their new son; envied her mother the company of her husband and children; envied the Rowan Afra . . .

Afra! What right had he to interfere, to reprimand her! His words still seared.

'You've been getting an almighty vicarious charge out of peeking in on Larak and Jenna. Scared Jenna out of her wits, lurking in her mind while she was in labour! You leave them both alone!'

Damia was forced to admit that such an intrusion had been the most shameless breach of good manners. But how had Afra known? Jenna hadn't even been aware until the split second when Damia had felt, as its mother did, the despairing birth howl of Jenna's son. Unless Larak had caught her as she withdrew from Jenna's mind and told him. She sighed. Yes, Larak would have known she was eavesdropping. Though he was the only T-3 among her brothers and sisters, he had always been extremely sensitive to her mind touch. How often she and Larak had been able to overwhelm any combination of others, even when Jeran and Cera had teamed up with Talented cousins against them. Damia had never tried to analyse the trick, but, somehow, she could switch into a higher mental gear, doubling the capability of other minds within her focus.

Afra's scorching rebuke had come as an intense humiliation: one of several she had suffered from him. The worst of that was that invariably Afra had been correct. Well, better by that yellow-eyed, green-skinned T-3 Capellan than her father, acting in his capacity as Earth Prime. She rather hoped that her father had not learned of that appalling breach of T-etiquette.

Odd, though, she hadn't heard as much as a whisper from Afra since then. It must be over seven months. He had listened in as she'd apologized to both Jenna and Larak, and then silence. He couldn't be *that* angry with her. Or maybe he could. Afra's Methody upbringing made him a martinet on points of etiquette.

Damia diverted her thoughts away from Afra, and went through the ritual of muscle relaxation, of mental wipeout. She must be back in the Tower very soon. In a way, the fact that she could handle Prime duties with no higher ratings than a T-6 to assist had certain disadvantages. The Tower staff could handle only routine planetary traffic, but she had to be on hand for all interstellar telepathic and teleportation commerce.

It would be wonderful to have a T-2, or even a T-3, to share her duties: someone who could understand. Not some*one* . . . be honest with yourself out here in space, Damia. Some *man*. Only men shy away from you as if you'd developed Lynx-sun cancers. And the only other unmarried Prime was her own brother, Jeran. Come to think about Jeran, the smug tone of his recent mind-touches as they exchanged cargoes and messages between Deneb and Aurigae undoubtedly meant that he had found a likely mate, too. When the Denebians paused to use their wits instead of their muscles, they discovered in themselves strong embryo Talents. Like her father, Jeff Raven, or, more to the point, her grandmother, Isthia, who had waited until her forties to make use of powerful innate Talent.

It was no consolation to Damia that her mother, in

a rare example of maternal solicitude, had warned her of this intense, feminine loneliness which she, too, had experienced. But Jeff Raven had appeared to breach the Rowan's Tower and the Rowan had at least had Afra's company . . .

Afra! Why did her mind keep returning to *him*?

Damia realized that she was grinding her teeth. She forced herself through the rituals again, sternly making specific thought dissipate until her mind drifted. And, in the course of that aimless drifting, an aura impinged on her roving consciousness. Startled – for nothing could be coming in from that quarter of space – she tightened her mind into a seeking channel.

An aura! A mere wisp of the presence of something. Something . . . alien!

Alien! Damia recomposed herself. She disciplined her mind to a pure, clear, uncluttered shaft. She touched the aura. Recognition of her touch! Retreat – return!

The aura was undeniably alien, but so faint that she would have doubted its existence except that her finely trained mind was not given to error.

An exultation as hot as lust caused her blood to pound in her ears. She was not wrong. The trace was there. And it wasn't Beetles!

Taking a deep breath, she directed an arrow-fine mental shout across the light-years, nadirward, to the Earth Prime Tower in the squat Blundell building which housed the administrative centre of Federated Teleport and Telepath.

I've caught something out here, Earth Prime!

Aurigae Prime, damn it, control. Control, girl! Jeff replied, keeping his own mental roar within tolerable bounds.

Sorry, but I'm aimed directly at you, Damia replied without real contrition. Her father was capable of deflecting her most powerful thrust.

Thank all the gods for that mercy. So what have you caught? Specify! His tone was official.

I can't be more specific. The alien aura is barely detectable, coming from four light-years galactic north-northeast, Sector 2. I arrowed in once I heard the trace and it responded.

It responded? And four light-years out? Damia, where are you? Jeff's tone was suspicious.

Slightly beyond Aurigaen heliopause, she replied, hoping that her father had no way of judging just how far she actually was. *I'm resting.*

Just how far are you from your Tower? Jeff demanded, more irate father than Earth Prime.

Only a light-year.

Leaving the Tower with only a T-6 in control? I thought we'd instilled more common sense than that in your head! Let's not get too cocky, Damia. Those hey-go-mad colonists are having a bad effect on you.

Damia chortled. *And here I thought the opposite was well reported.* Damia knew perfectly well that her father would have heard about her exploits with carefully chosen, energetic and chauvinistic young engineers and miners. But none of them had been the least bit Talented so her affairs had not harmed them. She'd never been able to forget Amr Tusel. If some of her partners thought she would favour their shipments over others because of her liaisons, they were soon disabused of the notion. In her Tower she scrupulously adhered to FT&T's business.

You are at least discreet, Jeff admitted, *but don't change the subject. Resting is good, but you can achieve as much rest beyond Aurigae's moons as you can a light-year out and not risk being irretrievable.*

Privately, Damia admitted that his point was well taken. *I wouldn't have impinged on that aura if I was only beyond the moons, Dad. Aren't we supposed to discover visitors,* and she added a mental grin for her description, *before they reach the heliopause?*

All right, all right, Jeff said, but Damia knew she hadn't convinced him. *Show me,* he added, his tone reproving.

She allowed his mind to join with hers as she led him

directly to the alien trace. The aura was palpable but so far away that only the extraordinary perception of two powerful minds could sense it.

I sense anticipation, curiosity, surprise, Jeff told his daughter thoughtfully as he withdrew from the tight focus. *And caution, too. Whatever it is, is approaching our galaxy. Damn, why couldn't we have at least a few peripheral sentinels for you beyond Aurigae.*

Mechanicals would be no good in this instance, Damia declared, irritated by the inference that devices would be more useful than she could be.

That's true enough, though the safest procedure is for mechanicals to inform humans.

So I've stolen a march on those much vaunted DEWs. And I can find out a helluva lot more than they could. Damia couldn't resist reminding her father of that.

Not at any time personally endangering yourself, Prime, Jeff replied, colouring the official concern with personal.

Of course not, Damia replied, fully confident in her own abilities. *But if I can establish some kind of communication with these visitors, I'll need someone to take over my Tower. Like Larak.*

I can't spare Larak immediately. He's training a T-3 to augment old Guzman at Procyon Tower. The old fellow tends to fall asleep and great tact is required to keep from irritating or humiliating Guz, neither of which temper keeps Procyon operating smoothly.

I thought you'd a dozen good T-2s coming along, Damia replied, for she kept informed of all matters concerning Talents.

I do, but there isn't a team working smoothly enough yet to take over on such short notice. I'll send you Afra. He'd be better anyhow.

Because Afra was involved with the Deneb Penetration? Damia asked, slightly supercilious. *And you don't think I'd know Beetle stink after a childhood on Deneb?*

Jeff chuckled. *Yes, I suppose you'd have learned that, too.*

Well, I'd rather wait until Larak's free if it's only a question of a few weeks. We've time in hand, I think, before the alien vessel gets anywhere near Aurigae's heliopause. And you know how Mother hates being deprived of Afra, Damia added, not quite leeching all the rancour from her voice.

Damia! and Jeff's tone crackled with disapproval. *I thought you'd grown out of that bit of childishness. Furthermore, I will not tolerate such disrespect of your mother, least of all from you.* He paused, leaving Damia in no doubt of his anger, a palpable bridge of tension between them despite the enormous distance that physically separated them. *By rights, I ought to saddle you with some T-2s and let you sweat out their teaming.*

Thank you, no, Dad. Not under the present circumstances. And Damia did not bother to hide her dismay at his suggestion.

Unfortunately the most useful pair are twins and as you never got on terms with the way Jeran and Cera operated, I doubt you'd establish a rapport with them either.

Sometimes, Dad, I don't think you like me.

Of course, I do, Damia, and a swelling of love, affection and approval laved her, *as your father. But,* and now Jeff's voice turned droll, *as Earth Prime, I'm as aware of your strengths as your weaknesses. You operate far more effectively with T-3s and under. I just don't happen to have any T-3s but your brother.* There was a note of wistfulness in her father's voice that Damia understood all too well, to both her amusement and chagrin.

Your dynastic plans will bear better fruit with Jeran, you know. He's been awful cocky lately. Only don't let him settle for anything less than a T-4.

She grinned to herself at her father's startled pause.

You haven't been eavesdropping again, have you, Damia?

She parried that surprise with a quick, *After Afra reamed me for that with Jenna? Not bloody likely.*

Oh, so it was Afra. Your mother thought it might have been

Isthia. Your grandmother had a rare Talent for knowing when one of her charges was up to mischief.

The trouble with telepaths is that sometimes they think too much, she remarked acidly, infuriated afresh to realize that her mother also knew of that incident.

Damia! Jeff's tone was unusually severe. *Better than anyone else in this galaxy, your mother understands your Tower isolation.*

Is that why she handed me over to Isthia to raise? Damia flashed back.

To give you a safe ambience when you were too damned precocious to appreciate the dangers of living in the Callisto dome. And I know you remember Afra hauling you out of a freighter a split second before your mother was about to launch it to Altair.

Damia did remember but she didn't like to and she hated for her father to bring it up.

Furthermore, and she had to set her teeth as her father continued on that tack, *let me try to seal it into your stubborn head that it was I who insisted that you go to your grandmother on Deneb, not your mother and it was Afra you were clinging to like a barnacle when it came time to be put in the capsule for the trip.* Right now Damia particularly didn't like to be reminded of that fact, not when Afra's silence had lasted seven months. Her father sighed, abruptly breaking off that familiar lecture. *You and your mother are so much alike.*

Damia snorted. She was not the least bit like her mother. There was absolutely no resemblance between them. She was Jeff's daughter from her slender height to her black hair and vivid blue eyes. Jeran, yes, and Ezro, too, took after the Rowan. But not she. Of course, her mother had an exceedingly strong and diverse psionic Talent or she wouldn't be Callisto Prime, but Damia felt that she was just as strong, and she had the added advantage of that catalytic ability as well.

Well, Jeff was saying in a resigned tone, *you'll see it one day, my dear, and I, for one, will be immensely relieved. Your mother and I love you very much and we're damned proud of the way you've been managing Aurigae Tower. Professionally I have no quibbles with you.* Damia basked in her father's praise. He didn't give it lightly. *I'll send Afra on directly,* he added, spoiling her pleasure. *I can trust his impartiality,* and to Damia's amazement, her father chuckled.

She stabbed at his mind to find the basis for the amusement, but met a blankness as her father had turned his mind to some other problem.

'Impartiality? Afra?' The sound of her own voice in the little personal capsule startled her.

What on Earth was that supposed to mean? Why would Afra's impartiality be trusted – above hers – in identifying or evaluating an alien aura?

But Afra was to come to Aurigae.

After he had broken contact with Damia, Jeff did not immediately turn to other problems. He mulled over the subtler aspects of that vivid contact with his daughter. Damia's mind was as brilliant as Iota Aurigae, and right now blazing with excitement over the contact. He didn't like her recklessness but, in this instance, he could only be relieved that she had been in position to catch the aura.

Odd that she could still be so angry about being sent to Isthia. Odder still, that she could still deny that it had been Afra she'd clung to, and cried for, not her mother. Jeff knew very well that, once Damia had settled in with her grandmother and her cousins, she'd been extremely happy and benefited tremendously by the Special School for Talent that Isthia had set up. Jeff sighed. The decision to send Damia to Isthia had been one of the hardest he had ever had to make, personally and professionally. But she'd come early into her extraordinary mental powers, frightening everyone on the station with her antics and incredibly dangerous use of telekinesis. Only Afra had any control over her and even his patience had ended with her capsule stunt.

Under Isthia's calm, unruffled discipline, and with a huge planet to roam in and myriads of cousins to keep tabs on her, Damia had learned how to use her Talent without abusing it, herself, and anyone in her immediate vicinity. She became sincerely fond of her grandmother and would obey Isthia where she argued every request from her parents, especially her mother. Strange that it was the Rowan whom Damia still blamed for fostering her.

Rowan, Jeff called out to Callisto Tower and sensed that his wife was resting as the interchanges on Callisto's cargo cradles filled from Earthside.

Her mind linked with his gladly, just as if they hadn't breakfasted together on Callisto a few hours earlier.

I've a message of extreme importance to impart to you, luv. Open to me.

Damia's made contact with an alien aura? The fleeting maternal concern was quickly supplanted by professional curiosity as the Rowan scanned Jeff's recent experience beyond Aurigae. *Of course Afra goes. I can't think of anyone better.* Her tone was slightly ironic until she caught the thought that Jeff tried to lose. *But why on Earth Damia would think that you can't assign Afra wherever he's needed, I just don't understand. Oh, well. I don't understand that child. I'll take a pair of those T-2s you're training until he comes back. Twins, huh? Well, Mauli and Mick have been a superb team, and Jeran and Cera accustomed me to fraternal language.* She added with a sigh, *I'll miss him.*

You always do, Jeff replied teasingly, to divert the Rowan from scanning the recent conversation too deeply, *Good thing I trust that yellow-eyed Capellan . . .*

Jeff Raven, there has never been an improper thought between Afra and myself even before you lurched in from Deneb . . .

Jeff laughed and she sputtered at him indignantly.

Actually, she continued, *it'd be a relief for me to know that Afra's out with Damia. I really do worry that she might get besotted with one of those brawny Aurigaen types she plays about with.*

The last thing Afra'd do is interfere with her pleasures.

The Rowan let out an exasperated sigh. *But those pleasures do nothing to relieve her loneliness. Sometimes . . .*

I know, said her husband with considerable sympathy and then his tone hardened. *She wouldn't BE lonely if she hadn't been so heavy-handed with every other high T young male . . .*

She resents our matchmaking as much as I resented Reidinger's.

There's no guarantee she won't find a Denebian, too, you know, Jeff replied, allowing his voice to become so lascivious that the Rowan pretended shock. *When can you spare Afra from doing your work?*

Afra? Doing MY work? Just wait till you get home. And she pretended to ignore his response to that threat. *Afra? Jeff requires your attention.*

Jeff caressed her with a genuinely affectionate thought before he felt Afra's mind touch his.

Are you sure you're still only a T-3? he asked, surprised at the firmness in the Capellan's contact.

I'm in gestalt, after all, Afra replied, adding a mental shrug at Jeff's surprise. *What else could you expect after twenty-odd years of proximity to two of the strongest Talents in explored space? It's no wonder I've learned a few tricks from the pair of you. From the expression on Rowan's face, I'd hazard that Damia has lately been discussed. What's she up to now?*

Damia had just returned to Aurigae when she heard the Rowan giving the Tower official warning of the transmission of a personal capsule.

Afra? Damia exclaimed, reaching back along her mother's touch to Callisto.

Damia! Afra said warningly but too late.

Without waiting for the Rowan to launch the capsule towards Aurigae, Damia blithely drew the carrier directly from Callisto, ignoring her mother's stunned and angry reaction to such bad manners.

Damia regretted her impulsiveness immediately. But Afra's capsule was opening and he was swinging himself out. She could not have missed his trenchant disapproval if she'd been a mere T-15. He stood, looking down at her though she was tall enough to look most men in the eye, as imperturbable as ever. As aloof and contained as always. Did Afra never alter? Did he never give vent to his feelings? Did he have any? Unfair of her for she knew he did – even if he seemed to expend most of them on barque cats and Coonies. She really shouldn't have snatched his carrier from her mother: that had been childish and she so wanted Afra to notice how well she managed Aurigae Tower with a minimum of Talented staff and a maximum of efficiency. She sighed for she knew she hadn't impressed Afra at all.

Instinctively, she straightened as if to minimize the difference in their heights. Even so, she still only came to Afra's shoulder.

'You will apologize to your mother, Damia,' Afra said, his unexpectedly tenor speaking voice a curious echo of his quiet mental tone. 'Isthia taught you better manners even if we never could.'

'You've been trying to lately, though, haven't you?' The retort came out before she could stop it. Why did she always feel like an errant child in Afra's presence? Even when she wasn't at fault.

He cocked his head to one side and regarded her steadily. She sent a swift probe which he parried easily.

'You were distressing Jenna unnecessarily, Damia. She appealed to me because she did not wish Jeff to know of your indiscretion.'

'She chose well.' Damia was so appalled at the waspishness of her tone that she extended her hand to him apologetically.

She could feel him throw up his mental barriers

and, for a second, she wondered if he might refuse what was, after all, the height of familiarity between telepaths. But his hand rose smoothly to clasp hers, lightly, warmly, leaving her with the essential cool-green-comfortable-security that was the physical/mental double-touch of him.

Then, with a one-sided smile, he bowed to indicate he was flattered by the compliment of touching but allowed a recollection of herself, clad only in drypers, cross his public mind.

She made a face at him and substituted Larak's son. Afra blandly put 'her' back beside her nephew.

'All right,' she laughed. 'I'll behave.'

'About time,' he said with an affable grin. 'Now apologize to your mother.'

Damia made a face but she sent a suitably contrite message to the Rowan who accepted it with only a modicum of disapproval. When she had done that, Damia saw Afra looking about him. He would have seen Aurigae through the perceptions of herself and Keylarion, her T-6.

The Tower occupied a position beyond the edges of, and on a height above, the sprawling colony town which had been built on both sides of the river that flowed into Aurigae's southern sea several kilometres beyond. A fine straight road linked Tower and town, but there was little traffic on it now in the early evening.

Unlike other Towers, there was no staff compound, for most of the Talents preferred quarters in the nearby town. So, late in the evening there weren't even any ground vehicles about the Tower buildings and only the two personal capsules in the cradling yard. The sweet-scented breeze sweeping down from the high snowy mountain range was lightly moist and the atmosphere had a high oxygen content, exhilarating him. Afra took a deep breath and exhaled.

'It's a lovely world you have here, Damia.'

She smiled up at him, her blue eyes brilliant under the fringes of long black lashes.

'Yes, isn't it? Young and vigorous. Come see where I live. And see how well all the Coonies have adapted to Aurigae.' She led the way from the landing stage to her dwelling.

Her house, a cantilevered affair on several levels, perched on the high plateau above the noisy metropolis. Its randomly sprawling newness had a vitality which the planned order of both Earth and his native Capella lacked. Afra found the view stimulating.

'It is, isn't it?' Damia agreed, following his surface thought. Then she directed his mind to her day's discovery, giving the experience exactly as it had happened to her. 'And the touch is unlike anything I've ever encountered.'

'You certainly didn't expect it to be familiar, did you?' Afra asked in dry amusement.

'Just because they originate in another galaxy doesn't mean they can't be humanoid, and thus somewhat familiar,' she replied.

'Dreamer . . . '

They both heard an excited chatter as they started up the last flight of shallow steps to the main entrance to her quarters. She grinned over her shoulder at Afra.

'They know you're here,' she said just as a tumble of brightly furred bodies squeezed out of their special door, sorting into five separate entities. Squealing and clicking with delight, they swarmed up Afra's long legs – one Coonie making a splendid leap from the top step directly to his chest. Laughing, Afra reached up to keep the daring Crisp from losing her grip on the smooth fabric of his tunic. Meanwhile, Arfur scrambled to his shoulder, twining his banded tail around Afra's neck, just as Merfy arrived on the other shoulder and Priss and Scrap argued with each other for Afra's crooked right arm. Merfy was disgusted and leapt to Damia's shoulder, scolding her siblings impartially as she proprietorially threaded her tail about Damia's neck.

'Aurigae's unscrewed all their training, too,' Afra remarked as he carried his squirming load into the house. But his smile took the sting from his words. 'I'm positive that Crisp and Arfur have put on kilos since they left Callisto.'

'They've filled out a lot. The hunting's good,' Damia said.

'They're foraging?' Afra was both surprised and pleased. Coonies were infinitely adaptable which was why they fared well wherever they were raised. This litter had been born on Callisto – under Damia's bed, if Afra remembered correctly. They had always been Damia's but had included him in their exuberant affections.

'Daily, or should I say nightly? What they don't eat they deposit very carefully in my bathtub – where it's easy to clean up.' Damia made a face. 'Are you hungry? I've probably interrupted your normal shift.'

'Oh, don't go to any trouble for me,' he said, settling on the long deep couch in the living area so that he could pet the Coonies who rapturously exposed their white-furred bellies for his special attentions.

'No trouble at all,' Damia replied. Mischievously she kinetically started several cooking operations at the same time, each one a dish which she knew Afra particularly enjoyed. For quite a few minutes, the kitchen was full of flying utensils, condiments and raw materials being processed.

'Always the thoughtful hostess,' he said, graciously inclining his head. 'How fast is this alien closing on Aurigae?'

'Give me a break, Afra! I only know it's there! How could I possibly judge relative speed? I've got to establish some frame of reference.'

'Well, you've always been precocious.' He had to duck a vegetable peeling which she flung at him in her pique.

He neatly launched it into the disposal unit. 'Seriously, Damia, how long do you think you'll need?'

Appeased by a reasonable request, she considered. 'I should have some idea of relative speed in a week or so. Maybe even sooner, but I doubt it.'

Absently fondling soft, silky Coonie bodies, he watched her as she ended the telekinetic preparatory ballet of edibles, and began to sample what she was cooking, corrected seasonings and added final ingredients. Like most T-1s, she enjoyed manual work and kept her house without relying on the mechanicals which most households considered essential. In a very short time, she prepared a perfectly cooked, attractively presented meal at which he glanced casually, seemingly reluctant to disentangle his hands from the Coonies' playful paws and teeth.

'Scatter, kids,' Damia said, firmly separating the little animals from their willing victim.

With startled squeaks, the Coonies fled from the couch to positions where they turned to glare in her direction, muttering Coonie imprecations. Afra glanced at her, his eyebrows raised in mild rebuke.

'They had a good romp with you,' she said, 'but I went to a lot of trouble to give you a decent meal and I don't like my efforts wasted.' She sat down across from him, plate in hand.

'Your efforts are not wasted,' he said, putting his fork in the crispy ginger chicken served with mangetout. 'Tasty enough.'

Damia made a face at him. '"Tasty enough?"' She mimicked him. 'Can't I ever impress you?' she asked, half-wistful, half-sharp.

'Why should you want to at this late date?' he asked, amiably. 'I've never forgotten our introduction.' And he grinned.

'Oh, that!' As always, that reminder caused her to flush. 'It's not fair of you to continually bring that up.

So I smiled at you until Elizara took me from you and then began to bawl my eyes out. I was hardly aware of what I was doing, now was I? a bare hour born.'

'My dear Damia,' and he chuckled appreciatively, 'you have always been aware of your effect on an audience.' He bowed his head towards her. 'But let us attend to the business at hand. How can I help you? Shall I take over the regular Tower workload and leave you free for surveillance?'

'I think you'll have to. When I got back in from resting, before mother despatched you, Federated Mines and Ores notified me of intent to forward nine drones to the refinery on one of Betelgeuse's outer planets.'

'Nine shouldn't be a problem with David to catch,' Afra replied.

Damia rolled her eyes. 'Big daddies, every one of them, not those small interstellar drones you and Mother play with.'

'The big ones?' And Afra regarded her with some concern. 'And they expect you to manage such mass with only a T-6?'

Damia grinned with satisfaction at his response. 'I always do manage, you know,' she said with considerable pride.

'Still jump-starting other peoples' Talents?'

'There's nothing wrong with that, Afra, if it helps me spin off the workload they expect of me.'

Afra leaned forward, lightly touching his finger to her hand. 'There's such a thing as being too stiff-necked proud, Damia. Especially as you might put your T-6 at risk of burnout. Did you think of that?'

'Yes, I have, but Keylarion is sturdy. She doesn't have much finesse but she sort of sets her heels down and pushes.' Damia gave a little laugh. 'We might need more generators if this traffic in big daddies continues.'

'Earth Prime has the right to know when his people are overloaded.'

Damia found it difficult to evade Afra's yellow eyes. 'I would have mentioned it if the heavy traffic keeps up, Afra. I'd thought of insisting on the linked pod configuration you initiated, but it's more a question of mass than convenience. Up till some dork thought of the big daddies, Keylarion and I have been able for all they've asked.'

'At least you had sense to ask for help today,' Afra said, and then shook his finger at her, simulating censure. 'I think I'll recommend that you're allowed a T-4 . . . Ah ah, Damia,' and held his finger in a sterner pose, '*I'll* have made the recommendation if I judge the traffic requires it. You won't have to admit you're unable to handle it.'

'I *am* able to handle it,' and she jerked her chin up in challenge.

'Indeed, but not if you've got to play sentinel, too. I should imagine that your staff will give a collective sigh of relief to know you're being reinforced.'

Looking down to artistically rearrange the vegetables on her plate, she found that Afra was, as usual, correct in his supposition. The tip of his finger touched her chin and, with a deft kinetic tilt, he made her look him in the eye. His mind touch was so sympathetic and understanding that she smiled ruefully.

'I don't have a big staff,' she admitted, adding hastily, 'but we really do work well together. And I haven't heard so much as a wisp of complaint at the workload.'

'Then you've a good loyal group who will be delighted to see me appear in the Tower to help one and all move those ponderously packed pachydermical projectiles. When we've done that, your retiring in your capsule for a spot of peace and quiet will seem quite in order. Right?'

'As always, Afra.'

He regarded her steadily. 'Is that so hard to take from me, Damia?'

She mushed up the vegetables on the end of her fork

and replied honestly. 'No, not from you, Afra. Never from you. You don't change,' she added, rather more tartly than she intended.

He grinned at her. 'Good old reliable Afra, consistent and constant.'

She wrinkled her nose at him, experiencing an odd twinge of regret for his flippant self-description. 'You're not that old.'

'No, actually I'm not,' he said enigmatically and served himself a second helping from her pots and pans.

That pleased her and she rediscovered her appetite. Having Afra recommend what she herself hadn't wanted to request restored her self-confidence. She was exceedingly glad to have Afra here just now, and not merely to help her shift cargo that was beginning to tax her strength, but because she was still absorbing the effect of touching that alien aura. She was excited, too, that she, Damia Gwyn-Raven, should establish such a first contact. Almost as if it had been preordained – though she had never succumbed to the immature curiosity that sometimes preoccupied lesser Talents to seek hints of their future from clairvoyants.

'You know,' she began, wanting to clear the air between them completely, 'you were right to call me to task for "tasting" Larak and Jenna. But I did want to know how a lasting love feels in the mind. So I'll recognize it when it happens. And what it's like to give birth.'

Afra raised an eyebrow quizzically. 'And . . . '

'Apart from the pain, I guess it's rewarding enough.'

'You don't sound too sure.'

Damia cocked her head and traced an involved pattern on the table with her index finger.

'I suspect the firsthand experience is more intense, no matter how deeply one scans.'

A trace thought behind her shield, triggered by her observation, sent a stab of apprehension through Afra that he barely managed to contain. She was unconsciously censoring, and it had to do with the alien aura and with her own desire for the experience of motherhood. But trace thought it was, and he had only that nano-second impression, tantalizing, terrorizing.

'You're young yet, Damia,' he said, keeping his voice light, 'and it's really important for you to consolidate your abilities as a Prime before you have conflicting loyalties. You know how hard it was for your mother to juggle Prime duties and motherhood.'

Damia cast him a jaundiced glare. 'Not that old homily again,' she said in disgust. 'From Mother and Isthia it's bad enough, but not you. And why does it seem to affect women more than men? Look at Larak: he's got Jenna and he's two and a half years my junior!'

'Cera's not involved . . . '

'Oh yes, she is, even if he's not very Talented. Oh, is that news to you?' She was pleased to surprise him. Restlessly, she launched herself physically from the table in one lightning move, startling the Coonies who had been nestling in one of the lounge chairs.

'Cera could always keep her own counsel,' Afra replied.

'Why is it that Primes have such a hard time, Afra? We can do so much more than . . . ' She discontinued that thought for one of the strictest precepts of her upbringing was to avoid the arrogance of ability.

'Compensation,' Afra said in the languid drawl he reserved for these moods of hers. 'There are some experiences in life which are worth waiting for.'

She whirled, scowling at him, looking even more lovely than ever. 'So I should just wait in my Tower? As Mother did? Passive?'

Afra let out a roar of laughter that startled Damia as much as it did the Coonies. He laughed until his eyes were tearing. 'My dear Damia, there is nothing passive about you, or don't you remember how you dismissed young Nicoloss . . . '

'Nico! That adolescent mess!'

'He's a good reliable T-5 and he's a superb second at Betelgeuse.'

'David's welcome to him!' Damia's eyes flashed blue sparks of outrage.

'Well, now, girl, you know you need a steadying hand . . . '

'Oooooh! Steadying hand . . . I'll steady you . . . ' and Damia lifted her right hand.

Well acquainted with Damia's tendency to dramatize, Afra deposited Crisp in her open palm. Crisp blinked and cheeped in surprise.

'Ah, yes, I see I was mistaken,' Afra said as she closed her fingers reassuringly about the Coonie, drawing it in to her breast. '*YOU* have the steadying hand.'

She regarded him darkly, tapping her foot, her lips compressed.

It had become second nature, Afra decided, to deal with Damia's moods. To be sure, they were more complex since she became interested in the opposite sex – or, to be precise, the lack of partners, steadying or otherwise. These times tried his resolve despite the fact that his diversions were usually effective. One day he might graduate from the avuncular stance he had had to adopt and be able to give free expression to his deep-hidden desire. But, from the day that Damia's imminent puberty had forced him to realize how much she meant to him, he had given a great deal of thought to the variables and knew that he could only wait. It was hard. Certainly as hard as it was for Damia to watch others pairing off, achieving the enviable total rapport that telepaths enjoyed, and for which she was so eager. Her very brilliance and beauty caused many otherwise willing mates to shy away – Nicoloss being only the latest one of a long line. At least she had never repeated the Amr tragedy. Usually she would talk herself out of these libidinous moods but tonight Afra sensed a new pulse that was dangerous in its intensity.

'Is that why you so eagerly await the arrival of the aliens?' Afra said in his soft drawl, deliberately leeching all emotion out of his words. 'On the extremely unlikely chance they're biologically compatible? Do you envision your soul mate winging across the void to you?'

Her eyes dilated in anger and the hand caressing Crisp stilled.

'That was unworthy of you, Afra,' she said in a hoarse whisper.

He knew that, but the thought was better aired between them where it couldn't fester in her mind. He inclined his head in apology.

'Better get some sleep, Damia. We're pushing big daddies tomorrow,' he said gently and gave her a little mental shove toward her bedroom.

She scowled, still smarting from his facetious observation but allowed herself to be swayed by the nudge. 'Well, you know what a romantic I am, Afra,' she said with a rueful grin and hitched Crisp to her shoulder where the Coonie had snuggled happily against her neck. 'And I do need my sleep. That contact was quite a high. No action without a reaction, after all,' she added in a philosophical tone but the sadness in her smile touched Afra to the heart.

He nodded understandingly, keeping a tight grasp on his emotions. Again Afra caught the unmistakable and unconscious suppression of a thought within the maelstrom of her weariness.

As Damia turned, she made a sweeping gesture at the other Coonies and, with squeals of delight, they erupted out of the chair and scurried after her.

Afra dared not relax until he was certain Damia was fully asleep. So he tidied away the remains of their meal, filled the Coonies' water and dry feed dishes, and then watched the sunset turn the plateau a deep tangerine before diminishing in the west. Brooding over the nuances of the evening's conversation, he waited until the roiling activity of Damia's mind subsided into the even beat of sleep. Then he, too, went to bed.

To his surprise and delight, Scrap and Arfur appeared in his room to sit on his bed, clearly awaiting his company for the night. He was touched by their presence and settled himself down quickly, performing the obligatory caresses until they arranged themselves against him. Comforting creatures to have. Not what he really wanted but better than nothing. Carefully, just as he was on the edge of sleep, he reinforced his mental screens so that none of his longing for Damia would escape. He wondered, in that honest interval between consciousness and dreaming, if he would have enough strength left to cope with a third generation of such women.

8

The next day, Damia introduced Afra to her Tower personnel. Keylarion was visibly relieved to see him for he had been her training mentor at Callisto. How Damia managed with only seven in staff, and all under T-8 apart from Keylarion, Afra could not imagine. Yet they had; there were no complaints from the Aurigae Management. Which, in point of fact, being so new a colony, could not have afforded the rates a large number of high Ts commanded in FT&T.

He perceived that Damia was popular with her staff, male and female. The T-9 stationmaster, Herault, was infatuated with her, a condition of which Damia was clearly unaware while Afra picked it up instantly. But then, he knew the signs so well. It was also apparent to Afra that none of them realized that Damia's catalytic gift boosted their performance levels above their T-designation. He was relieved that she had finally learned not to reveal that aspect of her Talent. It had taken him long enough to get that message through her Talented skull.

'I've got the placements for the big daddies, Damia,'

Herault said, shaking his head. 'And they've instructed us to pick 'em up at the mines again.'

Damia nodded curtly to Herault, pursing her lips in annoyance over that as she glanced over at the generator boards where Xexo was monitoring their performance.

'We'll have full power in another ten minutes. The two spot's going to need servicing soon, Damia,' the T-8 engineer said, shaking his head at the unwelcome necessity.

'Blast!' Damia allowed her anger to show. Afra could scarcely blame her. With what she had to teleport, she'd need all four generators giving her top power. 'And they're too broke to buy me a spare.'

'Backtrack a moment,' Afra said, holding up a hand. 'You have to pick up the cargo at the mines?'

'We have to,' Damia said with a meditative shrug and a gamine grin. 'They don't possess a land vehicle strong enough to transport them even the short distance from the mines.' She jerked her thumb over her shoulder in the general direction of the rugged foothills behind the town.

'Nonsense,' Filomena, the T-9 expeditor, said sharply, 'they don't want to gouge ruts out of their new roads which they didn't construct correctly to carry the heavy loads they ought to have known they'd have to transport. This IS a mining planet!'

Afra regarded Damia sternly. 'They're abrogating FT&T regulations . . . '

'I know that,' Damia responded tartly, 'but,' and she sighed, 'I can try to oblige them and save a lot of hassle – which transport would be—'

'To say nothing of the wear and tear on you and your staff—'

'Afra! *This is my Tower and I'm running it my way.*'

Afra inhaled deeply. It was improper for him to challenge Damia in her own Tower. He exhaled, lifting his hands in a gesture of yielding. 'I just hope that Aurigae appreciates you. All of you.'

At that instant both Damia and Afra heard the generators reach their peak.

'Well, folks, let's speed the daddies on their way while we're fresh and eager. It's also morning on Betelgeuse so David'll catch efficiently. Afra?' And she led the way into the Tower.

To his surprise, a second conformable chair stood next to hers, complete with a secondary board, screens and a terminal.

'Thank you,' he said as he settled himself.

'You deserve no less,' she said at her sweetest and he curbed an impulse to 'see' what she was up to. 'Placements!'

Both tower screens showed the huge ore pods, dwarfing the men on the ground in the mine yard, and even the heavy cranes and flatbeds that had helped load them. Beneath the picture were the coordinates for delivery at Betelgeuse's outer planet.

Betelgeuse Tower, Aurigae here, she said, observing protocol.

Damia? Morning, replied David of Betelgeuse. *The refineries have been screaming for this shipment.*

You're likely to have a hernia bringing 'em in, Damia said.

Too much for you, darling? David asked archly. Afra knew the older Prime enjoyed taunting Damia.

Not for me, she replied, projecting a broad and confident grin. *Ready?*

Damia! Afra sent the warning on a tight shaft, having heard just that tone of voice from her mother.

Don't Afra. You'll spoil my fun! Damia shot back and began the lift. Because he'd been forewarned by her mental tone, Afra was ready to follow her mind to the immense drones in the yard and felt himself strengthened, by the incredible catalytic link she could establish. Effortlessly they 'ported the first big daddy towards its destination.

What under the stars are those Aurigaens trying to prove?

David exclaimed and both of them heard him work to receive her 'port.

Your principals were screaming for the shipment, weren't they? Damia's voice was smooth and silky with satisfaction. *Ready number two?*

Ready when you are, and there was determination in David's voice.

By the ninth 'port, Afra knew himself to be tiring and wondered at the energy Damia exuded.

That is the last of such weights I will accept from Aurigae, David said. *And I'm registering a complaint against the mines with Earth Prime. I can't imagine why you haven't, Damia. I don't mind cooperating with management and industry but nine of those is stretching both of us. Do not, I repeat, do not accept such monsters again. Why, I could shift a battle fleet more easily.*

Damia's grin at irritating David altered to a frown and Afra sensed her sudden apprehension.

A random remark, and those daddies would weigh the same. You've had your fun. Leave it, Afra shot at her. 'You do have coffee here, don't you?' he asked, looking about the Tower.

Two steaming cups and a plate of energy biscuits appeared and one cup homed in on Afra, the plate following it.

'You're guest,' she said with an unrepentant grin and a shrug of her slim shoulders. 'I don't have enough staff to adhere to strict protocol.'

Refreshed, they were shortly ready to 'port and receive incoming cargo, none of which was anywhere near the weight or mass of the morning's first delivery. Damia worked without affectation, Afra was pleased to note: a Prime in easy command of her skills. There was an excellent harmony with every one of her staff. Aurigae was a more than adequate testing ground for Damia. Afra wondered if she'd been apprised that she would succeed Guzman at Procyon when the old

Prime was finally persuaded to step down. Despite her youth, FT&T would have insisted on his retirement if they'd known how frail the old man was but Jeff Raven, and others, conspired to deceive the administration. And they'd continue to do so as long as necessary.

Shortly, all the incoming loads had been cradled and the light afternoon traffic processed. Damia, her eyes glinting with mischief, slid out of the conformable chair and signalled for Afra to take her place. When the focal Talent of the gestalt went from one to the other, not even a half beat of the pulse of the Aurigaen Tower was missed. Damia used the Tower exit to reach her capsule and informed Afra of her departure. He let up on the gestalt long enough for her to 'port her own launch before he picked it up again. She was gone too quickly for him to keep even the most negligible of contacts with her.

So much for that notion. However, her absence would permit Afra to use gestalt to communicate with Jeff should he need to. The Tower's work proceeded smoothly. There was, in fact, rather more traffic than Damia had anticipated, but no more big daddies, though several medium drones of refined material had to be despatched to various destinations. Inbound supplies arrived sporadically but nothing that an experienced T-3 couldn't handle. However, number two generator was definitely ailing and Afra was concerned. Xexo tinkered and fiddled with it whenever he could but the machine needed more than adjustments. Fortunately, Damia would not require full station power to assist her comings and goings so, once the day's work was done, Xexo could begin to dismantle it.

In terms of intergalactic distances, the aliens approached at the proverbial snail's pace: by interstellar references, incredibly fast. Such a feat argued for a highly sophisticated technical species. On the evening of the eighth day, Damia returned from her quest, bursting with news. She 'ported herself from her capsule right into the lounge area where Afra was amusing the Coonies.

'I made individual contact,' she cried. 'And what a mind!' She was far too excited to notice Afra's flare of apprehension. He told himself this was just Damia being her usual melodramatic self. 'And what a surprise he got,' she went on.

From the first words out of her mouth, Afra knew that the mind was male.

'Really?' and he injected genuine interest into his response. 'A Prime Talent?'

'I can't assess his abilities. He's so . . . different,' she exclaimed, her eyes shining and her mental aura dazzling with her success. 'He fades and then returns. The distance is still immense, of course, and there isn't much definition in the thoughts. We can only deal in abstracts.' She laughed tiredly. 'As scientists have often maintained, I made a start by reciting the periodic table of chemicals and basic atomic structures to establish at least some level of communication.'

'Surely an intergalactic ship would utilize a more sophisticated source than atomic power?'

'I'm sure it would have to, to travel such distances,' and Damia threw herself on the long couch, pushing back her long hair in a tired gesture before she let her hand drop bonelessly to the cushioning. 'I can't be bothered at this stage of interaction to deal with minor details.'

'Minor details?'

'Oh, don't fuss, Afra,' she said irritably. 'Considering our space travel experts postulate drives as far beyond fusion as the wheel from mixed fuel space drives, we can posit that they would have to have developed an efficient drive. At least I could project mutually understood abstracts. I'm exhausted. I haven't had this sort of a workout since Larak and I played dodgeball against all the cousins. Let me grab a little nap before I contact Dad.'

'Xexo's patching that ailing generator.'

Damia scowled, then shrugged off that complication. 'All the more reason for me to have an hour's snore.'

'You don't snore,' Afra said firmly, giving her a mock-stern glare.

She managed a grin for his loyal denial.

Afra waited until she relaxed into sleep. Putting ethics aside, he tried to reach this experience in her mind, below the emotional level, only to find himself overwhelmed by the subjective. Damia was indulging in a high emotional kick! He recognized that she had every reason to be proud of herself in establishing any sort of contact with an alien but he was afraid for her, with a fear deeper than any he had ever touched personally or vicariously. Afra withdrew, troubled. Crisp and Merfy crawled over to him, whining softly as if they felt his concern. Soothing them, he managed to disperse his presentiment.

He let her wake up naturally and was proud of her now calm and balanced mind. As she 'reached' Jeff, she was totally the Prime, giving a considered and professional report of the contact. Not a trace of the excitation Afra had probed coloured her thoughts. When she had finished 'pathing, Jeff inserted a private query for Afra but he could only confirm Damia's report. He saw no point to mention vague forebodings but he did mention the matter of overweight drones. Jeff had received a formal complaint from David of Betelgeuse and there was to be an official protest from FT&T to Aurigae Miners.

The next day, Damia tossed off the few live 'portations and departed for her surveillance. And Afra contained his presentiments. She returned so shining from the second session of communication that Afra had to clamp an icy hold over his mental reactions.

'We're making great progress in conceptualizations,' she told Afra, pirouetting with abandon into the lounge and flopping on to the long couch, her eyes glowing. One long tress, half black hair, half white, fell across her flushed face.

'Such as?' he enquired in a politely interested tone. She was so absorbed by her accomplishment that she didn't react to his ironic tone.

'Once past simple atomic weights, we've,' the pronoun, an innocuous detail in itself, raised Afra's hackles, 'gone on to solar systems. His has twelve planets and two asteroid belts.'

'What sort of planet does his species inhabit?'

Damia shot him a quick glance, then laughed uneasily. 'That's strange. We didn't establish that.'

'And how did you answer his query about Aurigae?'

She was more alert now and her eye contact was wary. Then she grinned cockily. 'I gave the same detail he did. Without, dear Affa,' her use of her baby name for him underlined her impudence, 'disclosing any more than the number of planets, moons et cetera. I'm not a fool!' She hauled herself out of her semi-recumbent position and made a show of tossing her hair back.

'You've never been a fool, Damia,' Afra replied coolly. 'Nor am I catechizing you. I cooked dinner tonight.'

'Did you?' and she seized on that topic with obvious relief. 'You're a better cook than any other man I know.'

Afra decided that she had redeemed her use of 'Affa' with that unsolicited praise. One day, maybe, they'd confront each other as functioning adults . . . Ruthlessly he suppressed the *eros* and reinstated the *philia* and began to serve her a much-needed meal.

The third morning, as Damia sat in the Tower, she worked with such haste that Afra was obliged to reprimand her. She gaily corrected herself, making far too negligent a response. Then, eagerly she propelled herself out to make the rendezvous. When she returned that evening so tired that she reeled into the room, Afra took command.

'I'm going with you tomorrow, Damia,' he said firmly.

'What for?' She glared at him from the couch into which she had sunk. 'I'd know the sting-pzzzt of Beetles.

And there isn't even a trace of that about Sodan.'

'Sodan?'

Damia flushed at the crack in his voice but did not evade eye contact with him. 'That's how he identifies himself. Furthermore, I inserted the concept of other sentient life forms and he denied knowledge of any.'

Afra decided not to challenge that information. 'What do you mean by the sting-pzzzt of Beetles? The Deneb Penetration happened before you were even conceived.'

She rose and came to sit at the counter where Afra was fixing their dinner plates, she gave a casual shrug. 'When we were exploring around Grandmother's farm, we often found bits and pieces of Beetle metal. Uncle Rhodri was still paying by the weight for their junk.' She gave Afra a teasing grin. 'It made a comfortable addition to the measly pocket money Isthia allowed us. Larak and I decided that there was sting—' now she wet the tip of one finger and placed it on the counter surface, making the 'pzzzt' sound, '—in Beetle metal. There's no sting-pzzzt about Sodan.' She sounded entirely confident.

It disturbed Afra to know that this entity had a name. It made the alien seem amiable/approachable. Nor could Afra quite reason away the unusual lilt with which Damia spoke the name.

'Fair enough,' Afra said, with an indifference he didn't feel as he passed her a plate. 'However, the lack of sting-pzzzt is not going to reassure Earth Prime. Tomorrow take me along for the ride. There'll be no need to introduce me. All I need to do is confirm your sense of the aura. I certainly wouldn't want to jeopardize whatever rapport you've managed to build. He'll never realize I've been there.' Afra yawned.

'Why are *you* tired?'

'I've been stevedoring all day,' he said with a malicious grin.

'How? Who?' Damia demanded, indignantly. 'There was nothing urgent on the schedule when I went off.'

'No, there wasn't, but there was a minor mine disaster where the Tower could assist. Then a delayed shipment of spare parts was signalled in from Procyon, and a freighter with some perishables and a
covey of prospective immigrants came through.'

'Damn them! They were taking advantage of you, Afra! Towers have protocol to avoid collisions and confusions. Especially on inbound 'ports. Unscheduled shipments . . . ' Then she stopped for he was grinning at her. She let out a gusty sigh. 'I know.' She waved her hand irritably. 'Phrases out of mother's mouth. But . . . '

Afra waggled a finger at her. 'You set the precedent at Aurigae Tower, Damia, by being so cooperative that miners and shippers assume that you're ready, willing and able when need arises.'

'This smells heavenly,' she said artlessly as she loaded her fork.

'Hah!' Afra said, refusing to be diverted.

'And it is,' she said through her first mouthful. 'Lovely seasoning.'

'Thank you. By the way, that crew of yours is really excellent. Even the generator behaved. Have some chopped fruit. Takes the edge off that pepper.'

They ate companionably, though Damia's appetite seemed to be affected by her fatigue for she usually went for seconds of one of his special meals. She did ask for details of the mine problem – a line of ore carts had slipped off the cable, causing an obstruction in the shaft which Afra and the Tower folk were able to shift so there was no significant loss of time. When he asked her what else she had discussed with Sodan, she had trouble formulating sentences despite a resurgence of animation on that subject.

'Don't stand on ceremony with me, Damia,' Afra finally said when she didn't even have the energy to groom Merfy when the animal brought her the brush. 'Here, I'll do Merfy. You go to bed. Sleep well.'

Such exhaustion for one so vibrantly healthy worried Afra even more than her emotional involvement with this Sodan entity. It no longer mattered that the intruder was unrelated to the species that had attacked Deneb; he was a menace in himself.

The next day, after 'porting out medium-sized drones of refined ores, Damia told Keylarion to inform any callers that the Tower was on hold for repairs to the generator that Xexo now said were critical. Then she and Afra settled into their personal capsules. Afra followed Damia's thrust and held himself silent as she reached the area where she could touch the aura of Sodan. To his relief, Damia had no hesitation when Afra asked permission to establish a light link in her mind. So she carried them both to the alien ship. As soon as the alien touch impinged on Afra's awareness, much was suddenly clear to him: much seen, and worse, much unseen.

What Damia could not, would not, or did not see justified Afra's nagging presentiment of danger. Nothing out of Sodan's mind was visible: and nothing beyond his public mind was accessible. The alien had a powerful mentality. As a quiescent eavesdropper, Afra could not probe, but he widened his own sensitivity to its limit and the impressions he received served to increase his intuition of danger.

There was absolutely no comparison between Sodan and the Deneb invasion species. Damia was correct in that evaluation. One impression which surprised Afra was that of an almost interminable journey. And excitement at an end in sight. Yet how Afra could grasp that concept from a mind that did not yet speak in a known language, he did not know. But those were the impressions he grasped.

Damia would not expect Afra to linger once he had satisfied his stated errand. But, fascinated by the contact, he did linger, discovering other unsettling aspects. Sodan's mind, undeniably brilliant, was nevertheless augmented. Afra couldn't perceive whether Sodan was the focus for other minds on the ship or in gestalt with the ship's power source. Straining his nerves and senses to the limit without revealing his presence, Afra tried to pierce the visual screen or, at least, the aural one. All he received was a low stereo babble of mechanical activity, and the burn of heavy elements, the latter sufficiently disturbing in itself. Yet how did a species without a visual faculty function on such a sophisticated level? To be sure, antennae of various sorts relayed a tremendous amount of information to an intelligent mind: sensors and optics imitated vision but it was the sight of stars that had lured Mankind into space. What had been this alien's goad to cross intergalactic space?

Worried and frustrated, Afra withdrew, leaving Sodan and Damia to exchange abstracts that, to him, were also the ploys of emotional attraction. He returned to Aurigae and sought the Tower couch. He felt completely drained by the brief jaunt. That was in itself unnerving. He'd planned to contact Larak on Procyon without having to gestalt. But he knew that was impossible just then. Carefully assuming a light tone, he asked Keylarion to bring a generator on line for him.

'We've three if you need them,' the T-6 replied helpfully.

'No, one's enough.' And Afra hoped that it would be. For a T-3, one should be sufficient. He scrubbed at his face while he watched the gauge on number one generator climb to sending level. It was not, Afra assured himself, that Damia had deliberately concealed anything in her reports to him or to Jeff: she was entirely unaware that her usually keen perceptions were fuddled and distorted by the fatigue levels caused by contact with this alien. And Damia had been spending hours dealing abstracts at Sodan? He exhaled noisily and wondered if a cup of coffee would have a reviving effect. But the needle reached the required level even as Keylarion verified readiness to him.

Even with the gestalt, 'pathing to Larak was an effort.

Larak, Afra called, leaning heavily into the power and projecting his own mental/physical concept of Larak to aid him in reaching the boy's mind.

Man, you're beat, Larak answered, his touch sharp, clear, green.

Larak, relay back to Jeff that this Sodan—

It's got a name?

It's got more than that and Damia is responding on a very high emotional level, Afra sighed heavily. *This entity has no resemblance to the Deneb Penetration species. No Beetle sting—*

What? Oh, yeah, I remember. Larak's projection of a grin was oddly comforting to Afra.

But there's something very insidious about this Sodan individual. A few moments in its company and I'm so shagged that I needed gestalt to reach you.

You? That was enough to remove the grin from Larak's voice.

Please inform Jeff that I consider this situation of a highly volatile – and possibly dangerous – nature. I want you out here as soon as possible on any pretext so I can get through to Earth Prime without requiring either Damia or gestalt. And— Afra paused to emphasize the next request, *please ask both Jeff and the Rowan to remain available to me on demand.*

What has my darling sister found this time! Larak responded with an impressed whistle.

Get Mick and Mauli to push you out here as soon as you can relay that message, huh, Larak, like a good lad?

Coming, Larak responded crisply.

Afra leaned back in the couch and flicked off the generator. The exchange had taken no more than thirty seconds: not long enough for Keylarion to take particular note or even log it into the station records. Not that Damia would check the station log if she returned: she'd be too tired, he thought grimly. How did that entity cause such enervation? Why? Afra brooded. Perhaps he was being over-sensitive because Damia was so absorbed by this contact. He had half-hoped, when Jeff told him to go to Aurigae, that he might have a chance to attract Damia as he had so long wanted to do. Perhaps he was acting prematurely to call Larak in. Perhaps he could handle the Sodan mind himself.

No, Afra told himself candidly, not when you're reduced to a limp rag after a vicarious touch. And not with the competition Sodan was providing.

Hey, Afra, what does a guy have to do to get your attention? was Larak's cheery greeting as he bounced up the Tower steps.

His energy seemed almost obscene to the weary T-3.

'Knock twice!' Afra replied but he grinned gratefully as he extended his hand to the visitor. The vigour which Larak exuded was as much a restorative as the infectiousness of his smile. The resemblance between Larak and his sister was pronounced, even to having the Gwyn slash of white in the same position on their black-haired heads. Larak was not quite as tall as his sister who was unusually tall, and more slightly built than his brothers. But he had full measure of the Raven charm and Afra found the energy to return the boy's smile.

Hands now touching, Afra conveyed the one impression he had not included in the broadcast.

Damia's infatuated with this peculiarly dangerous alien? Larak murmured, surprised, and looked hard into Afra's eyes. 'Wouldn't you know she'd have weird and exotic tastes!' He let his lips turn down sympathetically. *Why can't she pick on the home-brewed?* He cocked his head at Afra.

Afra felt it expedient to ignore that comment. 'A very dangerous alien, unfortunately. Do you remember that old scare tale about soul-eaters?'

Larak rolled his eyes wide. 'You just bet I do. Damia terrorized me into starting a forest fire with that tale of hers. Wait a minute. You think this alien's a soul-eater?' Larak was almost indignant at the notion. 'Hey, Afra, that was kid stuff.'

'I can't think of another analogue. I spent no more than ten or fifteen seconds, in a light secondary link, and I had to use gestalt to reach you at Procyon.'

'That's not good,' Larak said. 'That's very bad. What's wrong with Damia? Doesn't she realize . . . No, obviously she doesn't.' Larak slid into the second comformable couch, his eyes flickering as he considered and discarded thoughts.

'Damia mentioned the residue you two felt from Beetle artifacts. There's something comparable to your sting on board Sodan's vessel. And it's not comfortable.'

'Fissionables?' Larak asked.

Afra shook his head. 'It is very alien. I couldn't define it.'

'Can Damia?'

Afra grimaced. 'She's involved in translating abstracts.'

'Those'll be a great help if he plans to blow us up.' Larak tensed. 'What has she said about us? The League?'

'From what she reports, she's been discreet.'

'That's a mercy.'

Afra could sense that Larak's flippancy disguised a concern for Damia as deep as his own. Larak had always been closest to her. 'I wouldn't mind what they discussed,' he said, 'but Sodan leaves her so drained.'

'New kind of weapon – total enervation before annihilation?'

'That's not as outrageous as you think,' Afra said grimly. 'There's a tremendous power source in the ship . . . '

'There'd have to be to push it between galaxies . . . '

'But that's all I could sense. Beyond the public mind, I met an impenetrable wall. Granted, Damia's much stronger than I am . . . '

'But she hasn't tried?'

Afra frowned, and rising, began to pace restlessly back and forth in the narrow Tower.

Larak held Afra's glance, and then sighed.

'But there's been no overt act of aggression?'

'That depends on what you call "aggression". I believe that Sodan is subtly trying to destroy Damia in the process of this peaceful exchange of culture and information. In my lexicon, eroding her mental capability is an assault with intent to maim or kill.' He saw that remark succeeded in arousing all Larak's natural fraternal concern and protectiveness. 'I could be overreacting. I'm no pre-cog but there are instances in which one doesn't need to be to guess intent. Judge for yourself when you see Damia this evening.'

Larak did not bother to shield his anger. 'I will but I've never seen you overreact, Afra. Apart from the danger to my sister, just how close is this Sodan to Iota Aurigae? Close enough to recognize this system as Damia's point of origin?'

Afra managed a wry grin. 'You're a real Tower-man, Lar.'

Larak gave a quick unhumourous grin. 'A Gwyn-Raven, body, blood and brain!'

'Logically,' Afra continued, 'we have to allow him the same sophistication in monitoring devices as he has in travel capability. So he's certain to detect sufficient activity on this planet to attract,' and Afra paused, searching for the appropriate phrase, 'his attention. Since a high tech society gobbles ores, minerals and rare earths at phenomenal rates, it is reasonable to assume that he's crossed to our galaxy to find new sources.'

'Are we assuming aggression where none exists?' Larak asked, playing devil's advocate.

Afra paused, 'We could be. The Beetles made their plans exceedingly clear but they might be exceptions to the rule of peaceful exploration. Only I cannot get it out of my mind that the Sodan is deliberately depleting Damia's energy to reduce her ability to defend herself. And I've never had such a presentiment of danger before – not even when I was mind-merged with the Rowan-focus over Deneb.'

'If we must eradicate the threat this Sodan entity poses, I'd say it would be wiser to do it now, rather than later when he's closer to this system,' Larak replied, pressing his lips tight against that expedient. 'Should we call for naval backup?'

'Ha! Sodan'd be orbiting Aurigae before the Fleet would bestir itself to action,' Afra replied derisively.

'Especially right now,' and Larak's grin was amused, 'when they're investigating the nibbles at Procyon's DEW system.'

'What?' Afra stared at Larak, struck by a horror of several Sodans converging on the Nine Star League.

Larak was delighted at the effect of that casual statement. 'They're keeping it to a need-to-know basis but don't worry. So far it's been limited to unidentifiable impingements,' and Larak shook his head vigorously to reassure the Capellan, 'and neither the scouts nor all that sensitive instrumentation has revealed anything in the least bit hostile. Those sentinels are sensitive enough to be set off by spaceflot or cometaries. This Sodan's *modus operandi* seems to be entirely different. We Talents destroyed the Beetles more or less by ourselves. I think we can handle this mental giant.'

Afra gave a mirthless laugh. 'We'll be lucky if we can.' He nodded briskly when Larak regarded him with astonishment. 'Oh, yes, that mind is incredibly powerful. Not at all like the Beetles where there were only sixteen control beings that had to be diverted. And, if he has been insidiously reducing Damia's strength or getting past her shields . . . ' Afra paused, adding very softly, his yellow eyes clouded, 'he could quite possibly destroy us.'

'Let's get Dad and Mother in on this,' Larak said in sudden resolution.

Together the two soberly presented their conclusions to Jeff and the Rowan.

Surely if you were an alien contacted by a strong mentality, you would exercise caution in revealing details? the Rowan suggested. *I would, if I met a mind in outer space.*

You did, Jeff reminded her, *and I was very friendly indeed.*

Jeff!

If this Sodan is draining Damia, he means her, and us, no good, Jeff went on, speaking in an official tone. *We are agreed that Afra does not cry panic unnecessarily so we must act on his recommendations and now, before this entity gets close enough to investigate the Aurigaen system. Especially before he discovers the Aurigaen system and the rich lodes on that planet. I'm also keenly aware of how little defence Iota Aurigae has against space attack.*

You concur with Afra that he's prospecting for new sources of raw materials? the Rowan asked, in a tone of indecision.

That's our main push in finding new planets, isn't it? Larak said.

If Damia is as exhausted as you suggest, Afra, how can we use her as focus? In the first place, she's not likely to agree to take aggressive action against an entity she considers friendly. She spoke as Damia's mother, not Callisto Prime.

No, she's not, Afra said sourly.

And yet we need to use her link to his mind to make our own contact. There's also the point that, Jeff continued, not at all liking the expedient, *if we do discover, and prove to her, that this Sodan entity is truly dangerous, to her, to Aurigae, to us, that we may need her catalytic ability to increase our defence against him.*

Each day Damia returns to Aurigae a little more tired than the previous one, Afra said slowly. *I was immeasurably drained after only a few moments in link. That's never happened to me before.*

I think Afra's correct to call him a soul-eater, Larak put in.

There's no such thing, the Rowan said sharply.

I don't know what else to call him that's as accurate, Afra said. *Or how else to describe the effect he has on her.*

In any case, Jeff said firmly, *I find it disturbing to think of her immense natural energy being depleted.*

Highly unlikely. The Rowan bristled with indignation.

Let us conclude this swiftly, Larak cautioned them. *Damia's returning and . . . WOW! Is she dragging!*

Afra suppressed annoyance that the curious childhood link between sister and brother gave Larak the edge in sensing her return. But, as Afra reached out to touch her mentally, her aura was very dim indeed. He concentrated on the lightning debate that Jeff, Rowan and Larak carried on, as decision and strategy were settled in the moment before Damia's capsule landed in its cradle.

'Larak, I couldn't believe I felt your touch,' she cried happily as she saw her brother, the picture of casual relaxation, perched on the edge of the console.

'Believe it, sister dear, your favourite bro is here,' he said, rising to embrace her. 'This alien sure has got you wrapped up and tied like a present. See how the mighty have fallen.' When Damia flushed, Larak roared with laughter. 'I've got to meet a guy who can do this to my sister.'

'Really, Larak, how puerile! You obviously have no conception of what a momentous occasion this is. I've always felt that I was given unusual strengths and abilities for a special reason,' Damia said, her eyes shining, 'and now I know what it is!'

'The whole planet will know in a moment if you don't reduce your output,' Afra said sharply, to give Larak a chance to control his shock at her extraordinary remark.

With some resentment, Damia dampened down her emotional outpouring.

'I suppose you arrived with an appetite like a mule,' she said with some resignation.

Larak's expression was a study of innocent hurt.

'I'm a growing boy, and while you're out courting, Afra's getting overworked, leaner and hungrier.'

Damia looked guiltily at Afra.

'You *do* look tired,' she said with concern. 'Let's all push over to the house and have dinner. Larak, why are you here?'

'Oh, Dad wants Afra to pinch-hit on Procyon. Those two Ts who're buffering Guzman are down with one of the local viruses and traffic is backing up. You know we have to jolly Guzzie along but he hasn't much stamina these days. He's complained that I'm too young for such responsibility,' and Larak's grin was pure malice. 'Say, what's this alien ship of yours like? Crew or full automation for a void trek?'

Hand poised over the cooking dials, Damia hesitated. She regarded her brother with a blank expression.

'Oh, you men are all alike. Details, details!'

'*Details* like that may bore you, sister heart, but they fascinate me. But if you want to continue on the abstract level, let me catch such mundane details for myself.'

'You can't reach that far.'

To Afra her tone was protective as well as defensive.

'Let me hop a ride with you tomorrow, then,' Larak snagged a raw vegetable stick from the crisper and seemed more interested in its taste than her agreement.

Damia hesitated, looking for support from Afra, who shrugged 'why not' as he followed Larak's example and savoured a crunchy white root with a slightly aniseed flavour. She caught no more than that from Afra's mind when she sent a swift probe. And, he was certain, no more than that from Larak's if she tried her brother. Even as close as they were, her probe was a poor imitation of her customary mental dig.

'C'mon, sis, what's to be coy for?'

'I'm not being coy!' Her temper flared in irritation, then subsided. 'It's just that . . . just that . . . these are very delicate stages in establishing a rapport . . . '

'Delicate? Rapport?' Larak blurted out, staring at her as if he couldn't believe his ears. 'You're making a first contact, not a first date! That is, if it's even marginally humanoid.'

'His is a true mind, brilliant, powerful,' she said haughtily. 'The form is immaterial.'

'Oh?' Larak's mobile face expressed extreme doubt. 'Never thought you'd fall for the cerebral type, Damia, not the way you've developed.' He eyed her, not as a brother, but as an interested male.

Damia reddened, half with fury and indignation, and half with a sudden virtuous embarrassment for her brother's accurate jibe.

'Ever since you and Jenna propagated a child, you've turned insufferable! Why, if I hadn't been out here, we wouldn't have been warned at all.'

'Warned?' Afra leapt on the choice of word. Perhaps she was not as completely bedazzled as they'd thought.

'Of this momentous occasion,' she went on, oblivious to the implication. 'You've touched Sodan, Afra. Don't you agree that his feat of crossing to another galaxy is momentous?'

'Yes, it is,' Afra said tactfully. 'Only a brilliant mind could accomplish such a feat.'

Damia caught an undertone he wasn't quick enough to suppress. 'Oh, you! You're jealous! Jealous?' Damia eyed Afra closely, plainly struggling with this new dimension to her oldest ally.

'And you're also letting dinner burn,' Larak said, pointing to a sizzling pan.

'Don't either of you know better than to distract a cook with stupid questions?' she demanded, quickly shifting the pan. 'It's a mercy nothing *is* burned!'

She served them, irritated that her dinner was not as perfect as usual, and the two men could think of no way to break the strained silence, especially as both had to concentrate on maintaining a convincing level of trivial surface thoughts. They hardly needed to use such a subterfuge because Damia went off into a private reverie, ignoring them completely.

Finally, Larak pushed back his plate, having finished every scrap on his plate and what was left over in the pans.

'Even with half your mind on what you're doing, sis, you're a great cook,' Larak said, wiping his mouth and sighing with repletion. 'So! This Sodan entity is clearly not a new reconnaissance device of the Deneb Beetles?' Larak looked from Damia to Afra who shook his head quickly in denial.

'No question of that,' Afra replied. 'Totally different mentality . . . ' He ignored Damia's snort, 'and vehicle. There is an impression of immense distances traversed, far longer than the twenty years since the Deneb Entanglement.'

Larak whistled appreciatively, as if this was news to him.

'You didn't happen to catch any details about propulsion and power which my sweet sister would not deign to notice?'

'No, actually, for there were no obvious visual images to be sensed and I was only concerned with identification. Clearly this entity isn't a Beetle.'

'Stop calling Sodan an "entity",' Damia said. 'That's rude. And he has eyes,' she added defensively. 'We've discussed the concept of sight. You must take into consideration that he is also in control of the ship, and the drain on his energies to reach me as well as manage ship function and crew is enormous. It certainly is on me.'

'Yeah. You could do with some beauty sleep, sis,' said Larak.

'Thanks muchly,' she said, bridling.

'Children! Cut it out!' Afra intervened out of habit.

Larak and Damia glared at each other, but the long habit of obeying Afra held.

‘Get to bed, the pair of you,’ he added. ‘Snarling at each other in the worst example of sibling rivalry I’ve seen since you graduated from Isthia’s fosterage,’ and now he gave Damia his full disapproval. ‘Makes me wonder how your father dared install you as Aurigae Prime.’

‘If there’s anything that annoys me more than Larak acting fraternal, it’s you, Afra, being avuncular.’ She spoke coolly, but her flare of temper had been controlled.

Afra shrugged, relieved that his diversion had worked before Larak inadvertently disclosed to Damia why he was fielding these particular queries.

‘At least this avuncular entity has sense enough to go to bed when he’s out on his feet,’ he murmured. As he passed Larak, the boy winked.

The next morning at breakfast, no-one looked particularly rested by a night’s sleep. Afra kept a surface rumble going on his mind to mask both tension and anxiety. Larak delivered a running monologue about his son’s developing intelligence and Jenna’s maternal charms. Damia was also closely shielding. When the three reached the Tower, Damia took the most cursory glance at station business, noting that cargo was light and the few messages were standard communications.

‘I’ll take you out now, Larak, and then you’ll be free to handle the afternoon despatches.’

‘Fine. Dad wants Afra on Procyon as soon as I’ve taken over from him.’

Damia hesitated, then jutted her chin out. ‘I suppose you want to come along again, too,’ she said, flinging the challenge at Afra who merely shrugged.

‘I wouldn’t mind another gawk. Fascinating mind,’ Afra said casually. He was intensely grateful to whatever quirk had prompted her to make such an offer. He’d thought he’d have to surreptitiously follow Damia and Larak. With such distances to travel, he’d been nervous of losing even their combined touch.

'You two get settled. I can follow if Damia's leading,' Afra said, boosting the generators to their peak. Xexo had got the ailing one back on line, for which Afra was extremely grateful.

As Damia and Larak left the Tower for their capsules, he contacted Jeff and the Rowan to stand by, then settled into his own shell, reassured by their sustaining presence in his mind.

Is there any possible chance we're wrong about Sodan's intentions, or the depth of Damia's emotional commitment? the Rowan asked hopefully.

Less and less, Afra told her grimly. *We'll know soon for certain. Larak needled her last night. She'll have to check to make sure he's wrong about Sodan.*

Then Afra touched Damia and Larak, and all three went the mere half light-year further to the ship, and Sodan.

You have rested well and are strong today, was the cool greeting after an instant's welcoming flash.

Damia instinctively covered against the discovery of her co-riders, but the greeting stuck in her mind. She could not escape the inference that Sodan was displeased with her strength, yet a tinge of relief coloured that fleck of thought.

You come nearer to physical contact with us every day, she began.

Us? Sodan queried.

My planet, my people . . . me.

I'm only interested in you, he replied.

Damia was unable to censor from Afra and Larak the pleasure she felt in that qualification. *That is between us but my people will be interested in you,* she said adroitly.

There are many people on your planets? he asked.

Planet.

Doesn't your sun have several life-supporting satellites?

That is why I must know more about your physical

requirements, Sodan, Damia replied smoothly. *After all, my home world may not have the proper atmosphere.*

My physical needs are admirably sustained by my ship, Sodan said brusquely, with the slightest of emphasis on the second word.

It was the Rowan who caught the infinitesimal break in his shielding, and simultaneously all four minds stabbed at the gap to widen it. Sodan, torn by this powerful invasion, lashed back in self-defence with a vicious blow at Damia who, he thought, had perpetrated the onslaught.

No! No! Not I, Sodan, she shrieked. *Larak, what are you doing?*

Struggling frantically, Afra tried to become the focus of the other minds, only to find himself caught in Larak's mind with the Rowan and Jeff, as the curious bond between brother and sister snapped into effect.

He must be destroyed before he can destroy you, Damia, the Larak-focus said, tingeing its inexorable decision with the regret it felt.

No! I love him. His mind is so brilliant, cried Damia, pitting her strength against her peers to defend her lover. The Larak-focus staggered, unable to prosecute their attack against such a combination.

Damia, he is only a mind!

Stunned, Damia hesitated, and the Larak-focus plunged forward again, battering against Sodan's shielding.

Only mind? she gasped, begging Sodan to deny it.

Why no vision? Why no sound? He is only a brain, devoid of all except remembered emotion. He is slowly depleting your strength so that he is free to attack this system. You are its only defence. Did you never realize that? Feel the dangerous substances this ship carries? Is that customary for a peaceful exploratory expedition?

You're against me, against me. No-one wants me to be happy, cried Damia, suddenly aware, terribly aware of her loving blindness. *He loves me. I love him.*

If he has nothing to hide, he will reveal his reason for crossing the void, the Larak-focus said, implacably intent. *Is it truly peaceful? Or is it acquisitive? Why do we search out new worlds? Or is it because his galaxy is so depleted that he must search elsewhere for the rare metals that are required for more vessels like his?*

Reassure me, Sodan, Damia pleaded, desperately, hopefully. *Tell them you come in peace? To find other sentient beings, to establish friendly relations?*

For what seemed an eternity, Sodan hesitated.

If I could, I would, he said softly and with honest regret.

Like a vengeful blade, her mind, freed from the infatuation which Sodan had artfully fostered and, strengthened by her righteous indignation, launched itself with the others to destroy the aggressor. For Damia could now comprehend Sodan's purpose and knew his disembodiment. The battle was waged in the tremendous space between two heartbeats. Sodan, his mind fortified by the exotic power of his ship, was stronger than their conservative estimates. Almost negligently, he held the Larak-focus at bay, his mind laughing at what he considered their puny efforts.

Then, the veil of her romantic illusions stripped from her perceptions, Damia increased her pressure and aligned herself with the Larak-focus. Sodan called for more power within himself. The scorching blaze that fed through Damia's resurgent and catalytic mind flashed through and stripped him bare, lashing beyond to trigger the metallic structure of the ship into instability. Involuntarily, and for a microsecond, the Larak-focus caught a glimpse of what Sodan had been.

Once, generations ago, embodied, he had breathed an alien air, propelled his curious body along alien roads; until his brain had been chosen to undertake the incredible enterprise of crossing the galactic rift.

In my fashion have I loved you, he cried to Damia as he

felt her reach the fuel mass. *But you never really loved me,* he added with intense surprise as her mind, vulnerable in the instant of that massive thrust, was open to him. *And he shall not have you!*

With his last strength, Sodan sent out one final mental flare just as the ship exploded.

Even as Damia felt herself blacking out from the tremendous battering, she frantically tried to deflect that shaft.

As a kingpin flattens a row of its fellows, so Sodan's blast, striking through the Larak-focus, caused a wave of mental agony to roll backwards to Aurigae where station personnel grabbed at their skulls in anguish and all four generators seized up in overload; to Earth and Callisto where T-ratings cringed in pain and on to Procyon where old Guzman's valiant heart stopped. Horrified crews found Jeff Raven and the Rowan unconscious in their Tower couches and sent for Elizara and her teams. Jeran on Deneb had certainly been aware of an incredible psionic backlash. He was hastily summoned to Earth since FT&T command devolved to him in the emergency. Jeran took time to assure himself that with sufficient rest his parents would recover, then he officially informed the Nine Star League of the event. He was requested to join, and 'port units of a Fleet squadron to Aurigae. In his turn, he sent for his grandmother, asking Isthia to bring the specialists she had trained to revive overstressed Talents. With Elizara's help, he and Isthia were able to extract gently from Jeff's taxed mind the position of the three personnel shells.

As the Fleet squadron neared the relevant spatial co-ordinates, Jeran and Isthia on board the flagship could 'hear' nothing. Then the ship's sensitive equipment located the three capsules.

It is possible, Isthia said, trying to be positive in the absence of any mental aura from the shells, *that all three are in very deep shock. The power in Damia's final thrust!*

Damia cannot be dead. Jeran allowed himself the luxury of believing in his grandmother's optimism. *We cannot lose her!* He had forced himself to accept other losses. *Sodan may have been powerful but is there a T-rating in the galaxy who didn't feel her hit him?*

'Ah!' Isthia gave a sharp gasp. *I have them.* And she signalled for Jeran and her team to assist, leaning into the ship's engines to 'port the capsules aboard.

'Damia's alive,' Jeran cried in relief, having made that his first priority. *I thought I felt them all die.*

'Afra lives, too, but he's very faint. Larak . . . ' and Isthia's voice faded. *Why did the focus have to snap through him?*

They opened Afra's capsule first, and sighed with pity at the lean form drawn up in the foetal position of complete withdrawal. Jeran thought his heart would break, remembering the vibrant man who had been as much a part of his life and learning as his parents.

'He's so badly hurt, Isthia. Can we save him?' *Should we . . . if he'll be psionically numb for the rest of his life?* he asked on the tightest possible band.

Isthia raised her eyebrows in a scathing rejection of that suggestion. 'I've pulled minds back from worse than this, Jeran Gwyn-Raven. Move aside.' With a touch skilled and delicate, she put her hands on Afra's temples. Jeran saw her eyes cloud with anxiety.

She sighed, for a brief moment depressed by her examination. 'His dominant desire is death. Which is so totally unlike Afra that I shall ignore it. I don't intend that he should succumb to death right now. However, his life force is critically low and must be carefully revived.' She gave rapid mental orders to the medics standing by so that, within seconds, Afra was receiving emergency injections and two highly skilled metamorphic practitioners began the routines that had once restored her son, Jeff, from a nadir that bordered extinction.

Afra'll need some subtle encouragements, Jeran, to overcome that death wish. Divorce your emotions, Isthia told him sharply. *Put your fingers over mine. Help me reach him. We have to reverse that wish before it succeeds.*

Jeran gave himself a stern shake and, holding his breath, placed his fingers lightly over Isthia's at Afra's temples.

He let his mind be guided by hers in the gentlest of probes, ignoring the mental anguish they experienced at having to touch so torn a mind. Uppermost was the thought that both Larak and Afra had shared: Sodan striking at them and Damia, exhausted, trying to block his final shaft.

He'll kill her! He'll kill her! was the repeated cry of terror, a curious melding of both Larak and Afra, swirling in the pain of Afra's mind. *No, Damia! Don't try! I waited too long. No, Damia! You'll be killed. You mustn't. Why did I wait so long? Too long. No, Damia. Don't try . . .* and the sequence was repeated.

Damia lives! Damia lives! Isthia accepted the fact that Afra would not care to live if he thought Damia was dead. But she was alive and he must be convinced of this. She urged Jeran to reinforce her message. He provided a baritone level to her soprano chant. *Damia lives. Damia lives, Afra. Damia lives!*

Damia lives? Damia lives, Damia lives. The response was the merest whisper of hope from an overtaxed psyche.

Isthia caught Jeran's eyes, hope widening hers.

Yes, that's exactly what he needed to know. Let's reinforce it. Together they repeated their encouraging litany. *Afra, Damia lives. She rests. She waits for you. Damia lives, Afra. She waits for you.*

Sleep, Afra, Isthia added then with the most delicate urgency. *Sleep and rest. Damia lives.*

Damia lives? Damia lives? Damia lives!

With a shudder, Afra's subconscious finally accepted that reassurance. His body relaxed from its foetal curl. For one terrifying moment, he was absolutely still. Gasping, Isthia dipped way down into the suddenly tranquil mind before she realized that Afra had merely slipped into deep sleep.

'He's badly hurt,' Isthia admitted sadly as they watched the medics wheel Afra away to a tightly shielded room where no mental noise could intrude. 'But he'll live.' Jeran did not try to read whatever reservations she might entertain.

They opened Damia's capsule together. She lay on her side, looking very young, but there were marks that showed the effects of that meeting of minds. She had bitten through her lower lip; a trickle of blood had made a scarlet line across her cheek. Her face was streaked with tears. Her fingernails had cut into her palms when she had clenched her fists. Her closed eyes looked bruised by deep and dark circles.

With great compassion, Isthia turned the girl on to her back and laid both hands lightly on Damia's temples.

I can't reach them. I can't get there in time. I hurt. I've got to try. I burn. Oh, will I lose them both? Isthia could hear the words, a faint loop of thought in the deepest recesses of a scorched and overstretched mind.

With a sigh of relief, Isthia straightened.

She's badly burned? Jeran asked anxiously, having waited outside Isthia's contact but aware it had been made.

Scorched, overstretched right now, and deeply hurt. Damia's been reduced, Isthia remarked ruefully, *in the terrible way that only the very bright and very confident can be diminished.*

Diminished? Jeran was both Prime and brother at that moment.

In pride and self-confidence, Isthia qualified with a sad smile. *Her Talent is far too robust to suffer any permanent effect. Her ego, however, will. She'll never forget that she underestimated Sodan's potential danger because she became infatuated with her perception of him.*

For all of that, if she hadn't touched him first, where would we be with such a menace zeroing in from space?

That's the Prime in you speaking, Isthia said, but her

tone was complimentary. *Although let's hope that eventually Damia can see this incident from that perspective. Right now she'll grieve terribly because her lapse in judgement caused Larak's death and has seriously injured Afra.*

But, Isthia, once the attack on Sodan began, nothing could have saved Larak as focus-mind. Death is far kinder than being burned out. She's not to blame for that.

Isthia shook her head sadly. *She'll never see it that way. But I devoutly hope that it never occurs to her that, in the final moment, instinct overrode reason and it was Afra she struggled to save.*

Afra? What the hell? Jeran stared at her blankly before he followed her thought to its conclusion. *Sodan tried to kill Afra? Wasn't he aiming at the entire focus?*

Not from what I gathered from Jeff and Rowan.

Isthia signalled to the medics to administer deep-sleep drugs and intravenous nourishment to Damia.

With great reluctance then, they turned to Larak's shell. Because they had to, they opened it and saw with some little relief that there was no mark of the violence of his death on the young face. A curiously surprised smile lingered on his lips.

Isthia turned away in tears and Jeran, too numbed by the total tragedy to display his own sorrow, put his arm around her to lead her away.

'Prime,' the captain of the ship said respectfully when they entered the control room, 'we have located the debris of the alien ship. Permission to recover the fragments?'

'Permission granted. Isthia and I will return to the Tower. Signal when you're ready to be 'ported, Captain.'

'Very good, sir,' the captain said and stiffened to a rigid attention. The unashamed tears in his eyes and his very crisp salute expressed wordlessly his pride, his sympathy and his sorrow.

Struggling against a will determined to keep her asleep,

Damia fought her way to semi-consciousness.

'I can't keep her under. She's resisting,' a remote voice rang in peals.

As distant as the sound was, like a far echo in a subterranean cavern, each syllable fell like a hammer on her exposed nerves. Sobbing, Damia struggled for consciousness, sanity, and a release from this agony. She couldn't seem to trigger the reflexes that would divert pain, and an effort to call Afra to help her met with not only the resistance of increased agony but a vast blackness. Her mind was as stiff as iron, holding each thought firmly to it as though magnetized in place.

'Damia, do not reach. Do not use your mind,' a gentle voice said in her ear. She recognized the voice as Isthia's and her grandmother's presence restored her wavering sanity. She felt the touch of Isthia's cool capable hands on her forehead.

Damia opened her eyes and tried to focus on the face above her. With trembling, weak hands she pressed Isthia's fingers against her temples in an unconscious plea for relief of pain.

'What happened? Why can't I control my mind?' Damia cried, tears of weakness streaming down her face.

'You rather stretched yourself, destroying Sodan,' Isthia said. 'But you did get him, you know.'

'I can't remember,' Damia groaned, blinking away tears so she could at least see clearly.

'Every rating in FT&T does.'

'Oh, my head. It's all blank and there's something I've got to do, Isthia.' Damia tried to rise but, though Isthia exerted little pressure, she sank weakly back into the bed. 'I've got something I *must* do only I can't remember what it is.'

'You did do what you must, dear, I assure you. But you've suffered a tremendous trauma, and you must rest,' Isthia said, her voice in the croon that had soothed Damia as a rebellious child. Cool hands stroked her face and she welcomed the relief for her skin felt so hot and hard. Each caress seemed to lessen the terrible pain inside her skull. 'I'm putting you back to sleep now, love,' and Damia felt the coolness of an injection pop into her arm. 'We're very proud of you but you must sleep. Only sleep can heal your mind.'

' "Great nature's second course, that knits the ravelled sleeve of care." What's knitting, Isthia? I've never known.' Even Damia recognized that she was babbling as the cool scalliony taste in her throat heralded the spread of the drug.

Again, after what seemed no passage of time at all, Damia was inexorably forced to consciousness by her indefinably relentless need.

'I can't understand it,' came Isthia's voice. This time it did not reverberate across Damia's pained mind like tympani in a closet. 'That last dose was enough to put a city to sleep.'

'She's worrying at something and probably won't rest until she's resolved it. Let's wake her up and find out.'

The second voice was masculine and sounded vaguely familiar, also vaguely annoyed. With a grateful smile, she labelled it 'Dad'. She felt her face gently slapped and, opening her eyes, saw her father's face swimming out of an indistinct background.

'Dad,' she pleaded, not because he had slapped her but because she had to make him understand.

'Dear Damia,' he said with such loving pride that she almost lost the tenuous thought she tried to hold.

Her body strained with the effort to reach out only a few inches a mind that once had blithely coursed light-years, but she soon managed to communicate her crime.

Larak and Afra! They were ahead of me in the focus. I killed them when I had to destroy Sodan. I must have killed them because I'm still alive!

Behind Jeff she heard her mother's cry and Isthia's exclamation.

'No, no,' Jeff said gently, shaking his head. He placed her hands on his forehead to let her feel the honesty of his denial. 'You're not at fault, dear Damia. Yes, you drew power through the Larak-focus to destroy Sodan and succeeded. Only you were capable of such a magnificent thrust! Furthermore, without you to throw *us* into high gear, Sodan could have destroyed every Prime in FT&T. And that's the truth your mother will verify.'

Damia heard the Rowan murmur affirmatively.

'But I can't hear anything right now,' and in spite of herself, Damia felt her chin quiver and tears of pure terror welled out of her eyes. 'Have I lost my mind?'

'Of course you haven't,' and the Rowan elbowed Jeff to one side to kneel by her daughter and tenderly stroke her hair back from her flushed and tear-stained face. 'You saved us, you know. You really did.'

Isthia moved the Rowan gently but firmly to one side.

'You must go knit some more sleeves of ravelled care, Damia,' Isthia said with therapeutic asperity. 'You knit like this,' and she inserted a visual demonstration of the technique of knitting into Damia's mind. It was an adroit gambit, designed to fragment concentration but Damia saw it for the evasion it was.

'I must be told all that happened,' she demanded imperiously. A wisp of memory nagged at her and she caught it. 'I remember. Sodan made one last thrust at us.' She closed her eyes against that recall, remembering too, that she had tried to intercept it and, 'Larak died,' she said in a flat voice. 'And Afra. I couldn't shield in time.'

'Afra lives,' the Rowan said in a steady voice.

'But Larak doesn't. Why Larak?' Damia demanded, desperately striving to uncover what she felt they were still hiding from her.

'Your brother was the focus, Damia,' the Rowan said softly, knowing, too, that Damia would never absolve herself of Larak's death. 'Afra was supposed to be the focus, being the experienced mind, but the old bond between you and Larak snapped into effect. You tried to shield Larak but he couldn't draw sufficient help from you. Your father and I also tried to support him but he was the focus. Without you to help, we couldn't even have cushioned Afra in time. Sodan's was truly a powerful mentality.'

Damia looked from her mother's face to her father's and knew that they spoke the truth. But a reservation hovered in their eyes and their manner.

'You haven't told me everything,' she said, fighting both immense fatigue and the drugs.

'All right, sceptic,' Jeff said, lifting her into his arms. 'Though there's nothing wrong with your hearing so why it hasn't been assailed by his snores, I do not know. Everyone else is using ear plugs,' he added as he carried her down a dim hall.

Pausing at an open door, he swung her so she could see into the room. A night light hung over the bed, illuminating Afra's quiet face, deeply lined with fatigue and pain. Denying even the physical evidence, Damia reached out, touching just enough for reassurance the distressed mental rumble that meant Afra inhabited his body.

'Damia! Don't do that!' Jeff roared, hurting more than her ears as he bore her back down the hall to her room.

'I won't again but I had to,' she sobbed, her head ballooning with agony.

'And we'll make sure you don't until your mind is completely healed. Out you go, missy,' and she was powerless against the three minds that reinstated the welcome oblivion of sleep.

An insistent whisper nibbled at the corners of her awareness and roused Damia from restorative sleep. Cringing in anticipation of the return of pain, she was mildly surprised to feel only the faintest discomfort. Experimentally, Damia pushed a depressant on the ache and that, too, disappeared. Unutterably pleased by her success, she sat up in bed. It was night and the gentle breeze wafted scents which she recognized as Denebian. She stretched until a cramp caught her in the side.

Heavens, hasn't anyone moved me in months? she asked herself, noting that her mental tone was firm. She lay back in bed, deliberating. *Poor Damia,* she said in a self-derisive tone, *ever since that encounter with that dreadful alien mind, she's been nothing but a T-4. T-9? T-3?* Damia tried out the different ratings for size and then discarded them all, along with her melodrama. *You idiot. You'll never know till you try.*

Tentatively, without apparent effort, she reached out and counted the pulses of another – no, two other – sleepers. Afra's was the faint one. But, Damia realized in calm triumph, it *was* there. Which brought her up sharp against the second fact.

She slid from her bed to stand by the window. Sometime during her last deep slumber, she – and Afra – had been moved to Deneb, to her grandmother's forest retreat. This room looked out on to the back of the clearing in which the house stood. Beyond the lawn of evergrass, beyond the bank of the stream, to where the forest began her glance travelled. And stopped when she saw the white oblong. Instinct told her that Larak was buried there and the thought of Larak buried and his touch forever gone broke her. She wept, biting her knuckles and pressing her arms tightly into her ribs to muffle the sound of her mourning.

Out of the night, out of the stillness, the whisper that had roused her tugged at her again. She stifled her tears to listen, trying to identify that sliver of sound. It faded before she caught it.

Resolutely now, she laid her sorrow gently in the deepest part of her soul, a part of her but apart for ever. No matter what Jeff and the Rowan said, she had caused Larak's death, and maimed Afra. Had she been less preoccupied, less self-centred, she would not have been dazzled by the fancy that Sodan was her Prince Charming, her knight in cylindrical armour.

Such a spoiled child she'd been: egotistical, arrogant, proud, making demands she had no right to request, wanting privileges she had not earned, rewards she was too immature to appreciate . . .

The whisper again, fainter but somehow surer. With a startled cry of joy, Damia whirled from her room, running on light feet down the hall. Catching at the door frame to break her headlong flight, she hesitated on the threshold.

She caught her breath as she realized that Afra was sitting up. He was looking at her with a smile of disbelief on his face.

'*You've* been calling me,' she whispered, half-questioning, half-stating.

'In a lame-brained way,' he replied with a wry half-smile. 'I can't seem to reach beyond the edge of the bed.'

'Don't try. It hurts,' she said quickly, stepping into the room to pause shyly at the foot of the bed.

Afra grimaced, rubbing his temples. 'I know it hurts but I can't seem to find any balance in my skull,' he confessed, his voice uneven, worried. 'Even as a child, I always had that.'

'May I?' she asked formally, unexpectedly timid with him.

Closing his eyes, Afra nodded.

Sitting down as if her slender frame might jar the bed, Damia lightly laid her fingertips to his temples, and touched his mind as delicately as she knew how. Afra stiffened with pain and Damia quickly established a block, regardless of the cost to her own recent recovery. She drew away the pain, laying in the tenderer areas a healing mental anaesthesia. Jealously, she noticed someone else had been tending the damage.

Isthia . . . has . . . a . . . delicate . . . touch, too. He sent the thought with deliberate and slow care.

'Oh, Afra,' Damia cried for the agony the simple phrase cost him. 'You *aren't* burned out. You're no lame-brain either. As if I would let you be. You'll be just as strong as ever. I'll help.'

Afra leaned forward, his face close to hers, his yellow eyes blazing.

'*You'll* help?' he asked in a low intense voice as he searched her face. 'How, Damia?'

Her fingers plucking shyly and nervously at his blanket, Damia could not look away from an Afra who had altered disturbingly. Damia tried to fathom the startling change in this familiar figure. Unable to resort to a mental touch, she saw Afra for the first time with only physical sight. And he was suddenly very different. Very masculine! That was it. All at once, Afra appeared startlingly male to her.

She was appalled to think that she had blundered about so, looking for a mind that was superior to hers: a mind that demanded her respect and admiration, that could lead hers, and support her with sure understanding and empathy. And that mind had always been available! Every time she had needed it – on Deneb, on Callisto, everywhere she'd ever been. Only she hadn't *looked* for it.

'Damia? Speechless?' Afra teased her, his smooth tenor voice tender.

She nodded violently as she felt his warm fingers closing around her nervously plucking hand. Immediately she experienced a profoundly sensual empathy.

'Why, you wanted me even then, on Callisto, when you denied me? Didn't you? You just waited . . . and waited . . . Whatever for? I've always needed you, Afra! Always! Why do you think I've been so lonely?' The words burst from her.

With a low triumphant laugh, Afra pulled her into his

arms, cradling her body against his and settling her head against his shoulder.

'Familiarity breeds contempt?' he asked, mocking her gently with her own words.

'And how could you . . . a T-3 . . . manage to mask . . . ' she went on, fuelling her indignation.

'Familiarity also bred certain skills, Damia.' And he chuckled, holding her firmly despite her half-hearted attempt to struggle free. But he was physically stronger than she imagined, delighted by that as well.

'You and that aloof attitude of yours. When you wouldn't take me on Callisto I was sure it was mother—'

'Your mother was no more for me than Sodan was for you,' Afra said, his eyes stern as she stared up at him, shaken by his harsh tone.

His expression altered again, his arms tightened convulsively as he bent his head and kissed her with an urgent, lusty eagerness.

'Sodan may have loved you, in his fashion, Damia,' Afra's voice said in her ear, 'but mine will be far more satisfying for you.'

Trembling, Damia opened her mind to Afra without a single reservation. Their lips met again as Afra held her tightly in what shortly became far more than a mere meeting of minds.

9

Damia roused the morning, aware first of having slept very deeply. Then of feeling unusually refreshed, relaxed and self-satisfied. Having established those states, she was abruptly aware of what had transpired the previous night. And sat up in the bed.

Curled on his side and still sound asleep was Afra, his long arms dangling over the edge of the bed. She couldn't see his face but she gave him just the briefest mental touch and sighed with relief: his mind-tone had noticeably improved overnight.

That can be a fringe benefit of loving, you know, said Isthia in a whispery mental voice.

Grandmother! Even as Damia bridled at Isthia's amused observation, she also noted that receipt of the carefully tendered message caused her mind no pain.

I would have had to be mute or dead not to hear the way you two were vibrating. Isthia kept her 'voice' quiet but Damia could not miss the amused quality of it.

The two of us? Then Afra's able to 'path?

Well, let's just say that there are certain emotions that

broadcast in spite of themselves. Just let him find his own balance.

Isthia appeared in the doorway, a cup in each hand. Entering the room quietly, she gave Damia one cup and then went to the other side of the bed, to scrutinize Afra's sleeping face. Damia bristled possessively.

Down, girl, Isthia said with an ironic smile, *I'm on your side. Afra has been special to me, too, for vastly different reasons.*

Damia wanted to discover them but Isthia waggled a finger at her the moment she felt Damia's pressure.

Don't, Damia. Enough that I'm on your side.

Damia tried a different tack. *What did you mean then? Let him find his own balance?*

Isthia's expression became rueful. *I couldn't help overhearing your very creditable offer to him last night. But that won't be needed. Nor any notion of yours to sacrifice yourself to restore him. Now, now, don't hackle at me. Professionally, I've every reason to believe that he'll make a full recovery, given time and plenty of quiet. That's one reason I convinced your parents to let me bring you both here to Deneb. Callisto's far too frenetic a place for mental convalescents.*

Any Tower would be, Damia thought, and sipped at the hot brew, eyeing her grandmother speculatively.

Then what did you mean – you're on my side?

Isthia regarded her with exaggerated incredulity. *You mean, you think you can jump from mooning over that Sodan character to a liaison with Afra and not expect repercussions?*

It's NOT a liaison. It's a bonding! Damia said in an unequivocal tone. *You should know that . . .*

Isthia held up one hand in rebuke. *I closed my mind when I realized which way your . . . ah . . . suddenly discovered rapport was heading. I do practise discretion as well as metamorphics, you know.*

Mother will object. Damia gritted her teeth. During last night's passionate consummation, she certainly had had no time to consider 'repercussions'.

Well, she has had Afra's support for many years and she'll be annoyed at having to replace him but I suspect you'll find that your father might have more cogent objections.

Dad? Why should he mind? He's far more likely to suggest that Afra will be just the stabilizing influence I need!

Possibly.

Damia frowned, regarding her grandmother with apprehension. Isthia had a habit of predicting reactions.

How could they object to Afra? They both know him so well. And he's a T-3.

He's also nearly a quarter of a century your senior.

Don't put it like that, Isthia. It's not as if age makes that much difference for Talents! Damia was openly scornful. *I know Mother won't like it.*

Isthia perched on the low chest, sipping her drink.

Nonsense, although you may hear words like 'backlash', 'martyrdom', 'self-sacrifice', 'compensation'. You'll improve your position if your attitude towards him is devoid of guilt or the least tinge of reparation for the Sodan disaster.

Damia flinched, hunching against the pain of that reminder.

Sorry, love, Isthia shot back in sincere apology.

Do they hate me? For not saving Larak?

Slipping off the chest, Isthia embraced Damia in tender, loving arms. *No, love. No-one hates or blames you for that. Nothing could have saved Larak. Unfortunately!*

I will never, never, NEVER, let anyone else be focus! Damia said resolutely.

The focus-mind is always at risk in a merge, Damia love, and never is a long time. Don't store guilt for future use.

Afra stirred and Isthia rose to her feet.

Get him out of that bed and to my kitchen table. He hasn't eaten properly since we got him here. And you've both got to start moving about on your own. Now mind, no mental games until I give the go-ahead! Isthia stood, but her piercing gaze and stern face stressed that prohibition, and the force of the tone she used, no longer a whisper, set Damia's mind to throbbing: the clearest possible demonstration of her invalid state. Then her whisper returned. *I shouldn't even be talking to you like this now, but* you're *able for short distances and I wanted to clear the air privately,* she added as she left the room then.

Mulling over what Isthia had said, Damia watched as her lover restlessly turned on to his back, and flailed an arm against her. That woke him and he shot upright in the bed, anxious eyes seeking hers, a hesitant, shy smile on the lips that had tantalized her the night before. She found herself blushing and evaded his gaze. Giving herself a stern shake, she lifted her head and met his eyes.

Damia blushing? he teased her, lifting his hand to caress her cheek in a lingering fashion.

'You're not supposed to 'path, Afra,' she scolded, more because his 'tone' was so weak compared to the mental touch he had always projected.

His expression altered subtly and his hand dropped to her bare shoulder.

My love, I will do what I can with what I have, and his tone chided her. *And what I have is much better this morning, thank you.* 'Thank you!' he added aloud and, tilting his head, kissed her pursed lips.

The intimate touch was shatteringly electric and once again swept away any half-formed resolution of circumspect behaviour while Isthia was in range.

Hold breakfast, she managed to convey to Isthia on a tight thought.

Was that Afra's soft chuckle for her willing compliance in her mind or Isthia's for their delay?

'Actually, it's lunch,' Isthia said blandly when they finally did appear in the kitchen. It was a very pleasant room, south-facing, with windows that opened on to the front with a view of the lane that wound through the forestry to the major link road with Deneb City. Isthia preferred to know who was approaching her retreat so that she could take evasive action if necessary. When she had begun a profound enquiry into metamorphic treatments, she had needed such a refuge. She had no neighbours nearer than sixty kilometres and that family had absolutely no Talent.

With the courtesy that was second nature to him, Afra settled Damia into a chair at the long table that was work-space as well as dining surface. Then, turning his chair around he sat, his arms crossed on its back. He didn't appear to be watching Isthia intently but Damia knew that he was. Of Isthia's earlier observations, Damia had only told him that Isthia had said she was on their side. One of his eyebrows had quirked slightly and his lips had twitched but he didn't make any further comment. With Isthia's emphatic ban on 'pathing, Damia did not try to 'hear' what thoughts had crossed his mind.

As Isthia served them coffee, she wondered how her mother and father handled that intimate aspect of their life together. She knew they always kept a light touch but, in each other's minds constantly? Of course, right now, even the most delicate link could exacerbate. But she could watch him, learn every subtle nuance of his body language: had Afra always had such an expressive face? Droll, humorous, pensive, observant? Though he was listening to Isthia, he winked at her.

'I think you two are now able to handle your own convalescence,' Isthia was saying, ladling one of her hearty soups into bowls. She brusquely waved Damia back into her chair when she started to rise and help. 'I've laid in plenty of supplies. Damia, you are not to "reach" for anything yet. Use the communit,' and she grinned as she pointed to the unobtrusive set in one corner of the big room. 'Prosaic, I know, and nowhere near as swift as "lifting" something but, if I feel either of you "lifting" anything, I'll slap you back into deep sleep again. Your minds have to rest to recuperate, have to be free of even the pulse of other minds. You won't be bothered by casual visitors because this place is known to be off-limits and I've made it plain that I'll flay anyone who disturbs you. Anything you should require,' and her tone suggested that she'd be surprised if she hadn't anticipated every need, 'can be delivered.'

Afra nodded, glancing at Damia to be sure she was as obedient. 'What I don't know is how long we'll be convalescing. I have absolutely no idea how much time has already elapsed.'

Damia winced at even that tactful reference and, her appetite abruptly disappearing, she put down her spoon.

Isthia gave one of her evasive sniffs. 'Sleep,' and she bent a stern look on both Damia and Afra, 'was the best remedy. You've been kept quiescent – when we could—' and there was an element of exasperation in her manner as she pinned Damia with her stare, 'for sixteen days.'

'Oh!'

Isthia laid a comforting hand on Damia's head as she put her own bowl on the table and sat down beside her granddaughter.

Afra gave an odd chuckle. 'No wonder my legs are rubbery.'

Isthia gave one of her sniffs. 'A great wonder you've been able for anything!'

He refused to rise to the jibe.

'Mother and Dad?' Damia asked anxiously, irritated that it was only now that she thought to enquire.

'I kept them asleep for four days. You deflected a lot of that final thrust, Damia, and saved them from the worst of it. Believe me, you did,' Isthia added when Damia seemed to droop further, remembering who she hadn't been able to save.

'Who ran FT&T then?' Afra asked in a brisk tone. 'Jeran?'

Isthia nodded. 'With Cera. They made a formidable team.'

Afra chuckled. 'I expect they did. So long as they didn't

noticeably improve on what Rowan and Jeff can do.'

'Some detractors,' Isthia said with a snort of disapproval, 'feel that the Gwyn-Ravens have far too much power in FT&T chain of command.'

'Then let them breed up their own Prime Talents,' Afra replied abruptly. 'Meanwhile, they should be immensely grateful that Jeff's planned for every contingency. Who's working Callisto with the Rowan? Gollee?' When Isthia nodded, he shrugged. 'In that case, I have no need to hurry back. Frankly, this will be the first proper holiday I've had, bar the occasional weekend, since I had the gall to apply to the Rowan twenty-eight years ago.'

Damia stared at him, appalled. 'Twenty-eight?'

Afra regarded her levelly. 'That's right, love. That's how long I've been Towered. Not that I minded, for I'd nothing else to do with my spare time.'

'Nothing?' asked Isthia sardonically.

'Nothing,' he said, giving her the same level regard, 'that mattered. Unlike you dilettantes, we Tower folk become dedicated—'

'I'd call it enslaved,' Isthia said with a sour look.

'Inseparable from the needs and deeds of our particular Tower.'

'Who's managing Aurigae?' Damia asked in a guilty panic.

Isthia chuckled, her eyes sparkling. 'They're going to appreciate you when you return, Damia!'

'They do want me back? I will go back?' She hadn't quite dared to ask yet.

'Since they have to tailor their exports to the abilities of a young T-4 . . . '

'Who?' Damia was abruptly jealous of anyone taking over her Tower, however briefly.

'Oh, Capella lent a promising trainee: your oldest nephew, I believe, Afra; your sister Goswina's son.'

'Veswind?' Afra was mildly surprised. 'Yes, I suppose

he *is* old enough for responsibility. Gossie would be pleased. I wonder she never mentioned it.'

'They wouldn't, would they?' Isthia said in a mildly barbed voice.

'No, come to think of it,' Afra replied and broke off a piece of bread to soak up the soup juices at the bottom of his bowl.

'How soon?' Damia asked Isthia.

'How soon what?'

'How soon can I go back to work?'

Eyebrows raised quizzically, Isthia favoured her granddaughter with a very long and piercing look. Then sent a mental probe that made Damia gasp with pain.

'When you no longer have that sort of reaction, my dear. I repeat, since you have a hard time absorbing the information, you'll both recover, and with no reduction in potential. But it will take time, peace, quiet and no messing about.' Isthia waggled a finger first at her granddaughter. 'Have I made myself plain?'

Damia swallowed, her head throbbing. 'Completely.'

Immediately she felt a kinder touch and the throbbing was reduced to a minor ache.

'Have I made myself plain to you, too, Afra?' Isthia now turned on Afra who had gone slightly paler. 'Yes, I see I have. Now, will you both stop worrying about the galaxy and eat my nourishing soup? You need to reintroduce your abused stomachs to real food instead of nutrient sprays. I've prepared a diet sheet which,' and again she pinned them with her forceful stare, 'you will both follow assiduously.' When they nodded meekly, she went on. 'I'll leave tomorrow since a third party is unnecessary – or should be. You certainly are adult enough, Afra, as well as old enough to admit, and yield, to your current physical and mental disabilities.' She gave a sniff. 'And to bore each other in close proximity. Nothing like that to demonstrate compatibility.'

'Grandmother!' Damia cried in protest for she *knew* that Afra and she were already bonded.

'Damia, stop doodling and start eating. You'll have more soup, Afra,' she said in one of her quick shifts of mood. 'When you've finished, I suggest that a gentle walk about the cabin will be about all the physical activity you'll be able for today. THEN,' and she shook a stern finger at each, 'you will rest in the porch hammocks so I'm sure that you *are* resting.'

'No quarrel there,' Afra said with a droll grin of apology to Damia.

'Hear me, Damia? Give him a chance to regain his strength!'

'Grandmother!'

'Don't grandmother me, young woman. Learn the joys of anticipation!'

A slight shake of Afra's head cooled Damia's heated response. And the warm look in his yellowy eyes promised her that he'd make it all up to her later.

'It is peaceful here,' Afra said as he and Damia obediently took their stroll. He had linked his warm long fingers in hers and such tactile contact was unusually reassuring, and curiously satisfying. Almost as good as the now forbidden mental link would be. Especially since the touch-sense of Afra had taken on an added dimension – no longer merely cool-green-comfortable-secure: a vibrancy threaded through the cool-green, and 'comfortable' had definitely lazy-sensual elements, while 'secure' had intensified into a deeply rooted foundation that could never be attacked. Occasionally Afra's long thigh brushed against her leg, and their bodies swayed together, to touch at the hip, while her shoulder often encountered his arm.

Damia took in little of their surroundings during that slow saunter: she just revelled in the purely physical contact with a subtly altered Afra. She still couldn't believe her stupidity. But then, Afra'd *always* been part of her life: how could she have known he'd assume such a vital role in the rest of her life? She refused to consider problems. Nothing must mar this tranquil moment.

They rounded the corner of the cabin and made for the short flight of stairs to the veranda where two hammocks swung idly in the afternoon breeze. The few stairs put an unexpected strain on her thighs. She thought of the big daddies she had once so effortlessly transported. Well, she'd do them again! She was even panting a bit when they reached the porch. So was Afra so she didn't feel quite so decrepit. But this was a splendid spot for napping, shaded as it was from the direct rays of the sun.

Afra held the cords of one hammock while she eased herself into it. Then he bent and, at the last moment, altered his target and kissed the side of her neck.

'Your mouth, love, is far too inviting,' he said with a low laugh and set her hammock to rocking.

'Why are the swings set so far apart? I want to keep in touch,' she complained, extending her arm as far as it would go towards him. He laughed as he settled himself and, with one quick push, set his hammock into a gentle swing.

'We're to rest, remember, love? And since I want nothing more than to be rested . . . ' and he laughed softly, suggestively, 'I'll obey.'

Surprising her, Afra began to hum a melody she faintly recognized. And hearing it, she fell asleep.

Afra almost botched his attempt to invoke that old preconditioning: in the first place, he couldn't sing and laugh at the same time and then, when Damia's breathing obediently slowed to a sleep rhythm, he was both surprised and gratified that that old trigger still worked.

He let the lullaby die away, watching Damia's face which still showed the marks of her ordeal and grief. He hadn't liked to see her so painfully thin, either, but Isthia's threatened diet ought to repair that damage. He wished he could restore her as easily as he had put her to sleep. He sighed, and clasped his hands behind his head, shifting his gaze to the cabin's incredibly serene setting. Gradually he became aware of discrete sounds; Isthia moving about inside; insect and bird song drifting from the trees; the soughing of the breeze. He was also calm within himself for the first time in years: perhaps, he amended, in his adult life. Certainly since Damia's ripening sexuality had stunned him – what was it, only seven years ago?

Last night had been completely unexpected: a boon he could never have anticipated – a boon which might yet cause him more anguish than he had already endured. And yet, *this* time Afra Lyon had no intention of standing patiently by and permitting Damia's incredible gift of love to be wrenched from his grasp.

Hadn't she come to him of her own volition? Seen him with eyes no longer clouded by old perceptions and the anathema of 'familiarity'? And her dear nonsense about sharing her mental strength with him? Well, he'd just see if that was ever needed! How devoutly he hoped that Isthia's prognosis was correct! Keeping up with Damia would require Afra Lyon in top form.

On the other hand, Damia might have turned to him as an anodyne to the devastating experience of misjudging Sodan, and Larak's loss. They had been so close, those two. Had she turned to her oldest and most trusted friend only for solace? No, Afra told himself, he had not misjudged the look on Damia's face, the amazement in her eyes as she had *really* looked at him, Afra Lyon, the way her hands had caressed him were revelations for them both. She had undergone a shift, a realignment of senses, a translation of preconceptions that had been far-reaching. That he had shifted from old family friend to potential lover years before was immaterial: in her eyes, she herself had made the final adjustment to accepting the steadfast and silent love he had for her.

Afra smiled wryly. He had stunned Damia with his

mention of twenty-eight Towered years. But his love had to face the fact that he was twenty-four years her senior. Rowan would mention it and possibly Jeff. He did wonder how they were going to receive the news. He could hear the Rowan roaring – she'd have to break in a new assistant – unless she could persuade Gollee to stay. Or install Veswind? Would she be willing for another from the Lyon line?

Afra smiled again as he remembered how often Jeff had teased him about starting his own family. Jeff had never had Damia in mind for Afra's mate but would he really object? Damia *was* younger by over two decades but how much could that matter?

Especially now that Damia had gone through such a tempering and maturing crisis. Afra saw it in the lingering sadness in her eyes, heard it in her subtly altered voice, felt it in her abandoned response to their impassioned consummation. He wished she had not been subjected to such a harsh, unforgiving, sacrificial rite of passage. He could have wished it had been easier on her – but surely both Rowan and Jeff would recognize her new maturity. Afra shifted restlessly, his thoughts turning to the unexpected victim. Dear, dear Larak! That vibrant, amiable, loving boy, gone in a flash of alien anger. Afra forced himself to face that hideous moment, if only to defuse the emotional burden, but his mind refused to focus. In fact, it hurt . . .

Afra, came Isthia's admonition, *don't think about that yet. You can't alter what has happened.*

He didn't try to reach her telepathically, just let his reply sit in his public mind. *I must, however, confront what did happen and sort it out for peace of mind.*

Not now, not today or for several weeks to come, Isthia replied, and what she did next, Afra never knew, but sleep overcame him. To achieve the restoration of her patients, Isthia wouldn't cavil at planting a few irresistible suggestions of her own.

★

'Tomorrow you can catch your own,' Isthia told them as she served them a dinner of fish, tiny vegetables and a salad of mixed greens, 'and scavenge your greens from my garden. I ask only that you eat everything you catch and pick. You know the drill on Deneb, Damia.'

'Waste not, want not,' Damia dutifully chanted as the delectable odour of the pan-fried fish made her mouth water. 'Fish is brain food, Afra,' she added pedantically. 'High protein, low fat. Is there a limit on a day's catch?'

Isthia snorted. 'Of course not. I stocked the lake myself so it's not part of the official resources.'

Damia leaned across the table to Afra, her eyes dancing with mischief, 'That means that Isthia reserves the right to fish the lake to herself. Deneb can't use it in time of famine.'

'Deneb hasn't endured a famine, has it?' Afra was astonished enough to stop eating.

'Of course not,' Damia said.

'Famine and planetary emergency.'

'Such as the Beetles?' Afra asked.

'Exactly,' and Isthia looked slightly grim, 'first they filled our lakes with contaminants, then they blasted them dry. Took years to get our reservoirs rebuilt and full. So a fish-stocked lake can be considered a natural resource and could be added to planetary food reserves. Fortunately, I made sure I had a few perks.'

'This isolated site is one?' Afra asked.

'Took me nearly a year to find exactly the right land when the grant was bestowed,' Isthia said, 'but it's worth every bit of the fuss it caused.'

'Fuss? With all you've done for Deneb?' Damia said, indignant.

'That's why there was so much fuss,' Isthia replied and related to them the struggles she had had with local and central administration, builders, naturalists, as well as medical boards which did not want her so far from population centres. 'I was blocked on minor points for nearly another two years. But I got the place I wanted, where I wanted it, and no-one can revoke my title to it, nor my heirs.'

'What do we fish for?' Afra asked.

'Rainbow sparklers,' Isthia replied. 'Bait your hooks and throw 'em in. The fish eventually get interested.'

'It's a novel idea to catch one's dinner, too,' Afra added.

'You can, though, can't you? It's not something Capellans are against?' Damia asked, realizing how little she really knew about Afra Lyon.

'No,' he assured her with a grin, 'nothing in my upbringing prevents me from fishing for food.'

'I'll show you the lake after we eat. There'll be light enough,' Isthia said. 'In fact watching the sunset there can be rather spectacular.'

And that evening Deneb put on quite a display for them. The lake was reached by a narrow track that threaded its way through a thick stand of Denebian softwoods: single trunk spires with short, full-leaved branches. The lake, dewdrop in shape, was deceptively large for Isthia led them out at its narrow end where the tributary stream flowed down from the hills to their right.

'I've constructed a perch,' Isthia said, directing them along the bank to their left where several large flat black rocks formed an irregular bench.

Some sort of spidery multi-legged insects skimmed across the lake and occasionally an aquatic denizen broke the surface into ripples, snagging the water runner. Sleepy avian and nocturnal bug noises punctuated the evening air as they seated themselves.

Afra threw a jacket across Damia's shoulder, for the air at the lakeside was chillier than at the protected cabin. She leaned into his touch, avid for physical contact. He settled his arm about her shoulders and drew her against him as if this casual sort of contact was long established. Afra was having no trouble, she thought, with their new relationship. His fingers pressed against her arm and she glanced at him, suspicious that he was disobeying Isthia. He bent his head towards her.

'A touch is just a touch, Damia love,' he said quietly, 'so don't get fussed. More than you, I can't afford to risk the healing process.'

Damia shot a quick look at her grandmother who was sitting, with the discretion of a duenna, at the opposite end of the rock couch. Isthia gave every evidence of ignoring them. Which, Damia realized, was probably genuine. Isthia would hate having to leave this place with its insured solitude. She must remember to thank her for that sacrifice.

'Sacrifice,' Damia thought, her heart heavy. So many little things reminded her of Larak. Once again Afra's fingers took a new hold on her arm and she shook her head of such wounding reflections.

'See!' Isthia pointed at the cloud formation now tinged with a delicate shade of peach as the sun began its final descent behind the hills.

So they watched, awed by the beauty, by the silence of the wood and lake about them, a reverence for the display and for the tranquillity of the night to come. When the last colour faded from cloud and sky, Isthia sighed, a sound of intense satisfaction, and rose.

'Don't stay too long. There's a chill in the night air,' she said, and thrusting one handlight at them, she departed, playing hers on the track as she made her way back to the cabin.

For Damia, who had always been physically restless, this sort of inactivity was novel, yet she would not have broken the quiet mood for anything on any world she had ever trod. What was even more amazing was that she was sharing – truly sharing – this magical serenity with Afra. From the corner of her eye she snuck a peek at him and saw, in the crepuscular twilight, that he reflected her own tranquillity. Why had she never noticed what a strong profile he had: a high straight forehead, a straight nose jutting at a fine angle, the generous gap between nose and upper lip, and the strong well-modelled wide mouth, the firm chin and jawline. He had nice ears, too. But there were undeniable flecks of white in his blondy hair. Not much, but noticeable.

Self-consciously, she fingered back the white-flecked lock that always fell across her face.

'I've got more white hair than you,' she remarked.

'But not in the same number of years, love,' he replied equably.

'Is that going to matter?' she asked anxiously.

He looked down at her, smiling at her concern. 'It oughtn't but it's bound to come up. Does my seniority bother you?'

'You're always "Afra" to me,' she said, surprised at how she identified him within herself.

He chuckled. 'As you have always been inimitably "Damia" to me. D'you know? I heard you protest your birth.'

'That's not fair!' She did not like him to remind her of moments like that.

'When does "fair" enter into any relationship? Suffice it to say, that I have known you since the first breath you drew and, strangely enough, it makes you dearer to me.'

The look in his yellowy eyes, the tenderness in his mouth, the appeal in even the way his shoulders inclined towards her, and Damia had to admit that she could have no objection to what lay behind that soft declaration.

'Oh, Afra! Why did you wait so long?'

His lips turned up and his eyes danced. 'I had to. Until you were ready to look *at* Afra.' With such laughter in his eyes and mouth, he had a careless boyishness about him that cancelled further discussion of age.

Larak had been little more than a boy at his death. Unbidden, the comparison had crossed her mind.

Afra's hand covered hers instantly. 'I can see that you're thinking sad thoughts again, love. What this time? Tell me!'

Damia smiled ruefully up at him. 'As I told you all my small troubles?'

'I'm able for the big ones now.'

'I keep thinking of . . . ' She faltered.

'Larak,' and his fingers caressed her gently. 'I think of him a lot myself.'

Damia burrowed her head into his shoulder, hooking one hand about his neck as she had done so often as a child. But it was not as a child that she clung to him now.

'I'm told such pain eases with time,' he said quietly, 'and there has not been enough of that between us and his death.'

Damia sat upright. 'Who is taking care of Jenna right now?' Her tone was stricken for she had been thinking more in terms of her own grief and loss from this wretched Sodan affair.

'Isthia can tell us . . . no, don't reach,' he said and Damia let out an exasperated sigh. 'We'll *go* and ask.'

'It takes getting used to, this limitation,' she replied caustically.

'In a good cause, love,' he said and, smoothly rising from the warm rock, pulled her to her feet.

'Jenna?' Isthia said, surprised at the question when they returned to the cabin. 'Jeran sent Ezro to her, but she has a big family and they're Talented enough to give her comfort and sufficient solace to ease her heart.' Isthia's expression altered to one of amusement. 'After all, she has not only her son but also another child on the way.'

Damia stared at her grandmother. 'Oh!' she exclaimed indignantly. 'Larak didn't? Why, he's . . . ' She stopped short. 'Under the circumstances, I guess I'm glad. Lord, but we Gwyn-Ravens are prolific.'

'Tell me about it,' and Isthia threw her head back and howled with laughter. 'Remember, *separate* rooms tonight. I'm not going to explain *that* to your parents, Damia!'

When Isthia entered Deneb Tower, her grandson Jeran had just finished with the incoming traffic.

'How are they?' he asked urgently, rising from his conformable chair and embracing her. She rather liked his strong young arms about her: made her remember Jerry.

'They will both recover completely,' she said, and then gave him a warning glare, 'if they are allowed to recover at their own rate. No unexpected visits, no shafts of enquiry, no exercise of 'path or 'port whatever!'

'How's Damia taking that kind of a prohibition?' Jeran asked, raising his eyebrows.

Isthia considered, careful not to let any of her more recent conclusions be accessed by her clever Prime grandson. 'Better than you'd expect,' she replied, with just a slight emphasis on the pronoun. 'Of course, once she regains her health—'

'What?' Jeran's exclamation of alarm was genuine.

'Oh, she's battered physically as well as psychically, Jeran. And genuinely distraught about Larak. It'll all take time . . . '

Jeran frowned. 'How long?' Now an FT&T Prime spoke.

'As long as it takes,' said Isthia with a shrug. 'I'd like to reassure Jeff and Rowan—' she added, gesturing towards the board.

'Certainly,' Jeran said, stepping well away from the conformable chair. 'It's break time for me anyway. Will you be going right back?'

'Heavens, no,' and Isthia grinned as she settled into

the chair. 'When I meant no mental exertion, I meant none, which includes me leaking metamorphic theory all over them. Physically, they're well able to take care of themselves, and each other.' She shook her head, thinking of how true that was and trying very hard not to chuckle at her private merriment. 'You're stuck with this white man's burden again.'

'Never stuck, Gran, glad to have you any time.'

Isthia snorted, knowing perfectly well that Jeran was rapidly reviewing how to conduct his current affair with his grandmother in the same house. 'Or, I can always move into Kantria's digs. Yes, that makes sense and she's on the outskirts of the City anyway. Do be tactful and ask her first, Jerry.'

She laughed as she caught the quickly-suppressed ripple of consternation from Jeran as he hurriedly closed the shielded door behind him. That should divert him sufficiently from speculating further about his sister and Afra.

Then she settled back in the chair and, picking up the pulse of the generators, sent her mind ranging the long distance to Callisto.

Isthia? the Rowan caught her up immediately and did not moderate her understandable anxiety. Damia was foremost in her mother's mind.

They're both well and they will both recover, Rowan.

Mother? Instantly Jeff's mind joined the link. *Without loss?* Afra's recuperation worried Jeff more but only because he felt Afra had been in more jeopardy than his daughter.

I don't foresee any diminishing in either mind. As I told you, rest from any mental stress, plenty of sleep and solitude will cure them.

Relief flowed from them to her and back again.

Any idea when their cures will be complete? Jeff the Prime spoke.

I haven't a clue, Isthia blithely reassured them and felt their misgivings. *Heavens, I've never treated such overextended minds before. Metamorphically, Damia buffered Afra and you two cushioned her even as she blocked and destroyed Sodan.*

There was a brief pause. *Does she blame herself for not saving . . .* The Rowan's voice faltered.

Yes, but that was inevitable and we cannot spare her that grief. You will be surprised when you do see her, and Isthia was rather glad there was no-one in the Tower room to see her smile. She liked and admired her son's mate. It was scarcely Angharad's fault that she had overcompensated her children for the vicissitudes of her early childhood.

Surprised? Jeff asked.

Agreeably, Isthia replied. She might as well predispose them. *The incident has matured the girl.*

Rite of passage? Jeff asked.

A rocky grievous one, to be sure, but considering Damia's personality, only that sort of experience would produce the proper tempering.

Aren't you being hard on Damia? the Rowan began.

I'm being objective, I assure you. You should be grateful for her fortitude and resilience. She could have been consumed and broken.

But she is well? She will recover?

Given time. No more headaches, Angharad, or lapses of concentration? Isthia asked, skilfully diverting the contact into a new channel.

No, because we've cut down the traffic, Jeff replied brusquely. *Sometimes FT&T expects too much of its Primes. Both of us,* and he sent his mother a rueful grin, *are letting our assistants handle inanimate stuff. Gives them a feeling of accomplishment and us a brief respite. And Aurigae got their ears bent for the sort of loads they were having Damia 'port. She's not to do that again. You did say that Afra's going to be all right?*

Isthia chuckled. *Oh, you'll notice a change in him, too. All for the good.* Then, before her inner amusement broke through, she hastily ended the contact. *Goodbye now. Jeran wants his chair back. I'll keep you informed.*

10

Because they were so isolated and because they had been in the habit of being wide-open in every sense to each other, Damia and Afra both experienced the first tendrils of query.

Damia censored the incident. Afra ignored it. Neither mentioned it; Damia because she wasn't going to get caught twice the same way; Afra because he didn't trust his mind.

Not only had Isthia left them a diet sheet – easily digestible foods at first, graduating to some of her more esoteric and exotic combinations – but also she had left them a work sheet. As her note reminded them, the cabin was not automated.

'Nothing to tax your energies but light chores to keep the place ticking over and to combat boredom.'

'I'm not sure that I like her going on about boredom,' Damia told Afra as they looked over the roster.

Afra's eyes gleamed, but his finger running down her cheek took the sting out of his words. 'We both know our quick-silver Damia, restless, curious . . . '

'I need rest,' and Damia pretended a haughty air, 'and I got an overdose of curiosity too recently to indulge in another. I shall vegetate, right along with you, Afra Lyon!'

'We are not precisely vegetating, love,' Afra said and demonstrated.

They were, however, scrupulous about doing the various tasks Isthia had set: keeping the cabin neat and clean, tending the garden planted around it, weeding the vegetable plot, reinforcing the guard fencing to prevent forest life from browsing the young plants, and fishing. The lake was stocked with many tasty varieties.

Damia liked fishing, liked the excuse to sit beside Afra, shoulders and legs touching as they sat on the bank waiting for the sparklers to rise to the bait. The enforced idleness of angling permitted Damia to satisfy her insatiable interest in every facet of her lover's childhood and early training, though she forcefully denounced such heartlessness.

'I guess I was a lot luckier in my parents than I knew,' Damia had to admit when he had finished with his early childhood trials.

'Even being sent away as an infant to Deneb?' Afra asked, his eyes intent on her expression.

She grimaced with chagrin. 'Yes, I was a right wagon, wasn't I?'

'Heavy duty big daddy wagon.'

'You don't have to agree!'

'Why not? I knew what you admit to.'

'But you're not supposed to agree!'

Afra chuckled. 'If it's true, why not? It's perspective that counts, love. It isn't that I don't know your faults – as I have tried to admit to mine – it's that I love you more because of them.'

'Love me for my faults? How stupid!'

'Should I ignore them because I love you?'

'Well . . . '

'Nonsense. It's those odd quirks of yours that are endearing, not your very stellar qualities which I respect and admire. That could get tedious . . . '

'You mean, boring?' Damia suggested, eyeing him speculatively.

'No, tedious, because then I'd have to watch everything I said and did, trying to be equally respectable and admirable.'

Damia's eyes widened in protest. 'But you are respected and admired.'

'By you?' His soft voice was entreating and his look made her melt.

'I think,' she said in a deliberate way, playing with the long fingers that held one of her hands captive, 'that I have always admired and respected you, Afra. You always *listened* to me, even when I was a baby. You always made me feel as if you had time for no-one else in the Tower.'

'That's true enough, love.'

'Did you love me then as a baby?' Damia could not quite erase the wistfulness.

'I loved you as a baby, but as a man loves an adorable, winsome child. I love you now as a man loves a vibrant, talented, sexually aware young woman.'

'Love me then, do.'

At first, they kept about the house. Afra taught Damia how to do complicated origami until she was almost as fast fashioning them as he was. She taught him – or tried – to ride ponies from the small herd that often drifted to the lake in the evening. He had to keep his long legs either drawn up, nearly under his knees, or straight out on either side of the pony or they would drag on the ground. Damia found either position hilarious but mastered her mirth rather than prejudice Afra against the ponies as transportation.

As physical strength returned, they ranged wider; in

part in response to the list of Isthia's chores. She was keeping track of some Earth species which had been judiciously added to Deneb's ecology. One such species were breeding pairs of raptors which had been established in the rough hills above her cabin. Isthia wanted to check on the nests and the success rate of fledging. With her maps and backpacks of food and trail supplies, Damia and Afra took advantage of a fine bright morning to accomplish that task.

'You have the longest legs,' Damia told him, somewhat admiring them, lightly haired, well-shaped, sinewy and tanned from long sunning. 'Nice knees.'

'I can say the same of yours, love,' he responded equably.

'Can't I ever get a rise out of you?'

'Oh, you do indeed,' Afra said mischievously, 'you do indeed.'

'I didn't mean that! But you *never* lose your temper, or is that your Methody upbringing?'

'Losing one's temper over a trifle would definitely be considered unmannerly,' he replied.

'Maybe I'm the one who should have been raised by your parents,' she said with some exasperation.

'No, love, no!' he replied so fervently that she turned to look at him over her shoulder and managed to collide with a tree. 'Are you hurt?'

'What? From that little bump?' she demanded, annoyed with herself for being so clumsy. The sapling had caught her from cheek to knee and the impact had stung. She rubbed herself fiercely, gave the tree a pat. 'I probably hurt it far worse. Look, I've taken off all its new growth!'

'Hmmm, so you have. Let's hope Isthia does not intimately know every tree she planted.'

Damia watched her way after that, wondering just how the bruises would come up. But shortly she was far more interested in the beautiful landscape for they had left the sheltering belt of forestry and were out on the rough hillsides, stepping from rock to grassoid clump, or cutting through a bracken-like vegetation which, bruised by their hiking boots, gave off a pungent astringent odour.

They rested often, in deference to slack muscles and their convalescent state, but by midday had reached the craggy outcroppings where the raptors had nested. Using the high-power binoculars, Afra located the right cliff and the first nest.

'No birds, no egg shells. Is that good?' He passed the glasses to her.

'We might try looking at the base of the cliff,' she said after a careful sweep. 'Seems to me the raptors clear the debris from the nest.'

They had to climb over uneven ground to reach their objective but found nothing beyond fragments of shells and bones, many of those cracked for the marrow.

They pushed on to examine the other four nests Isthia had listed and found two more before they came across a gushing mountain stream where they decided to eat their lunch. They had appetite for everything they'd thought to bring, washed down by the clear cold water of the creek. Then they went on, still climbing up the tumbled greystone cliff. When they finally came out on the height, Damia paused and, shielding her eyes, turned slowly, taking in the panorama below and almost all around them.

'It's breathtaking,' Afra said. 'I'd forgotten there could be so much world to see from one spot.'

'It's a far cry from Callisto, that's for sure,' Damia replied. 'And yet,' she added loyally, 'I'm fond of that moon! All the world I knew until I . . . ' she cut off, frowning.

'What's wrong?'

She was turned towards the rise beyond the saddle on which they stood. She bit her underlip, puzzled, twitching her shoulders restlessly.

'There shouldn't *be* any more. There shouldn't be any *more* here.'

'Any more what?'

'Well, I've got to go see, don't I?' she said enigmatically.

'See what, Damia? I can't read your mind, you know.'

'You don't really want to, Afra, but you'd best come see.' She started scrambling up the steep rock face and gestured for him to follow.

'What should I be looking for?' he asked tactfully.

'You *should* be sensing it,' she replied, her tone almost angry. 'Beetle stuff. Don't you *feel* the . . . '

'Sting-pzzzt?' he asked, half amused.

'Yes,' and she was very angry, 'the sting-pzzzt. It's very loud.'

Afra paused, trying to sense what she did. 'I *hear* insects buzzing.'

'No, you feel Beetle metal. Look around, do you see any insects up this high?'

Now that Damia had mentioned it, he didn't, but she was setting quite a pace and he had to work to keep up with her. When they reached the top of the next rise, he looked about him expectantly but Damia turned right and started purposefully up the next slope and abruptly halted, staring at a groove in the fine grey granite – a groove that was not natural and from which protruded a ragged shaft of metal. The buzz that Afra had thought insectoid was louder, and every breath he drew had a sharp metallic taste to it.

'Sting-pzzzt is really accurate,' he said, gazing down at the artifact. Then he paced it out, along the impact split in the rock. 'Fifteen metres visible.' He knelt down and, somewhat gingerly, poked his finger at the nearest surface. 'Part of a hull?'

'Looks like it,' Damia replied, beginning to take an interest in it. 'Pitted. I didn't think there'd be anything left to find. My Uncle Rhodri spent the last nine years of his life tracking pieces down.'

'This is a rather inaccessible spot,' Afra observed.

Damia sighed. 'We'd better get back and report this.'

'Why? It's been here twenty-odd years—'

'One reports finds like this. And it's awfully near the fourth raptor nest.'

'There'd be a problem?'

Damia shot him an irritable glance. 'Can't you taste it in the air? Feel it? Can you imagine what effect it would have on hatchlings?'

'There is one?' He curbed a growing irritation with her cryptic remarks. 'I may have helped blast Beetles out of the sky but that contact was at an exceedingly long range.'

'Well, there's nothing long range about the way this metal affects me,' she replied tersely and started to climb down. 'I can't get away from here fast enough.'

'Oh, is that what's wrong with us?'

'Yes, indeed!' She snapped that out, almost spitting the ds at him. 'Let's get away from here!' Her tone was desperate.

He bit back an angry comment about how fast she'd climbed to get to the artifact. Damia did not slow her descent until they were back at the stream, panting for breath and sweating with exertion.

'I think that's far enough,' she said in gasps and flopped down by the stream, to splash water on her face and neck and then grinning with a return of good humour, at him. They both drank deeply, washing the metallic aftertaste out of their mouths.

'Why did you let me eat all my lunch?' Damia asked. 'I'm starving.'

'I saw some berry bushes,' Afra suggested.

'Hmm. Good idea. Sorry about the temper, Afra, but Beetle metal really agitates.'

'What I find amazing is that it retains that effect so long.'

Damia grinned. 'Uncle Rhodri was determined to

find out why. He wasn't sure if it was caused by emanations of the alien ore or vibrations induced by the Beetles for defence. He suspected the latter since it would be very difficult for attackers to approach the vessel when grounded.'

'What was his final conclusion?'

'Oh, he died before he arrived at one. High Command took over the project. They're still here. They're the ones I'll call when we get back to the cabin. C'mon.'

Though Afra did not protest the brisk pace Damia set back to the cabin, they were both exhausted when they got to the clearing. Afra paused long enough to get a drink but Damia went immediately to the communit and dialled the number.

'Damia Raven-Lyon,' she said to his astonishment and delight, 'I've found an artifact, buried in the hills above Isthia Raven's cabin.' She gave them the coordinates from Isthia's map. 'Yes, it's still emanating. Couldn't leave the area fast enough. You could land a vtol on the saddle below it. Yes, about fifteen metres long, maybe more. It buried itself into the ravine. Looks like hull.' She grimaced. 'Feels like hull. Yes, of course, we'll be here.'

Afra handed her a cool juice drink as she replaced the handset.

'Damia Raven-Lyon?' he asked softly as he slid an arm about her shoulders to pull her close.

She gave him a sideways glance, her blue eyes sparkling in her tired, sweaty face.

'Well, it'll be obvious!'

An officer rang through, requesting permission to land at the cabin clearing. On the porch to greet him, Damia and Afra saw the giant removal unit, the jagged hull piece suspended from massive cables, as it thumped ponderously east towards the naval research facility. One of the escort vehicles peeled off and landed.

'That was a grand find,' the lieutenant-commander

said, beaming from ear to ear as he presented himself and saluted smartly. 'Thought we'd gathered up all the debris. Let us know if you find anything else, will you?'

Damia felt a convulsive shudder go down her backbone. 'We certainly will. Don't want so much as a sliver of that stuff nearby.'

'How do you mitigate the effect, Commander?' Afra asked.

'What effect, sir?' The man was surprised. 'Oh, you'd be Talented then.' He gave them a slightly patronizing smile. 'Doesn't affect us types at all. But I'd heard it can be pretty potent for sensitives.' Fortunately he turned away then, and trotted back to his skycar.

'The nerve . . . ' Damia began. 'Potent for sensitives . . . Indeed.'

Afra chuckled. 'At least we know we're sensitive again.'

Damia blinked. 'I hadn't thought of that aspect.' Then her face brightened. 'D'you think that means we're healed?'

'On our way to it, certainly.'

The dreaming began that evening. And, at first, Damia did subscribe it to the alien metal. Yet these weren't nightmares: more pictures imposed on her dreaming mind, a kaleidoscope of images. She didn't wake in an uneasy state of mind, but she could vividly recall the night's fantasies.

She did get in touch with Isthia, mentioning the Beetle find and its effect on them.

'I would say that you are healing well. Don't rush it, Damia. Too much is at stake.'

'We've been here seven weeks.'

'Bored yet?'

'Grandmother! I'm not bored. D'you want us to go back and see what effect the Beetle fragment had on the last nest on your list.'

'Hmmm. Yes, there could be problems. Leave it until the next good rainstorm, let that taint wash away. You don't need alien pollution at your stage of repair.'

'Are you so eager to get back to a Tower, Damia?' Afra asked when she broke the contact.

She chuckled. 'No, I'm not. Nor am I bored. Isthia says—'

'I heard her—'

'Afra!' Concerned, Damia seized at his shoulder.

'I'm not deaf and Isthia was perfectly audible without any "sensitive" assistance.'

After two weeks of nightly episodes, Damia was getting worried. Her uncle had never been able to explain how the Beetle metal could continue to emanate but he had insisted that all fragments be contained in shielded bunkers with six-foot walls of the toughest plascrete. He had recommended that those with any vestige of Talent be barred from the research compound. But the substance of her nocturnal images held neither threat nor malice. In fact, they seemed to repeat in a pattern, unusual enough in itself, and gradually the pattern became so predictable that Damia could step from one sequence to the next . . . as if she were turning pages.

Easing from their bed early one morning, Damia slipped to the kitchen and dialled Isthia's number. Her grandmother was an early riser. Contact came on the third ring.

'Grandmother, did Uncle Rhodri ever discover a long-term contamination from Beetle metal?'

'What do you mean exactly?'

To Damia, her grandmother sounded so casually alert that she felt no further reluctance in bringing the phenomenon up.

'I've had dreams for the past two weeks, ever since that hull piece was found, only they're not threatening, or evil, or particularly unnerving. They are repetitions of the same images.'

'What images?' And again Isthia's detached query suggested to Damia that the phenomenon might not be limited to herself.

'I get a pleasant setting, then figures – too distant and fussy to be described – coming up a long road to another group of six figures. Both sets sit down. The atmosphere is peaceful and it seems to be as if the two groups are talking. Then the visitors, for that is the impression I get of them, turn and go back the way they came to what looks like a vessel of some kind.'

'What kind?'

'I can't discern that, Isthia. I just identify it as a vehicle. An opening appears and the visitors go in it. Then everything starts all over again. Now, tell me that other people are having this same dream?'

'I am,' Afra said, having entered the kitchen quietly.

'Afra says he is.'

'That doesn't surprise me, Damia. What does surprise me is that you two would be among those contacted.'

'Those? How widespread is this?' Damia wasn't certain whether she was relieved or annoyed.

Isthia chuckled. 'This time it's not just the females who're getting it.'

'WHAT?' Damia beckoned urgently for Afra to come closer so he could hear what Isthia was saying.

'Well, your Uncle Ian as well as Rakella and Besseva have been having much the same nightly visitations. Yours are the clearest.'

'You said "contact" a minute ago?'

'I did, and that's what I think it is now that you've amplified what the others only guessed.'

'I'm not sure I like this,' Damia said, noticing that her hand was beginning to tremble. Afra put his arm about her waist, and the other hand on her shoulder, steadying her. She leaned back against him. 'What does Jeran think?'

'Ah, that's it. Jeran isn't included in the chosen,' Isthia said. 'Of course, he spends most of his free time with a blonde he's courting.'

'He's serious?'

'I suspect so. When Jeran makes up his mind, he's unswervable.'

'Have you asked him to try?'

'To dream requires sleep,' Isthia said pointedly.

Afra smothered his laugh in Damia's loose hair, pressing his face against her neck which he then nibbled. She jerked her shoulder, giving him a hiss to behave. He was totally unrepentant.

'So what do we do? Have you told my parents?'

'Hmmm, no, not yet. It's been too nebulous.'

'I can also hear what the Rowan and Jeff would say,' Afra remarked, projecting his voice so Isthia heard him, 'about a third Denebian Penetration.'

'It's not penetration,' both Damia and Isthia said together.

'Really?' Afra regarded his lover with quickened interest. 'An interesting reaction.'

'Plainly dream-generated,' Isthia added. 'Look, since you've been having these visitations, and clearer ones than anyone else, I think I'll join you there, if you don't mind . . . '

'If you wouldn't be bored . . . ' Damia could not resist the jibe.

'My dear, boredom has a certain appeal for one who has never known what it was. Now, go get me some fresh fish for lunch.' She broke the contact.

'I'm not sure I like this,' Damia said, replacing the handset.

'Why?' And Afra turned her around in his arms, to hold her comfortingly against him. 'I had no impression of danger or menace or jeopardy. As you did, I had the feeling of visitation, a peaceful one.'

Cushioned against her lover's body, Damia sagged

against him, unconsciously seeking reassurance which he willingly gave.

'I'm not sure I'm up to another visitor,' she said glumly. She gave a second convulsive shudder. 'The last one cost us too much.'

'What? My brave Damia sidestepping a challenge?'

'Your cautious Damia not rushing in, blind,' and her tone was sardonic.

'Let's see what Isthia says. Meanwhile, I could use some coffee, and maybe even some breakfast before we go fish for her lunch?'

'You're trying to make light of this whole thing,' Damia accused, pushing away from him.

He disclaimed that immediately. 'Far from it. The prudent would examine the whole imposed dream sequence with an open mind . . . '

'If we're allowed . . . ' Almost absently, Damia began to prepare the coffee and other elements of a breakfast.

'We must be, if we've had the clearest dreams . . . '

'But they began the night we found that Beetle artifact . . . '

'They did at that,' and Afra frowned over the coincidence as he took the skillet from her hand and started cooking the eggs. 'We'd best weed that front bed, too, or Isthia will have words about negligence.'

It afforded Damia some relief to yank out weeds and fork up the soil to be sure she'd got the root systems as well. And, although Damia enjoyed fishing, today it was only a way to pass time until Isthia came. As is sometimes the case when one doesn't care, the fish bit well and they landed ten good-sized white-bellies before they realized they had more than enough. When Isthia arrived with both Ian and Rakella, they had just enough.

Afra hadn't seen Ian for quite a few years and he was surprised at how much the young man resembled his older brother. Though he had not quite the same forceful personality, he had sufficient of the inimitable Raven charm.

'Niece, you've improved past all recognition,' he said, dropping the flat black carrying case to warmly embrace Damia. After giving her a rib-cracking hug, he held out a hand to Afra. His eyes were somewhat paler a blue than Jeff's but as full of vitality, good humour and delight in their company.

'I second that,' Rakella said, kissing Damia's cheek. 'You were in a woeful state when you got here. I helped nurse you, or did Isthia ever bother to mention that?' She did not bear much resemblance to her older sister, Isthia, but the family stamp was in the set of her eyes and her generous mouth.

'For that, my deep gratitude,' Damia said, 'for I've no recollection of much beyond the most thundering headache imaginable.'

Isthia clapped her hands sharply together four or five times – claps which Damia heard echoing in her skull – and proceeded to order them to gather at the dining table. Damia noticed that she was also doing a quick check of her premises as she shooed them into the dining-room.

'White gloves, Grannie?'

'I wouldn't need them,' Isthia replied blithely. 'Look, Ian has some sketches to show you. See if you recognize anything from them.'

'They're pretty vague,' Ian said, obediently opening the portfolio he had brought with him. He slid pencilled drawings out, across the sleek surface of the table, so that some faced Afra and others Damia. 'I don't always sketch what I dream but, by the fourth or fifth repetition, I felt I had to.'

Damia held up one, showing the long road and the two blurs of figures. 'That's exactly what I see, only, there are at least twenty figures advancing and only six receiving, as it were.'

'Six?' Isthia looked pleased. 'That's us, counting in Besseva who couldn't come today.'

'And we're all high Talents, aren't we?' Damia said, glancing at her grandmother for reassurance. Isthia gave a wave of her hand, dismissing Damia's self-doubt.

'Why isn't Jeran affected?' Ian asked and, when Isthia smothered a laugh, he added. 'Oh, I suppose that would affect his judgement, if not his receptivity.'

'So what exactly is this?' Damia asked almost petulantly.

'Has it anything to do with that nibbling on the DEW net off Procyon?' Afra asked, startling Damia.

'What nibbling?'

Afra regarded her steadily for a moment. 'Larak mentioned it. The Fleet had been sent to investigate and found nothing.'

'From Procyon to Deneb is a long distance,' Ian said thoughtfully. Damia caught her breath.

'True, but longer distances have been covered recently,' Afra replied and Isthia nodded.

'And with devastating effect,' Damia said, feeling a tense anger and denial building in her.

'Is it wrong to suppose that all . . . ah . . . visitors have to be unfriendly?' Afra asked calmly, reaching under the table to put a steadying hand on Damia's leg.

'We've had more of the one than the other,' Isthia replied mildly. 'I'd certainly prefer that Deneb wasn't always the target.'

'It wasn't,' Damia said in a flat hard voice.

'Two out of three are not good odds,' Rakella said drily, 'but are we sure what these dreams mean? That there's some other species out there, asking to visit?'

Isthia gave her sister a sharp look. 'Is that how you'd put it?'

'I think I would,' Rakella said after considering her reply. 'The dreams have not been threatening. They have been quizzical. Yes, that's the word I want, quizzical. Like neighbours who do not wish to intrude but would like to make friends.'

'I find myself in agreement with that,' Afra said.

'And I,' said Ian.

Damia stared at the sketch, at the clump of figures struggling up the hill towards those waiting at the summit. She waved at the drawing. 'I don't know if I want to understand that. I don't know if I'm afraid of what we will discover.'

'That, at least, is honest,' Isthia said but there was approval in her expression.

'Only a fool doesn't learn by mistakes,' Damia said in a bitter tone and felt Afra's fingers tighten, this time warningly, on her thigh. 'Well, we should profit by my mistake in this. They seem to be offering something, too.'

'On the contrary, Damia, Sodan offered nothing. And he took – subtly and brutally – all your energy, your strength, and your perception,' Afra said, his tone very gentle, his eyes entreating her forgiveness for his candid words.

She stiffened, catching her breath until she could not deny the love, encouragement and understanding which flowed into her mind from all those around the table. Afra's fingers dug into her thigh, rousing her from her bleakness.

'And my brother,' she added. 'Why should we believe this – this intruder is any different?'

'Well, for one thing, whoever they are have had the courtesy to *request* admission into this system,' Isthia said. 'That's my interpretation of the dream sequences.'

'Who – what – are they?' Damia asked bluntly.

'We'd all like some reassurance on that score,' Isthia said. 'On the way out here, Ian, Rakella and I worked out a plan. Ian's willing to be subject and Rakella and I will implant a response to the dream sequence which ought to give our visitors – not invaders, I think – an answer to their query.'

Damia regarded her young uncle with admiration and some consternation. He was by no means as strong a Talent as she was, nor had he spent much time developing his innate Talent. But she held back her protest. She had no wish to tempt a repetition of the Sodan affair. She did give Isthia a long and worried look.

'Shouldn't we inform Earth Prime?' she asked.

'I'd rather we had something more concrete than a nebulous pattern of dreams,' Isthia replied. 'Jeff's still trying to calm everyone down,' and then she laughed, 'and help Cera deal with the Procyons who feel she is far too young to be responsible for that system . . . '

'Cera's the most responsible of us all,' Damia said indignantly.

'Exactly,' Isthia said, smiling at her granddaughter. 'But you can quite appreciate why we must be circumspect with this latest—' She jiggled her hand, searching for the appropriate word.

'Flap?' Afra suggested blandly.

'Flap'll do. There're only the six of us, having the dreams. Now if more had been involved – even just Jeran—'

'Good ol' prosaic Jeran,' Ian said disparagingly and Damia suppressed a giggle.

'Isn't he just,' Isthia said at her mildest. 'At any rate, until I feel we have sufficient evidence to require an alert of any degree, I think we keep this among ourselves.' She sent a querying look around the table. 'Very well then. We'll proceed with Plan A. And when is lunch going to be ready?'

Of them all that evening, Ian seemed the most relaxed as he submitted to the hypnotic session, woke, joked that he didn't remember a thing, and ate a huge supper, consumed most of a bottle of Isthia's treasured pre-Beetle vintages before taking himself off to his bed. During the afternoon, Afra and Damia had brought two conformable chairs into Ian's room where Isthia and Rakella could be comfortable during their vigil.

Damia had been generous to her own wine glass at dinner but she found it difficult to relax once she and Afra had gone to bed. She couldn't find a comfortable position though she tried several as surreptitiously as possible, not wanting to rouse Afra.

'I can't sleep either,' Afra said, though even his quiet tone startled her in the dark room. He turned her on to her back and gathered her into his long body. 'Shall I sing you a lullaby?'

'I'm not a baby any more, to be lulled asleep by a song,' she protested but she did not resist his comfort and settled her head on his chest.

To her surprise, not only did he begin to sing softly but also he rocked her gently against him. And, before she could protest his nonsense, her eyes got too heavy to remain open and her mind darkened responsively.

This time she seemed to be awake even as she started the visitors' dream sequence. And Ian's drawings became part of it – part of it, expanded by it and interpreted in it. The long uphill road was a dark one, many stars above it, passing by in an endless stream. A small globe appeared and the visitors abruptly stopped their upward progress. Then, very carefully, several visitors picked the globe up and put it to one side for it apparently impeded their forward progress. Then the file of visitors became twenty separate figures: long, thin, with spindly anterior segments which propelled them and upper extremities which were held forward in entreaty. The dream seemed endless to the sleeping Damia and she felt exhausted by its length, fervently wishing for action. There had been some before. The visitors had reached the top of the hill and met the six. The six also extended long, thin limbs but, though they advanced a few steps towards the visitors, no real progress seemed to be made in establishing a contact.

Contact! Damia woke with a start, sitting bolt upright in the bed.

What is it, Damia? Afra asked her, and the question was repeated by Isthia.

We aren't making contact. They wish to make contact. Then she covered her face with her hands and dropped her head to her bent knees, shuddering violently. She felt Afra's arms enfolding her and she leaned into his protective clasp.

'It's all right, Damia,' Isthia said, gliding into the room.

'What did Ian dream? Did your plan work?' Afra asked her.

'I don't know yet,' she said, sitting down on the side of the bed and stroking her granddaughter's hair. 'It's all right, pet.'

'I'm not a child any more, Grandmother,' Damia murmured and gave one last shudder before she looked up. 'It's contact they want, though. Afra?'

He shook his head. 'I only dreamt the usual sequence.'

When Ian finally woke the next morning, he had done no more than that. 'I tried, Mother,' he said ruefully. 'I knew I had something to tell them all night long but I couldn't get a word in edgewise.'

Damia felt close to panic and that must have shown in her face for both Isthia and Afra moved to touch her reassuringly.

'I don't want this,' she told them, 'I don't want any part of it.' Then, before she could see the pity in their faces, she slammed out of the house and down the narrow track to the lake.

She had been sitting for a long time in her favourite fishing site before Afra joined her. She could hear him coming, 'heard' his anxiety, too.

'I'm a coward, Afra,' she murmured when he reached her spot. He hunkered down beside her and his 'concern' was a shield between her and the reality she wanted to escape.

'No, but you're understandably cautious. I think we ought to inform Jeff, especially when you had such a definite response.'

'It was Ian who was supposed to get one. I'd rather it was he, anyway. I didn't handle the last one very well.'

'Isthia doesn't want you to handle this one at all,' Afra said, a little ripple of amusement in his voice.

Surprised, she looked up at him. 'And?'

'Despite what you may think of your initial attempts at establishing contact with an alien life form, you handled the actual link extremely well.'

'You have the nerve to tell me that?' Shock poured through her and she stared at Afra as if she had learned nothing of the man in the past two months.

'Telling the truth doesn't require nerve, love,' he said with a little laugh. 'The problem lay in Sodan and his long-term plans, not in your management.'

'I don't believe what I'm hearing.'

'You should,' Afra said blandly. 'You had bridged a communication gap and had established frames of reference. You've always had that gift. Look at how well you get on with barque cats, Coonies and the pony. Not to mention how good you were at teaching. Or have you forgotten Teval Rieseman?'

' "Friends don't throw rocks"!'

'These may be friends. And you have to learn their language to translate their message.'

Damia took in a long breath, held it, seeking that younger so-self-confident self. Sodan had damaged more of her essential being than she'd realized.

'He has certainly robbed you of self-esteem and confidence,' Afra said. 'I'd hate to think he'd won on that vital count.'

She stared at him, her beloved with whom she had shared so much, and here he, Afra the cautious Capellan, was suggesting that she . . .

'You're the only one of us who could make the contact they wish—'

'But—'

'I'm serious, Damia,' and Afra nodded his head urgently, 'you're the only one capable of doing it.'

'Only if you're with me . . . ' That plea came out of her mouth before she could stop it.

'I'd insist on inclusion.'

I'll be coming, too, Isthia said.

Are we allowed to think again? Damia asked sarcastically.

I applaud it.

Was that what your clapping meant? Afra asked as he locked eyes with Damia.

They were both answered by Isthia's laugh.

I had to be certain you'd obey my injunction, so I added a deterrent. Please come back to the house, Damia, Afra. Her request bore no hint of command.

Sighing at the inevitable, Damia got to her feet and, with Afra's long fingers twined in hers, made her way back to the house.

'Are we telling Earth Prime now?' Damia asked as they joined Isthia in the kitchen. Neither Rakella nor Ian were present.

'No, not yet.'

'Is that wise, Isthia?' Afra asked.

Isthia leaned forward across the table, still littered with Ian's sketches. 'Look, you two, I have survived two invasions of a highly inimical force, bent on total destruction. I do believe I can tell the difference when – ah – visitors do come in peace.'

'Remembering that the reason for most stellar travel is to provide colonists and mineral wealth for the explorers?' Damia asked cynically.

'I don't have much precognitive Talent,' Isthia surprised them by saying, 'but what I have is straining to make that contact. Ian's dream last night did have one positive result,' and she flicked one of the drawings on the table towards them, 'if you'll notice the stars?'

Damia drew the sheet towards her, frowning, for the seemingly random scatter of stars gradually became familiar to her.

'These are the constellations above Deneb!'

'Exactly. And this globe has protuberances suspiciously like the DEW sensors beyond the heliopause.'

'Oh,' and Damia's single syllable came out on a long sigh of denial.

'That's not so far to take a personal capsule. Is it?' Isthia asked softly.

'No,' Afra replied equably. 'Damia went much further than the heliopause to reach the Sodan entity.'

'I'm not sure,' and Damia spaced her words carefully, 'that I could go that far again.'

'Ah, but you won't be going by yourself, pet,' Isthia said comfortably.'

'I shouldn't be going at all.'

'That's why you must,' Afra said, gently pushing his index finger into the soft part of her arm. She felt not only the vibrancy of cool-green but a resolution she could not fight. She'd been terribly wrong once, and Afra had suffered. Afra and Larak. She must trust Afra now if his feeling was that strong.

Isthia was shaking her head slowly. 'I wish we had a reliable way to convey a response.'

'What do you mean, Isthia?' Afra asked.

'I mean, I send a message by Ian and Damia gets the answer.'

'Send the question by Damia then.'

'If Damia doesn't mind . . . ' Isthia looked hopefully at her granddaughter and Damia conceded gracefully. 'Then we'll try it tonight.'

'Why wait until tonight?' asked Afra.

'Sleep seems to be the vector,' Isthia said.

Afra chuckled. 'Then Damia can go to sleep.'

'I what?'

Afra rose, took Damia by the hand and, with a perplexed Isthia following, stalked out to the corner of the porch where the hammocks swayed gently in the breeze. Afra sat Damia down in one, picked her feet up and motioned for her to get comfortable while he set the hammock swaying.

'I can put Damia to sleep any time,' he said, grinning broadly.

'Now, wait a minute—' but Damia's protest was cut off as Afra began to croon the same song he'd sung her to sleep with the night before. She had no choice in the matter but her last outraged thought was that she'd settle this with him when next she was awake.

The sequence started instantly, only this time Damia took control and, as the visitors made their way up the hill, she separated a figure from those at the top and walked it down towards the visitors. She stopped it at the globe. Then, beckoning broadly to them, she urged them to follow her back up the hill. She was then back at the start of the dream and repeated her reassurance, to be sent back to the beginning at which point she was becoming rather annoyed that they couldn't get so simple a message.

She woke up grumpy, her head loggy with sleep.

'Afra Lyon, you stop doing that to me,' she said, shaking a finger under his nose.

'Works, though, doesn't it?' He was not the least bit repentant.

'How?' asked Isthia, mystified, but she regarded Afra with considerable respect.

'Goes back to when Damia wouldn't sleep at night. The daycare Talent and I used a prudent post-hypnotic suggestion and, with a bit of rocking and a line or two of a lullaby, Damia would drop off to sleep just fine for her mother.'

'And it has lasted this long?' Damia was incredulous.

'I've proved it. Mind you,' and Afra's voice held

the note that meant he was teasing, 'I wish I'd been forethoughtful on other matters.'

'As well you weren't,' Damia said direfully.

He helped her up out of the hammock and hugged her.

'So, tell us what happened?' Isthia asked, getting back to the more important matter.

'I told them we'd meet them at the DEW, and indicated that we'd welcome them. That's what you wanted, wasn't it?'

Isthia nodded her enthusiasm. 'Now, do we get Jeran's assistance?'

'We'd have to explain everything,' Damia said with an exaggerated groan. 'You know how Jeran is. A, B, C and D!'

'Damia, did you feel threatened by the dream?' Afra asked, no hint of levity in his expression.

'No. I'd like to believe Isthia's intuition is correct.'

'Like to believe?' Isthia asked.

Afra held up his hand. 'That's fair, Isthia.'

'I suppose so. Well, let's tell Ian and Rakella. We'll need their help anyway.'

The one vehicle at Deneb Tower which could carry three long bodies was a medium-sized rescue pod with four conformable seats. It had probably been left behind by a liner for its engine was missing but it still had working directional thrusters. They put in fresh oxygen tanks and dusted down the console, rather pleased to have a vehicle that had standard communications as well as a viewplate and external sensors. Jeran was not on duty, which was no problem as Ian and Rakella knew how to run up the generators. Damia could feel her palms sweating and her stomach was griping badly as she settled herself into her chair, Isthia on one side, Afra just behind her.

'I'll make the lift,' Isthia said, settling her hips deeper

into the seat. 'You're completely cured, Damia, but you save your strength for the contact.'

Damia had a moment of panic for that decision, but Isthia had never lied to her and probably wasn't now. It just would have been so reassuring to push off again, as she used to do so blithely.

You could now, too, love, said Afra in a fine thin tone. He reached forward to give her shoulder a reassuring squeeze. *Relax!*

She was quivering with tension and forced herself to unwind. She could, however, sense the rising keen of the generators and felt Isthia tense as she waited for exactly the right mo . . .

She launched them, a good strong thrust that Damia could objectively admire. It was good to be in deep space again. And then the pod's proximity alarm beeped urgently.

'Bring up the screen, Damia,' Afra said, leaning forward to peer over her shoulder.

'There it is!' cried Isthia, unnecessarily pointing, her expression exultant.

'It' was not a large ship, which immediately encouraged Damia to believe in amicable motives. 'It' was also a deep-space craft, having the usual haphazard design of ships that were never intended to land. It did have what looked very much like weaponry: wide-mouthed orifices that were stained with old fires and long snouts pointing outwards and looking effective.

Ian, turn off the DEW, Isthia said. *We don't want the Fleet charging out here and blowing us and our visitors up. Yes, that bunch of toggles under the red rimmed glass panel. Turn 'em all off. The disconnection won't show up for an hour or two. At which time we'll know one way or the other . . .*

'I think I have to go to sleep again,' Damia said drily. 'Will just the song do it, Afra? These seats aren't made for rocking.'

'I could rock the pod,' offered Isthia.

'We'll try without that, thank you,' Afra said and, with his hand on Damia's shoulder, began to sing the potent lullaby.

She knew she was shaking her head as sleep once more claimed her.

The pattern was gone. Instead she was inside the other ship, looking out at her tiny cargo pod. This time other figures were clearly visible and they were definitely alien. Despite their unusual appearance, she could sense no danger, nothing 'heavy', only relief. The 'visitors' looked to be tall though she had no gauge by which to compare them, save the bulky equipment. They did not sit, but stood on the three rear appendages, stubby legs which ended in splayed feet with three thick 'toes'. The upper limbs had five longer digits, one on each side of a squat 'palm' and three along its top. The heads were long, tapering to what appeared to be a muzzle but she could not see a mouth. One eye of a composite nature crowned the thick 'head'. There seemed to be dorsal ridges along the backbone. Maybe one of the three feet was actually a caudal appendage. Their skin or pelt, she couldn't discern which, was sleek and varicoloured, ranging from greys through green, brown and a slaty blue. Some were definitely taller than others but she didn't think the smaller ones were immature or of another sex.

Instantly her dream self turned towards a flat surface, set at a distance above the deck. This surface abruptly lit up and images began to form. More of this species, racing to enter what she had to identify as shuttles. These took off into space and she watched them link up with larger versions of the ship she was dreaming on. In a massed array, this fleet left its orbit, obviously in battle readiness.

To her shock, she saw their objective: a Beetle Hive Sphere. She watched the battle, saw 'her' ships being destroyed, saw the Hive sphere send its fighters out, watched them being destroyed and then, with great relief, saw the Hive ship suddenly explode, sending huge chunks spinning off, sometimes colliding with 'her' ships and demolishing them.

Abruptly those scenes segued into huge fragments turning end over end against . . . Suddenly the background changed and it was the Denebian system from which the twisted detritus escaped.

Then all the dream figures turned inwards to face her and she was overwhelmed with a sense of urgency, of interrogation, of fear.

In yet another wrench of perspective, she was back in the pod, crying out.

'They know about the Beetles. I saw them destroy a Hive. Then there was all this debris spinning in space, away from Deneb.' She turned first to Isthia and then to Afra for a reassuring interpretation of what she'd seen.

'Are they warning us then?' asked Isthia.

'No, they know we've been attacked and survived, as they have survived,' Damia said, choosing her words slowly.

'Then what do they want of us now?' Isthia wanted to know.

'Just don't put me back to sleep again,' Damia said flatly, rubbing at her temples.

'It seems an admirable way of communicating between species,' Afra said, teasingly, but he patted her arm sympathetically.

'The universe doesn't have to be full of species who are inimical,' Isthia said. 'Perhaps what these folk need are allies against the Hives. We've survived an attack so we'd make good allies.'

'They've certainly gone to great lengths to explain,' Damia admitted. She was beginning to believe that Isthia could be right. Her mind had not been overwhelmed or raped during this closer encounter. They had managed to convey vital information.

'Isthia, can you put me into a hypnotic sleep?' Afra

asked. 'I was part of both mind-merges: the first Rowan-focus, and then the B-Raven section that sent the Hive Sphere into the sun. I can at least give them our battle account.' Then he settled himself in the comformable and linked his hands across his thin waist.

Damia had an impulse to protest but Isthia unfastened her safety harness and drifted to Afra, holding herself down with one hand while she placed the other firmly on his left temple. Afra seemed to collapse into sleep.

She turned to look out at the visitors' ship, now noticing how pitted its surface was, how worn and scratched the symbols on what she took to be its bow. There were other ideograms elsewhere, some more legible than others. A complicated language rendered in bars and dots and occasionally cross strokes. Not as complex as some of Earth's oriental scripts, if that was the right word for them.

'How long did I sleep that last time, Isthia?'

'About half an hour. I didn't think to time it,' she said, floating back to her own chair. 'Fascinating. Absolutely fascinating.' Then she let out a big sigh. 'I suspect my son is going to be vastly annoyed with his old mother,' and the eyes she turned on Damia hadn't the slightest gleam of repentance. 'I really should have taken training much earlier. I could have been Deneb's Prime.'

Damia regarded her grandmother with wonder.

'We tend not to make the most of our chances,' she went on. Extending a hand, she lightly touched Damia's arm. 'Make the most of yours, dear child. But then, you are, aren't you?'

'Do you think they are emissaries of an altruistic species?'

'I'm quite attached to that notion,' Isthia said comfortably. 'I wish we'd thought to bring some provisions.'

Damia laughed. 'This was sort of a scramble. Oh ho!' Her throat went too dry for more words and she could only point at the vessel which was clearly moving under power.

'Let's get out of its way,' Isthia said and frantically reached a hand out to Damia.

Damia, following Isthia's thought, pushed the pod back so forcefully that the vessel became only a darkness.

'Not that far.'

'It's following us,' Damia decided after a moment's observation. 'What *is* Afra telling them to do?'

'Come on in, the water's fine,' Isthia replied facetiously. 'This must be the right way to handle this.'

'I thought it was, too.'

'This time it is right, Damia.'

'Yes, it is,' Afra said, though his words were slightly slurred. 'At least I have extended the invitation. I've no gauge to guide me but they appeared to be amazed at how we conduct our battles. I think that's a good impression to give them.'

'Now, what do we do?' Damia asked, watching as the alien vessel continued to close with them.

'Now, we inform Earth Prime that we have concluded opening talks with an alien species,' said Afra so calmly that Damia knew he was very nervous.

11

Deneb Prime Jeran gave them a prolonged demonstration, at the top of both lungs and mind, of what they might expect from Earth Prime. The local Fleet Commander appeared at the Tower, apoplectic to have found an alien ship orbiting the planet when the warning system hadn't so much as burped.

I TOLD YOU WHY IT IS NECESSARY TO PURSUE THIS COURSE OF ACTION, Afra roared with such vehemence that Isthia and Damia regarded him with astonishment. Cut off in mid-spate by Afra's uncharacteristic bellow, Jeran glared at the Capellan.

'You had no authority to do so,' Jeran said in a terse tone, clipping his words; expression and stance illustrating his indignation.

'He obeyed me,' Isthia said calmly and took the conformable seat. Ian and Rakella were still backed in the corner where they had retreated from Jeran's angry harangue.

Somewhat to her surprise, Damia could regard the scene with objective detachment – or perhaps, she amended, she was merely too stunned by the whole episode to be able to react.

Jeran turned on Isthia. 'Grandmother,' he began.

'Did you bother to inform Jeff or have you just been enjoying this exhibition of vituperation too much?' Isthia had a distinct gift for putting people in their places.

'I have first,' Jeran said in a loud voice, enunciating very, very clearly, 'to ascertain just what has transpired before I can send a rational report. They,' and he jerked his head at his uncle and great-aunt, 'gave me some hoodle-hoop about dreams and being called. Dreams,' and his scorn would have scarified a lesser personality than Isthia Raven, 'hardly constitute an intelligent reason for admitting strangers past our perimeter defences.'

'The dreams constituted a contact which cleverly surmounted a language barrier,' Afra replied, 'and provided us with sufficient information to wish to investigate more thoroughly, up to and including personal confrontation.'

Jeran stared at him, his nostrils flaring, fists on his belt, one foot tapping as he struggled to leash his temper.

'Between Isthia, Afra and myself,' Damia said coolly, rather delighted to see her phlegmatic brother moved to temper, 'you must admit, Jeran, that we would have experience in recognizing threat. This species does not pose one. In fact, hostility is furthest from their thoughts. Their worlds have suffered from Hive attacks. They urgently desire to know how we repelled the Leviathan.'

'As I was part of that assault, I explained how we contrived,' Afra went on conversationally. 'The Mrdinis were very impressed that we had needed no recourse to armaments to destroy it.'

Jeran rolled his eyes, noting the distraught expression on the commander's face. 'That was even stupider, Afra. Giving *away* information about our defence? That's the most horrendous breach of security that . . . that . . . ' Words failed him.

★

WE'RE COMING IN, and Jeff's words rang in everyone's ears. Damia had to blink, because her father's bellow did not reverberate in her head. She glanced anxiously at Afra who closed one eye in reassurance.

You see, you can even take my son's bellow without wincing, Isthia said in a finely-tuned thought. *I did make one slight error though,* and Damia and Afra turned to her in surprise for her expression was fleetingly rueful. *I set a sending constraint in your minds so you wouldn't inadvertently 'path, but I didn't restrict receiving. Never thought you* would *be in receipt of anything. Everyone* knew *not to 'path you until I gave permission.*

So that's how we were able to receive the Mrdinis' dreams, Damia said and hid her smile behind her hand. *How reassuring to know that you can be fallible, Grandmother.*

The opposite would make you unbearable, Afra added with no rancour.

'I simply don't understand your reasoning in this,' Jeran was saying, 'any of you. Especially you, Damia, since you nearly—'

WE WON'T GO INTO THAT, JERAN! Jeff's forceful words echoed and Jeran bowed his head, scowling blackly at the floor, around him, at anything but his sister.

Jeran didn't have to say it out loud, Damia thought bleakly, though she was grateful to her father for stopping him.

The Mrdinis are an entirely separate affair, Isthia said gently.

Entirely, Afra added and twined his fingers in hers. Damia shifted restlessly, knowing that Jeran would not be the first to remind her of that Sodan stupidity. When Afra also edged slightly in front of her, Damia realized his intention. It wouldn't be the first time he had protected her from her father's censure but this time she would take her fair share so she eased forward to close the gap.

Abruptly the largest cradle in the Tower yard held one

of the fast Fleet courier vessels and the orbital alarms indicated the emergence of four large ships in space above them.

'They *are* upset,' Isthia murmured, grinning.

Damia envied her grandmother that superb self-confidence but, oddly enough, she began to feel more positive about her part in this encounter.

Wearing a ferocious scowl, Jeff 'ported into the Tower, the Rowan beside him. The next few seconds were full of such heated exchanges of accusation, refutation and explanation that Rakella, never a strong Talent, folded against Ian, moaning.

'Oh, do cool it, Jeff,' Isthia said commandingly, her blue eyes flashing with a reciprocal outrage. 'I most certainly do want you and the Rowan to enter into discussion with the Mrdinis. That's what they're here for. Both Afra and Damia support my evaluation that these are allies, not aggressors. We exhibited reciprocal good faith by inviting them within our defences.'

'That's why I'm raging, Dad. Letting aliens into Deneb's skies is totally irrational!' Jeran exclaimed, gesturing wildly. 'We haven't yet got over the psychic scars of the Beetle Penetration and then my grandmother—'

'One unarmed vessel? One small unarmed vessel is no threat. It is usually regarded as an emissary,' Isthia replied, her patience fraying. 'Oh, do be sensible, Jeff.'

'Sensible is using the channels and procedures that are set up to deal with occurrences of this sort, Mother,' Jeff began, his temper only just contained.

'Wait a moment, Jeff,' the Rowan said thoughtfully, 'Isthia may have acted impetuously but I can sense the Mrdinis. They are very open. I'm not getting a shred of hostility from their minds and there's certainly nothing "heavy" on this alien ship.' Her glance slid across Damia and back to Jeff. 'I'd know,' she added gently, putting her hand on Jeff's arm so that the contact would emphasize the impressions she had just gained from her mental probe.

Jeff regarded his wife for a long moment and then the anger seemed to drain out of him. He gestured to Jeran to relax and smiled reassuringly at the pallid Rakella whom Ian was supporting.

'Who made first contact?' he asked, looking from his mother to Afra and then Damia, where his gaze lingered.

'We all had contact,' Isthia said, 'though Damia's was the clearest.'

Jeff nodded, accepting the statement without challenge.

'I put a restraint on them 'pathing,' Isthia went on, in a slightly apologetic tone, 'but I forgot to inhibit receipt. Damia would, of course, be both more receptive and more vulnerable in post-convalescence.' Isthia shrugged. 'After two weeks of nightly dream sequences, I had to accept the fact that the pattern could not be random, had to be an imposition. I couldn't establish a source for it. I was more than surprised when first Rakella, Besseva, then Ian, and finally Damia and Afra informed me that they were also receiving similar sendings.'

Jeff turned to Jeran expectantly: his eldest son shook his head.

'I can't imagine why Jeran didn't receive, too,' Isthia remarked drolly. 'But he didn't. We six got together, to compare notes, and tried to figure out a response to what was patently a friendly overture. Damia volunteered.' When the Rowan looked apprehensive, Isthia raised her hand in a placating gesture, 'I would scarcely undo the patient work of several months, Angharad. Knowing the martial mind, I decided that we'd check as far as we were able to. The Fleet takes so long to mobilize, doesn't it! So we made visual contact, established communications and extended an invitation to the emissaries. Now you, Fleet and the League can handle future negotiations.' She let out a sigh as she propelled herself out of the chair. 'Now, it's been a busy few hours and I look forward to some unstructured sleep. Come, Damia, Afra! We'll all rest better back at the cabin. I don't want you exposed to the emotional levels that will shortly be rampant around here.' Then she turned to Ian and Rakella. 'You two come as well. You look as shagged as I feel. See you later, dears,' she said, blithely flinging her fingers at Jeff and the Rowan. 'Come *on*!' and she imperiously gestured for obedience to her orders.

'Dad, Mother,' Damia said with a tentative farewell smile.

As soon as Isthia had admitted to fatigue, Damia had felt it creeping along her nerves. Not disastrously, merely informing her that rest was a good idea. Swift on that thought, she felt Afra's agreement and they both 'pathed back to the cabin's main room. Isthia, Ian and Rakella arrived more prudently on the lawn and joined them inside.

'Plainly you've recovered when you can 'port that neatly,' Isthia said with an approving nod. 'Now, what shall we have for lunch?'

Jeff and the Rowan asked permission to join them late that evening.

'Damia, Afra, we've got to whip up a meal,' Isthia said with a show of energy. 'Neither of them have eaten all day. I wonder if we have anything left after that mountain Ian and Rakella put away at noon.'

Damia scurried about the kitchen, checking what was available, remembering that her father was only out of temper when he was hungry. He may have absolved them of an impulsive act in contacting the Mrdinis, but she was certain that some reckoning was due.

Jeff doesn't hold grudges, love, Afra murmured, winking at her. 'Shall I uncork some of that excellent mountain white of yours, Isthia?'

Isthia grinned. 'Clever Afra.'

Five minutes later, the two Primes arrived on the lawn and, daringly, Damia 'felt' for their mood. Both her mother and father were tired but their public thoughts were tinged with a satisfaction that bordered triumph.

'Well?' Isthia said, handing each a glass of the chilled white wine as they reached the porch. She gestured for them to be seated while Damia offered the small hot pastries she had managed to prepare.

Jeff took a sip of the wine, smiled and nodded appreciatively at his mother.

'One of these days, Isthia Raven, you're going to land out on a limb I can't get you off of,' he said and then he relented.

Isthia looked smug. 'I told you they were not hostile. Did you have pleasant dreams?' she added slyly.

Jeff laughed and even the Rowan began to smile.

'A novel but effective means of communication. You should be astonished to learn, Mother, that we also got Commander Curran in on one conference . . . with Rowan doing the hypnotic link.'

The Rowan chuckled. 'I don't know who was more surprised, him, me or them. But the conference sank all his ifs, ands and buts.'

'So you can now support our contention of their peaceful intentions?' Isthia asked.

'Indisputably,' Jeff said, leaning back in his chair. 'Commander Curran will so inform High Command and put forth an urgent request for priority conferences.' Then Jeff looked keenly at Damia. She returned his gaze calmly, keeping a firm grip on her emotions and hectic thoughts. 'They asked for you, Damia.'

'It's too soon . . . ' the Rowan began.

'No, it isn't,' Isthia said, smiling to soften her contradiction. 'There's nothing wrong with Damia's mind, I assure you. She is completely recovered. So is Afra.'

Damia glared at her grandmother for the sly smile on her face.

'I'm relieved to hear that . . . ' the Rowan began again and then broke off, staring at her daughter.

Damia felt her mother's mental 'nudge', verifying

Isthia's medical clearance, felt her mother's inability to get past her shields, 'heard' her mother's annoyance alter to irritation.

'Possibly you will also be relieved,' Afra said as he moved to stand behind Damia, his hands lightly clasping her shoulders. She could feel the intensity of his emotions and knew that he had opened his mind, and his heart, to the two Primes. ' . . . to know that Damia and I enjoy a meeting of minds.'

Her mother turned white and her hands grasped the arms of her chair as she stared back at them. Damia received a shaft of denial coloured by a sense of betrayal before the Rowan exerted a clamp on her emotions. Her father did not have quite so violent a reaction but surprise was uppermost in his mind, and consternation, before he closed off.

'The bonding is remarkably complete,' Afra went on in his quiet voice. Only Damia knew that he was trembling, for she could feel it through his hands on her shoulder. Once she would have been defiant and hurt that her parents had shut their minds to her. 'Though I have known my own heart on this score since Damia returned from Deneb, I could do nothing until she recognized in me a genuine suitor.'

'I do not feel alone any more, Mother,' Damia said with gentle intensity. 'Please understand that. You should understand that!'

'But with Afra?' cried the Rowan.

To everyone's amazement, Jeff started to chuckle, rubbing the side of his face in a restless gesture and shaking his head. Then his chuckle became more relaxed and his shoulders shook with genuine mirth. 'How often, Rowan dear, have we told Afra that he should form an alliance? How often have we tried to find the right person for him? Not to mention trying to pair Damia off to any young,' and Jeff emphasized the adjective, 'Talent we could find. Come, now, Rowan love,' and he leaned across the distance that separated them, 'it's a surprise, even a bit of a shock, but who better than Afra? If you consider it objectively?'

Jeff rose then, and took the few steps to the couple. He kissed his daughter in the most benevolent fashion – though he also subjected her to the most intense probe. Then he embraced them both warmly, his blue eyes sparkling with a mixture of amusement, surprise and – Damia noted with intense gratitude – acceptance.

'Mother?' she asked, timidly extending a hand in the Rowan's direction.

'I just don't understand it,' the Rowan said, not looking at anyone. 'I've known Afra for twenty-eight years and I never expected . . . ' She halted. A rueful look crossed her face and, with a huge sigh, she regarded them. 'Afra, you have always been part of our family, a cherished friend. But it's going to take me a little while to get used to thinking of you as a son-in-law.'

'Well, don't make a big thing of it, Angharad,' said Isthia, who had maintained a tactful silence long enough. 'You certainly know that Afra doesn't jump into things . . . '

'Oh, but he does, and has,' the Rowan replied, jerking her chin up and reminding Afra of exactly how he had come to Callisto Tower. Then, with a characteristic twitch to her shoulders, she began to relax. 'It'll still take some getting used to. And,' she frowned with some petulance, 'I'll have all the bother of training a new assistant. I'm not sure I'll forgive you for that, Damia.'

'I thought Gollee Gren was working out well for you,' Afra said.

'Oh, well enough,' and the Rowan dismissed that notion with a flick of her hand, 'but he's just not you!'

'I could remain at Callisto,' Afra offered and Damia caught her breath, not finding that solution palatable at all for reasons she could not immediately identify.

'No, no,' and Jeff waved that aside, and he began to

pace up and down the porch. 'Afra and Damia have to stay here with the Mrdinis so he couldn't come back to Callisto for a while anyhow: at least not until verbal communications have been established between our species. You work far better with Gollee than you know, luv. Once you accept that the appointment is permanent, you'll relax into a good partnership. Have you any more of those hot pastries, Damia? I'm starved. Never thought sleeping half the day would increase my appetite.' He turned his charismatic grin impartially on all.

'Oh, you!' his wife said, exasperated as well as outmanoeuvred.

If the subsequent excellent meal had its moments of tension, Isthia deftly turned the conversation back to the Mrdinis and how to improve communication with them.

'Always supposing that I'm not kicked out of my Tower for this,' Jeff said.

'They couldn't, could they?' Damia asked, appalled at the thought.

'Not likely,' Isthia said tartly. 'They need him, and you all, too much.'

'Well, getting Curran on our side is a distinct advantage, considering his initial reaction at Deneb Tower,' Jeff replied. 'There'll be the usual bureaucratic waltzing about, throat-clearing, data-collecting, hemming-hawing, all that fugue,' he went on, pushing back from the table, tilting his chair on to its back legs, and ignoring his mother's disapproving glare. 'However, their final analysis will have to be that getting a powerful ally in the Mrdinis compensates for any eccentricities.'

'Remember to mention,' Isthia said with one of her enigmatic smiles, 'that the Mrdinis made the initial contact. And, by the way, did you find out why the Mrdinis approached the Denebian system?'

'Yes,' replied Jeff, his expression lighting with a grin. 'Remember in the initial battle how we flung the one ship back the way it had come? As a warning? Well, Mrdinis had been monitoring the Leviathan, to be sure it wasn't headed in the direction of their colonies – and they've been extremely candid about how many they have and what systems they've explored – so they saw the ship return. Which evidently those ships don't do.'

'That made the Mrdinis very interested in whoever had been so bold,' said the Rowan, her eyes gleaming as she took up the tale. 'They took a fix on the Leviathan's course and direction but had to return to their home planet for instructions and provisions. The instructions took longer than the provisioning,' and she grinned maliciously. 'I suspect there might also have been a perfectly understandable reluctance to annoy a species that could lob back a Beetle scout ship.'

'Which is one reason why they were hanging about beyond the heliopause when they found the DEW devices,' Jeff went on. 'They weren't even sure they'd got to the right place because, at first, they couldn't find any trace of the Leviathan. In their lexicon, Hive ships are invariably victorious.' He turned to Damia and Afra. 'It was your discovery of the Beetle hull fragment, and then its transportation back to the City, that registered on their equipment. They've been probing every planet in the system: probes that were too small to register on the DEW net, but sensitive enough to pick up traces of Beetle metal.'

'So that wretched artifact prompted the dreams,' Damia said.

'Exactly. So the Mrdinis broadcast to this area, hoping to make contact with minds that were, as they put it, sensitive to and repulsed by Beetle metal.'

'We were so lucky to be able to turn that Leviathan from Deneb,' the Rowan said, shaking her head at the narrowness of that escape.

'But we'll make that extremely clear when we speak to the League,' Jeff went on. 'The Mrdinis gave us chapter and verse on Beetle colonization procedures: brutal. If we hadn't had held . . . ' He reached out, cupping the Rowan's silvered head with a grateful and affectionate hand. 'The Beetles are compulsive colonizers, driven by the fact that the queens tend to massacre each other, the winner devouring the eggs of the loser. To prevent that, Hive ships leave the home world – and the Mrdinis are still trying to locate that system – and find likely worlds. First, scouts are sent off to locate planets. On finding one, ships are despatched to 'prepare' the planet for occupation, which means, ridding the surface of any other life-forms. The Beetles are basically vegetarian. The initial force lands and begins digging out caves for the Mothers' eggs. When the Hive ship arrives at the prepared planet, the ships transfer the eggs to the caves: then they are free to repeat the process. When that planet can support no further Hives, the Mother ship is stocked up with appropriate workers, and they go on the prowl again. According to the Mrdinis, there are far too many Mother ships roaming in space. The incredible part is that the Nine Star League has only had the one incursion.'

'That's not good news,' Isthia said.

'Not at all,' Jeff replied. 'We've been far too complacent and our luck could run out anytime. That's one reason the Mrdinis had been so urgently trying to warn us, despite their apprehension about our abilities. The Deneb DEW net is all well and good, they tell me, but we all know that not all the League systems are protected.' He frowned, ducking his head as he paused in reflection. 'You know, Damia, Afra, there's no reason you two couldn't as easily work with the Mrdinis language people on Aurigae as here on Deneb . . . '

'First, we have to get League permission, Jeff,' the Rowan reminded him.

He waved aside that contingency. 'I only need to get a few sensitive senators to sleep with the Mrdinis and we'll get some immediate action.'

'Senators?' Isthia gaped at her son, her eyes bright with merriment, 'Sleeping with Mrdinis? Jeff, you are the living end!'

'So long as I'm still living in the end, I don't care what it takes to get the necessary done. But we can't have a weak link in the defensive chain and a T-4 isn't sufficient to protect Aurigae.'

'Remember that nibble at the DEWs in Procyon, was that the Mrdinis?' Afra asked.

'I haven't established that yet, Afra,' Jeff replied, 'but it certainly wasn't the Beetles. They'd've just plunged through the system.'

'Dad,' Damia began hesitantly, 'there's no chance, is there, that the Leviathan could have got a message back to other Hives when Mother and you destroyed it?'

Jeff shook his head and gave a cynical laugh. 'You mean, like "stay away from here – bad vibes"?'

As she nodded, the Rowan answered with a shake of her head. 'No, we had the minds paralysed and nothing left the Leviathan when the Raven-merge plunged it into the sun. The Mrdinis believe that the Beetles are fearless. They are also numerous.' Her expression turned grim.

'Their basic drive is species-propagation, nothing more.' Jeff turned to Afra. 'Your account of our self-defence made a tremendous impression on them, and reinforced their desire for an alliance with us.'

'Oh?'

'They've been battling the Beetles' incursions for a long time – how long we haven't established yet – but a long time. So far they've found only one effective way to destroy a Leviathan,' Jeff replied, 'and that at great loss of life. It involves suicidal missions of cruiser-class ships diving into the Hive and blowing it up. They have to send as many as forty such ships in the hope that one will survive to penetrate the Mother Hive. That's why they want desperately to know how we effected such a kill.' Jeff grinned.

'Yes, it worked that one time,' Afra began.

'If necessary it will work again,' Jeff said. 'The Beetles have no imagination. They just keep on repeating what they've done before.'

'Nothing succeeds like success?' asked Isthia drolly.

'Theirs or ours?' the Rowan responded. 'Successful or not, I really wouldn't like to have to make a career of merges that exhausting.'

'Wouldn't be exhausting now, luv,' Jeff said in an off-hand manner. 'We've three times as many top Talents now as we had then.' He snapped his fingers carelessly. 'We could take out as many Leviathans as we needed to.'

'Jeff!' the Rowan exclaimed in rebuke.

'How much mental power do the Mrdinis have?' Afra asked, curious.

'They understand mind power, but I don't think they are developed enough for a mind-merge or a focus,' Jeff said. 'They have been successful with one or two other species in dream communications. We seem to be the most advanced species they have met. That's another reason for their jubilation. And, frankly, mine. I welcome,' and when Damia felt his eyes on her, she was aware of his compassion, 'the chance to make contact with an alien species. I will have no hesitation in recommending to the League that we move forward to an alliance with no hesitation and great haste. We are aware of the dangers of the Beetles and we cannot be complacent behind the DEW.' He let his chair down with a thump and stretched his hand across the table to Damia. 'You're needed at Aurigae, daughter. It's also a very handy place to send the Mrdini delegation for language study. And,' then he flashed her a grin, 'I'm not as hard-hearted as that old geezer Reidinger was. Afra can keep you company.'

'Father,' Damia began formally with a twitch to straighten her shoulders, 'why would the League trust me with Aurigae?'

Jeff Raven blinked in surprise. 'Why shouldn't they?'

Then he gave her one of his lopsided grins. 'The miners have been griping over your absence something fierce.'

Damia felt her mother's touch, gentle but authoritative.

'I think Damia is concerned with the report on Sodan, Jeff,' the Rowan said.

'Oh,' was Jeff's response, his blue eyes clouded and his face expressionless as he said, 'Earth Prime reported to the Nine Star League that Aurigae Prime contacted an alien ship and, on discovering its hostile intentions, requested sufficient Prime assistance to destroy the intruder, an action that took the life of Larak Gwyn-Raven—' He paused and both he and the Rowan looked towards the peaceful spot where their son was buried. '—and severely injured Damia Gwyn-Raven and Afra Lyon.' With an abrupt change, Jeff regarded his daughter with his usual charm. 'Why?'

Damia faltered, as much because she felt the ache of Larak's loss as because she didn't want to admit how Jeran's remark in the Tower had affected her.

'Jeran,' the Rowan said cryptically and Jeff nodded with understanding. 'You two have never quite mended your sibling quarrels, have you? Well, Jeran is only human . . . '

Isthia rolled her eyes. *That is still debatable.*

'And you did,' the Rowan said bluntly, 'run rough-shod over his authority by contacting the aliens without notifying him.'

'We didn't know where he was,' Isthia said slyly.

'Oh?' Jeff asked and, as he regarded his mother, his eyes became intensely blue.

Grinning, she waggled a rebuking finger at him. 'Let's not try that on your mother, dear.'

Jeff threw back his head and laughed. 'I shouldn't, should I?'

'You're nearly as arrogant and audacious as Pete Reidinger was, Jeff Raven,' Isthia went on.

'He is not,' the Rowan said loyally.

'Not around me, he isn't,' Isthia said.

Earth Prime, and Jeran's formal address reached all the telepaths, *you are requested to return to Deneb Tower. Fleet and League representatives are urgently requesting transfer to Deneb to discuss the alien situation.*

With a sigh, Jeff heaved himself to his feet, extending a hand to the Rowan to help her to rise.

'No rest for Earth Prime, arrogant or audacious,' he said, putting on an air of martyrdom and letting his back sag as if he supported an unmerciful burden. 'Will you two be ready to go back to Aurigae tomorrow?' he asked in a serious tone.

'Yes, of course,' Damia said, nodding her head just as Afra, beside her, murmured agreement. His fingers squeezed her.

'Excellent.' Jeff bent to kiss his daughter's cheek, then slapped Afra's shoulder with every evidence of his usual affection for the Capellan. 'That'll soothe ruffled feelings: Gwyn-Ravens nobly respond to the demands of their League!'

In taking her leave, the Rowan gave Damia a brief caress on the cheek, her grey eyes thoughtful. 'It *will* take time, you know,' she said, twitching her eyebrows in annoyance. She turned to Afra. 'Gollee Gren is good but he just doesn't have your subtlety.' She sighed. 'But I'll manage.'

Jeff laughed, gave his mother a swift hug and kiss, and, folding both arms about his wife, 'ported out of the kitchen.

'Show-off,' Isthia muttered before she turned to regard Damia and Afra with a speculative gaze. 'Wriggled your way out of that one, didn't you? Nothing like an emergency to get a family to close the gaps, is there?'

'Isthia,' Afra said, drawling her name reprovingly, his expression amused, 'if Jeff is arrogant and audacious, what are you?'

'An interfering *mater familias,*' Isthia retorted with an

unrepentant grin. 'I'll clear up here. You two have a lot to organize before the morning, as well as getting a good night's rest.'

'I can always try a lullaby,' Afra said and ducked away as Damia swung at him, only half in play.

He continued on out of the kitchen, down the corridor to their room and she followed.

'Afra, is there any way of cancelling that dratted command?' she asked. 'It could become exceedingly awkward.'

'Why?' and Afra's yellow eyes danced with amusement. 'It's been exceedingly useful of late.' Then his expression altered to one of sudden and delighted comprehension as he sent a quick probe which Damia, laughing, did not resist. In a swift stride, he closed the gap between them, pulling her into his embrace with one arm while he laid the other hand on her abdomen. 'So! How could I have missed this?'

Shyly she smiled as she looked up at him. 'Too many lullabies.' Supremely content, she nestled against him. They were turned towards the window from which she could see Larak's grave.

'Can we call her Laria?' she asked softly.

Afra held her more tightly, opening his mind as completely as she had hers in this special moment, letting her see how long he had yearned for a child of his body – for *her* child; the blazing joy that burned through him for the gift of her love, for the new life within her, for the end of his solitude. For all this new and unexpected joy, and a restatement of the devotion that was so strong a bond now between them. Within him now swelled the resolve to manage a third generation of Rowan women.

'I'm glad we have a meeting of minds on that score,' she murmured. And because she felt his urgency rise to hers in that deserving and marvellous moment, their agreement was shortly expressed in another fashion, immensely satisfying to both.